HOT RUBY

LORENZ HELLER

INTRODUCTION BY
GREGORY SHEPARD

STARK HOUSE

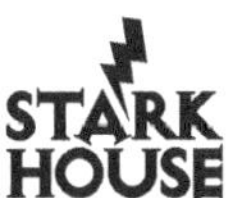

Stark House Press • Eureka California

HOT / RUBY

Published by Stark House Press
1315 H Street
Eureka, CA 95501, USA
griffinskye3@sbcglobal.net
www.starkhousepress.com

ISBN: 978-1-951473-75-4

Cover design by Jeff Vorzimmer, ¡caliente!design, Austin, Texas
Book design by Mark Shepard, shepgraphics.com
Proofreading by Bill Kelly
Cover art by Rudy Nappi

First Stark House Press Edition: August 2022

HOT

Vince Ewell and another man had robbed a bank and now Ewell is doing the time. So when a prison break sends him on the run, everyone expects him to head for Bonnie. Beautiful but not-too-bright Bonnie, his faithful wife, now living in Henry Crane's private suite and singing at his club. And completely surrounded by cops. Vince's brother Steve wants to help his brother get straight, but to do that, he will have to convince Bonnie to betray Vince and get him to hand over the stolen loot and name his accomplice. But Bonnie has other plans—she wants the money for herself. She may not be too smart, but she knows how to get what she wants.

RUBY

Everyone in town knows that Ruby is trouble. She drinks too much, spends the night with too many men, has quite a reputation. So no one is that surprised when she ends up dead on the beach with an ice pick wound in her heart. But Joe Latham is particularly hard hit. He never has been able to get her out of his system. Then detective Keeler comes sniffing around, implying that Latham had something to do with her death. Latham figures he better do some investigating of his own, and soon discovers that Ruby had been friendly with a lot of men: the casino owner, a local gambler, several older businessmen, and even her banker boss. Now the banker is dead, too, a suicide, and $200,000 is missing… and everyone assumes that Latham is the one who knows where it is.

LORENZ HELLER: HOT AND RUBY
BY GREGORY SHEPARD

"… the dialogue is crisp, the story edgy and populated by eccentric, volatile characters who just can't get a grip on life."

—Paul Burke, *CrimeTime*

Author Bill Crider called him "another one of those forgotten paperbackers who deserves to be remembered." Quite an epitaph. Lorenz Heller certainly does deserve to be remembered. He never quite achieved the heights of a John D. MacDonald, but as a fellow Florida crime writer, he kept close company. And he entirely supported himself with his writing, not something that a lot of 1950s authors could say.

Lorenz was born in West Hoboken, New Jersey, from fourth generation German-Americans, which might account for his first name. Lorenz is German for Lawrence. Everyone, of course, knew him as Larry. In fact, as Larry Heller, he wrote *I Get What I Want* and *Body of the Crime,* plus one short story, "Blood is Thicker." Lorenz wrote under many names, but published most of his novels under his "Frederick Lorenz" pseudonym.

As Frederick Lorenz he wrote six crime thrillers for Lion Books, beginning with *A Rage at Sea* in 1953 (a treacherous tale of revenge reprinted by Stark House Press, 2020), and quickly followed with *Night Never Ends* (a slice-of-life story involving an arrogant photographer and the couple he manipulates), *The Savage Chase* (a quirky kidnapping tale, reprinted by Stark House Press, 2019), *A Party Every Night* (about a bartender who is inadvertently framed for murder, also Stark House Press, 2020); the two novels in this collection, *Ruby* (a man is unjustly accused of murdering the town tramp), and *Hot* (in which the brother of a bank robber must deal with his conniving wife); plus a juvenile delinquent novel for Chariot Books called *Dungaree Sin,* a seedy romp through the author's Jersey days.

And then there are all the books written as Laura Hale (crime fiction with strong female protagonists), not to mention the Larry Holden stories from the late 1940s and early 50s—over 100 of them—written for such magazines as *Detective Tales, Doc Savage, Dime Detective Magazine, Shadow Mystery* and *Thrilling Detective.* Seven of these pulp stories feature detective Dinny Keogh, who seems to solve most of his crimes through brute luck more than careful deduction. But when you're writing for *Mammoth Mystery*, you don't want a main character who is too cerebral. Fast action and heavy gunplay is the name of the game.

Heller wrote three novels as Larry Holden as well: *Hide-Out* (originally published in 1953 by Eton Books), plus *Dead Wrong* (published by Pyramid Books in 1957) and *Crime Cop* (a police procedural originally published by Pyramid Books in 1959). All of these have been reprinted in new Stark House editions.

But for all that—all the many pseudonyms, and all the various publishers he worked with, all the hardboiled titles—Heller was a character-writer more than an action writer. In a 1956 interview that appeared in the *Sarasota Herald-Tribune*, he confessed to being "interested in characters, not plots." This was his defining quality as a writer. In another interview, this one from the *St. Petersburg Times* later that same year, Heller said simply, "the plot is less important than putting characters in conflict." Characters, he said, "must be alive and have dimension. The reader should be able to see every character in the book." And because he placed more emphasis on characterization than plot, Heller was able to allow the action to take a lot of unpredictable turns.

Heller always puts his characters through the wringer. He himself led quite an adventurous life. After running away to sea on a freighter at a young age, he then jumped ship with the entire crew and found work in Puyallup Valley, Washington, picking raspberries, baling hay and building barns. Heller then returned home and got serious about his life. He wrote his first book, *Murder in Make-Up*, in 1937 when he was 27, and got it published by Julian Messner, Inc., under his given name, Lorenz Heller. According to the St. Petersburg interview, it was his return home to West Hoboken that made him finally decide it was time to either get a job, or commit to his writing. Of course, like many young men, Heller took some time out of his life to serve in World War II, working at the Aircraft Radio Corporation war plant. But it wasn't too long after the war that his first stories began to appear. Then he moved to Florida.

Heller may have grown up in New Jersey, but he didn't grow old there. "I came down to Florida because I could not stand the snow," he said. First he moved to Nokomis, on the Gulf Coast, then built his own home in nearby Venice, sailing and fishing the Keys and islands when he wasn't working at his writing. The goal was to write 2,500 words a day, and sometimes Heller would be at it for 12 hours a day. That's how you support yourself with your writing. And Heller was dedicated to it.

He wrote 18 novels in all, not counting the four Laura Hale books he adapted for Beacon Books from earlier works. Heller also wrote six TV scripts during the 1950s as Burt Sims. His last book appeared in 1962, the previously mentioned Larry Heller title called *Body of the Crime*, a cop drama reminiscent of the Ed McBain 87th Precinct mysteries and a sequel of sorts to *Crime Cop*. His only other Larry Heller novel, *I Get What I Want,* was published by Popular Library in 1956.

Hot, one of his Frederick Lorenz novels, starts out as the story of an escaped convict, but quickly becomes instead the story of the convict's brother Steve, who has just returned to town after spending time as a merchant seaman. Steve still believes in his brother's essential goodness, but the truth is, there's not much left of Vince to like. His wife only wants him for the heist money that everyone thinks Vince hid before he was sent up. Most of the town just wants him gone, before there's any shooting. And somebody wants him dead. But nobody knows where he's hiding.

The most interesting aspect of *Hot*, as in any Heller book, is the characters. There is nothing predictive about them. Heller seems to delight in creating stock, hardboiled characters and then turning them into interesting, 3-dimensional characters through their conversations and adverse actions.

The convict's wife is a sexpot, but she's no femme fatale. In fact, she's not very bright. She really only has two things on her mind, and most of them are money. She's living with a nightclub owner who instead of being the usual oily fellow is rather fey, with a giant Great Dane for protection. His conversational gambits are some of the most intriguing in the book. Steve is a big burly guy but doesn't mind feigning weakness to keep himself alive. And Vince, the man they are all trying to find, used to be a good-looking man, always in charge, loved by all the women; but time has honed him down to the bone, stripped him of his humanity and most of his power. What happens to these folks over a short period of time in a small, heatwaved New Jersey town is predictable in a general sense, but filled with interesting little twists and turns along the way.

Ruby also has a sexy, misunderstood woman at its core, but the first time we see her, she's dead. A precursor to *Twin Peaks*, Ruby is a victim of men's desire, a woman with a tortured past, filled with secrets; a different person to everyone she knew. To some, Ruby was a slut, an alcoholic who deserved no more than she got. To others, she was lovely, warm, passionate and generous. Latham sees himself as the man who loved her the most, and decides to find the man who killed her. But he is also a man with blinders on, and we feel his frustration mount as he blunders from one confrontation to the next.

Both of these novels were originally published by Lion Books in the

1950s as inexpensive paperback originals. They were presented as two-fisted, hardboiled novels. But unlike so many of the crime fiction books of this period, they were filled with interesting, quirky characters that become more of the raison d'être of the book than the actual plot.

As Alan Cranis wrote about Heller on *Bookgasm.com*, "Lorenz's characters are what keep the pages turning, as we wonder what new complications the players will encounter." Neither *Hot* nor *Ruby* disappoints in this regard. Heller gives us two great stories, filled with interesting characters, and doesn't waste a word doing it.

—June 2020
Eureka, CA
[revised May 2022]

Notes:

Rita Billingham's "Profiles from Venice" from the *Sarasota Herald-Tribune*, Sunday, October 14, 1956

Woody Thayer, *St. Petersburg Times Suncoast Skyway* Edition, July 22, 1956

HOT

LORENZ HELLER

Writing as Frederick Lorenz

CHAPTER ONE

Crouched among the marsh reeds about a hundred yards from the road, he burned with the stabbing pain in his leg, with the suffocating stickiness of the night heat, and with the prodding desire to get into the tavern at the edge of the road. Lyle would be there, probably—but what was more important, so would Pauline.

He knew how to handle Pauline, all right, and as he thought about her now, he knew how she'd be dressed, in all this heat, even how she'd be standing when he first saw her, with the bold side-thrust of one hip, the soft quiver on her full red mouth. He knew.

But right now ... It was hot, the steaming, sweltering miasma of mid-August. The entire countryside lay gasping in the grip of a record heat wave, drowning in the mounting humidity. For over a week the headlines of the newspapers had panted, HEAT TOLL SOARS, and in thousands of bedrooms they lay in small sleepless agony on sodden mattresses. Those with air conditioning units retreated to their chilled dens and hid from the heat, and in other homes the electric fans moaned and beat at the smothering air. It was the same from the seaboard to the hill and lake country as the temperature passed the hundred mark and hung there like a hot, clenched fist.

It had been a rainy summer and in the great salt marsh, locally called the Meadows, along the Hackensack River, the mosquitoes bred and multiplied and swarmed out of the swamp to sting and feed upon the suffering populace, making the nights just a little more horrible.

Vince Ewell crouched there among the reeds. The ground was firm where he sat, but he knew that all around him was bog and mud and that his life would hang in the balance with each step when he crept out from among the reeds that towered ten feet above his head, for a man floundering alone in a bog in the dead of night would not have long to live once the mud took hold. He was dressed in a gray prison shirt, gray pants, coarse gray socks, heavy shoes and work gloves, and a second shirt was wound around his head and face to protect him from the mosquitoes. There were two holes in the back of this shirt and a great, stiff, brownish stain that had once glistened red with new blood. Into the waistband of his pants was thrust a powerful Colt .45 automatic from which three shots had been fired.

He was sitting on an empty, rusting, five-gallon oil can with his left leg stretched stiffly before him, and whenever he shifted a little he groaned and gripped his thigh, pressing against the thick bandage he had wound around it. He had been shot.

From time to time he made an angry gesture with his hand to sweep the thrumming mosquitoes away from the narrow aperture in the swathing shirt through which he peered.

He muttered, "Bitches!" for while in prison he had been informed by a lecturer from the County Mosquito Control Commission that it was only the female mosquito that bit. The female mosquito lived for only two things, the lecturer had said, feeding and breeding. And the convicts had laughed, but the laugh had not been entirely whole-hearted, for dark in their minds they had drawn a parallel and thought of their women. Later they had thought of the lecture and their women again and had muttered angrily, "Just like a damn dame!"

Vince Ewell muttered the phrase again as he flapped the mosquitoes away from his face and peered through the reeds at the red neon BEER sign of the Regal Bar and Grill up on Burns Road. He was feverish and his mouth was parched and he swore monotonously and clasped both hands over the throbbing wound in his thigh. His throat worked painfully as he thought of a tall, beaded glass of cold beer and the futile fury swelled in his chest because he had to crouch out there in the swamp until the tavern closed.

He had not the faintest idea what time it was. It could have been nine in the evening or it could have been after midnight. He had no way of telling. Time had been a nightmare of pain and hiding and pursuit from the minute he and Marky had broken out of prison and had raced for cover with the sirens screaming after them from the walls. Marky was dead and it was his shirt that Vince had wound around his head, and it was Marky's pants he had ripped up to make the bandage for the wound in his thigh, and it was Marky's gun in his waistband. Sweltering though he was, Vince felt the touch of a cold probing finger when he thought of how Marky had died with two bullets through his lungs, drowning in his own blood. He could have been the one who had gotten it. That slug through his leg, it could just as easily have been a little higher and gotten him in the guts and he would have been lying back there with Marky. *So what, so what?* he thought angrily, *it didn't, so what?* He had never been afraid of anything and he still wasn't afraid of anybody. Marky had gotten it and he hadn't and that was all there was to it. But there was a small, rotting spot of fear in him now, a spongy thing of creeping growth. It would make him timid and vicious and dangerous with the ever-increasing need to deny to himself that it was there at all.

Half out of his mind from thirst and pain and fever, he peered through the tall reeds at the neon sign until it beat like his own pulse against the darkness of the night. And he rocked to and fro with it, clutching the pain of his wound, raging against the owner of the tavern, a man named Lyle Ferenc. That lousy Hunky would stay open forever to squeeze another stinking nickel out of his crummy ginmill.

Suddenly Vince started. The neon sign no longer stabbed the night and the juke box had stopped. Shaking, sweating, he groped for the maple branch he was using as a crutch, and painfully hoisted himself to his feet.

Hesitantly, fearful of the swamp, fighting the terrible pain in his leg, he made his way to the stony, grassed shoulder about ten feet from the road. He collapsed again, sucking in short harsh breaths which burned deep into his throat. His leg was on fire and he sensed an oozing wetness that told him the wound had reopened.

He heard a car approaching slowly from the south. He flattened, scrunching deep into the grass as the car passed by. Vince waited until the taillights disappeared over the rise and then pulled himself to his feet. Despite the knifing pain in his leg, he hobbled clumsily across the road. Panting, he leaned against the gray side of the building that housed the tavern, hidden in the shadows of both the dwelling and the thick, muscular oak tree that grew beside it. The ground under the tree was littered with beer cans, empty cardboard cartons, newspapers and other refuse.

Vince was not particularly tidy, but he muttered, "Pigs," contemptuously and glanced up at the second floor where a window glowed with a drawn shade behind it. Lyle Ferenc lived up there with his wife, another dumb Hunky just like him. Pauline. Pauline Salaski her name had been. A Polack. Ferenc was a kind of Lithuanian or something, a dumb Hunky in any language. Pigs. Vince eyed the house and the lighted window with an air of savage contempt.

There was a stairway to the second floor in the bar, but the main entrance was on the side of the house where Vince stood concealed. The door was only about fifteen feet to his left, but he made no move toward it. He ran his tongue over his lips and huddled against the side of the house, hesitating, undecided. Suppose the Hunky didn't own the joint anymore? A lot could happen in two years. Suppose somebody else had the place now. Suppose this guy came to the door and recognized him from the picture in the paper and ducked back inside and called the cops. He'd be a sitting duck. He couldn't run anymore, not with this leg, and they'd pick him like a daisy. Or suppose somebody had tipped off the cops and there was a stakeout upstairs waiting for him. Or the Hunky himself might go chicken and call the cops himself just to get out from under. Or that lousy Pauline might be the one to do it. You had to think of those things, you had to be ready for them. His face was drenched with sweat as he felt for the thick butt of the gun in his waistband. That was it. That would take care of everything. He turned and slowly hobbled toward the door.

Vince wet his lips again and sharply turned the bell key three times and grasped the butt of his gun. A light went on in the hallway and Vince flattened against the side of the house so that it would not shine in his face. Heavy clumping footsteps descended the uncarpeted stairs and a moment later the door opened. It was the Hunky, big, blond, flat-faced, his shirt unbuttoned as if he had been undressing to go to bed. There were dark fatigue pouches under his eyes, but he looked as he always had. Dumb.

Vince whispered, "Ferenc," and pulled the gun from his waistband.

The man said, "Who's that?" and poked his head out through the doorway. At the sight of Vince, his jaw sagged and his face went white. He stood there petrified, incapable of speech.

Vince said harshly, "Douse that light and let me in, damn it!"

Ferenc nodded hurriedly and fumbled on the wall to his side for the light switch. Vince hobbled into the hallway and closed the door behind him.

"Now help me upstairs," he ordered, prodding Ferenc with the gun. "I got a bum leg."

The man babbled, "That's okay, Vince, that's okay, that's okay, that's okay, Vince—" and shrank away from the gun.

Together they lurched and stumbled up the narrow stairs, Ferenc holding Vince around the waist. Vince felt the man's thick arm trembling and he was grimly satisfied. He'd have no trouble keeping the Hunky in line.

A door opened at the head of the stairs and a woman's voice called, "Who was it, Lyle?" And then she saw Vince and her striking, high-boned face went rigid. "Oh my God!"

Vince snarled, "Shut up and get inside."

Jerkily, she moved aside as the two men entered the room, Ferenc hurriedly closing and locking the door. This was the living room. There was a broken-down, overstuffed sofa, two beat-up arm chairs, and a ratty rug. The wallpaper was bubbled and discolored from the leaking roof, and, from the woodwork, the paint peeled in leprous scabs. But at the far end of the room, facing the sofa, was a brand-new, shining mahogany TV set. Vince staggered to the sofa and dropped into it. For a moment he sat with his eyes closed, hunched over his wounded leg. Fatigue was a pulse and his body rocked slowly with it. When he opened his eyes again, the two Ferences were still standing at the door, staring fearfully at him, standing very close together as if for mutual protection. Vince gave them the bare bones of a grin, all teeth. He was holding the gun naked in his lap.

"Expecting me?" he asked.

Ferenc could not speak at all, but the woman managed to stammer, "What—what do you want, Vince?"

Vince turned his grin on her alone. He was feeling better now. There had been nothing to worry about. Everything was under control. They were both chicken, scared spitless, and that was the way he wanted it. The Hunky wasn't worth bothering with, but the woman had some guts. She had taken off her dress and was standing there in a thin slip that showed plainly the bold lift of her big breasts and the outline of her legs which were strong and full. Not bad looking, not bad looking at all for a Hunky.

"You're going to put me up for a while, Pauline." He patted his thigh. "Till my leg gets better."

The woman said, "Here?" and looked horrified at her seemingly paralyzed husband. Ferenc had not uttered a word since they had climbed the stairs.

"Yeah, here," said Vince, still grinning. "We're old friends and you wouldn't turn down an old friend, would you?"

"The—the police—"

"Friends of yours?"

"No, no, but—" Pauline's thin Tartar eyes fled to the gun in his lap. "They're looking for you."

"They've been looking for me for two days. So what? It's a big place outside. Let them look. Get me a shot of bourbon, Lyle. I ain't had a decent shot for two years."

Ferenc swallowed. "Sure, sure." He walked stiffly toward the stairway to the bar downstairs.

Vince said, "Wait a minute."

Ferenc stopped precariously. "Sure, Vince, sure."

"There's a phone downstairs, ain't there?"

"Yeah. That's right. Downstairs in the bar."

"Well stay away from it!"

"Oh, sure, Vince, sure, sure. I wouldn't—"

"Fine. Now get me that shot."

Ferenc plodded heavily down the stairs and Vince unbuttoned his pants and peeled them down over the crude bandage around his thigh. The wound was in one of its periods of just aching dully, but he untied the bandage carefully and unwound it. It stuck in the dried blood of the wound.

"Get me some hot water," he said without looking up. Pauline nodded and went out. Vince's heart had begun to beat a little faster. He had been shot yesterday morning and had been crawling around in all kinds of muck ever since. That was the way you got blood poisoning. The heat in the room was smothering, but the sweat that poured from him had nothing to do with the heat. That's all he needed was blood poisoning. When you got blood poisoning you had to have a doctor. Or die. The dumbest doctor in the world would see that he had been shot and the first thing he'd do would be to run to the cops.

He heard Ferenc coming up the stairs and he stiffened, sitting upright. Ferenc walked into the room carrying a glass and a bottle of cheap bourbon. His face seemed shrunken and bloodless.

"Pour it," Vince ordered, regaining confidence at the sight of the other man's fear.

Ferenc poured it with shaking hands. Vince drank it down in a single gulp and silently held out the glass for a refill, noting with satisfaction that his own hand was fairly steady. He felt much better after the second drink.

"Sit down, sit down, take a load off your feet," he said airily. "What're you worrying about? Nobody's going to look for me here. Sit down."

Ferenc sat rigidly on the very edge of the chair, his thick-fingered hands knotted in his lap.

"I suppose the papers're full of it," Vince said.

Ferenc nodded dumbly. Vince's contempt grew.

"What'd they have to say?"

"You—you busted out."

"I know that. What else?"

"There were two of you." Ferenc twitched and glanced at the door behind him.

"Relax. He ain't with me. He's dead. They put two slugs in him."

"The papers didn't say—"

"I know, I know." Then deliberately, "I tied a rock around him and sank him in the river. I thought it might make it a little tougher if they thought they were looking for two of us instead of just one. Anything else? Come on, come on, don't make me drag it out of you."

Ferenc looked sick when Vince spoke of sinking Marky in the river. "A—a guard. He was shot, too. He's in the hospital. They don't know if he'll live."

"Marky did that," Vince said quickly. "He had the gun. I didn't have nothing to do with it. What else did they say?"

"They think you're going to try to get in touch with Bonnie."

Vince started and compressed his lips, swearing to himself. They had hit that one right on the nose. That was exactly what he had been planning to do and if he hadn't been shot, that's just where he'd be now, trying to get in touch with her. The cold finger touched him again and withdrew. Luck, luck, just plain luck. He would have walked right into them. Bonnie was his wife. His hand tightened around the gun in his lap.

"Where've they got her, in that stinking jail up there?"

"Oh no no, nothing like that, Vince." Ferenc's words stumbled over each other as if he were anxious to say nothing that would displease Vince in any way. "They're just watching her, that's all. Just keeping an eye on her. Anyway, that's what the paper said."

Vince said, "Jerks." Letting it get in the paper like that. They might just as well of given him a map. But this made it easier. So long as they hadn't stuck her in jail, he could get in touch with her one way or another. Through the Hunky maybe. No, the hell with that. The Hunky'd drop dead if a cop looked at him cross-eyed. Pauline. She was the guts of the family. She was the one.

Vince leaned back in the sofa, easing his leg. It was beginning to hurt again.

"That all they had to say?" he asked. "Give me another shot of that rotgut."

Ferenc jumped to pour him another drink and hovered anxiously with the bottle until Vince waved him back into the chair. Ferenc sat down in exactly the same strained position as before.

"Now what else did the papers say?" Vince prompted him.

"Well, they think you might go to Philly, too, or maybe Albany. That's where this other guy's from, both places, and that's all except they got all the cops out, New York, Jersey and Pennsylvania."

"What's the matter with Connecticut?" Vince laughed. The liquor had made him very carefree. "I was up there once. And Staten Island. I was out there a couple times. Well, let them keep looking. It'll give them something to do."

Pauline returned from the kitchen carrying a kettle of steaming water, a washcloth and a bottle of mercurochrome. She had put on a pink rayon housecoat that you could see right through when her back was to the kitchen light. Her face was still taut, but she certainly wasn't scared spitless anymore and Vince didn't like that.

"I had to heat the water," she said. She looked at Ferenc. "Go to bed. I'll take care of this. You need your sleep."

"Yeah, beat it," said Vince.

Ferenc did not want to leave the room but he had no choice. "I'll—I'll leave this for you, Vince," he said, putting the bottle of bourbon on the floor beside the sofa.

"Good night."

"Sure, Vince, sure."

Ferenc walked reluctantly into the bedroom and closed the door. They heard the springs creak as he sat heavily on the edge of the bed. Pauline knelt on the floor at Vince's knee and wet the washcloth in the kettle of hot water.

"Why'd you come here?" she asked in a low voice.

"Where'd you expect me to go, police headquarters?" Vince grinned. "Ain't I welcome, kiddo?"

"You're here," she said shortly. "Hold still." She began to moisten the bandage with the wet washcloth.

Vince looked at the bedroom door. Ferenc was walking around in there now.

"He's not much good, is he?"

"He's all right if you leave him alone."

"I'll leave him alone if he don't get out of line."

"He'll be all right if you leave him alone!"

"Okay, sure, anything you say, kiddo."

She was bent over his leg, carefully peeling back the bandage from the bullet gouge on the outside of his thigh. Her housecoat hung open and he tried to slide his hand inside of it. She pushed his arm away.

"None of that," she said sharply. "That's over and done with."

"It's never over and done with, kiddo."

"With us it is. Now cut it out."

"Sure, kiddo, sure. For the time being."

She straightened up and looked steadily into his face. "All right," she said, "don't cut it out and see what happens. Lyle won't take it, not here in his own house right under his nose. He might not be much good when it comes to shooting people and breaking out of jail and acting tough, but there's a limit even with him."

"What'll he do, kiddo?" Vince asked softly. "Beat me up or run to the cops or what?"

"I don't know what he'll do, but I know he won't take it."

"I'm worrying."

"Oh, God!" she said bitterly, "I'm so tired of tough guys that think all they have to do is grab something when they want it; so for the last time I'm telling you leave him alone!"

Vince was shaken by her vehemence, but he concealed it and laughed, roughing her hair. "Maybe you're right. There's a time and place for everything."

"No more, Vince. Not ever again. I—"

"You what, kiddo?"

She lifted her head, facing him defiantly. "I was glad when they sent you to jail because that ended it."

"Well that's nice to know, kiddo. You were glad."

"Only because it ended it. I didn't want you in jail but—you got a wife and you say you're crazy about her. I don't mean nothing to you, so why mess things up for me? You know what you'd do if somebody messed around with Bonnie and—"

"Leave her out of it! She ain't like you, you dumb Hunky. She don't mess around. Now get that bandage off."

Neither of them spoke as she removed the rest of the bandage and gently washed the dried blood away from the wound. It was a clean gouge, bleeding just slightly, and there were no telltale streaks of red radiating into the leg from it. Pauline held the washcloth under his thigh to catch the drip and poured the bottle of mercurochrome into the wound. She took a roll of bandage from the pocket of her housecoat, made a pad of part of it and expertly bound it in place. She stood up wearily, bending again to pick up the water kettle.

"You can sleep on the sofa tonight," she said in a drained voice. "I'll fix a bed in one of the other rooms for you tomorrow. Do you want anything to eat?"

Vince was unbuttoning his shirt. "Beat it. I'm going to sleep."

"Want me to turn off the light?"

"Go ahead."

He took off his pants in the darkness and dropped them on the floor beside his shirt. He groped for the bottle of bourbon and took a deep swallow before stretching out on the sofa. He could hear the voices of Ferenc and Pauline mumbling in the bedroom and he strained to hear what they were saying, his eyes narrowed with suspicion. They were talking too softly and finally he got up from the sofa and hobbled painfully to the door, leaning close to it. He had the gun in his hand. Let them say the wrong thing, just one wrong thing.

"... the back bedroom. I'll put the bed together in the morning." That was Ferenc.

"The first thing, Lyle. We can't have him in the living room. Somebody might walk in."

"Sure, the first thing. His leg, how bad is it?"

"Not bad, but it'll be a week anyways."

"He'll pay, Pauline. Vince is okay. If he don't have the money now, he'll pay later for anything we have to lay out."

"I'm not worried about that."

"And don't worry about the cops. They won't bother us. They don't even know we know him."

"I'm not worried about that either."

"You're not sore, are you? I mean, because he—"

"No, I'm not sore. I'm just tired and I don't feel like talking."

"Sure, honey, sure."

There was a faint click and the thread of yellow light disappeared from under the door. Vince hobbled back to the sofa and lay down, thrusting the gun under the cushions close to his hand. Ferenc was just a mutt, but he'd have to keep his eye on that lousy Pauline. She was acting too damn smart. He lay in the darkness and listened to the heavy thudding of his heart in the deeper darkness of his chest. He was covered with sweat. It was hot.

CHAPTER TWO

Steve Ewell stood in the shade of the Rocky Hill Bank and watched the bus belch a cloud of blue exhaust smoke and lumber up the highway, noisily flatulent. His jacket hung limply over his left arm, his tie was pulled down from his collar and his white shirt glistened gray from sweat. It had been a two-hour trip from Newark and he had fairly roasted in the bus. Newark had been an inferno and it was scarcely any cooler up here in the mountains.

Steve flipped the sweat from his forehead with his thumb and, picking up his suitcase, plodded down the street toward Shorty's Bar next to the five-and-dime.

Shorty's was not air-conditioned, but the huge exhaust fan at the back sucked in a breeze through the open front door and made it cool enough. There were about fifteen men in the bar, vacationers, most of them, from the several lakes in the area, dressed in shorts and T-shirts, silently watching a baseball game on the TV. Even the bartender was leaning trance-like against the cash register with a forgotten cigar plugged into his mouth as if to keep the conversation from leaking out.

Steve rapped on the bar with his knuckles and called, "Hey, Shorty, give me a beer, will you?"

Shorty turned reluctantly from the TV screen and gave Steve an irritated glance that turned into a frozen stare of astonishment and fright. He recovered himself almost immediately but some traces of the fright remained in his voice when he said, "Oh—hi, Steve. Just get in?"

"On the bus, and I'm thirsty."

Shorty hustled a beer down to him. His interest in the baseball game seemed to have disappeared entirely, for he leaned against the bar and regarded Steve with an oddly covert glance.

"Still working on that boat, eh, Steve? Are you the captain yet?"

"Second mate." Steve was hot and tired and did not feel much like making small talk.

Shorty's eyes probed at him. "Been away quite a while this time."

"Two months."

"Where's that boat go, anyways? Europe?"

"Washington State for a cargo of lumber."

"Lonesome kind of life, ain't it? I mean, stuck on the same boat for two months. You have TV or radio or anything like that?"

Steve was amused at the thought of TV on the freighter. "If anybody tried to bring a TV aboard, the captain'd heave him and it into the bay before they got up the gangplank."

"You must get kind of out of touch with things then, don't you?" Shorty asked cautiously, still probing.

Steve shrugged. "We manage. Can I use your phone? I want to call Ida to pick me up." Ida was his older sister.

Shorty said, "Help yourself," and took the phone from under the bar and set it before Steve. He watched intently as Steve dialed the number and waited for his sister to answer.

The phone rang twelve times before Steve hung up. Shorty looked faintly disappointed. Steve dialed another number and ordered a cab from the railroad station.

Shorty hesitated, then said, "I guess you don't get much news from home while you're out on the boat, eh?"

"Ida writes twice a week. Give me another beer, will you?"

Shorty brought him a second beer, made another abortive attempt at his curiously probing conversation, then drifted up the bar to where the other men were sitting. Watching through the window for the cab, Steve scarcely noticed the whispering and the veiled glances. When the cab came he picked up his bag and trudged out to it. The driver started and gaped when Steve came across the sidewalk but, like Shorty, recovered and greeted him by name.

This time Steve noticed it more and, frowning with annoyance, said, "Take me out to the house, Wally." He lounged in the back seat and lit a cigarette. Wally was trying to make conversation, too, like Shorty, but Steve did not listen and discouraged it with monosyllabic grunts. He didn't like Wally. Wally was fat and sloppy and the town's worst gossip.

But when he got out at the house he felt that he had been unnecessarily surly and said more cordially, "It's sure nice to be back, Wally. There's no place like home."

Wally said, "Yeah," and looked back over his shoulder as he drove away.

Half-amused, Steve wondered if he had two heads or something, the way everybody was acting, but then forgot about it as he walked up the flagged path to the house. It was good to be home, and in another year or two it really would be home and he could forget about the boats and the sea and all the rest of it.

The house was not much to look at. It was just a house with a peaked roof and a verandah in front. It was freshly white in the sunshine and the grounds around it were as neat as a park. You could depend on Ida for that. Ida was sometimes a little too relentlessly neat, but it was better than coming home to a place that looked like a pigpen.

He and Ida owned, in all, about fifty acres of hilly, stony, untillable land with a pond at the northwest end of it. Vince had once owned a third of this, but Steve had bought his share for fifteen hundred dollars. The land had not been worth very much until Steve dammed the pond and made a good-sized lake of it. Next year he was going to put in a dock and rowboats, bathhouses, showers and toilets and open it as a public lake for swimming and picnicking. There were three public lakes in the area, but they were overcrowded every weekend. Steve knew that he would get the business when he opened the lake to the public, and at a dollar a car there was a damn good living to be made even though the season lasted only about ten weeks.

Next year they'd open for sure. The roads were in and Orv Burnett had been putting up picnic tables all summer. Right now it was known locally as Ewell's Pond, but they were thinking of changing it to something fancier to pull in trade. But they could take care of that when the time came. There were other things to think about right now.

He was changing into shorts for a swim in the lake when he heard the car crunch up the graveled drive beside the house. He glanced out the window and saw Ida and Orv get out of it. For some reason, Steve did not call out to them. Maybe it was the way they walked toward the house without speaking, as if they'd just had a fight. Ida was a little hard to get along with sometimes unless you knew how to handle her.

Steve put on a pair of tattered tennis shoes, threw a towel over his shoulder and went down the stairs whistling. Ida was in the downstairs hall and when she saw him she gave a scream and her hand flew to her mouth.

"I'm sorry, Sis. I—" Steve began contritely.

"Don't you ever do that again!" she cried shrilly. "I'm shaking all over."

Orv came running from the kitchen, carrying a rifle, and his jaw dropped when he saw Steve on the stairway. Steve looked from one to the other.

"What's going on here?" he asked. "What's the matter with everybody? And what's the gun for? Why're you gaping at me like that? Is everybody crazy?"

Orv stammered, "I—I thought you was Vince for a minute, Steve. You looked just like him."

Steve knew that he closely resembled Vince, his older brother. They were both big and both had red hair and the same lean kind of face, but they had always looked more or less alike, so what was there to get excited about? Vince was in jail, sure, but—

"Vince broke out of jail a week ago," said Ida, her voice still shrill. "They think he's hiding in the hills around here someplace and you come charging down the stairs like that!"

Steve said slowly, "Vince broke jail?"

"Didn't you know?"

Steve shook his head. "No wonder I've been getting funny looks from everybody. How do they know he's hiding in the hills?"

"They're pretty sure," said Ida, her lips thinning. "They're waiting for him to try to get in touch with Bonnie."

"There are police all over the place," said Orv. "He won't have a chance."

"Isn't Bonnie here?" asked Steve, coming slowly down the stairs.

"Here!" Ida laughed bitterly. "It was never good enough for Bonnie here. It was too respectable for her. She couldn't come and go as she pleased and traipse around with men. She left right after you did two months ago. The last I heard she was singing in that Field Stone Inn over on Lake Powhatan, that gambling place. But that's just her speed."

Steve did not reply to this. Bonnie and Ida had never gotten along, though Bonnie had come to live with them after Vince went to jail. It was plain from the beginning that she didn't want to, but Vince had told her to and she was afraid of Vince, even in jail. She was a beautiful girl, but sullen, and she had spent hours alone in her room doing things to her blonde hair, making up her face, manicuring her nails, trying on dresses, or just lying in bed reading movie magazines. It was obvious that Vince had sent her to the house so that Ida could keep an eye on her, because Bonnie couldn't be two minutes in a room with a man without—Steve did not want to think about Bonnie.

"Let's go into the living room," he said.

They went into the living room, Ida stiff-mouthed and grim, Orv slouching behind them with the rifle. Steve sat down in the wing chair and looked at them. Ida was twelve years older than he, a tall, spare woman with black hair going gray. There was a hardness in her face and eyes, and her mouth was thinner and more bloodless than he remembered it. Surprised, as if he had never really looked at her before, he saw an embittered woman, going harsh with age, her face now tight in anger.

"Did Vince break out of jail or did he just escape?" Steve asked, emphasizing the words to make the difference between them.

Ida remained standing, her hands tight at her waist. "He broke out, him and another man. The other man is dead. They found him in the Hackensack River. And a guard was shot in the prison. He might die."

"Did Vince shoot him or was it the other man?"

"What difference does that make? He's just as guilty if the guard dies. That's what the law says. It's not bad enough to have a jailbird in the family, now we'll have a murderer!"

"But that guard ain't dead yet, Ida," Orv said.

Except for an impatient noise in her throat, Ida ignored him and continued to address her anger at Steve. "Every time I go out there's a policeman watching me, even when I go to church or prayer meeting or the Ladies' Aid. I'm beginning to feel like a criminal myself."

"Nobody's treating you like a criminal, Ida," said Steve mechanically.

"No?" Ida's sallow face was very pale. "What do you call it when you have to sit and answer questions as though they were accusing you, and they've searched every room in the house, too. I suppose that was nothing at all. I suppose I should have welcomed them with open arms. How do you think I feel when I can't ask my friends to the house anymore for fear a policeman will stop them outside and ask them what their business is? The church supper's tonight, but do you think I'd dare go? Why, I'd be ashamed to show my face."

"You've nothing to be ashamed of, Ida," Steve soothed her, knowing how she could work herself into shrill hysteria. "I know Vince is our brother but—"

"He's no brother of mine!" she snapped. "He's a wild animal and I hope they hunt him down like one."

Steve was shocked at this glitter of crystallized venom. "You don't mean that, Ida."

"Oh, don't I? Well I hope he does try to get in touch with Bonnie. She'll turn him over to the police fast enough. He'll find out how much she wants him now, an escaped convict. She's no fool, no matter what else she is. You can't tell me anything about Bonnie. And I'll tell you something you don't know. She started divorce proceedings against him but called it off when he escaped from jail. Vince'd kill her if he ever knew she was after a divorce. And he'd kill her if he knew some of the other things about her, too," Ida added significantly.

In the same mechanical tone, Steve said, "Vince isn't going to kill anybody." He was still stunned by the news of the jailbreak.

He knew that Vince deserved to be in jail. He and another man had held up the Newberg Bank for thirty-seven-thousand dollars. Vince had been caught spending some of the money, of which the serial numbers were known. But he had refused to divulge the identity of his accomplice, just as he had refused to surrender the stolen money, and only the few hundred dollars were recovered that had been in Vince's wallet at the time of his arrest in Rocky Hill.

The bank guard had been shot during the holdup. The bullet had splintered part of his skull. He was still alive, if you could call it that. Bedridden and mindless, the only words he mumbled were, "Your face looks familiar," though he recognized no one, not even his wife. The insurance company had spent hundreds of dollars on doctors in the futile effort to restore his mind, for he was the only one who might have been able to identify the driver of Vince's getaway car.

Yes, Vince deserved to be in jail, but Steve remembered things about him that no one else knew. When he was about eighteen, Steve had worshiped his older brother. Vince had been big and tough and handsome and generous and always laughing and had taken him to shows and nightclubs in New York. He had also taken him to some pretty tough places in Jersey where men in shirtsleeves had shot craps in the back rooms of gin mills, and sometimes there had been four or five hundred dollars on the table awaiting the roll and bounce of the dice. And always there had been women.

Vince had had an enormous, confident vitality that had a tremendous attraction for women of all kinds. They just couldn't stay away from him.

"But don't let them kid you, Stevie. They're all pigs."

And many's the time when Steve had a date Vince stuck a folded twenty-dollar bill into the breast pocket of his jacket. *"That's all they want from you anyways, kid. Spend it on them and get what you want, too."*

Then he had disappeared for five years and it had turned out in the trial for the bank holdup that he'd been in jail for three of those years in Illinois.

Two and a half years ago he had come back to Rocky Hill with Bonnie. Pa had died and left them the fifty acres and Vince offered to sell his share to Steve for fifteen hundred dollars. Steve had been working on the boats and had two thousand saved. Vince had lived high and wide, gambling at the Field Stone Inn, buying Bonnie all kinds of fancy clothes, running around in a second-hand Cadillac, living at the Inn at fifteen dollars a day—until his luck broke at the crap table and he held up the Newberg Bank.

But you couldn't think of your own brother as a criminal, no matter what the evidence. Your memory was too full of all the everyday things from the time when he had not been a criminal.

"I suppose you're going to sit there and make excuses for him again, the way you always do," Ida said harshly, "in spite of all the disgrace he's brought down on us."

"I don't feel disgraced," said Steve with a sudden, inexplicable anger. "I haven't done anything to disgrace myself."

"That's all very well for you. You don't have to live here and face it and people whispering behind your back. What do you have to worry about? All you do is go merrily off on the boats, but I'm the one who has to face it. I'm the one they talk about. 'There goes Ida Ewell, her brother's in jail.' I hope they get him. I hope they've got him right now. I hope—"

Steve jumped to his feet. "Shut up!" he shouted at her. "Shut up, will you! Shut up! Shut up!"

Ida seemed to grow taller, more angular, harsher, a grim accuser in her relentless black dress. "You never would face the truth about Vince, never. He was never wrong as far as you're concerned and you even gave him fifteen hundred dollars for his share of the property when you knew very well it wasn't worth even twelve. You helped him in his life of sin and iniquity, and if there's any outside blame, maybe you're as guilty as he is in the eyes of the Lord!"

Crimson-faced, Steve yelled at her, "And your trouble is you always hated him because he had a good time and you never did. You hated him as long as I can remember."

"You're right. I did. I hated him because of his gambling and whoring and the disgrace he brought down on us."

Orv shifted uneasily from one foot to the other and rested the butt of the rifle on the floor. Steve looked at him.

"And what're you doing with that rifle anyway?" he demanded.

"He's helping the police just like all the other men," Ida said sharply. "And if you had an ounce of pride or decency, that's just what you'll be doing too!"

Ida lifted her chin triumphantly, turned and walked out of the living room. Her heels sounded like someone driving nails into the hardwood floor of the hall.

CHAPTER THREE

Steve walked heavily to the window and stood there though he could see nothing but the drawn blind.

"I shouldn't have gotten her worked up like that," he said.

"She wants to get married," said Orv in a matter-of-fact voice. "That's the whole thing. She ain't seen him since Vince broke out."

Steve turned incredulously. "She wants to get married?"

"Yep. A fellow down her church. Floyd Morley."

"Who!"

"Floyd Morley. He kind of works in the supermarket. The fat one."

Steve thought, *My God!* Morley was about Ida's age, but he was nothing more than a stock boy in the supermarket. He helped put the stock on the shelves, carried out packages, swept the floor and did other odd jobs. He was good-natured and didn't drink or anything like that, but he was so lazy that they called him the workless wonder. And he wasn't very bright, either. But bright enough to know that if he married Ida she'd take care of him for the rest of his life. Ida would have a pretty damn nice income when the lake was open to the public. But if he thought he was going to have a life of shiftless ease, he didn't know Ida.

But the whole thing was too ridiculous. Ida would never dream of marrying anybody like Floyd Morley. Ida had brains, she was a good manager and a good business woman. Then, uneasily, Steve remembered that Ida was far from young and had never been married. He had never thought of her as an old maid, but my God, that's what an old maid was, wasn't it?

And Orv told Vince about the police searching the house, asking endless questions, rounding up a posse which Orv had joined.

Steve looked at Orv's rifle and then at his long, bleak face. "You'd shoot Vince, Orv?"

"If he was shooting at me I wouldn't just stand there."

Steve nodded vaguely, but it was a kind of nightmare—Ida, Orv with the rifle, the police, and all the rest of it. "Is—Vince really hiding out there in the hills, Orv?" he asked heavily.

Orv lifted one thin shoulder. "I ain't seen him, and it ain't as easy to hide out there as it looks. I figure he's somewheres else and he'll come in after Bonnie when it suits him."

"Why should he come in after Bonnie at all?"

"That's what the p'lice say. I wouldn't know myself. Maybe she's got the money he stole from the bank."

Steve had forgotten about the money. Thirty-seven-thousand dollars. It never had turned up, except for a few hundred. Maybe it was hidden around the Valley somewhere, and you needed money when you were on the run. And maybe Bonnie did know about it. Maybe he had to get in touch with Bonnie.

And that was another thing Ida had been right about—Bonnie. Vince free and with money in his pocket was one thing, but Vince on the run was something else; and Bonnie was for Bonnie, first, last and always. God, if only he could get to Vince and tell him how things were. Maybe Orv—

"You and Vince used to be pretty good friends, Orv," he said tentatively, and then saw the uselessness of this in Orv's thin, bleak face. "Never mind. Forget it. Are you still working on those picnic tables around the lake?"

"I'll get back to them when this is over. I only got about ten more to put up, then I can start on the dock. I ain't got nothing against Vince, but the way I figure he's kind of like a fellow that's gone crazy and you got to go after him before he hurts somebody."

"Go on then!" said Steve violently. "Get out there with your gun. Maybe you'll be the lucky one to bring him in."

"Sure, Steve." Orv started for the door, but stopped and turned and said in his usual flat, matter-of-fact voice, "Mind if I say something, Steve?"

"What is it?"

"Well, just don't go getting any foolish ideas about helping Vince, that's all. Don't get yourself hurt, Steve. An escaped convict with a gun and in a killing mood ain't nobody's brother."

CHAPTER FOUR

On his return to the cab post in the Rocky Hill railroad station, Wally Kronk made several stops for the specific purpose of spreading the news that Steve Ewell was back. Wally could take the flimsiest bit of gossip and, with real talent, weave a seemingly stout fabric of innuendo with a faint pattern of the meager facts at hand. Perhaps he was not entirely to be blamed for the guinea hen clacking of his tongue.

Hacking in Rocky Hill did not have the variety of driving a cab in the city. There were long stretches of monotony when he did nothing but sit in his cab at the station and wait for the telephone to summon him, and perhaps this was one way of pretending that interesting things were taking place all around him.

But this time he had a bit of real news and he made the most of it.

"You hear the latest? Steve Ewell just blew into town."

"Steve Ewell? That's Vince's brother, ain't it?"

"Yep, and looks just like him too, red hair and all."

"Well. When'd he get in?"

"'Bout a half hour ago. I just drove him out to his place in the Valley. I couldn't get two words out of him all the way, and you should of seen his face. Brother! I took one look at it and kept my big trap shut."

"Sore about Vince, you think?"

"Sore! Man, he was boiling. You know how close him and Vince always was. As brothers, they were thicker'n thieves, and you know the old saying—birds of a feather. Why'd Steve just *happen* to turn up at this particular time?"

"I don't know. Why?"

"I don't know either, but it's a little funny when you stop to think about it, ain't it? Half the cops in the county and a posse of two hundred guys armed to the teeth behind every tree in the hills—and Steve turns up. Maybe there's no connection. I don't know.

"I ain't saying Steve is looking for trouble or anything like that. Hell, everybody knows Steve's a good, steady boy and never made trouble for nobody. He minds his own business and he's making a nice place out of that property of his in the Valley. But blood's thicker'n water, like they say, and what would *you* do if the cops were after *your* brother. Turn him in—or what?"

"Maybe you got something there."

"Me? I ain't got a thing. I don't know from nothing. I just drive a hack and Steve's turning up at this particular time is probably just one of them coincidences and that's all. Steve's too level-headed to go bucking the cops, even if Vince is his brother, and I'd be the first to say it."

"Yeah, but his own brother—"

"No buts about it. Steve's a tough boy, I grant you, but that don't say he's going to break any laws. Unless I'm greatly mistaken—"

And so on with variations on the theme, for Wally was a talented virtuoso.

Patrolman John Vacheresse was gassing up the prowl car in Henny's Service Station when Henny gave him the news which he had gotten directly from Chappy Collier who'd gotten it directly from the counterman in Woody's Diner who'd gotten it directly from Wally over a cup of coffee and a jelly doughnut. Patrolman Vacheresse had the eight-to-four tour. There were only three patrolmen and the chief on the Rocky Hill force. There was a radio in the police car, but Vacheresse used the telephone to call Police Chief Carl Winder at headquarters in the firehouse and tell him that Steve Ewell had turned up unexpectedly in town, spoiling for a fight. Winder, in turn, called the mayor, who was in his office in the south wing of the civic center. The mayor was boss of all town employees, but responsible, of course, to the four-man town council.

"This is Winder, Mayor. Vacheresse just told me that Steve Ewell's back in town and looking for trouble. Wally Kronk just drove him home in his hack. Groff and Ferris are watching the house, so we've got him covered for the time being, but I think we ought to look into this a little further. Want me to have Vacheresse bring him in for questioning? Him and Vince were pretty close."

The mayor was a retired states attorney, a shrewd courtroom campaigner and a shrewder politician, even though the Party had put him out to pasture. He had run for mayor, not to continue his political career—he'd had enough of that—but because he genuinely wanted to make Rocky Hill as fine a town as possible. Chief Winder was not his office boy by any means, but this was a big case and the mayor's experience made his advice a valuable aid.

The mayor deliberated. "No, Carl," he said at length, "I think it might be a mistake to question Steve at this point. We'll keep him covered twenty-four hours a day, the same as Vince's wife out there in the Field Stone Inn, but I don't think questioning would do us any good. If Steve is up here to help Vince, he wouldn't tell us and we couldn't make him tell us and there's nothing we could do about it. Steve hasn't broken any laws as far as we know. Furthermore, I think that a full-scale questioning would serve to make him only the more secretive. Let him think we're ignoring him. Tell Groff and Ferris to keep out of sight. There's a chance that Steve might lead us to Vince, and that'd be quite a feather in our caps. Just keep him well covered for the time being, Carl."

"I've got him covered, Mayor. We'll know if he brushes his teeth up and down or sideways, if he has eggs or oatmeal for breakfast, or what programs he listens to on TV. The boys are doing a nice job on that angle."

"I know I can depend on you for that, Carl. But you say he came back unexpectedly?"

"I haven't checked on that personally. Vacheresse just called me and I called you right away. From what I bear, Steve's a second mate on a freighter for the Trans-Ocean Line out of Port Newark, and he's usually away between four and five months. This time he came back in three weeks. How much truth there is in that, I don't know. I'm going to check with the Trans-Ocean Line office right away. Maybe Steve wasn't even on a trip this time, but I'm going to find out."

"Better let me make that call, Carl. I want to find out what kind of record Steve Ewell has with the company, too. You don't have anything on Steve yourself, do you?"

"Not a thing except a couple traffic violations."

"That's what I thought. I'll call you back after I talk to Trans-Ocean. Are those phone bugs still working?"

"Like a charm. Bus Taylor did a nice job on that. I'm monitoring every call to and from both the Ewell house and the Field Stone Inn."

"Is Bonnie Ewell still behaving herself?"

"Except with Crane, probably."

"Well—I'll call you back. Thanks for letting me know."

Doris Stewart was a brunette with smoldering undertones of red in her hair. Her eyes were a gold-flecked green and her lips had a definite and intriguing lift. She was five-feet-two and weighed a hundred and ten pounds, all of which seemed to have been quite well assembled. She was secretary to the executive secretary of the Rocky Hill Chamber of Commerce, who, as the boys said, knew how to pick 'em.

She heard the news about Steve when the president of the Chamber dropped in for a chat with the executive secretary, and her hands began to tremble just a little as she assembled the brochures which were to be mailed to a selected list of manufacturers who might consider Rocky Hill, with its zoning for light industry near the railroad, as a possible site for a small factory or assembly plant. She waited five minutes to steady herself and then went out to the pay phone in the outer office and called Steve.

"Welcome home, stranger," she said with a fair imitation of light-hearted gaiety. "Why don't you let a fellow know when you return from voyaging in far places?"

"Hi, Doris. I just got in a few minutes ago."

Doris hesitated and her hand tightened on the phone. "I—suppose you've heard about Vince."

"Yeah."

It was obvious from the shortness in his voice that he did not want to talk about it.

"You—haven't heard from him, have you, Steve?" she asked a little breathlessly.

"Heard from him?" He was angry about something. "Why should I hear from him? I haven't been in the house a half hour."

"I just thought that maybe—" She stopped and caught her lower lip between her teeth. She was being importunate and probably making a fool of herself, but she had to talk to him. "Would—would you like to have a cocktail with me after I finish work? It'll be nice to see you again, Steve."

There was a long pause and then he said slowly, "Sure, Doris. We can go over to Field Stone Inn. What time?"

"Five. A little after. Give me time for a new paint job and to wash the sludge off my hot and grimy little hands. Say ten after five here at the office of the Chamber."

"Okay. Ten after."

But she couldn't hang up. Lowering her voice, she said in little jerks, "You—really haven't heard from—Vince, Steve? Not at all?"

He said woodenly, "Maybe I should have told you this in the beginning, but the police are listening in to this call. They've got the line tapped. I can tell because I was in the Signal Corps in Korea and worked with phones a lot."

She said, "Oh," in a very small, chilled voice.

"Yeah. But that's their fun. I'll see you a little after five, Doris."

"I'll—I'll be looking for you, Steve."

She replaced the phone in its cradle and; shaking a little, wiped her hand down the side of her skirt as if she had picked up a piece of bacon rind by mistake. What an idiot he must think her! She glanced automatically at her wrist watch. It was quarter after four. She gasped, "Oh my!" and ran back into the inner office. The brochures had to be in the mail for the five o'clock train.

At ten past five she was watching anxiously through the window of the outer office. Her fingers were crossed and she was dreading that at any moment the phone would ring and it would be Steve saying that he couldn't make it. He drove up three minutes later in a black '51 Ford convertible, the top folded back and buttoned into the boot. Her heart swelled and pulsed and she tried to swallow the sickish feeling in her chest.

She jerked open the door and ran down the steps, crying brightly, "Hi, sailor, looking for a pickup?"

He said quietly, "Hi, Dorrie," and opened the door for her.

She chattered aimlessly as they drove out of town, but all the while she was watching Steve, comparing him to Vince. Steve watched the road, concentrating on his driving, letting her do most of the talking until they reached the Inn.

The Field Stone Inn was old, dating back to the Revolution. It was a gracious, rambling house on a hill overlooking the tailored, expensive placidity of Lake Powhatan.

Henry Crane, who owned it now, had restored the interior, keeping it

Colonial without distorting it. Of course, the dining room had been enlarged and a dance floor and band dais added. The white-paneled bar, with its marble fireplace, had originally been the north sitting room. There wasn't really a bar. It was called the Tap Room and you sat at small tables and were served by quiet waiters in gray jackets and dark blue trousers.

After they were seated, Doris leaned over the edge of the table and whispered, "Is there really gambling here, Steve?"

"Downstairs. A dice table and a roulette wheel and that's all. Everybody talks in a low voice and it's very respectable."

"How horrible. If I gambled, I certainly wouldn't want to feel respectable."

A tall, sandy-haired man, sitting alone at another table, rose and crossed the room, smiling as he patted Steve on the shoulder. "Well, well, well, home is the sailor," he said. "May I interview you, Mr. Ulysses? What is your opinion of American women?"

Steve said, "Hi, Ralph," and introduced him to Doris. Ralph Loriot, editor and publisher of the weekly *Rocky Hill News*. "Have a drink with us, Ralph. But no interviews." That was definitely a warning that he had nothing to say about Vince.

"You celebrities are all alike," said Loriot, sitting at the table opposite Doris, at whom he looked with cheerful admiration. "Though there's one question I won't have to ask you. I can see what you think of American women."

"I'm not American women at all," said Doris, wishing Loriot would go away so she could finally talk with Steve. About Vince. She wanted so desperately to talk to him about Vince! Now here was this Loriot character, all grins and sophomoric conversation. "American women are lady Congressmen, sewing circles and the Missionary Guild of the Methodist Church."

"You couldn't be more wrong," Loriot assured her. "As a matter of fact, there's no such thing as American women. It's a myth created by Petty."

Doris smiled absently. She was watching Steve. He was on edge. He was sitting with his arms folded over his chest and the fingers of his right hand drummed on the biceps of his left arm. He hadn't touched his drink at all and every once in a while he glanced sharply around the room.

He looked almost as if he had been expecting it when the waiter came to the table and said, "Mr. Ewell? There's a call for you, sir. The phone is at the service bar."

Steve jumped up, mumbled, "Excuse me," and strode quickly toward the bar. He spoke very briefly into the phone, nodded and strode back to the table. "Excuse me for a few minutes, will you, Doris? Mind her for me, Ralph. I won't be long."

And then he was gone. No explanation.

Loriot's lips bunched in a thoughtful pucker. And then he saw the remote, stricken, naked expression on Doris's face. He lifted his glass with an airy gesture.

"Well," he said, "perhaps I can interview you, Miss Stewart. What is your opinion of American men?"

She started and looked blankly at him.

CHAPTER FIVE

Bonnie Ewell was lying face down on a cot in the sun on Henry Crane's private terrace over the southwest wing of the Inn. The terrace was enclosed by canvas strips, which was just as well because Bonnie was not wearing even the token wisps of a Bikini sun suit.

Bonnie was bored and sullen. She had been terrified when Vince escaped from prison, terrified that he would come back for her. And so she was thankful when the police and the posse concealed themselves in the woods around the Inn. Four county detectives were in the Inn itself. One was the parking lot attendant, two were waiters and the fourth one was the doorman. Henry Crane always cooperated with the police, even in the matter of the gambling room, for which he had made suitable financial arrangements with the county officials.

But the fear had passed and now she was bored and resentful of the very protection that guarded her from Vince. It was as bad as being in prison herself. No matter what she did or where she went, there was somebody watching her. Men didn't make passes at her anymore. They didn't invite her out after her turn in the midnight show, or take her roaring around the lake in their speedboats. They didn't even ask her to dance with them. She was poison. She was Vince Ewell's wife, and though they came to stare at her, they didn't want any part of her.

Bonnie went through that phase of sullen boredom, and then she began to hope that Vince would break through. After all, he was crazy about her and she'd never really had any trouble handling him. She was terrified of him when he lost that wild, red-headed temper of his and he was like a maniac, but he was crazy about her and in the end she could always handle him. The cops and the posse out there were just a bunch of hicks in the sticks. Vince could walk right through them and out again.

And there was that thirty-seven-thousand dollars from the bank, and he wouldn't walk out without that. That would go with them in a box or a suitcase or something. You didn't realize how much thirty-seven thousand was until you worked for a hundred a week singing in this hick nightclub and figured how long it would take you to save that kind of money after paying your bills. Almost fifteen years or more. She'd be old in fifteen years, and anyway you just couldn't save that much money, something always turned up; but Vince had thirty-seven thousand in a lump.

She had no plan or anything like that. She never made plans, or if she did, they were just vague, formless things that she *hoped* would happen. All she knew was that Vince had thirty-seven thousand and she wanted it. The closest she came to planning a method to get it was knowing that she could handle Vince. And the proof of that was that he had broken out of prison just to get to her.

So she waited and the police waited but there was no Vince and it had been over a week since he had broken out. Nothing was going to happen. He had gotten the money from wherever he'd hidden it and was now on his way to South America or Canada or some other foreign country and maybe in a year or so he'd send for her, but that would be too late. Vaguely, but not knowing quite why, she realized that she would never see any of the money once it was out of the country.

And so the boredom set in again, heavier, thicker and deadlier because she had lost hope that Vince would even try to see her now. But the police still watched her, made her feel locked in.

She wished that Vince were dead, that they'd shot him like that other man when he broke out of prison!

She heard the snick of the catch as the French doors opened from Crane's suite off the terrace, but she did not look up. The suite and the terrace were forbidden to everybody but her and Crane. Passively she waited for him to come and pat her bare buttocks, as he always did. Just a casual pat, the way he patted that damn silly overgrown Great Dane of his. But this time he did not pat her and, with a small catch of fear, she turned her head to see if it were really Crane.

It was. He was standing at the French doors, smoking a cigar and scratching the ear of that damn Great Dane that should have been pulling a milk wagon instead of flopping around eating steaks all day.

"Why don't you say something when you come out," she said crossly. "How do I know who it is?"

He was a short, stocky man, swarthy and with black hair that looked as if it had been Simonized. He dyed it, Bonnie knew. His expression was that as if he were sucking something very delectable through a straw, and his eyes were large and almost liquidly brown. He looked like a pleasant, contented little stout man and very little like a gambling house operator—a fact that he disclaimed in any event. The gambling was merely a diversion for the patrons of the Inn, a profitable sideline. He was blandly contemptuous of gambling and gamblers, both of which he considered foolish. He was as hard as the blade on a bulldozer and as practical as a cash register.

"There's a man downstairs to see you," he said, ignoring her bad temper as he always did. He spoke with a slight accent.

"A man?" Bonnie sat up. "What kind of a man? Didn't he give a name or anything?"

"He gave a name. Steve Ewell. He told the parking lot attendant he wanted to talk to you. He did not know the attendant is a policeman."

"Steve Ewell! I don't want to see him. I don't want anything to do with him."

"He is the brother to Vincent, your husband, is he not?"

"I don't want to see him!" Bonnie cried stridently, jumping up from the cot. "I told you I didn't want to see him, didn't I?"

The Great Dane stiffened at this sudden action and Crane patted its neck reassuringly. "I'm afraid we have no choice in the matter, my dear," he told Bonnie. "The police wish you to see this man."

"I don't have to do everything they say, do I?"

"This, yes. We must cooperate."

"Why, tell me why!"

"Because the police are the police and they are the same everywhere. They can make difficulties and I do not like difficulties of any kind." The warning given, he went on, "Why is it that you do not wish to see the brother of your husband, my dear?"

Crane's manner had been bland and he had not raised his voice as much as the quarter of a tone, but Bonnie knew that she had been told off and she sat sullenly on the edge of the cot.

"Because he's a snoop just like that lousy old maid sister of his. He probably wants me to go back to that stinking old house and I'm not going."

"But he cannot force you, my dear."

"For Pete's sake, he can tell Vince, can't he?"

"Ah, would he, indeed? He knows then where your husband can be found?"

"You can say *that* again, brother!"

"I should think then, my dear, that you would find that a further inducement for having a tête-à-tête with him."

"Talk English for once, can't you?" Bonnie jeered.

Crane smiled faintly. "Put on your robe, my dear. I am going to talk to you for a moment and I do not wish to be distracted from what I am going to say."

Bonnie jeered, "More double-talk," but put on the expensive vicuna robe that she had dropped in a careless heap on the deck of the terrace.

Crane tapped the Dane on the shoulder and the animal obediently sat down across the threshold of the French doors. He picked up a light aluminum chair and took it to the side of the cot. He regarded her thoughtfully.

"I think," he said at length, "that it would be better if I put this in the form of an object lesson. Here is my watch." He removed it from his wrist and dropped it in her lap. "You have stolen it."

"Hey, wait a minute!" She looked at the watch, then angrily at him. "What the hell—"

"Please. Do not interrupt. Of course you have not stolen my watch. But this is an object lesson, which is merely the demonstration of a fact or theory to make it more comprehensible. So we will assume that you have stolen my watch. What are you going to do with it?"

"I ain't going to do nothing with it. Take it away. Put it back on. What do you think I am, a nutsy Fagin or something?"

Crane sighed. It was sometimes difficult to deal with a mind that was, at best, moronic. One had to be literal at all times, and more than literal, for the simplest things were often much too complicated for it to grasp even in essence and certainly not in detail. He had once mentioned the insurance policy on the Inn and she had hooted with laughter. "You got lots of dough, what do you need insurance? Out of purely clinical curiosity, he had questioned her. To her, insurance was, "Well, the guy comes around to collect it every week." But why did you pay it? "You got to pay. If you don't, they stop it." She was the same in all things. The movies? "You go to them." What was a bank, really? "They're glad enough to take your money, but just try and get a loan of some once!"

But there were compensations and, actually, conversations with women, especially intelligent ones, bored him. For him, Bonnie had all that was necessary for a woman to have and, with patience, she could be trained as easily as he had trained Tryggvi, the Great Dane.

He patted her thigh. "Of course you have not stolen my watch, my dear," he said, "but if it distresses you, we will assume that the watch was stolen by Jacob, the maître d'hotel."

"He's going to love this," she said sourly.

"Very well. Jacob has stolen my watch. It is worth fifteen hundred dollars. What is he going to do with it?"

"Hock it. What do you think?"

"Ah, but I have reported the theft to the police and you will observe that the watch is of a very distinctive design. Pawnbrokers will have been alerted."

"He can hock it in Chicago, can't he?"

"Of course, my dear. He could attempt to pawn it, let us say. But such a watch would arouse suspicion in any city and the pawnbroker would undoubtedly summon the police and Jacob would have to make a satisfactory explanation of his possession of the article or be arrested. Jacob is an intelligent man and he would know this and therefore he would not attempt to pawn it. Neither could he sell it unless he had a knowledge of the criminal market for such things, which is unlikely. It is not as simple to dispose of stolen goods as is popularly supposed."

Bonnie shifted peevishly on the cot. "So what?" she said irritably. "Jake or nobody stole the watch, so what?"

"Merely an object lesson, my pet. If Jacob can neither pawn nor sell the watch, what can he do with it? He wants the fifteen hundred dollars, but how can he go about obtaining it without being arrested for the theft? It would be extremely hazardous for him to approach either a pawnbroker or a reputable jeweler."

"He could go to somebody else, couldn't he?"

"To whom? An acquaintance? Does Jacob have an acquaintance who could or would pay fifteen hundred dollars for a watch? Even a friend would become suspicious under those circumstances. And it would be out of the question for him to offer it to a stranger. What, then, can Jacob do with the watch he has stolen?"

Bonnie scowled. "So he can't do nothing with it."

"Exactly. Jacob would be in the unfortunate position of having fifteen hundred dollars that he cannot spend, therefore he would have been very stupid to have stolen the watch in the first place. Is that correct, my dear?"

"It would be dumb," said Bonnie emphatically.

"It pleases me that you agree, my dear." Then very slowly and clearly he said, "Your husband is in an even more unfortunate position than Jacob would have been. Your husband has thirty-seven-thousand dollars that he cannot spend."

"You mean the cops'll get him first?"

"Even if he manages to evade the police he cannot spend the money, my dear. The bulk of the money he stole from the bank was a shipment of new bills from the Treasury Department, the serial numbers of which were on the consignment sheet that accompanied the shipment. The serial numbers identified the bills as having been stolen and caused his arrest two years ago. Upon his escape from prison, the numbers of the bills were again broadcast, so he still cannot spend the money without being arrested within a very short period of time, and anyone with him would be arrested also and sent to prison. Do you understand, my dear?"

Bonnie's jaw sagged in an expression of complete dismay. She understood and was a little afraid, too, for it was as if Crane had read her mind about getting her hands on the money.

Crane smiled. The point had been made, made and driven home. She was very transparent and he had known for some days that she had been thinking of the money, the obvious questions she had asked and things of that sort. He was quite fond of her and did not want to lose her. He knew she was greedy and stupid and lazy, but she was also voluptuously beautiful in the soft way he liked.

He picked up his watch from her lap. "Oh, dear," he said "We've been talking for fifteen minutes. Mr. Ewell must be getting impatient, and you still have to dress."

She stammered, "But—but—"

He patted her shoulder, ran his fingertips down her arm and squeezed it lightly. "There's nothing to be afraid of, my dear. I shall leave Tryggvi with you. Even if this Mr. Ewell is as violent as his brother, your husband, but observe—" He turned to the dog and said sharply, "*Alerta!*"

The animal sprang to its feet, its ears cocked sharply.

"You see?" Crane said to Bonnie. "Now if you were to raise your hand to strike me or if you produced a gun, a knife, a club or any other weapon, it would be very unfortunate for you. I will order him to protect you and all you will have to say is *alerta*. That is Spanish. I obtained Tryggvi from a Spaniard in Marseilles. Say *alerta*."

Bonnie ran her tongue across her lips and repeated the word mechanically. Crane nodded approval and spoke rapidly in Spanish to the dog, which sank back on its haunches, its eyes on Bonnie.

"Now repeat the word again, but sharply."

Bonnie said in a loud, frightened voice, "*Alerta!*" and the dog again sprang to its feet.

"As simple as that," Crane said. "Now dress yourself, my dear, and I will have Mr. Ewell sent up to you in ten minutes." He patted her delicately on the thigh and walked off the terrace, smiling quietly to himself.

It took a great effort of will for Bonnie to edge past the dog and go into the suite to dress. It rose and followed her, no more than a pace behind. She watched it fearfully as she dressed. She had never been alone with it before. It was as big as a horse and it kept walking around after her all the time. She felt as if she wanted to faint, and she cried out with almost hysterical relief when she heard the knock on the door and Steve's familiar voice, "Bonnie."

CHAPTER SIX

A waiter had taken Steve up the curving, mahogany-railed staircase to the second floor, but he left, as if on signal, when they met Crane in the hushed, carpeted corridor. The second floor with its tall, white-painted paneled doors and drowsy quiet was like an obscure portion of a museum and Crane, with his contented, fussy face and almost mincing gait, might have been its curator. Except for his eyes. No curator had ever lived behind eyes like Crane's. The crinkled sacs beneath them gave them an air of melancholic weariness, an effective disguise for the end-of-autumn cynicism in the brown pupils.

"Ah, Mr. Ewell." He gave Steve a small, plump, dry hand. "How very pleasant it is to see you. You remind me so much of your brother Vincent. That is, of course, a quite a superficial observation. The resemblance is merely physical. You are not like him at all. It is just that you recall him to me and it is pleasant to remember an old friend. Vincent was so impetuous and you, I suspect, have more reserve and think more within yourself. I am much the same, only more so because I am older; the thinking, the introspection, typical, I am told, of the Oriental mind. I am of the Near East, you know. I am Syrian. My name is really Hrand Krakorian, but it was much too difficult so I became Henry Crane. An ugly name, don't you think? I would much rather have become Henry Wadsworth Longfellow, a very beautiful name, but impractical. In business, short names are better in America, so I do not mind being Henry Crane in business, for inside I am still Hrand Krakorian. You have a very nice name, very musical. Stephen Ewell. Though I don't suppose you have thought about it very much."

"I don't think about it at all," said Steve, knowing that Crane must have a definite reason for delaying him with this scattered chatter. To give Bonnie time to dress?

"You're quite right, of course," Crane said. "Names have no importance except that of identification. Only egoists think of themselves by name, or those who identify themselves with a bigness. Caesar, Bonaparte, Hitler. That is when the thinking of the name becomes a danger, though it is always a dangerous thing. It is a matter of degree, of course. Such men insist that others think of them by name with the same seriousness. Render unto Caesar the things that are Caesar's. Caesar did not say that, but I am certain it was in his thoughts and naturally, in such cases, all things were Caesar's and that was the danger. I mean, the danger came when you did not acknowledge his Caesarhood.

Or his Ewellhood or his Krakorianhood. You see?" he smiled up at Steve. "There is always a little of that, yes."

"Now that you've made your point," said Steve, "I'd like to talk to Bonnie."

Crane's eyes grew round. "My point?"

"You were telling me hands off, weren't you?"

"I perceive that you are also a man of imagination," said Crane, as if amused. "I was merely being garrulous, the fault of barbers and hotel keepers. There is always the tendency to amuse the patron, to entertain. This facet of the ego, the name, has long been a small conceit of mine. I have talked of it many times and probably to the point of boredom."

"I'm not bored," said Steve. "I just don't like it when people give me long-winded warnings."

"My dear Mr. Ewell—"

"I don't like people to give me warnings of any kind, long or short. I have a tendency, as you'd say, to tell them to go to hell."

Crane pursed his lips and said, "Ah," and his eyes became remotely thoughtful. "You think, of course, that Bonnie is my mistress."

"I didn't think about it at all until you went into your song and dance."

"Ah, yes. You are quite right. Like all men who are overly fond of subtlety, I have the impulse to talk too much. Still, you are mistaken. Not entirely mistaken, but enough so that there is a distortion. Bonnie is not my mistress. I do not want a mistress. I have had mistresses when I was younger and sometimes they left me and sometimes I left them, but always it was a very unstable arrangement. When one is young, that is all right. It is even desirable. But I am no longer young. In fact, I am older than I seem and the notion of impermanence is distasteful to me."

"You mean you want to marry her?" said Steve incredulously.

"Is that so strange? Old men always wish young wives. It is the revenge they take, a cruelty, though of course I will not be cruel to Bonnie. She will not think it a cruelty. She is very lazy and very unintelligent. She will think me an old fool, but she will think of the amount of money I have in the bank and she will be content."

"But what about Vince?" Steve asked bluntly. "She's still his wife."

"Yes, there is Vince," Crane admitted. "She wished to divorce him, but at the moment she is afraid. Vincent is a violent and desperate man. However, he has the money that was taken from the bank, the thirty-seven-thousand dollars. Bonnie is afraid of him, but also she thinks of the thirty-seven-thousand dollars. I have more than thirty-seven-thousand dollars. I will be very generous with her, but not frivolous. I apologize, but Vincent has always spent his money frivolously. Bonnie is aware of this. She is frivolous as well as stupid. To spend money frivolously is to her an ideal existence. She would be very bad for Vincent. That does not interest me particularly, but it is a consideration, something about which to think. Sooner or later and probably unintentionally, she would betray him to the police and he would be put back in prison. Surely that should be obvious."

"If she's as dumb as all that, why do you want her?"

"As I would want a pet, a very beautiful Persian cat. If Bonnie were a woman of intelligence, of emotion, I would not think of marrying her. That would be a foolishness. Such women, if they marry old men, sometimes put arsenic in their food. On the other hand, Bonnie would be very happy with me because I would satisfy all her little greeds—a fur coat, expensive lingerie and rich foods, for she is very gluttonous. Some day she will be very fat, but it is feminine to be fat. I do not like your feminine ideal in the fashion magazines, who seem to me to be inbred and sterile. There is a fecundity in the fatness of a woman. The very fatness is a fecundity, do you understand? This, I know, is not an American point of view, but I am a Syrian."

A crafty bastard, thought Steve. Bonnie was his mistress all right, whatever that meant in Crane's language. A nasty language, and there was no doubt about that. The nastiness would be subtle and involved and concealed, but a nastiness none the less.

"Why tell me all this?" he asked. "I don't give a damn what Bonnie does."

"That is very possible, but still she is married to your brother."

"That doesn't mean anything either."

"Ah, then, you agree that he would be better without her."

"Look," said Steve impatiently, "this isn't getting us any place and I'm not in the mood for complicated conversations. If you've got something on your mind, tell me what it is. I don't care what Bonnie does, but I'll be damned if I'll pimp for you, if that's what you're driving at."

Crane said very softly, "No, Mr. Ewell, I would not dream of asking you to pimp for me. Neither you nor anyone else."

"Or maybe you want me to tell her what a great guy you are. Is that it?"

Crane sighed. "That's what it means to be young, now that I recall. So much truculence, so much violence, so much emotion, and so much suspicion. The simple fact of the matter is that I wanted your friendship, not your enmity. I know it has been said that your brother's wife is my mistress, and I thought that you might resent this and cause a disturbance that might embarrass me. It was merely to avert an unpleasantness."

"Then there isn't any little word you want me to take in to Bonnie? A thought for the day, maybe?"

Crane's face twitched and for an instant the muddy hatred in his eyes was revealed. Then he blinked and his eyes were as bland as chocolate.

"No, nothing, Mr. Ewell, nothing at all. I am very glad that there has been no unpleasantness. Her rooms are at the end of the hall. You will find her name on the door."

He smiled vaguely and walked down the hall with his peculiarly mincing step. Steve scowled but there was a touch of puzzlement in his face, too. Crane did not want a disturbance, but he carried a gun under his coat. Or was that his way of averting an unpleasantness? Steve gave his head a shake. He felt as if he had walked into a cobweb in the dark.

CHAPTER SEVEN

Bonnie answered his knock with a rush and cried "Stevie!" as she flung open the door. She had on a dress that was really quite simple, though on her it looked like something a stripteaser might wear when she first stepped out on the stage of a burlesque house. Most of Bonnie's clothes looked that way on her. The Great Dane stood in the middle of the floor behind her, watching Steve.

Steve looked at it and said. "What's that?"

"The mutt? Don't talk about it. But watch your step. It bites. It gives me the meemies. It's supposed to be a watchdog, but a thing like that, you could use it to watch Fort Knox or something."

"Crane's idea?"

"Well—it's his idea. But don't worry about it. It won't bite unless I give it the word. In Spanish yet," she laughed brittlely. "A watchdog in Spanish. Ain't that something? Come on, sit down. Want something to drink? You name it, I got it—Scotch, bourbon, rye, gin, rum, anything, I got it." She gestured jerkily at a chrome and glass portable bar at the side of the lushly furnished room. "There's even liquor I don't know the name of, we got so much. Maybe I ought to join the bartender's union. What'll it be?"

"Nothing right now," said Steve, looking around at the suite.

The living room was quite large and contained a graciously columned fireplace that made the portable bar look like a garish intruder. The bedroom, revealed by the partly open door, was almost as large and was a froth of organdy and frills.

Bonnie saw his probing glance and said uneasily, "This is only something he lets me use. He sleeps in a little room next to his office."

Steve shrugged. "That's your business."

"I'm telling you, that's all. I don't want you to go around thinking I'm sleeping with him here. What d'you think I am anyway? I'm just telling you."

"Fine."

"You don't have to believe me," she said angrily, "but it's the truth all the same. He sleeps in that little hole in the wall back of his office. I ain't no tramp."

Steve knew that this was only part of the truth, the façade, the part of it that was for public display, and he said dryly, "I don't care what you do, one way or the other."

"I'm not living with him, damn you!" Bonnie cried shrilly; her body was rigid and her hands were white, pointed fists at her sides. "I work here, is all. And what're you snooping around for anyways? I ain't done nothing. I sing here. It's a job. I gotta have a job, don't I? You expect me to live with your damn sister all my life, and her begrudging every mouthful she gave me and letting me know, too. I just work here."

The Great Dane lowered its head and snarled anxiously, inquiringly. There was something wrong and it knew that it was supposed to do something about it but the command had not been given. It gave another eager whimpering snarl as if to call Bonnie's attention to itself.

Steve said sharply, "Watch that damned elephant!"

Bonnie stared at the dog and it jumped to its feet, looking from her to Steve, letting her know that it was impatient for the command. She backed away from it, her face white.

Steve said soothingly to the dog in the crude Spanish he had picked up during the times his ship had docked at Vera Cruz, "*Sentarse, perro, sentarse. Si, si, bueno perrito, sentarse—*"

The dog looked bewildered. The screaming had stopped and the sound of the Spanish was quieting and at length it sank back on its haunches, relaxing its vigilance slightly. Steve went to the bar and poured some Scotch into a glass which he took carefully to Bonnie, approaching her slowly for the dog's eyes were on him. He said, "Drink this, Bonnie," but her hands were trembling so badly that he had to hold the glass to her lips. She swallowed and choked and shuddered.

"Let's sit down on the sofa," Steve said and, putting his arm around her as if to support her, he whispered, "Don't say anything yet. I think that old Syrian goat might be listening in and there are a couple things I want to ask you."

He went to the tall mahogany Governor Winthrop desk at the end of the room and went through the drawers until he found a pencil and a pad of scratch paper. He returned to the sofa and sat down beside

Bonnie. She snatched at the pencil and scribbled shakily on the pad.

"Get me out of here!"

"You can't leave?" Steve wrote.

"Cops—" And then she started to say, "They're all over the place—" but Steve placed his hand over her mouth and pointed at the pad. She wrote laboriously in a sprawling, childish scrawl, "Crane said they'd put me in jail if I tried to leave. Sneak me out. I'm going nuts here."

He took the pad from her and wrote on it, "Do you know where Vince is?"

"No."

"Has he been in touch with you?"

"No."

He reached for the pencil but she pulled it back and wrote sharply, "You no where he is. Dont kid me."

"I don't know where he is."

"Nuts. Get me out of here."

"I can't do anything until I get in touch with Vince."

"They can put me in jail?"

"I don't know. I think so. Or make you stay here. Tell me the truth about Vince. It's important. To you, too." He watched her clinically as she read what he had written. Bonnie had always been a liar. There had been times when she had lied for no reason whatever. She had lied merely for the sake of lying, or possibly because it had been easier to lie than tell the truth because the truth might have meant further explanations and she was lazy and didn't want to be bothered. Bonnie was not an accomplished liar and she could always be trapped if you wanted to, but usually there had been so little basis for her lies, that it wasn't worth the trouble.

He watched her as she wrote jabbingly, digging the pencil into the paper, "I dont no nothing about Vince."

He did not believe her and he held the pencil thoughtfully for a moment while phrasing his next question in his mind. Direct questions would not do. She would lie through choice on a direct question. An oblique question, however, might trap her into an admission.

"I hear Vince was shot," he wrote.

"That was the other guy."

"The one who was in on the bank holdup with Vince?"

She turned and looked at him with such astonishment that he believed immediately that she knew nothing of Vince's accomplice in the holdup. She grabbed for the pencil and wrote feverishly, "You no where they hid the money?"

And he was shocked by the naked greed in her face.

He wrote carefully, "I have to see Vince before I can say anything about that."

That, if anything, would open her up.

Her face became sly and veiled as she scribbled, "Maybe we can get together."

"Then you have heard from Vince."

She shook her head and wrote. "Not yet."

"They think he's hiding in the hills around here."

"Nuts."

"How do you know he isn't?"

"He aint been here."

"You're surrounded by police. How many police?"

She held up both hands with spread fingers and waved them several times to denote a large number. She wrote, "All over the place."

"Did he ever say anything about hiding out in any place at all?"

"All he said was hed bust out and get in tuch with me. If we had the money we could help him."

The money. That was clear now. She wanted the money. Crane had said that and it was true. Thirty-seven-thousand dollars. And she wanted it.

Money. To Bonnie, money was not a thing, but a place; a dark, warm enclosing; a safety and a satisfaction of all the small greeds and desires. Sometimes, in order to get money, there were inconveniences but you put up with them if you wanted the money badly enough—and Vince had been one of the inconveniences when she married him. Now there was a chance of getting the money without having the inconvenience of Vince. She would turn Vince over to the police if she could get the money, and it would not be a betrayal but merely an act like that of tearing an envelope to get the check it contained. She was completely amoral.

It might have been easy if, in his own mind, Steve had known exactly what he wanted. He wanted to get in touch with Vince and be sure that Vince was safe—but that was loose and generalized, and he had not thought beyond that. He was certain that Vince had shot neither the guard at the prison nor the guard at the bank. His memories of Vince rejected that. Vince would not shoot anybody or anything, except possibly by accident. He was not idealizing about this. This was precedent. It was impossible for Vince deliberately to point a gun and shoot a man. Ever since that day at the sandpit. The day Vince had shot Swoop McGoo.

Swoop McGoo was a cat. He was more like a dog, the way he used to follow everyone around, and even people who didn't like cats used to like

Swoop McGoo. They called it that because it used to take tremendous leaps from one limb of a tree to another, maybe pretending it was a leopard or something. Sometimes when you went for a walk in the woods, you'd look around and there would be Swoop McGoo going for a walk with you, stopping to stalk a bug or play with a leaf and then coming back to you, wanting you to join in the fun.

It was during the summer Vince graduated from grammar school that it happened. Vince and Steve were down in the old sandpit east of town shooting off their old .22 rifle, knocking off tin cans and soda bottles. Vince was in a very high state that day and he was shooting the necks off the bottles one after another, never missing, and telling Steve that he was going to be the first freshman letterman in the high school because he had already talked to the coach, or maybe it was the other way around, and it was practically settled that he was going to be at the very least the second string halfback. And then this old yellow Swoop McGoo had come creeping out of the bushes, long and flat, stalking a robin that was industriously jabbing for worms, and Vince had swung the rifle and snapped off the shot before either of them could think about it or say a word. There was a scream from the cat, but it was not dead because it had kept screaming and it was awful and the two of them had gone running across the sandpit to where the cat was trying to crawl back into the bushes, its hind legs bloodily dragging because Vince had swung the rifle too much and had caught it in the spine, paralyzing the hindquarters.

Vince didn't get sick, or anything like that, but his face had turned this veal color and all stretched tight, and he reversed the gun and hit the cat once very hard on the head and killed it, and, still holding the rifle by the barrel, he turned and swung it against the trunk of the nearest tree. That finished the gun.

Vince never had a gun after that, and in the Korean War Vince had got himself in a medical unit, giving first aid and carrying in the wounded and things like that. He could have gotten himself in the Quartermaster's Corps because Vince could always talk his way into anything, but the medical unit was up where things were doing and he still wouldn't have to shoot anybody. He never did touch a gun after that, and it wasn't the blood he minded because he'd fight anybody at the drop of a hat and some of his fights were pretty bloody because he always fought as if he meant it and would take on anybody, no matter how big he was.

So Steve knew that Vince had shot neither the guard at the prison nor the bank guard in the holdup. It was something he just couldn't do, that was all, and now he was out there somewhere, being hunted by men with guns and, even if he had a gun, he wouldn't use it to defend himself, so it was as if he were out there naked.

Steve stared at the pad. Bonnie had written, "He needs money," but she really meant that she wanted the money and the hell with Vince. That much was plain.

He wrote slowly, "The man who was in the holdup with Vince has the money, or knows where it is."

Bonnie grabbed for the pencil. "Its Vinces money. Vince went to jail for it."

"You visited Vince in jail?"

Her written answer was a stammer. "A couple times. It was awful. They made me feel like I should be in jail too. I told Vince and he said not to come back. Hed bust out."

That was a picture, those reluctant visits, grudgingly made, complainingly fulfilled. Could Vince have really been in love with her? She had a body, sure, and a bedroom face, but my God, she was practically a moron. And for the rest, she was selfish, greedy, lazy, gluttonous. What had Vince ever seen in her? But that was beside the point. There was a chance that she might be useful.

He wrote, "Did Vince ever say anything about the holdup?"

"No. Just wed be loded when he busted out."

"He wasn't worried about the money, afraid the man who was in it with him would go off with it?"

"He said he was okay."

"Did he say anything about this man?"

"Just he was okay." Her pencil hesitated. "Hes around here."

Steve wrote quickly, "How do you know?" That could be a lead, a way to get in touch with Vince.

Her pencil hovered indecisively and her face was bunched with the effort of trying to think. "Just the way he said."

"What did he say?"

"I dont remember," she wrote resentfully. She was tired of this and she didn't like the effort of thinking or the way he probed at her. "It was just the way he said. Somebody he knew a long time."

It didn't mean anything and it was no help. Vince had told her nothing. The man could be almost anybody. It was a dead end.

"I have to talk to Vince," he wrote. "He might phone you. The police will be listening in, but he might say something that will mean something only to you. So if he does phone you, try to remember every word he says."

"Yes. But he needs money. We have to get him money. If he tells us where the money is, we can help him."

He wrote stolidly, "Sure. We have to get the money to him. He'll tell me where it is." Then, urgently, "Don't call me if he phones you. Don't try to get in touch with me at all. I'll get in touch with you." He underlined it several times and punctuated it with exclamation marks and held it up before her for emphasis.

She read it and nodded.

He wrote, "That's all for now. I'll get in touch with you."

He tore the written pages from the pad and put them in his wallet. He returned the pad and pencil to the Governor Winthrop desk at the end of the room, and when he turned she was standing up with her hands bunched at her throat and her face was frightened. He could see that she was about to blurt something and he quickly put his finger to his lips. He was absolutely certain that the old Syrian was listening in. He crossed quickly to her.

The dog jumped to its feet and watched him. He slowed down and said soothingly, "*Buena perrito, sentarse, sentarse, perrito—*" Little dog, good dog, nice dog. My God, the thing was as big as a tank and just as dangerous and it wasn't *sentarse-ing* this time. It had probably made up its mind. Or had become confused, which was just as bad for then you couldn't tell what it would do.

Bonnie was aware of this and she whispered, "Get me out of here, for heaven's sake, get me out of here. I'm going nuts!"

Steve put his hand over his mouth and tilted his chin at the door. She went to the door with him. The Great Dane followed for two steps and then stopped, watching them.

"We'll get you out," Steve soothed her, "as soon as I get in touch with Vince. We can't do anything right now." Then, significantly, "This is the place Vince will try to get in touch with you and if you leave he won't know where to get in touch with you. It's important that you stay here. Do you understand that?"

She looked at the big dog and shivered. "But you *will* get me out?" she whispered.

He nodded. The lie was unimportant. Only Vince was important, Vince naked and defenseless out there.

She put her arms around his neck and kissed him then and, incredibly, it was the most terrific thing he had ever experienced. He had kissed women before and had been kissed by them, but it had never been anything like this. It was nothing a woman hadn't done for him before— arms enclosing, breasts, mouth giving promise and demand, the clinging and the significance. But it was different from that. In the act of kissing and molding herself to him, Bonnie changed. This was not the softness and the laziness and the greed and gluttony; this was what she really was, and though she was fully dressed, it was as if she were naked against him in the sensuous dark.

Steve thrust her harshly from him and the Great Dane leaped, quivering, to its feet, its whines intermingling with rumbling growls. Steve ignored it.

"That was quite a production," he said to Bonnie.

She smiled secretly. "It wasn't a production, Stevie," she said. "It's just I'm so glad you're going to get me out of this joint."

Now that the contact was broken, the crudeness was apparent again and he was incredulous that she could have aroused him so.

"I always liked you, Stevie," she said archly. "Some ways you were even nicer to me than even Vince. I mean, the way you stood up for me after Vince got sent to jail. With Ida, and how you told her not to keep nagging at me. You're better looking than Vince, too. You're bigger. I bet you got girls in every port, the way sailors do. Do you, Stevie?"

Steve concealed his revulsion because there was a chance that Vince might get through to her and she could be of some help that way.

"I better get back downstairs," he said. "I'll get in touch with you."

She smoothed her dress down over her long thighs. "I'll be waiting, Stevie," she whispered as he let himself out.

CHAPTER EIGHT

"You look as if you'd had bad news," Doris said anxiously.

Loriot, the newspaperman, had left to attend the weekly dinner of the Rocky Hill Merchants' Association, and she and Steve were alone at the table. He shrugged and looked abstractedly at his drink, twirling it so that the ice cubes clinked against the side of the glass.

"You were gone a long time," she said. "Over three-quarters of an hour. I thought you had walked out on me. Was it something about Vince, Steve?" She knew she shouldn't ask the question, but she could not keep herself from it, so achingly did she want to talk about Vince and find out if Steve had news of him. If only Vince had come to her. She would have hidden him and cared for him and in some way, somehow—because she loved him—she would see to it that he was freed and absolved.

Steve frowned, not answering, but Doris said doggedly, "I want to help, Steve."

There was something in her voice, an intensity, that caused Steve to lift his head and look at her in surprise. She returned his glance defiantly.

"He came to me once before for help," she said, and flushed because she knew that she had revealed herself to Steve.

"When was this?" he asked slowly.

"Before—before—"

"Before he held up the bank?"

"A—a little before that."

"Was he in trouble?"

"He—he was troubled, yes. But he wasn't *in* trouble. He didn't actually come to me. I met him by accident in the liquor store. He'd been drinking and he wasn't in any shape to drive and I—I took him to my apartment to sober him up. So that he wouldn't get into trouble," she added quickly, too quickly. "What he really wanted was somebody to talk to. He didn't have anybody to talk to and that was why he'd been drinking. You have to have somebody you can talk to once in a while."

This was spoken swiftly in embarrassed justification and Steve did not have to be told the rest of it.

Steve nodded. "You have to have somebody to talk to."

"It was his wife," she said tensely. "She was devouring him. He cursed her, Steve, he hated her. All she wanted was for him to buy her things. He said she was an incubus. She had some kind of emotional grip on him that he couldn't seem to break, even though he hated her."

Steve nodded without answering. He could see how a man might talk like that when he was drunk. And he could see how it could be with Vince and Bonnie.

Doris said pleadingly, "I wouldn't break up anybody's marriage, Steve. But he hated her and he needed me to talk to. We met several times after that. He needed that, Steve."

Steve thought—yes, that was the way it was with Vince and women, he had always been a great man with the women and it was not his triumph, but his confession of defeat. And now Doris, too, he thought with a flash of resentment. Couldn't Vince at least have left a decent kid like Doris alone? Did it have to be Doris, too? For a moment, an anger raged in Steve.

"You don't have to explain anything," he said stolidly.

She flushed even more deeply. "I just didn't want you to think—"

"I don't."

"But I want you to know that—"

"You're a big girl and you don't have to explain anything to me." Then, shortly, "I just talked to Bonnie upstairs."

She said, "Oh," and looked down at her hands. She had forgotten that Bonnie worked here in the Inn.

Steve went on. "You're right about one thing. She is an incubus, but I think he might try to get in touch with her."

She said, "Oh," again, and swallowed as if her mouth were suddenly dry. "He—he might think she'll help him."

"All she wants is the money from the bank robbery. If she can get her hands on that, she'll turn Vince over to the police without thinking twice. However, she might be able to help me find Vince, and I want to get to him before the police do."

The waiter appeared at the table with a menu under his arm. "Would you like to order dinner now, sir?"

Steve looked at Doris and she shook her head and Steve put a five-dollar bill on the table to pay for the drinks.

"Was he listening in?" Steve asked Doris in a low voice when the waiter left.

"I—I didn't notice."

"Damn. I should have thought of that." Then in explanation, "There are more people than the police who'd like to see Vince back in jail as quickly as possible."

She looked at him with worried, anxious inquiry, but he shook his head. The waiter returned within a few minutes with the unbroken five-dollar bill.

"The cocktails were with Mr. Crane's compliments, sir," he said.

The check had been for two dollars and Steve laid two singles on the table. "Thank Mr. Crane for the cocktails," he said. "The two dollars are yours. The service was excellent."

As they walked out, Crane waved his hand blandly from the end of the bar where he was talking to the head waiter. "Come again, Mr. Ewell. I am sorry that you could not stay to dinner."

"He's a cute little number," Steve muttered to Doris. "He and Bonnie should get along well together. We'll take a little drive up toward Lake Hopatcong and talk as we go. We'll have dinner later, if that's all right with you."

"I couldn't eat a thing now. I mean, I can't help thinking that Vince might be hiding out somewhere without food and—"

"Oh, I don't think it's as bad as that. Vince had a lot of friends. But just to set your mind at rest, I want to do all I can for Vince myself."

"You're going to help him!"

"I am probably," he said dryly, "going to get my teeth kicked in by everybody concerned." But he felt better about it as he told Doris his plan.

Vince would have to return the stolen money. That was the first thing. And he would have to go back to prison for a while. He had held up the bank and the returning of the money couldn't get him out of that. But if the money were returned a deal could probably be made with the authorities and a parole arranged within the next year or two. That was something he'd have to find out. The mayor of Rocky Hill had been in state politics and he would be the one to talk to first. He could at least give Steve some advice as how to go about it, to whom to talk. But all this was predicated on the return of the money.

"But there are two things that worry me," Steve said. "The bank guard was shot in the holdup and the prison guard was shot when Vince broke out, though I'm sure Vince didn't shoot either of them."

"The prison guard is out of danger," said Doris in a small voice. "I heard it over the radio this afternoon. They removed the bullet and he's going to be all right."

"That's some help, thank God. I think I can talk Vince into giving back the money. I'm not sure, but I think so because I own some property, that lake I've been developing and I think I can get a mortgage of about ten thousand from the bank on it. I'm going to tell Vince that when he comes out of jail I'll either give him a lump sum of money or make him a partner in the lake. Financially, he'll be better off if he takes me up on this, even if he has to go back to jail for a while. He can't spend that money he got from the bank. It's hot.

"He'd have to sell it to a fence and he probably wouldn't get more than twenty-five cents on the dollar—and the jail sentence would always be hanging over his head. I know there are a lot of ifs and maybes, but it's worth trying."

He stopped talking and it hung there, inconclusively, and he suddenly knew what was wrong with the whole thing and why it might not work at all. It was Doris who put it into words.

"There—was another man in the bank holdup," she said in a bleak voice. "He might not want to give up the money."

"He can be bought off."

But Steve knew that that was not the point. The authorities would insist that Vince name his accomplice, and the chance of Vince doing that was damned remote. But Vince wouldn't have to if Steve could discover who the man was.

But it was inconclusive and they both knew it and there did not seem to be much more to say at the moment because they were both depressed by the knowledge.

They had a sandwich and a cup of coffee at a roadside stand on the highway, for neither of them was hungry, and then Steve took Doris home.

"Well," he said lamely, "I'll start to work on this tomorrow and let you know."

She made no move to get out of the car. Her face looked a little bleak in the faded radiance of the street lamp on the corner. Her handbag was tightly clutched in her lap and she sat strained and hunched.

"Do you think he's hiding in the hills?" she asked.

"I don't think so. He knows he could be found too easily."

"There was some talk of getting bloodhounds," Doris said in a small voice.

"Bloodhounds aren't all they're cracked up to be. I doubt that they'll use them."

"Maybe—maybe he's hiding out at the Inn, Steve. He and Crane were quite friendly at one time. When Vince was living there."

"Vince the guest and Vince the escaped convict are two different people as far as Crane's concerned," Steve said dryly. "Crane isn't anybody's friend. Anyway, the Inn would dangerous. The police are watching it very closely."

"But I mean Vince's wife is up there and she might have a way. What—what is she like, Steve? What does she look like? I've never seen her."

So this was what she had been leading up to, Steve thought. He wondered if she had any inkling of Vince's casual way with women. Probably not. Or if she did, she would excuse it. She would find reasons why Vince had always turned restlessly from one woman to another. She would forgive him, she would understand him, she would cherish and love him, and she would be certain that she was the one Vince really needed.

"Well," he said, "she's blonde, about your height, but, uh, heavier."

"The phrase is better stacked, isn't it, Steve?"

"She's not my type," he said woodenly.

"She's—beautiful, isn't she? I've heard how men talk and, well, you know how men talk when they're impressed with a woman."

"I know how they talk about a dame like Bonnie."

"But she must have something outstanding, Steve."

"She has," he said, wishing that she would stop tormenting herself like that. "I can sum it up in three letters—s-e-x."

Doris lowered her head and her fingers kneaded her handbag. "You're prejudiced against her for some reason. Everybody says she's beautiful."

"Cut it out!" he said sharply. "You're just going round and round. I told you what she's like. She's greedy, she's lazy, and she's a moron. She's no good and that's all there's to it so let's cut it out. If you're trying to get me to say you're the better woman, okay, I'll say it. You're the better woman. Now are you satisfied?"

Her head was turned away from him but he could hear the sharp intake of her breath. Several pulsing seconds passed before she spoke again.

"I'm sorry, Steve," she said in a calm and rather remote voice. "It was rather neurotic, wasn't it?"

"Well," he evaded, "you're anxious about Vince, I guess."

"I am. Very. And believe it or not, I was also trying to find out if she could help him."

"She won't, Doris. All she wants to do is get her sticky little fingers on that thirty-seven-thousand dollars."

"Then it's up to us, isn't it, Steve?"

"It's up to me," he said. "I don't want you mixing in this. It can turn nasty."

"I don't care, Steve! I want to help."

"Well—" He frowned thoughtfully. "The best way you can help is by keeping police suspicion away from yourself. Just in case," he added significantly, "Vince needs you later."

"If you found out where he's hiding, I could go to him, couldn't I? I mean, without the police suspecting."

He did not mean to use her at all. The whole thing was too explosive, too dangerous, and he meant to keep her out of it entirely. "Something like that," he lied. "But in the meantime, don't do anything. Just sit tight. Promise?"

"Oh, yes, Steve! I'll do everything I can to help."

"Well, the best thing you can do right now is nothing. I'll call you at the Chamber of Commerce office and let you know how things are coming along."

"Oh thanks, Steve! You don't know how much better you've made me feel. I feel almost as if—" she laughed shakily, "as if Vince were out of trouble already, but I know it's not as easy as that. Call me tomorrow."

He said, "Sure," and then sat and watched as she slipped out of the car and walked up the flagged path overhung by the delicate branch ends of the weeping willow that rose as high as the roof of the little white-and-green house in which she lived. Unaccountably, he felt a little angry and muttered, "Oh, hell!" as he reached out and turned on the ignition key. Damn Vince for messing up a nice kid like that.

He waited until she unlocked her door, turned, half-waved and went inside. He beeped the car horn once. He felt a vague unease, almost a depression, when he drove away. And then he realized that he felt this way because he couldn't turn his thoughts away from the gold-flecked green eyes of Doris Stewart.

CHAPTER NINE

The road back to his house was a little-used one. It led to the farms deeper in the Valley after it forked from the road that led to Bear Lake. An old Ford pickup truck passed him noisily, going faster than was safe on this road, probably one of the farmer boys on his way home after an evening of beer and shuffleboard in town.

Steve was driving slowly and the close trees drifted darkly by on either side of him. Tomorrow, the first thing in the morning, he'd go into Rocky Hill and talk to the mayor. That had to be done first to find out where he—and Vince—stood. If there was no chance to make a deal, he'd have to think of something else. But there had to be a chance. There was that unrecovered thirty-seven-thousand dollars and lot of turkey could be talked with that much money at stake.

As he rounded one of the many curves in the road, his headlights caught the pickup truck and he jammed on his brakes. The truck was slewed broadside, its radiator against the bole of a maple tree on the left side of the road. No one was visible in the driver's seat or outside the truck. Steve grunted and slipped out of his car. The driver was probably lying on the floor either hurt or drunk. He walked over to the truck and opened the door. There was no one inside. As he stepped back, puzzled, he heard the slight scrape of shoe leather on the macadam behind him, but before he could turn something thudded against the back of his head. The road opened like a pit in front of him and he tumbled into it.

When he recovered consciousness he felt strangely unable to move and he thought to himself, *this is part of the dream*, the way you do early in the morning when sleep is ebbing away from you, leaving the flotsam of the dream on the beach of your mind. There was something pressing against his back. He was upright and sitting painfully on something that felt like rocks.

He could smell the heaviness of rotting leaf mold and the tangier scent of pine and, faintly, the sick-sweet odor of skunk. He was in the woods. He was leaning against a tree and his hands were tied behind him around the trunk. From the smooth feel of the bark, it was a scrub birch, the kind that grew in thickets all over the valley like weeds. His ankles were crossed and tied and there was a blindfold over his eyes.

A voice close to his ear said, "How do you like it, Ewell?" It was a disguised Donald Duck of a voice, a nasal falsetto. There was the sour smell of tobacco and bad teeth.

Steve said thickly, "What's the idea?" His bead hurt and there was a dizziness.

The voice said, "Don't try yelling, Ewell, or I'll give you some of this where it'll do the most good."

Something came down painfully on his thigh, like a blackjack or a length of rubber hose stuffed with sand and plugged.

"What do you want?" he asked, straining against the rope that bound his wrists.

Something tapped him lightly on the hand. "That won't do you no good, Ewell. You're snubbed tight. All we're going to do is ask you some questions and you won't get hurt. What did you find out from that whore up at the Inn?"

We. That meant there was more than one of them. Had Crane had him followed? "I don't know any whores," he said woodenly.

"Don't play it dumb, Ewell. You know who I mean, that whore-wife of your brother's. You're going to tell us what she said or we'll beat it out of you."

The man's breath was so nauseating that Steve felt his stomach churn. "Don't breathe in my face," he said. "Your breath stinks."

A hard palm cracked sharply across his mouth. "Keep that up and I'll fix it so you can't smell nothing. Now what did she tell you?"

"Nothing."

"Where's your brother hiding out?"

"I don't know."

"I'm going to straighten you out for the last time, Ewell. We've got wives and kids, understand? We don't want no shooting around here. So where's your brother hiding out?"

Steve said, "I don't know," and braced himself.

It came stunningly, a blow on the right side of the head, a kick in the kidneys. But not hard enough to knock him out. Dizzy with pain, gasping to draw a breath, he heard the voice cackle in that metallic falsetto, "We can keep this up all night, Ewell. And we can do worse, too, and don't think we won't. Now, what did you find out?"

The voice kept saying "we" but so far there had been only one voice. That didn't make sense. If there were others, someone else would have broken in with a threat or a curse or a question, and there would have been the sounds of other men moving around, but there was just the sound of this one man breathing beside him. Then there was the matter of the blindfold. That didn't make sense either. If this had been a group of self-appointed vigilantes, as the voice wanted him to believe, honestly indignant citizens, they would not have used a blindfold. They would have faced him and said, tell us what you know or we'll beat the hell out of you. And they would have gotten away with it, too. The whole countryside was frightened and the police would not have been too solicitous about one Steve Ewell, especially if he were suspected of aiding an escaped convict.

Steve was certain that there was just one man. *One man with a definite and personal reason! The man who had been in the Newberg Bank holdup with Vince, the man who would want to get to Vince as anxiously as the authorities, the man whose safety might depend on Vince's getting away. Or—or whose safety would depend on Vince's getting killed. The man who would then have the entire thirty-seven-thousand dollars for himself.*

Steve felt the galvanizing electricity of mounting excitement. There was a way to play this. Tell the man anything he wanted to hear. It didn't have to be the truth. But spin it out, gain time—and listen, listen, and wait for a slip that might identify the man.

"Bonnie didn't know anything," he said.

"We warned you for the last time, Ewell—"

"Wait, listen—" Steve spoke hurriedly, as if in fear. "Just think it over for a minute. How could she know anything? Ever since Vince broke out, she's been practically a prisoner up there in the Inn. The place is surrounded by police. How could she get in touch with him?"

"Maybe he got in touch with her, Ewell."

"How? The police have the phones tapped, they read her mail and they question everybody who even talks to her. Why, they questioned me tonight after I talked to her."

The man grunted, accepting the lie, but he did not change the assumed falsetto voice. "What's all this stuff you got written down on those slips of paper in your pocket?"

"Those are the questions I asked Bonnie. They left me alone in a room with her, but I was sure they were listening in. Read it. Go ahead. You'll find out that she told me several times that she knew nothing about Vince or where he is and that she hasn't heard from him."

"We read it. We know all about that, Ewell. But it says here too that she's sure he ain't hiding in the hills."

"She was just guessing. Read it. You'll see."

There was a definite pause and then the quick question. "What did she say about this guy that was in the holdup with Vince."

"If you read the notebook you can see what she said. It's someone from around here, someone Vince had known a long time."

"What else did she say that *ain't* written down here, Ewell?"

Steve started, "Everything she told me is down there in the—" but his words were cut short with a blazing slap across his mouth and cheek and he felt the slow crawl of blood down his chin from the end of his lips.

"Don't lie to me, Ewell!" The disguise had broken for a moment. The voice was shrill but not falsetto, a rising snarl, too strident to be identified, though there was something faintly familiar about it.

Steve knew that he was on the thin edge of violence and Steve whined hurriedly, "Don't—don't, I'm not lying," hoping that the whine would convince the man.

The blow came down painfully across his thigh again. "That's eighteen inches of hose stuffed with BB's, Ewell. How'd you like me to smack you across the jaw with it a few times?"

Steve whimpered, "I'd tell you if I knew, honestly I would, but I don't know. She didn't tell me."

The man made an angry noise low in his throat and then was no other sound for several seconds. Then, "Maybe you *might* know where he *might* be hiding out, Ewell. I just happened to think of that."

"I was away at sea when he broke out. I just got back. He couldn't get in touch with me at sea."

"I mean you know some of the places he used to hang out. What were some of them?"

"You'll have to give me time to think."

"Take all the time you want. But we ain't got all night."

Steve did remember some of the places where Vince had taken him from time to time, places where there was a poker or crap game going on in the back room, but he did not want to name any of those.

There was a place in Englewood Cliffs up on the Palisades, a place in Secaucus, a place in Hoboken, another one in North Laurel, a bar on Market Street in Newark, and that tough Irish place in Harrison. But, with a touch of chill, he knew that he could not name any of those or have the names forced from him because there was a chance that Vince might be hiding out in one of them, particularly that tough place in Harrison. Still, he had to name some places where Vince had been known, for this man—if he had been the accomplice—would also know some of Vince's habits. *Dear God*, he prayed, *don't let me make a mistake!*

"Well," he said slowly, "there was a place in Parsippany called the Four Winds—"

"It's out of business. Keep going."

"There was a place in Montclair called the Oasis."

"I know the place."

Steve felt a sense of grim satisfaction. He was certain that this man had been in the holdup with Vince and that he did live in the Rocky Hill area. To make certain, Steve named three other places not too far from Rocky Hill and the man knew all of them.

"Is that all?" the falsetto squeaked in his ear.

"Vince never took me around very much," Steve said, trying to sound apologetic. "He liked to gamble and chase after the women and most of the time he didn't want anybody tagging along. *You know how he was.*"

The last was thrown in casually and the man swallowed it. "Yeah," the falsetto squeaked with a tittering laugh, "he sure was a chaser. You know something, Ewell? You're as big as Vince and you look something like him, but you ain't like him at all. Vince would never crack when the pressure was on. Now I'm going to give you a little advice. Keep your nose out of this from now on—unless you want to get hurt."

"I don't want any trouble," Steve mumbled.

There was no warning, no sound, but in the last instant Steve knew what was coming. The blow came down on the side of his head and the blackness enveloped him in a thunderclap.

A blinding glare pierced his eyes and he turned his head away from it, slowly becoming aware that he was seated again behind the steering wheel of a car. His own car. The blinding light was a flashlight and beneath it was a hand pointing a gun at him.

"I'm sorry, Mr. Ewell, but I shall have to insist that you give me the notes you took while talking with Bonnie," said Crane's liquid voice.

Steve laughed. It hurt his head to laugh, but peal after peal of it rang from him and there was just a little touch of hysteria in it.

"You're too late," he gasped. "You're too late, Mr. Crane. Somebody else was interested in them, too."

"Ah, yes, there is blood on your face and your cheek is somewhat swollen. Were you robbed, Mr. Ewell?"

Steve's hand went mechanically to his hip pocket. His wallet was still there. "They, or he, wasn't after that."

"I know you have your wallet, Mr. Ewell. I took the liberty of searching you. Please step out of the car on the other side. I wish to examine the contents of the glove compartment."

Steve looked at the gun and laughed and slipped out of the right side of the car. He stood and looked up at the stars and whistled while Crane rifled the glove compartment on the dashboard.

"Mr. Crane," he called, "if you don't mind a suggestion, you might look in the trunk, too. Or under the front seat."

Crane smiled blandly. "Dear me," he said, "I seem to have been a little tardy. I won't make the same mistake the next time, Mr. Ewell. However, any time you wish to visit the Inn I shall reserve two excellent venison steaks for you. I hope you will forgive my rudeness—" he waggled the gun. "Good night, Mr. Ewell."

CHAPTER TEN

Steve awakened the next morning with a slight headache that disappeared after he showered, and had a cup of coffee which was served silently to him by Ida, together with a plate of bacon, eggs and toast. Her thin mouth was severely compressed and she did not reply to Steve's, "Good morning, Ida." She did not speak until he had finished his breakfast.

"I hope," she said curtly, "that you have made up your mind to aid the police."

"I am thinking first of Vince, Ida," he said. "But if it will make you feel any better, I am not going to help him escape."

"I don't want you in this house, Stephen, if you are thinking of doing anything illegal."

"I don't like to remind you of this," Steve said angrily, "but this house is half mine. If I bother you, you can live in the hotel down in town. I'll pay the bill."

She gave an outraged, "Oh!" and walked out of the room. Steve spread his elbows on the table and closed his eyes. That was a lousy thing to have said. He'd have to apologize. Later. He wiped his mouth on the paper napkin and went out to his car and drove to Rocky Hill.

Before going to the mayor's office he called Doris Stewart, not so much to tell what had happened to him the night before, though that was the excuse, but to hear the sound of her voice again.

Then, too, he told himself, she was the only one friendly to his attempt to help Vince. But he felt an unaccustomed stimulation as he waited for her to answer the phone and then a warmth at her throaty, "Good morning, Rocky Hill Chamber of Commerce."

Quickly he told her of what had happened on his way home the night before, leaving out the details of the beating. "I might be entirely cockeyed, Dorrie," he said, "but I think that guy is the one who was in the holdup with Vince."

There was a catch of excitement in her voice when she said, "That's *important*, Steve! You'll have to tell that to the police."

"Of course, Dorrie, but—I don't have very much to tell them. I haven't the faintest idea who the guy was. Wait a minute!" he snapped his fingers. "There is something. He drove a Model A Ford pickup truck and there aren't too many of those around anymore. The police could check on that easily enough. It's a starting point anyway."

"Oh, Steve, I never expected things to break for us so quickly."

He began to realize how full of holes his hunch was, but, not wanting to dampen her excitement, he said, "I'll keep working on it, honey. I'm going over to see the mayor now."

"Call me up the minute you get finished with him, Steve, I want to know what he says. You won't forget, will you?"

"No, I won't forget."

He hung up and pursed his lips thoughtfully as he walked back to his car. He had a starting point, as he had told Doris, but that was all. A Model A Ford pickup truck wouldn't prove anything against the owner of it, even if it could be proved that he was the man who had attacked him the night before. There were only two ways to get at him—to find the bank money in his possession or to get Vince to name him, but, knowing Vince, that wasn't very likely. Still, the police had to be told, even if they regarded the story as more fantasy than fact.

The mayor was surprisingly cordial when Steve got to his office. "Sit down, Ewell. What's on your mind? Something to do with Vince? Please have a cigar, Ewell." He smiled benevolently and pushed a box of slim, green-dappled panatelas across the desk to Steve. There was a slight tremor in his bony, mottled, old-man hands, but his eyes were as shrewd and alert as those of a questing mink.

Steve took a cigar and, while he was lighting it, Ike Winder, the police chief, opened the door and walked in, and Steve knew that the mayor had summoned him by pressing the buzzer button under the edge of the desk.

The chief gave Steve a small, noncommittal nod and leaned against the door and put a blue-headed wooden match between his teeth and chewed it slowly. Steve looked from one to the other.

"If you have anything to say about Vince, Steve," the mayor said, "I want Chief Winder to hear it."

"He can hear it," Steve said without expression. "I just wanted to ask a question. Can Vince's sentence be shortened if I can get him to return the money to the bank?"

The mayor and the chief exchanged a glance and the mayor asked, "You've been in touch with Vince, Steve?"

Steve shook his head. "I don't even know if I'll be able to, but if I can, I'd like to know if I can put a proposition up to him."

"Well—" the mayor rocked back in his swivel chair, "I can't make any promises. You know that, Steve."

"I just want an opinion."

"In that case, I'd say offhand that maybe something can be worked out. The money's important, but there's more to it than that. There were two men in the holdup. Could you get Vince to name the other man?"

"Would that have to be part of it?"

"I'm afraid you couldn't make any deal without that, Steve. With him *and* the money I think something could be worked out."

Steve drew a long breath and plucked a fleck of tobacco from his underlip, placing it very carefully in the ashtray. "Suppose," he said slowly, "I could help with that end of it, would it count for Vince?" Then, swiftly before they could interrupt, he told them of the man who had waylaid him the night before, adding, "And it makes sense because Vince told Bonnie that the other guy in the holdup was somebody from around here, somebody he had known a long time. And that Model A Ford pickup truck could be a lead. In fact, it's the only real lead I've got."

The chief said, "Uh!" in a grunt of disbelief and looked at the mayor and said hostilely, "This is getting too goddam tricky and complicated."

The mayor held up his hand. "Hold it for a minute, Ike. How much trouble would it be to check up on all the Model A Ford pickups in the Valley?"

The chief said impatiently, "That part of it's easy enough, but here's the snag. If this guy is what Ewell thinks he is, the other guy in the holdup, he wouldn't be dumb enough to run around in his own car. He'd swipe one. So where does that leave us?"

"If a Model A pickup was stolen last night, it would corroborate Ewell's story."

"I'll look into it. But," he turned unfriendly eyes on Steve, "I might as well tell you this. There's a lot of feeling in the Valley. People are scared. The men don't want their wives or kids hurt if there's any shooting, so this guy last night might have been on the level. People kind of tend to take the law into their own hands when they get scared, and an escaped convict with a gun is something to be scared of. So if you're being tricky, Ewell, I might as well tell you right now the mayor'd have to call out the state guard to protect you, and he ain't going to do that!"

"Don't talk like that, Ike," the mayor said severely. "I'd have the governor on the phone in two minutes if I thought there was any threat of a mob."

The chief shrugged. "It might happen too fast."

The mayor drummed stiffly on the desk with his aged fingertips. "I'm inclined to go along with Ewell for the time being, so see if there are any reports of a stolen Model A Ford pickup, will you, Ike?"

The chief said, "Check," and walked out of the room.

The mayor waited until the door closed and then he said, "He's right, Ewell. People are wondering. They're asking themselves how far you'll go and if there'll be any trouble. You can't blame them."

"The hell with them and the hell with Ike Winder!" Steve said violently. "I'm concerned with Vince and nobody else and I'm going to make the best deal I can for him. I can take care of myself."

"Like last night for instance, Ewell?"

"I won't get caught like that again."

The mayor shook his head. "Be careful, Ewell, be careful. I don't want anything to happen. It's a bad situation. But believe me, I hope things work out for you. When can you get in touch with Vince?"

"I don't know. I don't have the faintest idea where he is."

The mayor stood up. "Keep in touch with me, Ewell. And be sure you know what you're doing."

Steve said, "I know what I'm doing," nodded and walked out.

CHAPTER ELEVEN

Steve was drenched with sweat as be crossed the sunbaked street to an orange outdoor phone booth. His spirits lifted at Doris Stewart's breathless hello and he was enthusiastic in his description of the mayor's favorable reception of his proposition. He added, "I'm going to go home and change now and then I'll go nosing around some more. Maybe I can get a line on Vince."

"You've been wonderful, Steve," Doris said. "Keep calling me, please. I'll be home all night. Call me, no matter how late."

"I'll do that, honey," he said and hung up slowly and heavily.

She wasn't in love with Vince, he told himself. She was only in love with the idea of Vince, with that easy surface charm that made friends for Vince at first sight wherever he went. She didn't really know Vince, or that she wasn't his kind of woman at all. Bonnie was Vince's kind of woman, amoral, irresponsible, greedily lecherous.

But Vince was a wonderful guy, a really wonderful guy, despite that weakness in him, and he had been a wonderful brother. He had always been generous and loyal and he never gave you the brushoff when you needed him. He wasn't vicious and he would never hurt anyone deliberately. His selfishness wasn't the curdled, bitter selfishness of, well, face it, Ida. His selfishness was a weakness, and prison would ruin him forever unless he were given something to lean on, some hope. Vince was worth saving.

As he recrossed the street to his car, he saw the tall, sandy-haired figure of Ralph Loriot standing there on the sidewalk, fanning himself with a battered Panama hat.

He greeted Steve with a grin and said, "Hi, sailor, what's the scoop today, and for God's sake be unique and *don't* tell me it's hot."

"It's cool," said Steve, "real cool. It's snowing in the Yukon."

"Funny boy." Loriot's rimless glasses glinted in the sunlight, giving him the appearance of peering impersonally and clinically into Steve's face.

Steve lit a cigarette. He blew out a plume of smoke and watched it drift in the still air. "What's on your mind, Ralph?" he asked.

"The rumors are flying thick and fast, son, about how you have Vince hidden away, but discounting ninety-nine and nine-tenths of them, I'd say you're up to something. You saw Bonnie last night at the Inn and this morning you had a confab with the mayor and Ike Winder. What gives?"

"Sorry. Nothing for publication, Ralph."

"I know that, Steve. This is off the record."

"Sorry, Ralph."

"You know your little session with the mayor and Ike is going to be all over town in a half hour, don't you? People are going to say you're trying to make a deal for Vince."

"I don't give a damn what people say."

"They might even start thinking that you know where he's hiding out, son, and there are some hot-heads who might give you a bad time. There's been talk."

"Do you think the mayor and Ike would have let me walk out of that office if I knew where Vince was hiding out?"

Loriot leaned against the fender of the car and took off his glasses and wiped the perspiration from them with his handkerchief. "I think they might," he said thoughtfully. "The mayor's an old political fox from way back and I think he might wangle a deal for Vince, with the obvious reservations, if Ike could get the credit for the arrest. What've they got to lose? But it's you I'm thinking of, sailor. You're the one who's sticking out his neck.

"The word is that Bonnie has the bank money and that sooner or later Vince is going to come to town for it and there'll be shooting and people will get hurt. So you see what they're afraid of. They don't want bullets flying around our peaceful little hamlet. If you're helping Vince hide out, you might have to go into hiding yourself before this is over."

"I don't know where he is."

Loriot shrugged and put on his hat. "Well," he said, "if you do happen to find out, the best thing you can do is persuade him to give himself up and then make the deal, and the sooner the better, sailor." And then with an odd little grimace, "I always liked Vince. I wish—oh, hell, I hope something can be worked out for him. See you around, son." He turned and strode up the walk to the town clerk's office.

Steve drove stolidly homeward. Everybody liked Vince. But they all wanted to see him back in jail again. Except Doris.

As Steve walked up the steps to the front porch he saw the envelope thumbtacked to the door over the knob. His name was on it in Ida's stiff, prim handwriting. The note inside was brief.

"I have gone to the hotel. I can't stay here any longer with things the way they are. My advice to you, Stephen, is to get down on your knees and pray that God will help you think right again."

He went inside and called the hotel but Ida had not checked in yet. He went upstairs and showered and put on fresh clothes. He was in the kitchen drinking a glass of ice water when Orv drove up beside the house in his valve-noisy Chevrolet sedan. Steve walked quickly outside through the kitchen door.

"Did you take Ida down to the hotel, Orv?" he asked.

Orv's thin, bleak face looked unhappy. His long jaw moved slowly on his chew of tobacco. He shook his head.

"I took her down my sister's," he said. "I thought it would be better than sitting alone in a hotel room. You oughtn't of talked to Ida the way you did, Steve. She was crying all the way down."

"Hell, Orv, you know I didn't mean it. This is her house. I wouldn't drive her out of it."

"Ida's kind of touchy. You ought to realize that. She ain't got much, Steve. But maybe it's better she stays with my sister a while. It ain't good for her to be alone like she was here all the time."

Steve turned his head and looked at the house, the neat, sterile house, implacably clean, barren. Yes, it would do Ida good to be out of it for a while. He could call her up in a few days.

Orv crossed his arms on the steering wheel and said glumly, "And that fat bastard Floyd Morley, too."

"What's he got to do with it?"

"Well, you know him and Ida is kind of engaged. They got an understanding. You know."

"Well?"

"Well, I thought maybe Ida would like to see him so I dropped over the supermarket where he works and told him it would be kind of nice if he dropped in on her after work. Well, he fiddled and faddled and finally said maybe he'd call her up and tried to tell me Ida didn't want him to get mixed up with this as long as Vince was on the loose and people might think he was in on it, too. The son-of-a-bitch," Orv spat disgustedly. "He's the one that don't want to get mixed up in it and he's going to let her sit it out alone. I felt like banging one on his lousy fat chin."

"You didn't tell Ida, did you?"

"Hell, no. I know better'n that. But it'd be better in the long run if I did tell her. He's nothing but a fat slob. I'm hoping maybe she'll find out for herself. A man's no good for nothing if he won't stand by her at a time like this."

And Ida would see it, Steve thought. She would excuse it and tell herself that she forgave the weakness in Morley but hidden away would always be the hurt in the darkness of herself. If Vince had not broken out of prison, she might have lived the rest of her life with Floyd Morley, content even though knowing him to be ineffectual, and there probably would never have been a crisis to show her brutally that he could desert her.

In a voice of vague apology, Orv said, "I ain't a deppity no more, Steve. I resigned. Vince ain't no killer and I got to thinking what call did I have helping them hunt him down with a gun in my hand? Tomorrow I'm going back to work on your lake and finish up that privy on the north end."

"Thanks, Orv."

"No thanks coming." He looked unhappily at his hands, folded them and put them in his lap. "Let me know if there's anything I can do to help, Steve," he mumbled. "I mean about Vince. I know you won't do nothing that ain't right. You can call on me any time. You know that."

Steve said gratefully, "I know it, Orv, but the best thing you can do is go back to work on the lake. And thanks for taking Ida to your sister's house."

Orv nodded and scratched at a patch of dried mud on his jeans. He avoided Steve's eyes and his mouth was bunched and troubled.

Steve noticed this and said, "Are you worried about Vince and me, Orv?"

Orv made a vague, formless gesture with his hand as if to dismiss the thought and he said, "I don't know nothing about you and Vince. Is there something to know?"

"There are a lot of wild guesses going on around town. Have you heard any of them?"

"Here and there," Orv admitted. "One is you got Vince hiding out in the house here and the cops ain't doing nothing about it because you promised Ike Winder a cut of the bank money," he laughed without humor. "But that's about the worst of them. The other is that you're making some kind of deal with the mayor and Ike to get Vince off the hook if he gives back the money."

Steve was astonished at the accuracy of that guess but he said, "I don't even know where Vince is, Orv."

"But you're aiming to find out."

"So are the state, county and local police. Hundreds of them."

"But you might know something they don't. What I'm driving at is this, Steve—don't hesitate to call on me time you want."

CHAPTER TWELVE

The small room had the clenched, baking heat of a kiln. The two windows were open but the shades were drawn to the sills. Vince lay on the cot in his underpants, leafing listlessly through a back number of *Life*. There was a small, cheap electric fan on a chair beside the cot, but its ineffectual blades hardly stirred the torpid air and Vince's body glistened with sweat in the light of the single, naked bulb that hung from the middle of the ceiling.

The room, with its visual rot and smell of hidden decay, was more depressing than his cell had ever been. The cot was worse than his bed, the food was worse because Pauline did not know how to cook and chiefly served hamburgers or hot dogs on buns with coffee that tasted as if it had been made from dried liver.

There was no one to talk to except Pauline and Lyle and they had to spend most of their time in the bar downstairs from eight in the morning till two the next morning, and Vince had nothing to do but listen to the radio and look at magazines. That was the worst, having nothing to do. Your mind went around and around and around till after a while it felt like a drill boring holes in your brains.

The bandage around his thigh was white and clean and the wound bothered him hardly at all anymore and he could walk with almost no limp. It was practically healed and it was only three days. He had to give Pauline credit. She kept clean bandages on it, and as long as he took it easy and didn't move around too much, it'd be okay.

He wished Bonnie were here. The room wouldn't be so crummy with Bonnie here. What a time they could have, like the four days they holed up in that hotel in Niagara Falls, not leaving the room once. Niagara Falls. That was a laugh. Strictly a tourist trap, but Bonnie wanted to go to Niagara Falls on the honeymoon. She'd taken one look at it and said, "That all there's to it? Pete sake, you can't even hear yourself think." What had she expected, vaudeville? Ah, she was nothing but a big kid in a lot of ways. Yeah, but big enough and old enough in bed! He ached with the thought of her. The ache became an agony and he ground his teeth.

This lousy stinking crummy room!

But he couldn't leave it. Every cop in the country was looking for him and Pauline said his picture had been shown on TV. *If you have seen this man, report it immediately to your nearest police station. Take no chances. He is armed and dangerous.* The crumbs. That fixed it so if you stuck your nose outside the room there'd be a hundred jerks screaming "Cops!" The heat was really on and you couldn't move a muscle.

Then he heard the footsteps heavily climbing the stairs. He knew it was Pauline but all the same his heart lurched and pounded heavily and he slid his hand under the pillow and wrapped his shaking fingers around the butt of the gun. She knocked and he strode swiftly and silently to the door. "Yeah?"

"It's me," she whispered. "I thought maybe you like a cold pitcher of beer."

He unlocked and opened the door and limped heavily back to his cot.

"It still hurt that much, Vince?" she asked worriedly.

"Yeah."

"It's got me worried. It's almost healed and it shouldn't hurt that much. Maybe there's something else. Maybe we should try and get a doctor."

"There's nothing else," he said peevishly because he had exaggerated the limp as he always did when she came into the room. "It's the heat."

She wiped her face wearily with the hem of the apron she was wearing. "Yeah, I think it's worse at night. You can't sleep. I brought you some beer."

"Sit down and talk to me for a minute."

"Well—we're kind of busy downstairs in the bar, Vince."

"Damn it, you can spare me a minute, can't you? You can go nuts all by yourself up here alone."

She heard the genuine loneliness in him and was troubled by an odd note in his voice that she did not recognize as fear. "I guess I wouldn't like it so much myself," she said. "Here, have a drink of cold beer."

She had brought a glass, too, but he drank thirstily straight from the pitcher. He patted the cot beside him.

"Sit down for a minute, kiddo," he said. "You don't know what it's like being alone up here, hearing the juke box and the guys having a good time downstairs and knowing that you can't even stick your nose out of the room."

She sat down tiredly on the cot beside him, her hands limp in her lap. "Is there something I can get you maybe, Vince?" she asked. "How's about one of them jigsaw puzzles? I used to like working them when I was getting over my appendix."

He slipped his hand under her dress. "Yeah, there's something you can give me, kiddo—"

She grabbed his hand. "Please, Vince, no," she pleaded.

"Come on, kiddo. Lyle's busy downstairs."

"No—no—no, Vince. Please don't make me!"

He pulled his hand away. "I don't have to force anybody," he said sullenly. But secretly he was relieved. He hadn't really wanted her. He was too tense. He suddenly did not want her around.

"Get back to the bar," he said nastily. "I'm better off alone."

She stood but hesitated. "Let's not fight, Vince, I'm all worn out. I ain't had a night's sleep since you came."

Contritely he patted her hip. "Sure, kiddo. I'm sorry I made that pass at you. I was out of line."

"Want a hamburger or a hot dog?"

"No, thanks, kiddo. It's too hot to eat."

"I'll come up later and see if you want anything."

She walked out of the room with the heavy, springless step of fatigue. Vince took another drink of beer and stared morosely at the floor. What a stinking way to wind up when the only friends you have in the world are two dumb Hunkies like Pauline and Lyle. You might as well be dead as live like this. You'd be better off dead.

And he lay face down on the cot and bit the pillow as the self-pity inside him grew bigger and bigger and filled his throat and choked him.

It was about a half hour later when he heard the rush of Pauline's feet on the stairs again and be sat bolt upright, breathless, clutching the gun, shaking.

She burst into the room and stood with her back against the door, panting. "There's a man," she said, her eyes distended.

He tried to answer but something had him by the throat. Her hand made jerky motions toward the floor, indicating the barroom below. "He was asking if you ever came here. He didn't ask if you were here now, just if you ever came here, like he'd been here with you once before."

He tried to swallow the thing that was in his throat. "A cop?"

"I don't know. At least not from around here. Lyle knows all the cops here."

"What's he look like?" You were less afraid of something when you knew what it looked like, the kind of face it had, was it big or little, fat or thin.

Pauline moistened her lips. "He's big. He's got red hair. He looks like he ain't slept for a week. Lyle didn't tell him nothing."

Vince's hands began to shake very badly but it was from a new kind of surging inside him. "Wait a minute wait a minute listen—" the words tumbled out of him, tangling almost unintelligibly. "His right eye, look, right here on the forehead, right over the right eye, a scar right through the eyebrow about this wide almost a quarter of an inch, you can't miss it. Listen, find out if his name's Steve, that's all you have to do, just find out if his name's Steve?"

"Steve?"

"That's my brother. Steve. That's his name. My kid brother. Make sure though. Look at his driver's license. But if he's got that scar it's Steve!" In his eagerness, he jumped up and pushed her so that he could open the door and then he pushed her out into the hall. "Make sure it's Steve," he whispered, "then for heaven sake, bring him up!"

He closed the door and paced up and down, to the cot and back, to the shaded window, praying, *dear God, let it be Steve, let it be Steve. Steve, Steve!* He stopped and listened, holding his breath. They were coming up the stairs. There were two of them and for a moment he felt trapped and frantic. Suppose she had made a mistake? Suppose—

He darted across the room and flattened against the wall so that the door would conceal him when it opened. He couldn't breathe. He held the gun ready, pointing it at the door. He'd shoot. This time he'd shoot. But his terror mounted because his finger felt paralyzed on the trigger. *He'd have to shoot this time!*

The door opened and he thought he'd faint because it actually was Steve.

Vince cried, "Oh, kiddo!" and clutched Steve's arm. "God, it's good to see you, kiddo!" He pounded Steve on the back and clutched his arm again as if it were the only thing to which he had to cling.

They stammered and laughed and clutched at each other and slapped each other's shoulders and Vince tugged at Steve's arm and drew him over to the cot where they sat side by side and stared at each other.

But now that the initial elation and the incredulity of success was over, Steve looked at Vince with a sense of sick horror. Could this gaunt, unshaven, weeping, trembling man really be Vince? Big, laughing, confident Vince?

Masking the shock, he said, "It's good to see you, Vince."

"And you, kiddo, believe me. I've been going half-crazy up here. Have you seen Bonnie?"

"Yeah. I—saw her."

"What's the matter?" Vince asked sharply. "She's okay, isn't she?"

Steve cursed himself for not hiding his feelings better. "She's fine, Vince. She's working up at the Inn. Singing."

Vince scowled. "I don't want her working up there."

"She and Ida didn't get along very well, Vince. They both like to have their own way. You know what I mean. So Bonnie took this job up at the

Inn. I was away at the time."

"Yeah, Bonnie's pretty independent. Can you get word to her that I'm here? I mean, that I'm okay."

Steve felt as if he were walking in mud and sinking deeper at every step. "It won't be too easy, Vince. She's being watched. The police are expecting you to get in touch with her. The whole Rocky Hill area's practically an armed camp. There are police all over the place."

Vince laughed thinly. "That bunch of comedians. They're probably tripping all over each other."

"It's more serious than that, Vince."

"I know, I know, I'm not laughing. It's no joke having to hide out in a crummy hole like this. But—" and the fear quickened Vince's voice, "how'd you happen to find me here? You're being watched, too, aren't you? How do you know you weren't followed?"

He clutched Steve's arm, but Steve covered his hand with his own. "Easy, Vince, easy. I wasn't followed here. If anybody was following me, I lost him when I went through Bamberger's department store down in Newark. I ducked through the shipping department and out the loading platform and changed a couple buses before I took the one up here. This is the fourth place I've been to. You brought me here a few times, remember? Six, seven years ago. I was just shooting in the dark."

There was a shrill note in Vince's laugh and he gripped Steve's knee and shook it. "You're a smart kid." Then, sharply, "You didn't talk to anybody, did you? Anybody know you've been looking for me?"

"Don't worry, I didn't give anybody a lead," Steve said evasively. "I've worked this alone."

"You look all in, kiddo. I'll bet you haven't had a wink of sleep."

"You can't kill a Ewell. You know that, Vince."

Vince laughed loudly. "They sure tried though, kiddo."

He tapped the bandage on his thigh. Then uneasily, "But it was close."

"Oh, my God," said Steve, "I didn't even notice. Is it bad?"

"It's not good, kiddo. It's never good to be shot."

"Let me take a look at it. It might—"

"It's okay," said Vince hurriedly. "It's healing fine. Here, let's have a beer. It might not make you cooler, but it'll change your attitude." He laughed noisily and poured Steve a glass of the beer and he drank from the pitcher again.

They seemed to have run out of talk and they drank their beer in silence. There were things that had to be rearranged in Steve's mind before he could talk further to Vince. He had expected almost anything except this frightened, shaking, disorganized man. This was a Vince that he never suspected could exist. Or perhaps this was what had always lived under Vince's laughing, confident façade. The best thing, he thought, would be to state it flatly.

"I've got a proposition, Vince," he said.

Vince looked up and his eyes narrowed warily. "From the sound of your voice, kiddo, it's got something to do with me giving myself up."

"There's more to it than that, Vince. Just listen for a moment. That bank money is unspendable. The serial numbers are just as well-known now as they were right after the holdup. I think a deal can be made to shorten your sentence if you returned it and gave us the name of the other man in the holdup. Wait a minute. There's more. When you come out of jail, I'll have the lake fully improved and I can take a mortgage on it from the bank and give you enough money to get started. *Or* I can take you in as a partner and you'll be set for life."

"And what a life," Vince jeered, "renting rowboats to kids from now on. Now these are oars, kiddies, and you push them back and forth to make the boat go and please do Uncle Vince a nice favor and get drowned in the middle of the lake. No thanks, kiddo. They're not going to cage me up like a canary again. Thanks, but Bonnie and I have a little living to do."

"Bonnie's finished with you, Vince. She started divorce proceedings before you broke out."

"What the hell are you talking about? I wasn't served with any papers."

"She called it off—"

"Of course she called it off. She knows we can get together again now."

"She called it off because she's afraid of you, Vince, and that's the only reason. She's living with Crane up at the Inn. Everybody knows it."

"Crane!" Vince laughed jarringly. "That old poop? It's been thirty years since he knew what to do with a woman."

"He's rich, Vince, He's loaded."

"Loaded, schmoaded. Bonnie needs a man and don't you ever forget it. She wants me, kiddo. She'd be right here this minute if she could find a way."

Steve said slowly and with emphasis, "All she wants from you, Vince, is that bank money."

"She'll get both, kiddo, both. Me and the money, and you can't beat that combination with Bonnie."

In despair, Steve knew that he had made a mistake. He had made the proposition too soon and without proof of Bonnie's perfidy. But there was still time. Nothing had been settled. Vince had to stay in hiding. The next time he came he'd have the proof to show Vince how hopeless and even tragic his position was.

"Well," he said, "there's nothing we can do tonight anyway, Vince. Think over what I told you and I'll come back as soon as I can."

Vince picked up the gun from the cot beside him. "You know what this is?" he asked in an ugly voice.

"I know what it is, Vince. And I know you couldn't shoot anybody with it if your life depended on it."

"Things have changed, kiddo. I've learned how. So don't get any ideas about turning me in for my own good and trying to make a deal."

"Okay, Vince."

"You better be damn sure you mean okay, kiddo. Now see if you can figure a way to get Bonnie down here and I'll take it from there on in."

Steve nodded, discouraged, and stood up. "I'll do what I can, Vince."

Vince lay back on the cot, put his hands behind his head and scowled up at the leak-stained ceiling.

"On your way out," he said in a flat, hostile voice, "tell that bitch downstairs to bring me up another pitcher of beer."

He did not turn his head as Steve plodded from the room. Fury smoldered in him. Back to jail. Jesus Christ. Even Steve had turned against him now. Well the hell with them. The hell with all of them. He'd get out of this mess by himself. He'd done all right so far and he'd keep on doing all right. He didn't have to get down on his knees to anyone.

He heard Pauline's heavy footsteps mounting the stairs and he turned his head and scowled at the door and there was a narrow glitter in his eyes when she walked into the room, carrying the beaded pitcher of beer.

"Everything go all right, Vince?" she asked.

He sat up, watching her walk across the room toward him.

"Just fine," he said. "Just dandy. Couldn't be better."

He took the pitcher of beer from her and put it on the floor and, reaching suddenly, grabbed her wrist, pulled her down and rolled her on the cot, sprawling on her and covering her mouth as she cried out.

"Shut up!" he whispered harshly, pulling at her dress. "This time you're coming across, baby."

She struggled and pleaded, "Nonono, Vince, please no, please—"

He thrust the gun in her face and grinned when she drew back. "That's better, baby. I'm not taking no for an answer."

He hooked his fingers in the neck line of her flimsy cotton dress and ripped it from her. She moaned and the terror in her eyes was fuel to his excitement. His laugh was a savage cry of triumph and he threw himself upon her.

What followed was a madness and in the midst of it, as devastating as an explosion, the door slammed open and Lyle, his face congested, stood there roaring, holding a length of iron pipe in his hand. "So—you just bring him beer, eh! You bitch! You think I'm that dumb! You bring him beer once too often!"

Vince sprang from the bed and fell, dropping the gun. He rolled to the far corner and scrambled to a crouch, his eyes darting around the room for a weapon. Now roaring incoherently, Lyle leaped at the cot, swinging the pipe wildly at Pauline. She dodged from under it and the wooden frame of the cot splintered from the force of the blow. Cursing, Lyle swung at her again, the blow thundering against the floor as she sprang aside, screaming and snatching up the gun Vince had dropped. She backed away from him, pointing the gun at him with both hands.

"He made me, Lyle!" she cried. "He made me, he made me, I didn't want to do it, he made me!"

Lyle swore gutturally at her and stalked her with the pipe upraised. His eyes were not sane and there was a froth of white at the corners of his mouth. She dodged, pleading still, in front of the smashed cot and tried to get to the open door, but he circled and when he had her penned in the corner of the room he said, "Ah!" and swung at her, but the pipe was too long and it struck the ceiling.

Pauline screamed and fired, and when he staggered, she darted to the door. He bellowed and leaped after her with the blood streaming down the side of his face. Downstairs several men yelled and there was the sound of overturned furniture and a door slammed. Vince jumped to the window and pulled back the shade from the side. Still screaming, Pauline was running naked down the street and Lyle was pounding after her. She tripped and fell and Lyle cried out in triumph. He could not have been more than five feet away from her when she squirmed up on one hip and emptied the gun into him. He staggered as each bullet struck him, dropped the pipe, walked in a small, blind circle and then fell straight forward on his face. The men came streaming out of the barroom downstairs.

Vince dressed frantically and sprinted for the doorway, buttoning his shirt as he ran. He went out the back way and a few minutes later, as he plunged deeper into the frenzied darkness, he heard the high, keening wail of the police siren.

CHAPTER THIRTEEN

Taking the express turnpike, Steve was back in Rocky Hill within three-quarters of an hour. He stopped at a public phone booth on the outskirts of town and called Doris. By now they had developed a coded way of talking to each other so that if anyone listened in he would not realize the significance of what he heard.

"Hi, Dorrie," he said, trying to sound casual and cheerful, "I found my wallet today."

He heard the swift intake of her breath. "Was—was it all right, Steve?"

"It was all there."

"I'm so glad, Steve! I was worried that someone else would find it first. I suppose you're too busy to come over for a while."

"Yes, I've got work I have to get out of the way."

"Well—call me when you can, will you, Steve? I don't go out much these days."

"Sure, honey," he said, wishing that he *could* go over to see her.

He hung up and walked slowly back to his car. Now she knew that he had found Vince and that Vince was all right, but that nothing had been settled to get Vince to return the money and name the other man in the holdup. He glanced at his wrist watch and was numbly surprised to see that it was only nine o'clock.

He had to see Bonnie, but first he wanted a drink and he stopped in at Shorty's Bar on the main street of Rocky Hill. The bar was crowded and the bluish light from the TV set made corpse-like masks of the watching faces. Steve went to the end of the bar and ordered a gin rickey. He drank in silence, not noticing the covert glances darted at him by the heavy man at his side. The man was drinking whiskey with a beer chaser and he was a little drunk. He tilted back his head and stared openly at Steve.

"Say," he said in a loud voice of deliberate insult, "you're that Ewell son-of-a-bitch, ain't you?"

Steve looked up and saw that the fellow was drunk and tried to ignore him, but the man reached out and slapped him backhanded on the side of the arm.

"I said, you're that Ewell son-of-a-bitch, ain't you?" he said even more loudly.

Every head turned in their direction and Shorty came running down behind the bar, crying anxiously, "Now cut it out! Cut it out, Smitty! I don't want no trouble in here."

Steve put down his glass. "It's all right, Shorty," he said. "I was just leaving."

The big man shoved him back and stood in front of him, legs astride. "You ain't going no place yet, Mr. Son-of-a-bitch Ewell," he said belligerently. "I want to find out about that jailbird brother of yours. Where're you hiding him out, bastard?"

"Drink your drink," said Steve evenly. "I'm not hiding anybody. Don't make trouble."

"Trouble! You're the one that's in trouble, Mr. Son-of-a-bitch Ewell. Now answer me or do you want some of this?" He thrust his fist under Steve's nose.

Steve turned and walked toward the back door but the man sprang after him, seized him by the shoulder, spun him and aimed a wild, looping roundhouse blow at his head. Steve slipped inside and hit the man as hard as he could in the stomach. The fellow doubled over and fell against the bar, gagging.

Shorty said hurriedly, "You better go, Steve. It wasn't your fault, but you better go before—" he glanced down the row of hard faces at the bar.

Steve nodded and walked quickly out the back door. He was calm enough but his teeth were clenched. Smitty Horne was a loudmouth but he'd never had an original idea in his life. Somebody had been talking to him. Somebody had been talking it up against Vince all through town. Somebody who wanted Vince dead, somebody who wanted to inflame the mob into a lynching mood, somebody who wanted to make sure that Vince would be out of the way permanently. Of course, there was only one person—the second man in the bank holdup.

Steve was glad, eternally grateful, that he had kept Doris out of this. No one knew she was concerned, so she would be safe if anything broke loose, and thank God for that. Unhappily now, he knew that he was in love with her. He could close his eyes and see the curl of her hair, the way her eyebrows slanted to make her eyes seem oblique, the curling lift of her mouth when she smiled, and it was an ache inside him, knowing that she was in love, or thought she was, with Vince.

As he rounded the block to get to his car which was parked on the main street near Shorty's Bar, the police cruiser drew to the curb and Ike Winder hailed him from the near window. The patrolman on tour was Vacheresse, but Ike usually rode around with the cruiser for a few hours before going to bed.

"You're a hard man to get hold of these days, Steve," he said, his face hollowed with shadow and hostile in the feeble light from the dashboard.

"I've had things to do," Steve said. And then to Vacheresse, "Hi, John."

Vacheresse nodded impassively without speaking, and Ike demanded shortly, "What things?"

Steve hesitated, glancing at Vacheresse, and said, "You know what things."

"You've been in touch with Vince," Ike accused him, but there was something else in his voice, too.

Steve shook his head but it was an evasion for he said, "I was on the level with you and the mayor when I said I wanted to put that proposition up to Vince. Has the mayor talked to anybody about it yet?"

"He's working on it. But if I had my way, you'd be in jail right now and there wouldn't be any talk about deals, either."

His voice was hammering and resentful and Steve knew that the mayor was still holding the reins. That wasn't easy for Ike, Steve realized. He was a good cop and had been a lieutenant on the Jersey City force before he retired to Rocky Hill eight years ago.

Then abruptly before Steve could reply, "Where were you all day today?"

"Trying to find Vince."

"Where?"

Steve named all the places to which he had been but omitting the Regal Bar and Grill in North Laurel. "And you can check on it if you want," he said, "I'll give you the list."

"You're pretty cute, Ewell. You're too damn cute. Listen to me, boy. You don't know what you're fooling around with. Vince ain't the same guy you used to know when you were kids. He served a stretch out in Illinois and he held up a bank here and busted out of jail. He's your brother. Okay. I know how you feel, maybe, and that's why I'm talking to you like this. I don't think you realize what you're up against. Somebody's going to get hurt, and if you're mixed up in it, they'll throw the book at you."

"The only thing I'm interested in is making a deal for Vince," Steve said stolidly.

Winder slapped the edge of the window angrily. "Vince won't make a deal, you damn fool! He had his chance during the trial. The prosecutor put it up to him and he turned it down. You can't deal with a guy like that, and less now than ever before."

Steve said expressionlessly, "If he won't make the deal, I won't help him hide out," but there was a dry bitterness in his mouth because Winder was close, too close, to being right all down the line.

"Have it your own way," Winder said grimly. "But if this thing backfires, you'll be responsible. You and the mayor, but you'll be the one that gets it in the neck. Let's get out of here, John."

Vacheresse gave Steve a flat, unfriendly stare and turned the car away from the curb. Steve walked over to his own car and sat for a moment behind the steering wheel as he lighted a cigarette. He was tired, bushed, and he wondered wearily if there *would* be any end to this. He shook his head sharply and sat upright in the seat.

Why don't you break into tears, he thought with self-contempt. He had to keep moving. He couldn't string this out forever. It hinged on Bonnie now. If he could show Vince what Bonnie was really like, that might wrap it up.

It was nine-thirty when Steve walked into the Field Stone Inn, and Crane appeared from the bar, as if on signal. "You wish to see Bonnie, Mr. Ewell?"

"Were you expecting me?" Steve asked dryly.

"Naturally. Not tonight perhaps, but I knew you would return. Bonnie is singing for the guests at the moment. Would you care to listen from the bar?"

"No thanks. I've heard her sing."

"Have you indeed? But really, Mr. Ewell, she does not sing too badly. I, myself, do not care to listen to her either, but that is because I prefer more classical music. However, the guests appear to think she has a certain—ah, how shall I put it—"

"Sex," said Steve. "S-e-x. And it's certain, all right."

"Yes. Quite. But a marketable commodity, you must agree. Would you care to wait in her suite until she finishes?"

"Thanks."

"I'll go up with you. The dog is there, you understand, and sometimes he is most unfriendly. I do not think dogs should be permitted to grow so large. They become officious. We can use my private elevator. It is my secret extravagance but also somewhat of a necessity. One does not grow younger."

The elevator was in the office and there was barely room in the small cage for the two of them to stand side by side. It connected directly with the suite on the second floor.

"This would be most convenient if I were a younger man, Mr. Ewell," Crane murmured. "But as it is—" he shrugged. "However, being beyond the age has its compensations. It is a stress that has been removed, a periodic tension that no longer exists. There are times when I regret it, but not too often."

"I'll bet," said Steve.

Crane opened the door of the cage and the Great Dane faced them watchfully from the middle of the room. Crane spoke a command in soft Spanish and the dog sighed and sank back on its haunches. Crane did not leave the elevator but gave his small, plump, pampered hand a little sweep, the *maitre d'hotel* offering the guest the freedom of the house.

"Please make yourself at home while you're waiting, Mr. Ewell," he said. "Potables you will find in the cellarette in the corner of the room, where there is also a small refrigerator containing sturgeon, of which I am very fond, a fair caviar, a paté, sliced guinea hen and other delicatessen if you wish a snack. If there is anything else you wish you will find a buzzer for room service beside the door." He leaned out of the elevator and pointed as if anxious for Steve to identify the correct door. Then, with a smile, he popped back into the elevator looking very arch, and closed the mahogany panel.

Steve listened to the faint, well-greased whirr of the pulleys as the elevator descended, thinking, *You foxy little crud*. There had been no mention of Vince at all, no questions about his visit to Bonnie, no allusion to their last meeting when Crane had pointed a gun at him. Everything had been sweetness and light. Except for the huge dog that watched him from the middle of the room. Steve started toward the corridor door, but the dog was there first, standing in front of it. It neither growled nor showed its teeth. It merely looked interested and determined. Steve turned as if to go out to the patio, but the dog trotted around him and stood before the French doors.

Steve smiled thinly and said, "Nice doggie," and looked around the room. There was nothing heavy enough for a weapon that would stop a dog that size. The chairs that could be wielded were of aluminum and much too light. There were police all around the Inn but by the time they could get to the second floor the regrettable accident would have occurred and Crane would be desolate.

Mr. Ewell was trying to persuade Mrs. Vincent Ewell to leave here with him. Is that not so, Bonnie? I remonstrated with him but he became abusive. He wanted her to rejoin her husband, you understand. I sent Bonnie out of the room. I was thinking only of her safety. She did not wish to be associated with an escaped convict. Mr. Ewell then threatened me. I attempted to warn him but the dog, you understand, it has been trained. There was nothing I could do—

Steve told himself irritably that he was imagining things, that Crane would not go that far. But all the same, there was the dog at the door. Could Crane's infatuation for Bonnie be that insane? And then he remembered Bonnie 's kiss. She was a walking aphrodisiac and a man could go insane with the desire to possess her, even a man as old as Crane.

Steve looked thoughtfully at the planter at the window, out of which grew several varieties of cacti. Steve tilted his head. Cactus grew in sand. He walked to the chair beside the planter, sat on the arm and took off his left shoe and sock. He poured sand into the toe of the thick-ribbed sock until it rounded to the size of a small fist, and then he knotted it tightly and slipped it into the pocket of his jacket. He put on his shoe again and looked at the dog.

"Let us not have an unpleasantness, doggie," he said, thinly mimicking Crane.

He was sitting in one of the aluminum sling chairs, drinking a mild bourbon and soda, when Bonnie walked in ten minutes later. She was wearing a dark green evening dress that was slit up the side to show her leg to mid-thigh when she moved. The neckline ended in a rhinestone clasp at her waist but was so beautifully cut that it offered her breasts without quite fulfilling the promise. Her face was a blonde-framed sultriness.

Steve grinned at her and lifted his glass and said, "Hi, princess."

She put her finger to her lips and shook her head. She gave the dog a fear-tinged glance and warily crossed the room to Steve.

"He listens in," she whispered. "There's a microphone or something. He had a fit the last time. I thought he was going crazy. He wants to marry me."

Steve nodded. Then it was as bad as he had thought. "What did you tell him?" he asked, also whispering.

"What could I tell him? Marry him and Vince'd knock both of us off? I told him that after—" she caught herself. "I told him he was nuts. I'm married to Vince." Then, uneasily, "He gives me the creeps."

"But he's rich, Bonnie. He's got lots of money."

"I'd rather be with Vince. Vince's got dough, too."

"You mean the bank money."

"You seen Vince yet?" she evaded.

"Not yet, but I have a few ideas."

"What are they, Steve? I want to help."

"It's too early to say, but I'm working on it."

"Now don't give me the runaround, Steve!" she whispered nastily.

"Now why should I do a thing like that, Bonnie?"

"You know why—the money. Vince won't see none of it if you get your hands on it first." Then, wheedling, "He needs that dough, Steve. He can't get away without it. You can't get away without dough, Steve. He can't even hide out for long without it. You got to get to him. Where you think he's hiding out?"

"Out toward Morristown maybe."

"You got a lead?"

"I might have by tomorrow."

"You wanted to see me about something, Steve. What is it?"

"Well, I want you to write Vince a note. Just in case I have luck and can get in touch with him tomorrow. He'll want to hear from you."

She nodded eagerly. "Yeah, yeah. He's nuts about me. That's why he busted out. And I'm nuts about him, too," she added hurriedly. "I want to do everything I can for him. But I can't do nothing unless I have the money. Nobody can do nothing without money."

"That's right, Bonnie. That's what I want you to write to Vince. He won't tell me about the bank money, but it's different with you. He'd tell you where it is."

"That's right. Then I can help him, can't I?" she laughed a little shrilly. "I knew you was a right guy, Stevie. I knew you'd see you couldn't go it alone. I'm the only one that can help Vince and we're nuts about each other and it's different when you're nuts about each other. You'd do things you wouldn't do for other people, like me and Vince. Right, Steve, right?"

Much more of this, Steve thought, and I'll vomit.

But he whispered, "That's right, Bonnie. But suppose you can't get to Vince right away, what then? You'll have the money."

"You trying to say I'll gyp him?" she asked venomously.

"I was just wondering what you'd do, that's all."

"I'll hold the dough for him, that's what I'll do. I'll let him have some to get away and join up with him later."

"But suppose he gets caught in the meantime?"

"Then it's better I have the money than the cops catching him with it, ain't it?"

Steve patted her knee, "That's exactly what you should write to Vince in your note, Bonnie. Tell him everything. Tell him exactly how you feel about it. That's what he'll want to know—how he stands with you."

She eyed him with sudden suspicion. "You sound like you got an angle."

"He's my brother. That's my angle."

"Yeah, sure. But I ain't nothing to you. Maybe you're thinking of crossing me up."

Steve forced his lips into an insinuating grin and moved his fingertips a bit higher. "That's the last thing in my mind, Bonnie," he whispered.

Her eyes spread and then her lids lowered quickly to hide the high glint of triumph. She leaned into him.

She whispered, "Stevie—" Her hand touched his neck, cupped the back of his head and drew him down to meet the up-thrust of her parted lips. She moaned and moved her head as if to bury the kiss deeper. She moved against him.

"Hold me, honey," she whispered, "hold me, hold me—"

Steve put his arms around her, thinking, *You bitch you bitch you bitch*, but he ground his mouth against hers and held her until she struggled to break loose.

"No more, honey," she whispered, "no more right now. We don't want to get walked in on."

"I can't let you go, Bonnie!"

"We got lots of time, Stevie. It wouldn't be good if he walked in on us now. And I got to write that note to Vince."

"The hell with Vince!"

She smiled slyly. "Don't say things like that, Stevie. Vince knows where the bank money is, remember?"

"I forgot for the minute. You drive a man crazy, Bonnie."

She brushed his lips with hers and put the palms of her hands flat against his chest between them. "It's a lot of money, Stevie, and we'll need it later, me and you."

"But—what about Vince?"

"We'll take care of Vince. We'll give him getaway money. Now let me write that note."

He released her lingeringly, as if reluctant to let her go.

"I'm crazy about you, Stevie. Now I'll write the note. And don't worry," her smile was gloating and cruel. "I can put anything over on Vince."

The dog stood up, alert, when she crossed the room but subsided as she sat down at the desk. It took her about ten minutes to write the note.

"That'll take care of it," she said, recrossing the room. "Read it and tell me if I left out something."

He read it and it was everything he could have wished, naked greed in every word. Even to Vince it would be obvious that all she wanted was the bank money. He folded it carefully and put it into the inside pocket of his jacket. Bonnie smiled languorously and slid her arms around his neck, her body curving to his from thigh to breast—and that was the way they were standing when Crane stepped out of the elevator. He was deathly pale and holding a long-barreled Luger. He pointed it at Bonnie.

"Go," he said in a clotted voice, "go, go—"

Bonnie stared at him in voiceless horror and he cried, *"Go!"*

She ran to the door. It slammed behind her.

Crane said sharply, *"Alerta!"* and the big dog rose from its haunches and watched Steve, its ears pointed forward.

"You're making a fool of yourself," Steve said. "She'll double-cross you just the way she's set to double-cross Vince. She can't double-cross me because I don't want any part of her."

"Forgive me if I do not believe you, Mr. Ewell. I have eyes and I am not stupid."

"No? I wonder. If you're not stupid, why have you gotten yourself in an uproar over something like that?" Steve tipped his head toward the door through which Bonnie had fled.

"Why do you want her, Mr. Ewell? You were so clever, weren't you? It is not your brother you wish to help. You have hoodwinked everybody. Even the police do not suspect that it is Bonnie and the money you want. But that is all over now, Mr. Ewell. You have made the mistake of being too confident."

"Just as a matter of idle curiosity," Steve said, stalling, "why do you want her as badly as all this?"

Crane smiled in a mirthless display of false, too-white teeth. "Perhaps I am hypnotized, Mr. Ewell. Who can say? Or perhaps it is that I never let anyone take from me that which is mine."

Steve put his hands in the side pockets of his jacket and looked at the gun. "You won't shoot," he said, "You wouldn't stick your neck out that far with the police and you couldn't trust Bonnie to back you up."

Crane turned the gun in his hand and glanced at it. "You're quite right, Mr. Ewell," he sighed, his eyelids masking his eyes. "It would be very foolish of me, I thought perhaps I might intimidate you but—" and he shrugged, "it was a gesture I had to make." He threw the gun on the sofa, eight feet to Steve's right.

Steve whirled as if to dive for it and Crane spoke a sharp command. The dog whined and sprang and then uttered a yelp of surprise and pain as Steve flung the aluminum sling chair into its face. It sprawled on the floor, tangled momentarily with the canvas and aluminum tubing. Steve brought the sand-laden sock down squarely between its eyes as hard as he could. The dog's eyes glazed and it tottered. Steve hit it again at the base of the skull. It collapsed. Steve walked to the sofa and picked up the Luger. Crane sagged against the wall, speechless and sallow.

"Just for your information," Steve said heavily, "I was telling you the truth when I said I wanted no part of Bonnie. You're welcome to her and God help you."

He walked out and his feet felt as if they had been shod with lead.

CHAPTER FOURTEEN

Steve did not know what to expect when he walked down the stairs to the lounge on the first floor. Crane must surely know that Bonnie had written that note to Vince. He had probably been eavesdropping from the elevator right from the beginning and all the conversation had not been in whispers. They had forgotten themselves occasionally and the note had been mentioned several times, particularly at the end when Bonnie thought she had him hooked.

It had been easy to fool Bonnie, but to a man of Crane's shrewdness that note would mean only one thing—that Steve had made contact with Vince. And it would mean the same to the police. They couldn't prove anything, of course, and they couldn't make him betray Vince, but they could hold him in jail for a while and that would be almost as bad.

He had seen how desperate Vince was, and if Vince didn't hear from him within the next few days he might try to get in touch with Bonnie himself. And there was another thing, too. If anything went wrong at the Regal Bar and Grill down there in North Laurel, if the police were tipped off, then Steve himself would be linked with the hideout, having been there, and as Ike Winder said, they'd throw the book at him.

Steve wondered if these same thoughts crossed the minds of others who had helped their brothers or fathers or even cousins out of tight spots like the one Vince was in. Were they tormented by ignoble doubts when they thought of what might happen to them, themselves? Did they have the desire to run away from it, to wash their hands of the situation and leave the brother or father or cousin to fend for himself? And did they keep going in spite of the fear?

Steve wanted to run, to rush out of the Inn to his car, but he forced himself to walk out casually, brushing by the well-dressed couples on their way to the dining room.

The doorman touched his hat and held the door open. "Nice to have seen you again, Mr. Ewell, Thank you." He pocketed the half-dollar Steve gave him. "Shall I have your car brought up?"

"The walk'll do me good." It would have been impossible to force himself to stand there under the light and wait, though no one had tried to prevent him from leaving the Inn.

The parking lot attendant hoped Mr. Ewell had had a pleasant evening, took the offered half-dollar as if he didn't know what to do with it, and then went into his booth and called the Inn, asking for Crane.

"This is Farley out in the lot," he said. "Did Ewell see the dame? Did he say anything about his brother?"

"Just—just that, he hadn't contacted him yet, Mr. Farley."

"Was the bug switched on?"

"Yes, indeed. It was switched on the moment Mr. Ewell entered the Inn. The entire conversation was recorded. It was most, ah, most innocuous. There was nothing said, nothing at all, nothing of importance. Detective Lyons here listened to it and there was nothing of importance. They spoke chiefly in whispers, but it was obvious, very obvious, that Mr. Lyons, I mean Mr. Ewell did not know the whereabouts of his brother. Nothing, nothing of importance."

"What's the matter with you?" the detective asked suspiciously. "You sound as though you're talking through a mouthful of broken teeth."

"Mr. Farley, this whole affair has been very trying. I am not a young man. I am very tired. I think I shall go to bed."

Crane hung up and sat slumped in the chair at the desk, his hands dangling between his knees. There was a photograph of Bonnie in a wide silver frame on the desk. It was one of the publicity stills that had been taken when she first began singing at the Inn. Crane stared haggardly at it as if it were an evil from which he had lost all hope of escape.

Steve stopped on the way home and called Doris. Not to tell her about the episode at the Inn, but simply because he wanted to talk to her for a few minutes before going home and going to bed. She was surprised and a little alarmed.

"Did—did something happen, Steve?"

"Not a thing, honey. I've just been driving around and I thought I'd call up and say good night."

"You frightened me for a moment. It's almost eleven 'clock."

"I'm sorry, honey—"

"That's all right, Steve. I'm glad you called. I wasn't doing anything but looking at TV. Your—your voice sounds a little funny."

"I'm a little bushed, that's all, honey."

"I know. This has been hard on you. And I'll bet you haven't been sleeping well either."

"Sleep? How do you spell it?"

"Oh, Steve, I wish there were something I could do. You've been wonderful, do you know that? But you have to sleep. You'll have a breakdown if you don't sleep."

"I'm as tough as nails, honey. There's nothing wrong with me that a cup of coffee won't fix."

"Don't drink coffee. You need sleep. Go to the drugstore and get a bromide."

He wanted to say, *I love you, honey*, but instead he laughed. "I'll hire a small boy to hit me on the head with a mallet every half hour," he said. "That should keep me asleep till tomorrow morning. But why are we talking all this woe? I just called up to say good night."

"Sure," she said softly. "Good night, Steve. Try to get some sleep. And—I'm glad you called."

He felt immeasurably better when he hung up, though he could not define the reason for it.

There was a light in the kitchen when he drove up beside his house and he knew that Orv was up and waiting for him. Since he had started work on the lake again—he was building the refreshment stand at the boat rental dock now—he had been sleeping in the spare bedroom. He was sitting at the kitchen table, a pot of coffee at his elbow, playing solitaire. Steve was glad to see that homely, familiar face, the lean jaws moving rhythmically on the chew of tobacco. It was good to see any friendly face these days.

"Thought you'd never get home," Orv said, gathering up the cards. "You look done in. Cup of coffee?"

"I've been given strict orders against coffee," Steve grinned, "I think I'll have a cup of Ida's Ovaltine."

"I wouldn't touch that stuff. It makes me sick." Then off-hand as Steve went to the closet over the sink and took down the jar of Ovaltine, "Heard you had a fight with Smitty Horne in Shorty's Bar downtown."

"A fight?" Steve had almost forgotten the incident. "That wasn't a fight. He was drunk."

Orv turned in his chair and decreased the volume on the small radio that was playing on the counter behind him. "What was the fight all about?" he asked Steve.

"It wasn't a fight, Orv. He swung at me and I clipped him, that's all."

Orv growled, "That guy's a knucklehead. It's about time somebody smacked him."

"You know, Orv," Steve said thoughtfully, "I think somebody's deliberately been stirring up talk against Vince and me."

"There's talk, all right," Orv admitted.

"And well I knew. I've got an idea who started it, too."

"Ike Winder?"

"When I first talked to Bonnie, she said that the guy who'd been in the holdup was from around here, somebody Vince had known a long time. He'd have one hell of a good reason for wanting to get Vince out of the way now, wouldn't he?"

Orv grunted and rubbed the side of his jaw. "Never thought of it that way."

"And the bank money was never found, Orv. Who'd be the logical one to have it? The other man in the holdup."

"You know," said Orv, frowning, "I heard some funny talk over in Newberg last week but I didn't stop to think about it. All along everybody's been saying the other guy in the holdup with Vince. But there's a cop over in Newberg —the name's Henny Akrigg, he used to own Shorty's Bar in Rocky Hill—well, he's got the idea it wasn't a guy at all. He says it was a woman."

Steve was startled, "A woman!"

"Maybe he's got something. When you stop to think, how many men friends did Vince have? He never hung out with the guys, never went hunting or fishing or anything like that. Hell, I couldn't even name you one guy that you could call friends with Vince. Think it over. Can you?"

Steve cast back in his mind. In high school, of course, there had been the crowd that hung together, girls and fellows, but after he graduated, Vince never did hang out with anybody in particular. He had gone to

Atlantic City with Smitty Horne in Smitty's car a couple times, but they hadn't actually been fast friends. He shook his head. He couldn't think of anybody.

"Now on the other hand," Orv pointed out, "Vince was a ladies' man right down the line. Nothing against him, mind you. Some guys is like that, specially the way the women went for Vince, and he hardly ever went around with the same woman more'n a few times till he married Bonnie out there in Chicago. Now you take a guy like Vince, there's some women that'd do almost anything for him, even help him hold up a bank. I ain't saying this is what happened, but it could now, couldn't it?"

"Yeah," said Steve slowly. "It could." He gave his head a shake. His mind was sodden and it did not want to wrestle with a new line of thought. Anyway, this was just pure conjecture. He looked at the jar of Ovaltine in his hand and put it back on the shelf.

"I'm going to turn in, Orv," he said. "Right now I couldn't give you the answer to two plus two. The main thing is to see if a deal can be made for Vince and I don't want to think about anything else for the time being. I need some sleep."

"Take a couple aspirin," Orv advised. "Sometimes they help."

Steve nodded and walked out of the kitchen. He went upstairs and took a hot shower. He was standing in the middle of his bedroom, buttoning his pajama jacket, when he heard a crack from outside the house and a *thunk* behind him. He turned and looked bewildered at the plaster dust that drifted down from a hole in the wall. Suddenly he realized that somebody had taken a shot at him and with an involuntary yell, he dived for the floor, scooping the lamp from the bedside table with a sweep of his arm.

CHAPTER FIFTEEN

As he lay on the floor beside the bed, his face pressed close to the floor and smelling the dry dustiness of the rug, two things registered in his mind. The bullet pock in the wall had been high, very close to the ceiling. Unless it had been an extremely wild shot from a man perched in a tree, which was unlikely, it meant that the shooter had been very close to the house. The angle, intersected by his head, proved that. He lay very still, listening, waiting for the sound of a car to start and race away.

Then, hearing nothing but the music of Orv's radio playing in the kitchen, he crept over to the chest of drawers. The only gun he had, except the shotgun in the hall clothes closet downstairs, was a long-barreled, single-shot, .22 target pistol, an ineffectual weapon ordinarily, but Steve knew how to use it and outside the moon was high and bright. He moved to the window and, barely raising his eyes above the level of the sill, he scanned the lawn at the side of the house. Ida's rose bushes were there, but they offered no cover. At the far edge of the lawn was a stand of the usual scrub birch where a man could hide, but the shot, because of the angle, could not have been fired from there. A raccoon waddled out of the shadows, looked around and warily crossed the lawn toward the garbage cans at the rear of the house, and that told Steve that there was no one around any longer. The raccoon would never have ventured out into the open had there been a human being close by. The gun relaxed in his hand and he stepped back from the window, muttering, "Damn it." His chance at the shooter, possibly the second holdup man, was gone.

He dug his feet into a pair of slippers and went downstairs. Orv was still sitting at the table, hunched over his solitaire layout. He looked around as Steve entered the kitchen.

"I don't know why I play this damn game," he started to grumble, and then he caught sight of the gun in Steve's hand and grinned. "Going deer hunting, buster?"

"Somebody just threw a bullet at me. Didn't you hear the shot?"

"A shot!" Orv looked quickly at the window, then sprang and pulled down the shade. "You sure, Steve?"

"There's a bullet hole in the wall," said Steve grimly, "and it sure enough wasn't made by termites."

"Then you shouldn't be walking around in the light like you was, for the love of God, Steve!"

"He's gone."

"How can you tell—"

"The raccoons are coming out of the scrub birch," and as he spoke they heard the rattle of a garbage can cover outside the house. "There they are. I'm going out and take a look and see what I can find, if anything."

"I'll go with you."

He picked up his rifle, which was standing in the corner next to the door, and they went outside. They hesitated in the shadow of the porch and then walked out into the moonlight. Steve looked up at his bedroom window and then stepped backward until the angle was just about right. He looked down at the ground and gave an "uh" of disappointment. The grass was much too thick to show footprints. Orv shook his head and spat to one side.

"He's long gone, Steve. Or her," he amended. He squinted at the woods. "And to tell the truth, I ain't got no great hankering to go beating the bushes for somebody in a shooting mood. I'd see all them trees and shadows and say to myself, who's looking for who, anyways?"

"Let's get back in the house," said Steve after a reluctant look at the massed shadows of the trees.

The raccoons were silent and hidden as they recrossed the lawn. Inside, the music had been replaced by the sharp, barking voice of the eleven-thirty newscaster. Steve stopped with one foot poised above the first step of the back porch.

"—first clue on the trail of the escaped convict, Vincent Ewell. The woman herself, Pauline Ferenc, is in a state of shock and unable to make a statement, but according to witnesses who heard her first hysterical cries, she had been raped by Ewell. The dead husband, Lyle Ferenc, mistaking the rape for an affair between his wife and the escaped convict, attacked the woman with a length of iron pipe. She fled down the street pursued by the infuriated man, firing several shots into his chest and abdomen before he fell. The gun has been identified as the one taken from the guard in the state penitentiary by the now dead convict Frank Marky, Ewell's partner in the crash-out. A search of the rooms over the Regal Bar and Grill, owned by the Ferencs, revealed that Ewell had been hiding in a back bedroom. State, county and local police have thrown up roadblocks surrounding the area but at the time of this newscast Ewell is still at liberty.

"And now for a run-down on the political situation as four candidates for governor issued last minute statements on the eve of the primaries ..."

Steve and Orv stared dumbly at each other, and in a voice of awe, Orv breathed, "Holy God, that rips it!" Steve walked into the house as if stunned and turned off the radio. He gripped the back of Orv's chair with both hands and clenched his fingers until his knuckles turned white and pointed. He felt numb and hollow.

"Vince never raped that dame, Steve," Orv said, as if that might soften the news. "He'd never have to. He could get any dame he wanted just by raising his little finger."

Steve shook his head. What difference did it make if there had been a rape or not? This was the end of Vince.

The phone rang and Steve and Orv went as rigid as if a klaxon had sounded in the next room and both broke for it at the same instant. Steve snatched it up and breathlessly said, "Yeah? Yeah?"

"Hel-lo, Stevie. What do you think? Baby's lonesome."

Steve said, "Doris!" shocked at the blur of drunkenness in her voice.

"Heigh-ho, heigh-ho," she laughed inanely. "How's about taking baby out for a drinkie, Stevie, huh?"

No, she wasn't drunk. Her voice was higher than usual and though she slurred, he could now hear the quickening of urgency of it. Oh, God, he thought, she's heard the newscast.

"I was just going to bed," he said.

"Aw, come on, Steve. Baby's lonesome. Tell you what, lover. You be nice to baby and baby'll be nice to Stevie, mmmmmmmmmm?" she managed to make her voice throaty, insinuating and lascivious. "Come on, honey, buy baby juss one li'l ole drinkie down the Fireside Bar. The Fireside Bar, mmmmm? Juss one li'l ole drinkie?"

Her repetition and her insistence told him that she wanted to see him badly. "Well—" he grumbled, trying to sound reluctant. "If I'm not there, don't wait for me."

If the police were listening in on the call, that would sound like the brush-off.

"You'll be there, Stevie," she crooned. "Baby'll be awful nice to Stevie."

He said, "Okay," and hung up. Enough had been said.

Orv was bending close and Steve could smell his fetid breath, compounded of chewing tobacco, bad teeth.

In a falsetto, Orv cackled, "Baby'll be awful nice to Stevie," and that did it.

Steve sat very still, clenching his teeth, hoping that his face would not betray him. He had smelled that foul breath before and had heard that falsetto cackle. He had heard it a few nights ago when he had been tied to that tree and beaten with a length of rubber hose in an effort to make him divulge Vince's hideout. He felt as if he were locked in a glacial cold. Orv. Orv, the handyman. Orv, the friend of the family. Orv, whom he and Vince had known for years. *Orv, who had been in the holdup with Vince! Orv, who had taken a shot at him not fifteen minutes ago.*

Careful, he warned himself, careful. Don't go off half-cocked. Don't warn him. Wait. Wait till the police can dig that bullet out of the bedroom wall and compare the markings on it with the lands in the bore of Orv's rifle.

"Just a dame I've been trying to make," Steve said.

"Doris, eh? That'd be Doris that works down the Chamber of Commerce office. Sounded like her. I'll be damned. I never figured her for a little hot-pants."

"Not that one," Steve said quickly. "The waitress from the Rustic Cabin lunchroom."

"Oh, sure, sure," Orv winked. "That Doris. The one they call Gladys for short. That's who I thought it was all along." He tittered nervously. "Is she going to be disappointed!"

Steve stood up slowly, watching the rifle in Orv's hand. "No, I think I'll run down and have a drink with her. I could use a drink, believe me."

"And a little something else too, maybe, eh, Stevie?"

"Not tonight, Orv, not tonight," he had to keep this believable. "Not if they paid me."

"Yeah, I know, Steve. Maybe you'd better have a flock of drinks. Get soused for once. That's the way I feel, myself."

As he climbed the stairs to his bedroom on the second floor, Steve looked down and Orv was watching him narrowly, swinging the rifle slightly at his side.

"There's a bottle of cooking sherry in the kitchen closet, Orv," Steve said, "If you like sherry."

Steve felt the tension ease as Orv relaxed and nodded. "Yeah thanks, Steve, I think I'll try that."

Steve was dressed and ready to go in ten minutes. Orv was sitting on the edge of the kitchen table, examining the .22 pistol Steve had left there.

"It don't look like much gun," he observed, his eyes on Steve's face, "but I bet you could do damage if you put the pill in the right place."

Was it the prelude, was it a warning, or was Orv just waiting to see Steve's reaction? Steve shrugged.

"I'm a lousy shot," he said. "If I don't get home tonight, I'll be sleeping it off in the back room of the Fireside."

The gun, as if casually, had been pointed at Steve, but now Orv spun it on his forefinger by the trigger guard. "I don't blame you, Steve. It's been rough."

Steve said, "Yeah," and went out through the kitchen door, his back tight as if involuntarily bracing itself against the impact of a bullet. Before he climbed into his car, he looked back and Orv was watching him from the kitchen window. The breath did not loosen in Steve's chest until he eased the car down the driveway and turned into the road to Rocky Hill.

Steve slowed as be entered the town by the little-used road on the western outskirts. There was something wrong. Houses that would normally have been dark for the night had lights blazing from the windows and men stood in small, excited knots under the street lamps. Some had rifles and some had shotguns. With a sense of foreboding, Steve stopped the car at the curb and called out to one of the groups of men.

"Say, could you tell me how to get to the drugstore from here? The wife got a sudden attack and I have to have prescription refilled."

One of the men came over and peered in at him. "The drugstore's closed for the night, mister."

"I kind of thought so, but there's usually a number on the door that you can call in case of emergency."

"That's right. I forgot. Well, you go two blocks down to Ridge Road, that's the main street, then turn left. The drugstore's right across from the movies."

"Thanks, The wife gets these attacks every once in a while. Her heart." Steve looked up and down the street as if noticing the unusual activity for the first time. "What's all the excitement?"

"Excitement's right, mister," the man laughed nervously, without mirth. "That escaped convict, Ewell, is on the loose."

"Ewell? But I heard over the radio—"

"Yeah, I know, but he's right here. The police chief and one of the cops in the prowl car spotted him driving through town on the highway. They went after him but he run them in the ditch. The chief was bad hurt and the cop was knocked out. Ewell got away but they found his car, a black Studey, up the road with a flat tire. Stole, they said it was. If I was you, mister, I wouldn't stay on the streets any longer'n I had to. There's liable to be some shooting."

"This is terrible," Steve quavered. "I got to get this medicine for the wife."

"Well, just don't hang around too long, mister. Half the men in town's out with guns."

Steve drove to the first side street and turned right and parked the car in the shadowed darkness of a leaf-heavy oak tree that overhung the pavement. There was no question of his meeting Doris in the Fireside Bar now. He, himself, as Vince's brother, was in danger, and she would be too, if she were seen with him. She would realize that and not wait in the Fireside for him. But she would be frantic, he knew. He couldn't call her. The only public phone booth he knew was on Ridge Road and that would be thronged with men. Her house was three blocks away on a small side street. That street would probably be alive, too, but there was a way to it through the wooded lots behind—but God help him if he were spotted slinking through the trees! There were dozens of jittery fingers curled around the triggers of rifles and shotguns and if the cry went up, "There he is!" there'd be—Steve gave his head a short shake. There was no sense thinking about that.

It took him almost a half hour to reach her back door. Her house was dark, the only dark house on the street. He turned the doorknob and leaned into it, but the door was locked. He swore and jumped when the doorknob snapped back into place with a loud click as he released it.

He saw the drawn shade on the glass of the door move slightly and then the door opened. He stepped quickly inside and Doris was in his arms, clinging to him, saying something in a hysterical voice that she attempted to control. She dug her fingers into his arms and he could feel her regain command of herself.

"He—he's all right, Steve," she whispered shakily. "He's here."

His heart dropped like a stone in an empty shaft.

"But he's all right, Steve. He's safe. Nobody knows."

Steve clenched his fists. What could Vince have been thinking of, putting Doris in this danger. If he were found here—

As if sensing his thoughts, Doris whispered, "He's frightened, Steve. He didn't know where to turn."

"Sure, honey, but I'll have to get him out of here someway."

"But he can hide here, Steve. Nobody knows—"

"He can't stay here. I can't let him mess you up like this. I'll get him to a safer place. Out of town. I'll have to think."

"He's in the living room, Steve. He wants to talk to you. That's why I called. Steve, listen to me. Don't be angry with him. He's—terror-stricken. He's almost out of his mind."

The fury burned down, flickered, went out. But there was a bitterness. He had excused Vince as being weak, but there was an evil in weakness when, without conscience, it could destroy others. As Lyle and Pauline Ferenc had been destroyed. As Doris might be destroyed—

Steve walked into the living room, which was feebly lighted from the street lamp on the corner, two houses down the block. Vince was crouched on the sofa, his face scratched and stubbled, his hair matted, his eyes wild.

He cringed and whispered hoarsely, "Stevie!"

Steve was appalled. "Vince—"

"I knew you'd come, Stevie. I knew you'd help me out."

Steve felt only an arid, lifeless pity. What could he do for this trembling wreck who had once been his brother? What could anybody do? Lyle Ferenc was dead, Pauline was half out of her mind, Ike Winder was in the hospital, badly hurt.

Vince said whimperingly, "I—I want to give myself up, Stevie. I want to make that deal you talked about. I'll give back the money. I'll tell who was in the holdup with me. I'll tell them anything they want to know. Just help me, Stevie, that's all. Talk to the mayor and tell him I'll do anything he wants."

Steve took a breath and said gently, "Sure, Vince," as he might speak to a dying man who was pleading to live. He looked at Doris. Her eyes were large and dark as if she, too, knew that nothing could be done for Vince now.

"It was Orv who was in it with you, wasn't it, Vince?" Steve asked.

"That's right, Stevie. It was Orv. And he was the one that planned the whole thing right from the beginning. It was his whole idea. He talked me into it. I didn't even want anything to do with it—"

He was so obviously lying that both Steve and Doris turned their heads away as if by doing so they would not have to listen.

"And Orv has the money, Vince?" Steve asked woodenly.

"He's got it. He had it right from the beginning. See, I'm telling you everything, Stevie. I'm not holding out on you. You got to help me. You got to go to the mayor, you got to make that deal. Orv was the one who shot the bank guard. I didn't. I swear I didn't."

"Sure, Vince. We'll—talk to the mayor. Would you like to have a drink?"

"Jesus, kiddo, I'd give my right arm for a drink," he tried to laugh. "I've had it pretty rough."

"I have some brandy in the kitchen," Doris said in a low voice.

She walked to the door, stopped, and slowly backed into the room, her hand to her mouth. Orv slouched in the doorway, his rifle slowly swinging to cover all three of them. There was a little lift at the ends of his mouth, but it was not a smile.

"You know, Steve," he said, "I got to thinking. I said to myself, there's a nice girl like Doris Stewart, works steady, goes to church, lives decent, never a word against her. Now why, I said to myself, should she all of a sudden get soused and call up a guy late at night and invite him to come over and give her some loving. I said to myself, there's something fishy. That's exactly what I said, Steve, and now look." His voice hardened, "Hi, Vince." The slightly moving muzzle of his gun was like a weaving snake.

Vince was speechless with terror and his hands clutched the hem of Doris' skirt as if it were the last thing to which he had to cling.

Steve felt surprisingly calm and he measured the distance between him and Orv, but Orv looked at him and shook his head.

"It wouldn't do you no good, Steve. I wouldn't miss again, not this close."

"What now then, Orv?" Steve asked, knowing the answer.

Orv lifted one shoulder and let it drop. "Sorry, Steve, but a man's got to look out for himself and I ain't got no great hankering to go to jail for as long as they'd send me. It's your own fault for mixing up with this." He looked at Doris. "Too bad, miss, but you oughtn't of left your back door unlocked after letting Steve in like you did. You shouldn't of got mixed up with this, too."

Steve edged to his left, away from Doris and Orv barked, "Hold it, Steve!"

Steve whispered, "Wait, Orv—" and took another step away from Doris but not toward Orv.

The gun stiffened in Orv's hands, covering him, and he crouched a little. "Well," he started, "I might just as well get this over and—"

Vince uttered a shrill cry and, with a frantic sweep of his arm, sent Doris staggering and flailing straight at the rifle, sprang to his feet and dived through the front window, shielding his face with his crossed arms.

The shot was like thunder in the small room. Doris screamed and fell, desperately clinging to the rifle barrel, dragging it down with her. Steve swore and took two long steps and smashed his fist into the right side of Orv's lean neck. Orv made a horrible sound in his throat and fell back into the kitchen. Steve whirled to Doris but she had half risen, still holding the rifle barrel.

"I'm all right, Steve, I'm all right. Get Vince!"

Steve ran to the window. Vince was in the middle of the lighted street. He ran three steps toward the corner and stopped when he saw the men there. He turned and started in the opposite direction but there was another group of men and he turned again. For a horrible moment he made frantic steps one way and the other in a kind of demented dance, and then somebody yelled, "My God, there's Ewell!" Vince made a dash for the darkness between the two houses on the other side of the street.

Doris moaned and turned her face into the hollow of Steve's shoulder as the first shots rang out, so she did not see Vince stagger as the bullets struck him, did not see him fall and crawl for the curb, did not see his arms and legs collapse beneath him under the fusillade from both sides, did not see the last when he flattened on the macadam, one hand twitching at the very edge of the curb as the shouting men came running from either direction. Steve held her tightly. The trembling of her body subsided a little.

"He's dead, isn't he?" she asked in a muffled voice.

He nodded. He did not have to speak. She could tell from the shouts of the men on the street what had happened outside. Her hands twitched and she pulled him closer to her.

"I'm glad—I mean, it was better, quicker—oh, Steve, I was so frightened! I thought Orv had shot you. Oh Steve, hold me, hold me—"

He held her. She was crying, but later there would be an end to tears. He bent his head over her. Her hair was against his lips.

THE END

RUBY

·············

LORENZ HELLER

Writing as Frederick Lorenz

CHAPTER ONE

She was really very lovely. She had long, beautifully shaped legs, graceful hands and feet, a soft and completely feminine body. She had rather long eyes and a wide, generous mouth. Her blonde, cropped hair had already dried in the early morning sun and made a curly cap for her slim head. Her skin was a golden brown, as if she had sun bathed very often in the nude. She lay on the white sand, as she must have done many times, with the calm, lightly breathing Gulf of Mexico turquoise at her feet, her left arm curled across her face as if to shield her eyes from the climbing tropical sun, her legs relaxed, yet not sprawled.

There was a tiny round puncture under the strong curve near her heart, such as an ice pick might have made, but there was no disfiguring crust of dried blood because it had rained during the night. She had been dead about twelve hours.

Joe Latham sat cross-legged under the awning stretched over the stern cockpit of his half cabin cruiser, the *Belan*, mending a nine-foot circular casting net. The tarpon had been running in huge schools from Boca Grande to Sarasota, and this was the first day in three weeks that the *Belan* had not had a charter to take out a party of anglers. Latham was wearing only a pair of chopped-off blue jeans, and his heavily muscled body was sun browned with a burnished gold overlay of blond hair. He was a homely man, but pleasantly so, and women liked to be with him because of his easy manner and because of the enormous vitality that lay just beneath the surface of his seeming tranquility. People had been known to say, "I've never seen Joe Latham mad, but when he does get mad, watch out," but that was only because of something they felt about him. His bigness possibly, though people usually felt that way about a big man. He was six-feet-two and weighed a hundred and ninety-five pounds, but because of his carriage and the width of his shoulders, he gave the impression of being bigger. He could have had great success with a certain kind of woman, but there was something in him, a pride, that had kept him out of most of the beds that had been greedily thrown open to him. His love life was robust but casual, and he had never let the hungry ones feed on him.

He heard the heavy steps of the fat man walking up the dock from the shore, and he glanced back over his shoulder and then raised his right hand and rumbled, "Hi, Floyd, have I been doing something against the law, or something?"

The fat man plodded up to the boat, sat down on the dock and, grunting, slipped down into the cockpit. His dark blue sport shirt was black from sweat, and his face was scarlet from the heat, liquor, and high blood pressure.

"My God, it's hot," he complained. "You wouldn't have a beer in the ice chest, would you, Joe?"

Latham waved a beam-like arm. "Help yourself. And fetch me out one too, while you're at it."

The fat man waddled into the cabin and returned a few minutes later with two beaded bottles of beer and then, panting slightly, settling himself into one of the two fighting chairs with which the cockpit was fitted.

He was a detective on the Sanibar police force, and Latham, still working on the net, asked mildly, "Here on business, Floyd?"

"Sorry to say, Joe."

"What've I done that I shouldn't?"

"Nothing. Nothing at all. Not that I know of. Here, take a look at this." He handed Latham a photograph. "Know that mouse?"

It was a picture of a naked blonde girl. She appeared to be sleeping on the sand. Her left arm was curled across her forehead, as if to shield her eyes from the sun, and her long legs were relaxed and graceful. A second glance, however, showed that the ostensible repose was the unmistakable stillness of a corpse. Latham's big mouth tightened. The girl did not have to be shown nude; the picture could have been cropped, but Floyd Keeler was the kind of man who liked that sort of thing in his fat, sloppy, loose-lipped way.

"You know damn well I know her," Latham said shortly.

"What happened to her?"

"Take a look at her left breast. Somebody ran an ice pick into her."

Latham felt the sickness of brutal shock, but he concealed the emotion from Keeler. He knew Keeler, and he knew how, back at headquarters, Keeler would make a joke of it. "I'm telling you, you should of seen his snoot when I showed him the picture. He turned pus-white and when he opened his mouth, it sounded like the needle got stuck."

Latham handed the photograph back to the fat man and asked briefly, "What do you want me to do?"

"Identify her, that's all."

"You're a liar."

Keeler shrugged moistly. "Sorry, Joe, but that's what Hanna told me to do, take the picture around to all the guys and get them to identify her."

Hanna was chief of detectives, a dark, cold, handsome man, sometimes called the Indian and sometimes the Deacon, but never to his face. Latham knew him. That is, he knew him to speak to, but Hanna was not a man whom anybody really knew. There were only two things in Hanna's life—the police force and the First Church of Sanibar, and he divided his time between them. As far as anyone knew, he had no private life.

"Just following orders," Keeler said apologetically. "He told me to get identification and gave me a list and you're on it."

"Her name is—was—Ruby Lake. That all you want to know?"

"Just about, just about. You were engaged to her about a year and a half ago or so, wasn't you?"

"About that."

"And you broke up?"

"That right."

"Have a fight or something?"

"We just decided it wouldn't work," said Latham stolidly.

"Any reason?"

"She didn't like fishing."

"Not for fish," Keeler giggled. "Not the kind you catch in the Gulf."

Latham shrugged and kept his rising anger under control. He knew that Keeler was far shrewder and more dangerous than he seemed. He had been derisively called a "farmer," but Latham knew that he was one of the best detectives on the force. Keeler's sloppy, bucolic appearance fooled almost everybody, and he could needle a man into a rage and use it against him. Keeler liked being a policeman, and he had the feral conscience of a mink.

"Maybe not your kind of fishing, Joe," Keeler said. "She liked to fish on dry land, and she hooked some pretty good ones. Was that the reason you two broke up? She cheat on you or something?"

"If she did, I didn't know about it."

"You should see the list of guys Hanna gave me. My God! Half the guys in the county."

"That's a surprise to me," said Latham with no inflection in his voice.

"Now come on, Joe, what was the real reason you two broke up?"

"I didn't want to get married."

"She didn't even have the ring on her finger before she was two-timing you. You know that, don't you?"

"First I heard of it."

"You still haven't told me why you broke up."

Latham clenched his big fist and relaxed it immediately because he knew that Keeler's wet brown eyes never missed a trick.

"Okay," he said. "She broke it off. She didn't want to get married. She wanted somebody with a safe job and a steady income. In this charter boat business, you can make five hundred bucks in one week, and the next month you sit around listening to the sea worms eat holes in your hull. She didn't want any part of it, and I wouldn't switch over to anything else."

"So you got sore," said Keeler. "Not that I blame you. A mouse like that'd make anybody sore."

"I didn't get sore. She gave me back the ring and I took it and sold it for ten bucks more than I paid. Or what it was worth. I didn't pay anything for it. I won it in a crap game down in Key West from a sailor boy. So what was there to be sore about?"

"Right. You're absolutely right. But while you were engaged to her, she was, well, pretty free with you, wasn't she?"

"That's none of your damned business!"

"Sorry, Joe. Honest to God, I'm sorry. I was out of line on that one. You're right. It's none of my business." Keeler's moist brown eyes were intent. "But you know what I mean. A mouse like that, a guy hates to give it up, specially when he don't have to get down on his knees and beg for it. I wouldn't blame you a bit if you were sore. I'd be sore myself."

"Our breaking up," said Latham woodenly, "came merely because I refused to change my means of livelihood. I'm a fishing guide and I'll be a fishing guide till the day I die. If I'd had a job in the bank, we'd have been married and had kids by this time."

"Specially a job in the bank," said Keeler, tittering. "That was another angle she was strong on. As I remember, just about the time you two broke up, you had a string of hard luck with the boat and no charters. When you were in the dough, you were in—and when you weren't, you were out. Right?"

It was an actual physical effort for Latham to sit there and restrain himself from leaping to his feet and dashing his fist into Keeler's fat face.

But all he said was, "You couldn't be wronger. Money had nothing to do with it."

"Well, you got off easy, that's all I can say. By the way, did you know she was running around with Ross McElroy just about the time she was engaged to you?"

"That was later. That was after we broke up."

"Was it? I thought it was just about the same time. Her first date with him was November fifth, 1954. You were supposed to be engaged to her just about that time, wasn't you?"

Latham thought savagely, *you fat son of a bitch, you know damned well we were engaged at that time!*

Ross McElroy had charge of the craps table out at the Beach Casino on the Gulf. He was a big, florid man with the flamboyant manner of a used car salesman and the morals of a rabbit. A kisser and a teller, a boaster. It made Latham sick to think of Ruby with Ross McElroy. But who were all the others hinted at by Keeler? The sickness was a rotting inside him.

He had known that Ruby was an unhappy, tortured girl, but he had never known the reason. Keeler had supplied that. He didn't trust Keeler, but there was something about the fat man's gloating manner that told him that the detective was telling the truth this time. Using the truth as a needle, to be sure, but still telling the truth.

He said, "I didn't know that she was dating McElroy until afterward."

The fat man nodded solemnly. "Yeah, she was pretty good at that, from all I hear. Two, three dates a night sometimes, and nobody never the wiser."

Latham winced.

"Did you know that Hanna himself wanted to marry her about eight months back?"

"I heard."

"Well, it's going to be a rough investigation, that's all I can say. Hanna's a son of a bitch when he gets going, and he's got a kind of personal interest in this one. Anything else you want to tell me before I go, Joe?"

"Not a thing. Wait a minute. Let's see that picture once more." Latham held out his hand.

Keeler gave it to him. "Not that I blame you," he leered. "Really stacked, ain't she?"

Latham took the photograph and calmly tore it into tiny bits and threw it over the side of the boat into the bay. "Now get yourself a decent photograph to show around," he said.

"Or what?" asked Keeler, his eyes very bright.

"Or nothing. Just get yourself a decent photograph. There are decent people in this town and you might get yourself kicked off the police force for showing dirty pictures."

"Aaaah ..."

"Suit yourself," Latham shrugged. "But the church crowd wouldn't like it. Furthermore, I'll bet Hanna himself doesn't know what you've been passing around, and he's one of the church crowd."

Keeler licked his thick lips and Latham knew that it had been a bull's-eye. Hanna didn't know.

Keeler mumbled, "That's all they gave me," and Latham said, "You could have used a pair of scissors."

Keeler nodded. "Yeah. I'll do that."

He climbed heavily up on the dock and walked toward the shore. Latham looked at the bottle of beer beside Keeler's chair. It was still full. It had just been a gambit, that bottle of beer, a gesture to give an appearance of casual friendliness.

CHAPTER TWO

The sea gulls had found her first, and warily they kept away from her. A large flock of them stood in ranks on the beach about a hundred feet south of her, all staring out into the Gulf. They looked hunched and stuffy and cross, like people who had waited too long for the band concert to start in the park on a hot Sunday afternoon. They often stood like this on the beach and, when startled, they would rise and circle and complain in their harsh voices, and then settle on the sand again a little farther up the beach.

Some small white crabs, the kind called ghost crabs by some of the more imaginative tourists, were the next to find her. They scuttled around her but did not approach too closely, and after a while they popped back to their holes in the sand, reappearing from time to time to take another look at her and draw hurriedly back into their dens. They were very timid about anything of that size and shape, for too many of them had been chased down and used as bait by fishermen.

A long line of pelicans sailed by overhead, scarcely moving their wings, sixty of them in an undulating echelon. On the fringe of the beach, the clumps of cabbage palms stood dumpily, their fronds tousled and unkempt, and at their feet the fans of palmetto stood stiff and motionless in the still air. Out in the turquoise water of the Gulf, a pair of porpoises appeared to be playing leap frog, and high, high in the distant blue of the sky was the clean, swift silhouette of a solitary frigate bird. The water was so quiet that the surf barely creamed on the shore, and far out on the horizon a black-hulled freighter moved slowly toward Tampa in the north.

A large shaggy brown dog appeared up the beach, barking foolishly at the little white crabs. The sand was soft and powdery and the dog moved toward the girl in ungainly bounds. It was a happy, harmless dog, and it had too much energy for the serene peace of the morning. It stopped short when it saw the body of the girl. It approached on very careful feet, stretching its curly neck to sniff at it. It sniffed very slowly and for quite a while, and then it turned and walked silently away, looking back every once in a while.

A little later, a fat man in a flapping green and white striped cotton robe came down the wooden steps to the beach from the house that stood beside a massy grove of dense green Australian pine trees. He did not see the body at first. He removed his robe and very tidily folded it and put it on the sand beside his towel and sun glasses. He walked toward the water with mincing steps, humming a little to himself and thinking of the breakfast of eggs, bacon, hot rolls, marmalade and coffee that he was going to have after his swim.

He did not reach the water that morning. He stopped ten feet from the nude, graceful body and stared at it with surprise and a kind of pleasant shock. But then it came to him that she was too motionless. He circled her carefully, and then, with horror, he saw the small, round puncture. He stood stock still for a moment and then he began to tremble. He whirled and ran heavily toward the wooden steps to the house, panting hoarsely.

Before he left, Latham tore a check from his checkbook, first consulting his bank balance, and put the check into his wallet. He walked down the dock to the parking lot where his forest green Buick convertible stood under the exotic, aerial-rooted spread of a huge banyan tree. The banyan tree was famous in the area, and tourists often took snapshots of it. It was a leafy canopy a hundred feet in diameter, and the roots came down from the overhead limbs and sank themselves in the sandy soil, making a labyrinth almost as dense as a thicket.

Latham got in the car and drove directly to Younk's Funeral Home on De Soto Place behind the city hall. Walter Younk greeted Latham matter-of-factly.

"You've come to see her, I suppose," he said. "I've got her in the embalming room."

The air was colder there, and the only sound was the smooth purr of the air conditioning unit. Ruby Lake, under a rubberized sheet, was lying on a trestle table from which a rubber tube ran down to a drain in the floor.

"I haven't had time to work on her yet," said Younk, as if he were speaking about a car that had been brought in for repairs. "But she's in good condition and tomorrow'll be okay. In fact, I'm waiting to see if the coroner's going to order an autopsy, though I don't think he will. Autopsies cost money, and it's pretty plain to see what she got. Somebody stuck an ice pick in her. Want to take a look?"

Latham said tightly, no thanks, and Younk dropped his hand from the top edge of the rubberized sheet, looking at Latham with interest.

"Well you're the first," he said, "the very first. Everybody else wanted their money's worth. And they got it. Didn't have a stitch on, and they never found her clothes."

"Were there many?" Latham compressed his lips.

"Quite a few, quite a few. Keeler sent them in."

"That jerk."

"Just following orders, I suppose."

"The hell he was. He sent in all his friends. I know the bastard."

Younk shrugged. "It's all one and the same to me. All I know is that Keeler's Hanna's errand boy, and I'm not one to say yes or no where Hanna's concerned. He can be a very mean man when he puts his mind to it."

Latham remained silent.

"You here to identify her?" Younk asked

Latham shook his head. He had tried to avoid looking at Ruby, but she drew his eyes irresistibly. She looked so much the same that his heart clenched in his chest, remembering her. It took real effort not to look at her.

"I wanted to find out about the funeral arrangements," he said roughly.

"Services will be in the chapel here, conducted by the Reverend Alan C. McKechnie, pastor of the South County Presbyterian church, the day after tomorrow at two-thirty P.M. Interment will follow in the Sanibar Memorial Park."

"I mean, I want to pay for it," said Latham, in agony.

"Oh. That's all taken care of."

"She had enough money—"

"Hell no. She was flat busted, or almost. She had $31.75 in the bank. But it's been paid for."

"Who paid for it?"

"The name was asked to be kept anonymous."

"For God's sake, Walter—"

Younk shook his head and for the first time revealed a bit of gentle, human feeling. He put his hand on Latham's arm.

"I'm not allowed to tell you that, buddy," he said soothingly. "But it's been paid in advance, and she's getting a first-class funeral, the best. And for your information, I'm not making a nickel on it."

Latham gritted his teeth. "I'll pay the difference!"

"It's all paid, Joe, and I couldn't take your money if you pointed a gun at me. Much as I'd like to."

"Who paid it?"

"John Doe," said Younk expressionlessly.

"That guy from the Beach Casino—Ross McElroy?"

"The name on the receipt was John Doe."

"If it was that son of a bitch I'll—"

"Tear up his receipt? Relax, Joe. She's going to get a damn good funeral, and that's all that's important. There isn't another nickel to pay. It's all been taken care of, and I wouldn't tell you who gave me the money if you talked yourself blue in the face, so forget it."

Latham clenched his fists, towering over the stocky man. "Do the police know?" he demanded.

Younk was not intimidated. He had met raw human emotions too often to be impressed by them. "The police know everything," he said, "past, present and future. They know all, see all, and don't tell you a damned thing."

Latham swore, and Younk asked, "Was there anything else, Joe? I want to sneak out for a quick martini. Join me?"

Latham took a last look at Ruby's face above the rim of the brown rubberized sheet. No, she didn't look quite the same. She could never be the same with the quick, sick vitality gone out of her face. He shook his head.

"I just wanted to see about the funeral arrangements," he said heavily.

"Well, forget it, Joe. It's been taken care of."

Latham said, "Thanks," and walked out.

Before getting into his car, he took the blank check from his wallet and tore it into small pieces and dropped it through the grating of the storm sewer. He could never use it for anything else. It just wouldn't be right. Then he drove down to police headquarters and asked the desk sergeant if he could see Hanna.

The sergeant said, "He's upstairs, Joe, but I better call first. He's got himself in an uproar over this Ruby Lake thing, and I wouldn't touch him with a ten-foot pole if I was in Dade County. I'll call him. Is it on the Lake deal?"

"Something like that," said Latham laconically.

"I mean, he won't talk to nobody about nothing else right now. He's really on the prod. He was going to marry her once, you know. If it's not about that, my advice is go home and forget it for a while. He's on the prod."

"It's about that."

The desk sergeant said doubtfully, "I hope so, for your sake," and picked up the phone. He spoke respectfully and briefly and, hanging up, said to Latham, "He says come up. You know where his office is. It's got his name on the door."

Latham walked slowly up the mean-smelling stairs to give his nerves a chance to settle. He was churning inside, and he knew he couldn't face Hanna this way without doing something foolish, and the minute he did that, Hanna would put on the thumbscrews.

There was a uniformed policeman outside Hanna's office, and Latham gave his name, and the policeman went into the office. He returned a moment later and said Hanna would see him. His face was impassive, but it was obvious from his nervous manner that he wanted as little to do with Hanna as possible this day. Latham went into the office.

Hanna was sitting behind a scarred golden oak desk. He was a long thin man in a dark blue Palm Beach suit, and his coal-black hair and narrow face had earned him the sometimes nickname of The Indian. Some claimed that the nickname had come about because Hanna was not quite human, but that statement had been made by people who had never known Indians. Or Hanna.

He was a savagely handsome man, but the years of police work were beginning to groove his face in the deep lines between his eyebrows, the curving ones from the sides of his nose to the ends of his mouth, and in the decisive ones across his forehead.

Keeler was coarsely and sadistically brutal, but Hanna was as cold as the first thin, measuring touch of an executioner's axe. The first thing you felt when meeting Hanna was that you had to tread very carefully. He neither smoked nor drank, and the only woman anyone had ever known him to go with had been Ruby Lake, a strange alliance of extremely short duration.

He looked at Latham and said in a chilling, narrow voice, "State your business, Latham. I'm busy."

Latham's anger spurted within him like a punctured water main and he had to clench both hands to keep from exploding.

In a plodding voice, he said, "I want you to keep that bastard Keeler off my neck."

"Why?"

"I don't like him."

"I don't like him either, but he's a good policeman. Why exactly do you want me to keep him off your neck?"

"He enjoys his work too much. He wants to see you squirm."

"He gets results. But why did he bother you? Guilty conscience?"

"Guilty conscience hell!"

"Then he shouldn't bother you. He's only another cop doing a job. If you're in the clear, he shouldn't worry you. Are you in the clear?"

"I'm not saying he worries me. I'm just saying the next time he plants his fat bottom on my boat, he's going to get it kicked to hell right into the bay."

"Do that and you'll get *your* bottom in the stockade for a good sixty days. Keeler is doing a job and neither you nor anyone else is going to get in his way. Is that clear?"

"Very. But the next time he comes on my boat and puts the needles to me, I'm going to kick him right in the bay."

"Suit yourself, but I don't think it will be that easy. In fact, it's been tried and the Younk's ambulance has rushed many a man to the Memorial Hospital for emergency treatment. Keeler carries a gun, a blackjack, a pair of handcuffs, and he knows more about dirty infighting than you could figure out in a month of Sundays. Whichever way it goes, you can't win. Now what do you know about Ruby Lake?"

Latham said, taking angry delight in needling Hanna this time, "The same thing all the other boys know. All of them."

"What boys?"

"You know that better than I do. You were almost the last one to be engaged to marry her. My workout was over a year and a half ago."

"You were the one who made the statement."

"I retract it. But you broke off your engagement with her because you thought she was a whore. That's right, isn't it, Hanna?"

Latham could see that the narrow, dark man was shaken. There was sweat on his face and his hands trembled, but there wasn't the slightest change in his frozen voice.

"What boys are you talking about?" he asked.

"All of them. Everyone who knew her, and you know their names better than I do. She was a whore because she couldn't help herself."

"She *could* help herself!" Hanna said violently. "She chose the way she went. She was a Jezebel!"

Latham gripped the arms of his chair, and then opened his hands slowly and jerkily, as a man with painfully cramped muscles might spread his fingers. He thought he had himself under control, but Hanna was watching him narrowly.

"You were in love with her," Hanna said. "And you're still in love with her. Or what passes for love with men like you."

"I know damn well *you* were never in love, you lousy self-appointed saint. Ruby was a beautiful woman. She was made of warm, living flesh, and you wanted her just like all the rest of us. But you couldn't see beyond that. You couldn't see that she was a human being, sick and tormented and desperate. You could only see her in bed." Latham was talking louder and louder and his great voice filled the room as his anger mounted. "You could only see her for her body when she was begging you. Yeah, she begged you, didn't she Hanna? I don't know if she loved you or not. Maybe she did. She had a capacity for honest love that should make both of us self-righteous bastards ashamed of ourselves. That's one thing she really had. Bed was the sick part of her, and bed was the only part of her you wanted, but you'd never admit it, you damned saintly iceberg!"

Hanna's dark, narrow face and neck were as corded and taut as that of a man under a strain almost beyond endurance. "I never laid a hand on her," he said hoarsely, pounding the desktop with the flat of his hand. "I never so much as touched her."

"Why? Why not? Sometimes she wanted to give herself for love. Yes, love—l-o-v-e. She gave you the opportunity, why didn't you take it? What was the matter with you, Hanna? Had you built up in your own mind so much of a picture of yourself as the chief detective for the hosts of Heaven or something that you couldn't share a decent, honest thing with a woman?"

"I wouldn't touch a whore!" Hanna said furiously.

"So you kicked her out. Well, I'm as bad as you are. Worse. I kicked her out twice. A year and a half ago and again last week. You kicked her out and I kicked her out. We should form a club and call ourselves the Senior Order of Sanctified Stinkers. And we could have a special sign, too. When we meet, we should pat ourselves on the back."

Something went out of Hanna's face and suddenly he was as cold and intent as he had been when Latham first walked into the office. He put down the heavy glass paperweight that he had lifted from the desk and sat back in his chair. He drew the desk pad toward him and took a pencil from his pocket.

"You saw her last week?" he asked.

The fury had gone out of Latham, too, and he nodded, an empty kind of misery in his eyes. He made a formless gesture with his big hand.

"I saw her for a little while in the Flamingo Bar."

"Why?"

"No reason. We just happened to run into each other."

"By accident?"

"I went in for a drink and there she was at the bar, that's all."

"You followed her there. You made the 'accident.' You knew she was in there. You wanted to see her."

"I told you it was an accident," said Latham in a voice that now seemed tired and drained, "and that's all it was."

"You were in love with her and you wanted her back. You begged her. You asked her to give up the life she was leading and marry you. She turned you down. You got mad. You threatened her—"

"It was nothing like that, nothing like that at all."

"Why lie, Latham? This is something I can check."

"Go ahead. All we did was talk for about fifteen minutes, and then she left. She had a date."

"This wasn't the first time you followed her, was it, Latham? You followed her every chance you got, didn't you? You spied on her. You knew what men she went out with—where, when, how many times, and everything else about her. You spied on her apartment and probably called her on the phone and begged her to give up the life she was leading. Sometimes she was nice to you and sometimes she was drunk and laughed at you, and something kept building up inside you, didn't it, until finally you had to see her. You just couldn't help yourself anymore. You saw her again last night, didn't you, Latham? Last night."

"I didn't see anybody last night. I was tired and I went to bed early."

"Can you prove that?"

"I can show you the bed."

"In other words you can't prove it."

Latham shrugged and it was obvious that under these surface words, he was thinking of something else, and there was a deep sadness in his face.

"I'm not going to try to prove anything, Hanna," he said without much interest. "If there's any proving to be done, you do it."

The phone rang and Hanna picked it up and said curtly, "What is it?"

A voice cackled excitedly from the earpiece, and when it stopped Hanna said, "Have Sergeant Mulhern bring my car around immediately. Tell Griswald and Quinn to get over there right away, and you take care of the rest of the details." He jumped up from his chair and strode across the room and took his Panama hat from the clothes tree, saying crisply over his shoulder, "Beat it, Latham. I'll get around to you later."

Latham rose slowly from his chair. He stopped at the door.

"You know something, Hanna?" he said. "I feel sorry for you."

Hanna pushed him out. "Don't waste your time," he said shortly.

CHAPTER THREE

Police headquarters was in the southern wing basement of the combination city hall and courthouse, and Latham walked across the street to the inevitable bar that was close to almost every city hall in the country. He stopped first at the newsstand on the corner for the city edition of the *Tribune*, then went into the bar and ordered a bourbon and water. He drank it down and ordered another, but this time let it stand on the bar in front of him.

He did not immediately open the newspaper he had bought but laid it in his lap and stared drearily at the backbar, remembering another bar in which he had sat last week with Ruby for a dreadful fifteen minutes. It was a hot midafternoon, but cool inside, and she had been sitting there when he walked in for a John Collins. There had been shock in both their faces when they saw each other, and then she smiled a little tremulously and made a timid gesture toward the empty stool beside her. It had actually been a year and a half since they had last met. His pulse was definitely faster when he walked down the dimly lighted room toward her. At first they talked about odds and ends. She asked how the charter boat business was coming along, and he told her he was doing fine, just fine.

"The tarpon season," he said. "Except for a day here and there, the *Belan's* booked solid for the next six weeks."

"My, Joe, you'll be wealthy!"

"Just rolling in it, honey. The charters are coming in every day, and I'll be booked through the end of August when the tournament ends."

"Tournament? They have a tournament like tennis or golf?"

"Yes, they have a tournament," he said a little stiffly. "I forgot for a minute that you think fish is just something you get with the shore dinner at the Revere-Plaza at seven-fifty a plate."

"Don't be mad with me, Joe," she pleaded. "I didn't mean anything. Honestly I didn't. I wasn't making fun."

"Sorry, honey," he said, instantly contrite and miserable that he had started a squabble, or had tried to, before they were together even two minutes. "I'm a little bushed, I guess. I've had a charter every day for two weeks, a lot of them two, three days at a stretch down at Boca Grande, early morning fishing and nights and all in the same day, because that's the only way to get tarpon if you really go after them. And I've told you what it was playing nursemaid to some of those fish farmers I get. They all want to catch the record tarpon, but you got to bait up for them and when they get a strike, you got to hold them in your lap and give them blow-by-blow instructions, which they all want but won't listen to, and in spite of everything you tell them, they try to horse in their strike in the first three minutes, and naturally they lose it and blame you. I'm telling you, honey, sometimes I'd rather fish with women than some of those guys who once caught a catfish by accident in the duck pond back home in Ohio. Believe me, some of them are real comedians, whether they know it or not, and from the way they act, you'd think they expect me to dive overboard and come up with the tarpon in my mouth."

He was uneasily aware that, all the while he was talking, her eyes, huge and still pleading, never left his face. Which was the reason he had kept talking. To keep it impersonal. He didn't want this to get personal. He'd had enough of that. In fact, he had to hold onto himself to keep from getting personal. He wanted to. God, he wanted to, but it was a dead end.

"Don't try to fool me, Joe," she smiled. "You love it. You love every minute of it."

"I know, I know, but you have to complain once in a while."

He was trying to keep his eyes from the lovely lift of her slim face, but he wasn't doing a very good job of it. Just the barest glimpse of her high cheekbones was flooded with memories, and it wasn't what you were going through that tore you apart—it was the memories.

He saw that she was about to speak, and he said quickly, "When the tarpon season's over, I think I'll go down to the Bahamas with the *Belan* this year and take charters out of Bimini and maybe Nassau, though Bimini's best. Maybe Miami. Miami's really the best, as far as money's concerned, and it's cheaper to operate out of Miami with a boat, water, gas, provisions, tackle, and everything else. Too, maybe Cat Cay for the tuna tournament. There's real money there."

But he couldn't keep talking forever, and inevitably it got around to her and what she was doing.

"I'm working in the bank," she said. "The South County Bank and Trust. I'm secretary to the treasurer, no less. Stanley Wilfred Mays himself. You may not realize it, but I'm a very efficient stenographer and receptionist. Mr. Mays tells me very frequently that I'm one in a million."

"Mays, Mays—" said Latham. "Oh yeah, I remember him. A big young-looking guy about forty. Plays golf. A wife and two kids. Lives in the snooty Mediterranean Shores subdivision south of town. Drives a new Caddy convertible, went to Harvard, is a thirty-second degree Mason, thinks what this country needs is another Calvin Coolidge, less government control and a return to the five cent nickel, thinks the greatest mistake the workingman ever made was to join a union, married Colonel Dudley Freeman Rossiter's niece and thinks all blood is either blue or non-existent, and he is positive that if ever he needed a blood transfusion, he'd get it from a friend or perish. He doesn't believe in blood banks in hospitals. 'You never really know what you're getting now, do you, old boy?' A sterling character, Stanley Wilfred Mays!"

Ruby was laughing, and she was very lovely when she laughed. In repose, her face had beauty, but it was a still beauty like the head of the early Egyptian Queen Nefertiti. When she laughed or cried or was angry or passionate, there was nothing to compare with the living beauty that burst from her face and eyes and mouth and body.

"Well!" she said. "Somebody certainly gave you the Word on Mr. Mays."

Latham grinned. "He gave it to me himself. I met him the night he was plotzed in the Revere-Plaza Tap Room. The Yacht Club was closed for repairs or redecoration or something, and he was slumming. He was drinking Napoleon brandy 1812 and he was stewed to the ears."

Ruby frowned. "He was drunk?"

"Honey, he wasn't drunk, stewed or plotzed—he was *soused!* Remember, he was slumming. To him, the Revere-Plaza, after the Yacht Club, was practically skid-row and when in Rome, do like the tourists do, get soused. He hinted that he had a melancholy love life. Being a gentleman, he didn't come right out and say that his wife didn't understand him. In fact, at this point I could hardly understand him myself. He had a brandy snifter the size of a football and from time to time I had to catch him by the back of the neck so he wouldn't get his head caught inside it." Latham knew that he was talking too fast and too much, but there was the compulsion to keep talking because he had the feeling that if he stopped he would become involved with Ruby again, and he wanted it so desperately that he knew that this time it could be really destructive.

Ruby was still laughing and there was color high in her face and she was even lovelier. "You're making this up," she said.

"Hell no. I'm just giving you the Word on Stanley, King of England, or something. Ah yes, he had a very melancholy love life. 'Are you married, old boy?' he kept asking me. 'If you're married, you'll know what I mean. I have two wonderful children, two, smart as a whip, wouldn't be without them, but that's the end of it, know what I mean? *Pater familias*, and all that, live on your laurels, lot of men have to go through it, very sad, two kids, the end, very sad.' I had the impression, by this time, that he had to sleep on the sofa in the living room, and it was too short for him and his feet got cold."

Ruby's mirth was becoming almost hysterical and she gasped, "Oh no, no, please no, Joe!"

"Oh yes, yes. I'm not making any of this up. He sat right beside me and gave me the Word, and all the while diluting his Napoleon 1812 with a saline solution generally known as tears. Life certainly wasn't treating Stanley Wilfred Mays right that night, and he resented it. After all, my God, he had married Colonel Dudley Freeman Rossiter's only female niece, he was treasure of the bank, he lived in a fifty-thousand-dollar house in the Mediterranean Shores subdivision, and he had a right to some respect from life, which he wasn't getting. And after all this, he tried to get me to fix him up with some blonde or other, and I had all I could do to keep from poking him straight in his snoot. He kept saying that he knew I was the one who could do it and tried to slip me a fistful of money, and I'm telling you, honey, if the bartender—you know Mush, the barkeep, down there—hadn't seen the hurricane flag, I'd have poked that blue-blood louse right in the puss, and I mean it. I'm nobody's pimp, even if I do drink on skid row in the Revere-Plaza whenever I can afford a buck a drink. And then a crew of waiters turned up like pallbearers and carried him out to his car and all the while he kept moaning for me to fix him up with this particular blonde he had in mind. I'm telling you, honey, he almost committed unconscious suicide that night."

Ruby had stopped laughing and there was horror in the planes of her cheeks beneath her high cheekbones. "Please, Joe," she said faintly. "Please. No more."

"Yeah, you're right," he said moodily. "A guy like that, you can't feel sorry for him, but he gives you the creeps. I wouldn't have hit him. I was just making that up. I wouldn't smack a drunk unless I were drunker. I forgot he was your boss. I remembered him only because he told me he thought sportfishing was silly. Man versus fish. He implied that fish didn't have the advantages of modern science, such as the hydrogen bomb, and therefore was a pushover. Sorry, honey. I shouldn't have brought this up. When he's sober, I imagine he's all right."

"He is."

"Good. I shouldn't have talked like this. I was out of line."

"You're never out of line, Joe—"

He tried to dodge, but he could not avoid it. She wanted to come back to him. She loved him. She wanted to be married to him. She knew he loved her. They loved each other. They should get married. It was what they both wanted. He knew she meant it and God knew he wanted it. But there was this other thing and there was no getting around it.

"Have you seen the psychiatrist?" he asked her.

She looked down into her lap and shook her head.

"Why not?"

"I'm not crazy," she said in a taut, desperate voice. "I don't need a psychiatrist."

"But you do, honey," and his voice was just as desperate, knowing that this was *it*. "It's not a matter of being crazy. Lots of uncrazy people see psychiatrists to get themselves straightened out."

"I don't need one! I haven't—seen a man for two months. I'm not crazy. I don't need a psychiatrist."

"I'll pay for it, honey. I'll take you there and bring you back. I'll take care of everything. What are you afraid of?"

"I don't need one, I told you!"

"Why do you keep dodging it? Look honey, I love you. I'm crazy about you. Most of the time I'm half out of my mind just thinking about you. But I can't marry you *this* way, and you know that as well as I do."

He didn't mention the men, all the men, but he didn't have to. It was a barbed-wire barricade between them, and they were just talking through it. They weren't with each other and the wires remained between them.

"Listen, honey." He tried to take her hand but she jerked it away. "I'm not saying you're crazy or anything like that. Christ knows I don't think you're crazy! But I can't marry you this way. Why don't you go to this guy? I've got his name. He's a good doctor. He's down in Miami. I can take the boat down there and still make a living while you take the treatments. It won't be like going to the dentist. He's not going to hurt you. All he does is talk to you and straighten you out. That's all there's to it. What're you afraid of?"

"I'm not afraid of anything. I'm sorry I brought it up. I wouldn't want you to marry anybody you thought a half-wit."

"Honey—"

"Well, it's just one of those things, isn't it, Joe? It just wouldn't work. You're one kind of person and I'm another, so we might just as well forget it."

He had a fleeting glimpse of the dreary tragedy behind her eyes, but it was gone in a moment and all that remained was the flat, surface glance of resentment.

"Maybe you're right," he said. "It just wouldn't work."

"No hard feelings?"

"You mean no soft feelings. No, no soft feelings."

"Good. It's better this way, I guess."

"Why guess? We both know it wouldn't work. No guesswork involved."

"That's right. All you have to do is think about it for minute, and you know."

"That's the answer."

"I suppose I knew that all along, but you hate to give up, if you know what I mean. You have a terrific attraction for me, Joe. You know that, don't you?"

Now he definitely avoided looking at her. He stared down at the brown mahogany gleam of the bar. He said, "Well—" and shrugged. "It's not something you can live on."

"No, I suppose not."

The conversation continued for a few more aimless minutes, both of them ignoring the naked moment of tragedy that had appeared in her desperate face, the reason for it, the inevitable end to it, and the torment in between.

And then she stood back from her bar stool and gave her lovely shoulders a little shrug to settle her frock, and said just a little too brightly, "Well, I've got to run, Joe. I've got a date and I'm fifteen minutes late already. I'll see you around."

"I'll give you a ring," he said, not meaning it, yet wanting to.

"Fine, fine. But I have to run. Good heavens, I didn't know it was so late."

And she walked out, her heels clicking briskly on the hardwood floor.

A week ago, but it was as vivid in his mind as the black minute hand on the Western Union clock over the cash register behind the bar.

More so.

CHAPTER FOUR

Latham did not want to read the newspaper account of Ruby's death in that bald journalese that treated everything alike from a council meeting to the annual bazaar and flower show of the local D.A.R. Who, what, when, where, why. But probably that was better than a lurid account. He wanted the facts, which he had disdained to ask either Keeler or Hanna.

NUDE BODY OF WOMAN
IS FOUND ON BEACH

Sanibar: The nude body of Ruby Lake, 24, Sorrento Drive, stabbed through the heart with an ice pick, was found this morning at 9:55 by Herman S. Petersen, on the beach in front of his home on Pelican Key.

The woman had been dead for twelve hours, according to Coroner Robert B. Sibley, when found by Petersen on the dry sand above the high-water mark. Petersen immediately called the police. Sibley's verdict, without jury, was murder, and the police, led by Detective Captain Deke M. Hanna, have established the fact that the nude woman was killed in her apartment on Sorrento Drive.

The murder weapon, Captain Hanna said, was an ice pick from a cocktail set that included also a strainer, a bottle opener, a corkscrew, and a stirring spoon, all with staghorn handles from which it was impossible to obtain fingerprints.

Captain Hanna said that the woman had been killed in the kitchenette of her apartment, for there were several hastily wiped bloodstains on both the rubber tiling of the floor and the white porcelain of the sink and drainboard, and a washcloth, stained with blood, was found in the garbage pail beneath the sink.

There were no signs of a struggle and Captain Hanna ascribed the killing to a robbery attempt, pointing out that all the drawers from her bureau and dressing table had been emptied on the floor, and that the boxes and clothes from her closet had been strewn on the bed in the attempt to find valuables.

Captain Hanna called the killer an "amateur," and stated that the dead woman, a stenographer in the South County Bank and Trust Company, was earning a salary of only $75 a week, adding that it was extremely doubtful that she would have been wealthy.

As a secondary motive, Captain Hanna said, it was well-known that the Lake woman had had several "affairs" recently, and that the killer may have turned the apartment upside down in a search for incriminating letters.

Captain Hanna said that all known associates of the dead woman were being closely questioned. He doubted, however, that this line of questioning would give any immediate results.

"It looks like a plain case of attempted robbery to me," he said.

The clothes of the dead woman, nude when found on the beach by Sibley, were discovered in the bathroom of the Sorrento Drive apartment, hanging over the chrome rod of the shower. It is Captain Hanna's theory that the killer first washed the body so that he would not stain his clothes when carrying it from the apartment.

When asked why the killer thought it necessary to carry the body from the apartment to the beach, at considerable risk to himself, Captain Hanna said shortly, "There are screwballs in every field, and this is one of them. Possibly he was trying to conceal his crime, or divert attention from its source, until he had time to cover his traces."

Captain Hanna admitted, however, that it was entirely possible that jealousy had been a motive, as it had been discovered that the woman had been, in his words, "morally irresponsible."

Not discarding this theory entirely, he pointed out, however, that in most "crimes of passion," the murderer rarely displays the body of the victim on a public beach.

"They either flee the scene," he said, "or attempt to conceal the body. And records show," he added grimly, "that in most cases they confess within forty-eight hours, once the pressure is brought to bear."

Latham threw the paper aside. The story was nothing more than a Hanna news release, and contained little more than the facts everyone knew—excepting the information that Ruby had been killed in her apartment.

Latham threw down his drink and ordered another, staring drearily at the bar in front of him. The bartender filled his glass for the third time and gave him a professional, measuring glance. In the City Hall Bar, drunks were given the old heave-ho before they got to the obnoxious stage. Latham was drinking them one after the other, and the bartender made a mental note that just one more was the limit.

An hour later, he said, "By God, I could of sworn you'd of been ready to be mopped up with the bar rag by this time. Don't it affect you at all?"

"After 'shine, you can drink this crap like orange juice."

And two hours later, the bartender said, "Well I'll be damned. I'm going to have to slip you a mickey to get you out of here. Just between you, me and the lamppost, don't you feel it at all?"

Latham was drunk and he knew it, but he waved a big hand and said, "Sometimes it hits you and sometimes it doesn't. Tonight's one of those times."

"I don't know where you put it, that's all I can say."

"I'm not putting it anyplace. I'm saving it. Set it up again."

The bartender eyed the remains of a twenty-dollar bill that lay on the bar in nickels and dimes.

"This one's on the house," he said. "And by God I'm going to make it a double just to see you fall on your face."

"Orange juice," said Latham. "Not on that orange juice you call bourbon. You should drink 'shine."

"Sure, sure. But that's hundred proof bourbon you been drinking, friend."

"Proof-schmoof," said Latham. "You should drink 'shine. It ain't got no proof. They make it out of pure atoms."

"Hey, wait a minute. Maybe I'm wrong. I think maybe it is getting you."

"Look, friend, when I get drunk, I take a bartender in my hands and squeeze him dry and set up drinks for the house on the juice."

"One bourbon on the rocks coming up," said the bartender, briskly moving down the bar.

It was perhaps an hour and a half after that, maybe two hours, that Latham found himself wavering on the sidewalk in front of the Wingate Apartments on Sorrento Drive, where Ruby had lived. He had been to several gin mills since the City Hall Bar. He had been in two fights and there was a cut over his left eye and his jaw was swollen, and he stared at the green-and-white, wrought-iron decorated apartment with a glowering expression.

Ruby had been killed in there. She had an apartment on the first floor off the patio. He remembered it very well. She'd had this same apartment for two years. There was a fountain in the patio and in the middle of the fountain was the replica of a small naked boy, taken from the original in Brussels. The Wingate was supposed to be a very sophisticated apartment. They charged $150 a month for year-round rentals, and $250 during the season. It was a nice setup, but all they gave you for your money was the figure of the small boy in the fountain. They had made capital out of that kidney display.

In Latham's book, it was strictly for the birds. It had always irritated him. Now he stared at the dark windows of Ruby's apartment. He wanted to get in there, but he knew it was no use to ask Hank Wingate, who wouldn't point out the North Star on a starry night unless there was something in it for him.

Latham stared at the dark, blind windows. He had to get in there. At this point, he didn't know why he had to get in there, but he knew that he did. It had something to do with Ruby. It wasn't what they said. It wasn't any attempted robbery. Nobody in his right mind would think of robbery when he was in the same room with Ruby, much less stick an ice pick into her. The answer was in that apartment with the blind eyes.

And then he remembered that Ruby always left her kitchen window unlatched when not actually open. These were casement windows that worked with a crank, but that wasn't anything to worry about. He knew how to take care of that.

He walked carefully through the patio and slid into the shadows of the night-blooming jasmine that fingered the southwest wall of the apartment. He felt for Ruby's kitchen window. It was not open, but it was not locked, either, because there was a looseness to it.

He worked his hard, strong, blunt fingers into the slight opening of the frame. He pried it open another quarter of an inch and then gave a sudden wrench. The crank mechanism broke with a metallic clicking, and the window came open under his hands. Chuckling, he went in headfirst, feeling with his hands for the Formica top of the cabinet he knew was beside the sink. He was just about seven-eighths in when something crashed at the back of his skull and he collapsed limply.

CHAPTER FIVE

When Latham recovered consciousness, he was lying on the terrazzo floor of the kitchen. The floor was set with varicolored marble chips, smoothed and polished to a satiny gloss, and the colored spots swam before his eyes like tadpoles in cloudy water. His head was swimming and the surface was cool against his cheek and he did not want to move. About eighteen inches in front of him was a short dark line that shimmered and shimmered before it finally resolved itself into a black bobby pin.

To his right he could see two legs incased in wrinkled gray slacks, dark blue socks and dirty brown and white sport shoes. One foot was slightly lifted and was gently moving to and fro. The two inches of ankle between the top of the sock and the fabric of the slacks was veal-white and hairless, which gave Latham the odd impression that it had been embalmed, though none of this made any sense to him yet. His head throbbed painfully, and his stomach coiled and uncoiled as if it were on the verge of being sick. Through the nausea and fog he heard a voice ask faintly:

"Feeling better, Joe?"

He mumbled something and, with a tremendous effort, rolled over on his side. He sat up and looked blearily at the figure that leaned against the kitchen table, still slowly swinging one leg. The figure became Keeler, his fat face pursed in an expression of mock concern. He took the cigarette from his mouth and shook his head.

"That's a terrible bump you got on your head, Joe," he said. "If I got a bump like that, I'd be in the hospital. What happened, you trip over something?"

Latham did not reply. Holding the edge of the sink, he pulled himself painfully to his feet. He turned on the cold water tap and held his head under it until the giddiness left him and his stomach stopped churning. He was sober now and he knew that he was in the kitchen of Ruby's apartment, though he had not the faintest idea of how he had gotten there. He opened the cabinet below the sink and took one of the kitchen towels hanging there and dried his hair and face.

He winced as he toweled over a large bump above his left ear and for a moment his head beat with pulses of pain, which subsided gradually into a dull ache. He was sober, but his mind and body felt thick and clumsy and he shook his head as if to clear it.

Keeler regarded him with a parody of solicitude, his head cocked to one side, his eyes bright with amusement. He pointed with his cigarette.

"It's in the cabinet over your head, Joe," he said.

Latham stared dully at him. "What?"

"The bourbon, gin, rum, rye, vodka, a regular little liquor store. You could use a drink couldn't you? If I was in your shoes, I'd be screaming for a shot, a bump like that. Did you bounce off the wall or something?"

Latham's impulse was to turn and take down a bottle. He needed a drink badly, but not badly enough to gulp one down in front of Keeler, who, for some reason or other, seemed to be prodding him into hitting the bottle.

"I don't need a drink," he said heavily. He looked dully around the kitchen, still wondering why he was there and how he had gotten there. It was the last place he wanted to be, remembering now all the times he had come in there to mix a drink and carry it back into the living room to find Ruby dancing by herself to a Louis Armstrong record, or something by Jimmy Lunceford or Fats Waller or Sidney Bechet.

Those were in her relaxed moments and there had been few enough of them, God knew, but she loved to dance by herself, letting the music, the really good jive, flow through her and come out at her legs and feet, her head tilted back, a small gone smile on her lips, her short-cropped blonde hair a cap of shining gold, fine-spun and as alive as the voltage with which she was so charged. Those were the moments in which she really lived and in which she was Ruby. The rest of the time she was fighting that sickness and losing every round before the bell sounded.

I should have married her, Latham thought with a kind of agony, *why didn't I, what was it, pride or what, but I should have married her and maybe it would have given her a focus*. At the same time he knew that these were futile thoughts, for the thing that was in Ruby was beyond focus and that marriage would not have been a cure but only a temporary sedative and that within a very short time her sick spirit would have been roving again, prowling the alleys like a lean and furtive cat in the dark of the night.

Keeler was saying something, but Latham paid no attention. Keeler was of no importance. Nothing was of any importance except that perhaps, at long last, some measure of peace had come to Ruby. But no sooner had the thought formed than his mind revolted angrily. No! Peace could have come to Ruby in some other way and she did not need an ice pick through her heart to find it. She was lovely and warm and passionate and generous, and her murder had been needless and foul. She had never wanted the moldering peace of the grave; she wanted a living peace so that she could give and give from the infinite capacity for love that was in her. And she had deserved that—not the ice pick!

Keeler was drawling, "Hell, I'll have one with you. I feel a little clobbered myself. I ain't had no sleep since God knows when."

He slouched from the table and took down a bottle of bourbon from the cabinet. His body odor was acrid and sweaty as he stood beside Latham and held up the bottle to read the label.

"Old Grandpappy, one hundred proof, bottled in bond honest to God guaranteed bourbon." He shook his head "That chick really lived it up more ways than one. Me, on my salary, I'm lucky if I can buy a bottle of Old Horsey gin twice a week at two-fifty a throw. Virtue might be its own reward, but it sure don't buy good liquor."

He filled two cocktail glasses with bourbon and handed one to Latham, saying cheerfully, "It's on the house, baby."

Latham reached out deliberately and poured it in the sink. "I said I'm not drinking."

Keeler shrugged and sipped from his own glass. "Well," he said, "it's a good man that knows when to stop, I always say, but you sure smelled like you had a load on when I walked in the kitchen here. It stank like a busted distillery. I'm not saying you were soused, but a pickup might do you some good. You look like you been up all night licking the barnacles from the bottom of a cattle boat." He tittered and took another drink, eying Latham slyly over the rim of his glass. Latham knew then that he was being needled, specifically and for a purpose, and in a way in which Keeler was practiced, so he held tightly to his rising temper. Until he found out what Keeler was after. That was it. Play along until he found out. There were a lot of things he had to find out, and Keeler probably knew most of the answers. The thing to do now was find out who had killed Ruby, and when he did—the burst of savagery in him was like a lashing flame and for a moment he felt as if he were suffocating. It passed quickly and he felt icy cold, locked in a grimness that was a very glacier of frozen fury. Keeler was regarding him oddly.

"Were you the one who smacked me?" Latham asked without any particular inflection in his voice.

"Not this time, baby," Keeler answered, making it sound like an oversight on his part. "If I'd been here when you crawled through that window I would of, but I wasn't here. What makes you think you were smacked anyway?"

Latham knew he had been struck; he knew he had not fallen and hit his head on the floor—but he could not say how he knew. The reasons were hidden behind an alcoholic fog. *From here on in, I'm off the liquor,* he thought grimly.

"Well, maybe I wasn't," he said. "I was plotzed and maybe I fell. I came in the window? What window?"

"The one right behind you, baby."

Latham turned and saw the window swinging slightly in the light breeze and he knew that the locking ratchet had been broken. Vaguely now, he remembered something about breaking the window, but only vaguely.

"Yeah," he said, "maybe you're right."

"You're damn right I'm right, baby. One of the neighbors called headquarters and said a guy was crawling in here so I buzzed right over and there you were stretched out on the floor like a bar rag and stinking just about the same. You were *really* stinko, like they say. Wooten, that was the neighbor's name. Eugene M. Wooten. He's got the apartment straight across the patio, or whatever they call that hunk of grass out there. Eugene M. Wooten, a very nosey guy. And a real drinking man, too," Keeler nodded with pretended admiration. "We talked to him earlier in the day and you should of seen his joint. Bottles all over the place, on the floor, in the chairs, on the tables, under the bed, in the bathroom, all kinds of bottles including bay rum. There's a man that really likes a nip now and then. Eugene M. Wooten, Esquire, lives right across the way. A skinny little guy, about five feet five, and he's been on the sauce so long that he don't know what way is up half the time. A real lush-head."

Again Latham found Keeler eying him oddly, his eyes intent, as if there had been more to his speech than the idle chatter like which it had sounded.

"That makes two lush-heads," said Latham, playing dumb. "Him and me."

"Oh, he's okay, even if he is slopped up most of the time. All he wants to do is lap up the sauce and look out the window. He's all right, and he's playing right along with us, too, a regular mother's little helper, he is."

Thinking that Keeler meant the report that Wooten had made to headquarters that evening, Latham said indifferently, "Maybe you ought to put him on the payroll."

"He's better than that, baby. He might even turn out to be a witness. Yes sir, an honest to God guaranteed witness. As far as we know he's the only guy that saw the guy that killed Ruby."

Latham turned and said savagely, "*What!*"

Keeler grinned. "Don't get yourself in an uproar, baby. It ain't as good as it sounds. Yet. He tells us like this—he was sitting in his window like usual, enjoying the balmy Florida air and a little liquid refreshment, when he just happens to look across the patio. If you ask me, that was one of his favorite pastimes, just happening to look across the patio.

Ruby never shut her venetian blinds and he must of gotten quite an eyeful every now and again." His sly glance probed at Latham again and he chuckled softly at the rising blood in Latham's face. "Yeah, a careless dame like that, she must of given poor old Wooten quite a treat once in a while, him being the kind of guy that gets his kicks from just looking. Maybe you yourself was one of the guys he used to watch with her over here with the windows wide open. The floor show, he called it. Wooten, I mean. A real nosey guy, and he sure liked his floor shows, but you take a lush-head, all he *can* do is look. You gotta feel sorry for a guy like that *even if you happened to be one of the guys in the floor shows.* Right, baby, right?"

For an instant of terrible fury, Latham saw Keeler's fat, jowly face with almost microscopic clarity—the greasy overlay of sweat, the veal-white skin, the coarse pores in the fleshy nose, the loose mouth with that pendulous underlip showing yellow teeth. His teeth were small and his eyes were small, more ferret than rat. Latham held on tightly to the edge of the counter at the side of the sink until the wave of fury washed back. Keeler was giving him the needle, that was all, just giving him the needle, and he had to watch out for that. Wooten had never seen anything between Ruby and him, never.

"Now, baby," said Keeler's insinuating, probing voice, "you're not getting sore at a lush-head like Wooten, are you?"

"I just feel sorry for him," Latham said thickly.

"That's right, baby, that's the way. You gotta feel sorry for a guy like that, and he might even come in handy. Frinstance, the night Ruby was knocked off, he was sitting over there in the window, half-crocked or even more so. This was at night and the lights were on and he could see right in and he sees Ruby and this guy kneeling on the floor. They were playing crap, he says, and having a scrap over every pass. He couldn't tell us what the guy looked like. That's the rub. He was half-bagged, like I say, but he told us there was something familiar about the guy. That was his exact words, 'something familiar,' but he couldn't remember what it was. We figure it was one of the guys that used to come here quite a lot so there must of been something familiar about him. The point is that the guy was having a scrap with Ruby, and maybe it didn't have nothing to do with the dice. You don't stick an ice pick in a chick over a two-handed crap game. Hell, there just wouldn't be enough dough on the blanket, so the scrap must Lof been about something else. We're just sitting back and hoping that one of these days Wooten might happen to come out of his fog long enough to tell us what that 'something familiar' about the guy was. We could sober him up but he'd probably blow his stack if we took the sauce away from him after all these years. He'd just get the screaming meemies. But these lush-heads, it's a funny thing, sometimes all of a sudden they can remember everything back to the year one, or maybe something'll prod him and he'll put the finger on and say, 'That's the guy.' *It's been a year and a half since you been in here, you said, right, baby?"*

So that was the build-up, Latham thought, then aloud, "It's been just about that."

"Well, then you're in the clear, baby. Wooten wasn't even living there a year and a half ago, so he wouldn't know you from a hole in the ground and you don't have to worry about that 'something familiar.' And I mean worry," Keeler gave the words a special emphasis. "You take a lush-head, you don't know what he's going to come up with, his brains in a scramble all the time. He might just up and decide there's 'something familiar' about a guy that had nothing to do with it at all, know what I mean? Just some poor sucker, and he'd have a hell of a time trying to explain it in front of a jury. But on the other hand, Wooten could just happen to hit it right on the nose. Like I say, we're just sitting back with our fingers crossed."

Latham thought, *the hell you are*, but said, "What else can you do?"

"Nothing, I guess, but it's better than no break at all, though right now I wouldn't give a plugged nickel for a dozen Wootens and his brother. As far as I'm concerned, he's for the birds."

Keeler set down his glass on the counter beside the sink. it contained just about as much liquor as when he had poured it, though he had seemingly been sipping steadily at it. He stretched and yawned and blinked as if now there were no other thought in his head but bed. He rubbed his eyes and mumbled, "I'm clobbered, baby. This has been a day."

"Why don't you go to bed?"

"Yeah, I better. I can't even think straight no more. Let's get the hell out of here." Then, as if the thought had just struck him, "But what were you doing here in the first place, baby?" He blinked sleepily and grinned to show that the question had just been put out of idle curiosity, nothing else.

"I just thought I'd take a look around for old times' sake," said Latham ironically. "What the hell did you expect me to say, you foxy son of a bitch?"

"I just wondered, that's all, baby, just wondered, seeing what a mess you made out of the joint. Looking for something special?"

Latham said incredulously, "Mess!"

Keeler giggled. "Well, you left the walls standing, but that's just about all. Did you have something special in mind?"

Latham barely remembered breaking the ratchet on the casement window, but nothing of what had happened after that and very little of what had gone on before. Had he really gone through the apartment, as Keeler had said? But what for? Why? What was the point? He had no reason to go through Ruby's apartment. But why did you do the things you did when you were drunk, or why did you get drunk in the first place? You could add it up that way, if at all. But to make a mess out of the apartment, that didn't make sense, no sense at all. Still, when you're drunk … The thought disgusted him, and he kicked at the black bobby pin that lay on the floor at his feet. It spun against the opposite wall and bounced back under the table.

"Christ knows what I had in mind," he growled. "I was gory-eyed drunk."

"Could be," Keeler agreed. "The liquor fumes in here was so bad I was afraid to light a match. But whatever you was looking for, you sure went after it. Want to take a look? He tilted his flabby chins at the kitchen door that led to the living room. "The department went over the joint with toothbrush, you know, routine, but you must of used a baseball bat."

Latham said shortly, "Let's go."

"Whatever you was looking for, you didn't find it. I gave you a quick frisk and you was clean. If you could remember what it was, maybe I could help you. I been over this place myself, two-three times. I could be a big help to you maybe, baby."

There was a hidden eagerness in Keeler's manner that Latham could not understand, and he was instantly suspicious. Keeler was not needling him this time; he was after something. You never got something for nothing from Keeler.

"You've been a big help all along," Latham said sarcastically. "What more could I ask?"

"I'm serious, baby. I got this whole case in my lap. Hanna's in charge, but I'm the guy that does the leg work. All he knows is what I tell him, and in a case like this, you can't tell your boss everything till you can check it out, if you know what I mean. So maybe I got something you want and maybe you got something I want, and why not work together."

Latham said, "Do your own work," walked across the room and thrust open the swinging door between the kitchen and the living room. He stopped short in the doorway and stared aghast at the ruin before him. He heard Keeler chuckle behind him, but he paid no attention to it. A 'mess' did not begin to describe what had happened to the living room. The upholstered chairs and sofa had literally been torn apart and the springs and batting and down feathers covered the floor. The throw rugs lay crumpled in a corner, and the bookcase had been emptied and every book gutted. The radio was pulled out from the wall and wires dangled limply from the back of it as if someone had pawed impatiently inside with a heavy hand. The pictures were off the walls and broken, the lamps were overturned, and even the drapes had been pulled from the windows and the lining ripped from them. The devastation was complete.

Latham walked incredulously into the room, staring around him. A silver photograph frame lay on the floor at his feet and mechanically he stooped and picked it up, looking around for someplace to stand it. As he turned it in his hand, he saw with a poignant wrench that it was a picture of himself, an eight-by-ten blown up from a snapshot. He was standing on the flying bridge of the *Belan*, clad in a pair of swimming trunks and a Basque striped T-shirt, silhouetted against the clean sky, scanning the starboard sea. He remembered exactly when it had been taken—the first time he had taken Ruby fishing in the Gulf. One of the very few times, for she did not like either fishing or boats.

No, that was wrong. She loved the boat, the clean, honest lines of it and the swift flying freedom in the open water, but there was that sick restlessness in her and she could not stay in one place for any length of time. No matter where she was, sooner or later she had to be someplace else, anyplace, and it was an agony to her if she could not go, just go.

Latham took the picture from the frame and tossed the empty frame on the gutted sofa. Carrying the photograph, he walked slowly into Ruby's remembered bedroom. Here the ruin was just as complete as in the living room. The mattress and box spring from the bed were in shreds and the clothes from her closet were scattered everywhere. Her chest of drawers had been emptied on the floor, and her daintiest underwear mingled with the yellow-white cotton batting from the mattress and box spring. Something crunched under his feet, and when he picked it up, he saw that it was a piece of inexpensive costume jewelry. He glanced, stupefied, into the bathroom and saw broken glass and jars and towels all over the tiled floor, and in the midst of the debris was a tube of toothpaste on which someone had stepped and the white paste spread in coils like an obscene white worm.

He clenched his big, knuckly hands and said violently, "No! *Hell* no!"

"No what, baby?"

He turned sharply and saw Keeler regarding him brightly from the door to the living room. Latham swept his arm in a half circle.

"This! I didn't do this. I didn't have any part of that, and I don't give a damn how soused I was!"

Keeler rounded his eyes with pretended amazement. "No?"

"No, damn it! Look, her clothes—" He made an incoherent motion toward the torn and crumpled dresses and slips and underwear scattered around the room, as if someone had flung them every which way in a fury of impatience. "Her clothes, the things she wore. I wouldn't do that!"

Keeler looked owlishly around the room. "Maybe you couldn't find what you were looking for," he suggested.

"What the hell could I have been looking for to tear her clothes up like that?" Latham shouted angrily, his face flushed and congested.

Keeler said, "You'd know more about that than I would," but a note of puzzlement had crept into his voice. He had been very sure of himself before, but now he was uncertain "Well, somebody messed it up, if you didn't."

"Somebody was here when I came, you damn fool. I—" Latham stopped and snapped his fingers. He strode out of the room, across the living room and into the kitchen.

Keeler cried, "Hey, wait a minute there!" and ran into the kitchen after him.

Latham searched the floor with his eyes, then bent over and picked up the black bobby pin from under the kitchen table. He held it up in front of Keeler's face.

"There!" he said. "There!"

"There what?" Keeler backed away. "What is it?"

"It's a bobby pin, a black bobby pin. Girls wear them in their hair when they're making curls or waves or something."

"So what?"

"It's black. Can't you see it? It's black, and Ruby was a blonde."

"So she was a blonde. So what?"

"Blondes don't wear black bobby pins. They wear pins to match their hair. Anyway, Ruby's hair was too short. She wouldn't wear a bobby pin, black or otherwise."

"Ah hell." Keeler looked disgusted. "I thought you really latched onto something. Anybody could have dropped it here, when she was throwing a party or having company or anything."

"Ruby didn't throw parties. She went to them but she couldn't be bothered throwing one."

"Yeah, and the company she had didn't wear bobby pins," Keeler said maliciously. "Okay, but you still ain't nowhere. It could of fallen off the cleaning lady."

"She didn't have a cleaning woman. She did her own cleaning. She said she couldn't stand strangers handling her things and—" Latham stopped and, looking straight at Keeler, said softly, "And if you make any cracks about that, I swear to God I'll smack you harder than you've ever been hit before in your life."

"Why should I make any cracks?" Keeler's jaw dropped with simulated surprise, but his eyes jeered. "Hell, my wife's the same way. She wouldn't have a cleaning lady in the house, pawing over things, peeking in closets and all that. But maybe you got a point, baby. Let's see that bobby whatever you call it, bobby pin."

Latham gave it to him and he turned it curiously in his fingers. It was an ordinary bobby pin, shiny black.

"It was lying right there on the floor next to me," Latham said. "It was one of the first things I saw when I opened my eyes. Your boys would have spotted it when they went through here in the first place, wouldn't they?"

"Probably, probably. We usually go through a joint like this with a fine toothbrush."

"Now here's something else, this lump on my head, back here. I'd have to have fallen backwards to get a lump there, and when you trip, you fall frontwards. Now if I was crawling in through that window and somebody smacked me, that lump would be just about in the right place. That might not make sense to you, but it makes sense to me."

Keeler looked thoughtfully at the bobby pin again, walked over and glanced at the broken window, then stood to one side as if putting himself in the place of a person poised to strike as Latham crawled through the narrow opening. He nodded and slowly put the bobby pin into the pocket of his slacks.

"Well, well, well," he said vaguely, "what do you know about that now. You never know who's going to turn up next, do you."

"So you agree somebody was here before me?" Latham demanded.

"It sure looks that way, baby, though I wouldn't give odds on it. One lousy bobby pin ain't much to go on. Still ..." he frowned and glanced toward the wrecked living room.

"And I didn't do that either," Latham said forcefully. "My God, I don't care what I thought I was looking for, drunk or sober, I wouldn't do that to Ruby's apartment This was where she lived, this was her home, this was where she lived with herself—"

"All right, all right, *all right!* Shut up for a minute, will you?" Keeler walked to the doorway and scowled at the debris, his head moving from side to side as if trying to find a way through an impasse that had suddenly become too high and too wide. He swore thinly, pounding the side of his thigh with his fist. His face was bunched in an anxious pucker and the sweat hung in beads from his eyebrows and Latham could see that the fat man was more than ordinarily upset.

"What's the matter, pudgy?" he asked, grinning thinly. "You're getting yourself all worked up. Something go wrong?"

Keeler gave him a glance that was as savage as the bright slash of a fish gutting knife.

"My, my, my," Latham murmured, still half-grinning, "chubby's in a tizzy."

Keeler seemed on the verge of hurling himself at Latham. His pale eyes were distended and staring, his teeth chattered, and his thick hands half raised, quivering. Latham laughed.

"What's the matter, fat boy?" he jibed. "Can't you take it? I thought you were an expert, the way you dish it out. I haven't even started to needle you and you're all worked up. What you need is a few lessons in self-control."

Keeler's hand jerked and moved toward the pocket on his right hip, then dropped to his side. He laughed shortly.

"Yeah," he said, "we're a pair of comedians, ain't we, just a couple of clowns, anything for a laugh, shoot the works just for the ducks of it." He laughed again but there was something in his voice that promised Latham an evening of the score at a later date. He put a cigarette into his mouth and lit it, flipping the burnt match into the sink beside Latham. He took a deep breath and gave the living room another glance. Then he turned sharply and looked around the kitchen, which was the only room in the apartment that had not been torn apart ... He nodded, looked pleased and murmured, "Yeah, yeah, yeah, just about, uh huh." He glanced slyly at Latham. "Just thinking out loud, baby, figuring the way it might of been. When you came crawling in the window, this dame with the black bobby pin—no, wait a minute. There must of been more than just a dame. A dame couldn't handle that heavy stuff like the mattress and box spring and the way that big couch's been turned over. There must of been a guy with her, maybe two guys. Right?"

"It only took one to smack me," said Latham, wondering why Keeler was so excited about this and why the big build-up.

"But there had to be more than one, baby, and when you came in through the window, you scared them off. You must of made quite a racket, breaking the ratchet on that casement. So they smacked you and got the hell out of here, not even waiting to give the kitchen here a going over at all. They didn't even get to the kitchen. That's the only way it figures. Right, baby? You scared them off."

"Off from what? Why were they here at all?"

"Well, a dame like Ruby," Keeler said evasively, "a lot people figured she was loaded, the life she led, if you know what I mean, and don't get sore, I'm just repeating. She went around with some pretty high-class guys who were loaded, and it just stands to reason they would have given her a little present now and then, like diamonds for instance, and it don't take long for things like that to add up to real dough. If I could figure that much out, a couple of them sharpshooters that hang around the Beach Casino could figure it out too, and they went after it. Hell, five or ten grand in jewelry ain't to be sneezed at. Right, baby, right?"

"Ruby never took that kind of present from a man in her life," said Latham harshly.

Keeler held up soothing hands. "Take it easy, baby, take it easy. I ain't saying she did and I ain't saying she didn't. I'm just telling you the talk that's going round."

"It's not going around in front of me!"

"What're you going to do, fight everybody in town, baby?" Keeler jeered. "Everybody's talking about it, and I'm giving it to you straight. They say she took these guys for everything she could get. And there's no sense getting sore at me because I don't give a damn if she did or not. More power to her, I say. If a guy steps out of line with a dame, let him pay for it, that's my motto. And if she could get it, she had it coming. But if you say she didn't, that's okay with me too. It's no skin off my nose either way, but that ain't the point. The point is that somebody thought she was loaded and went to the trouble to take the joint apart to try and find it. It's as plain as the nose on your face." Keeler spread his hands persuasively. "Right, baby?"

"You're sure trying hard enough to convince me."

"Just thinking out loud, baby, that's all, just thinking out loud. A bad habit of mine. Most people do their thinking on the inside but I got to do mine on the outside," Keeler laughed. "And that brings up something else, too. It's been a year and a half since you had anything to do with that chick, baby. Did it ever cross your mind that people can change in a year and a half? Let's say a year and a half ago she wouldn't even take a hamburger from a guy, but suppose she suddenly said to herself, 'The hell with this,' and started taking everything she could get. Why give it away when you can sell it? She wouldn't be the first chick that turned sour, and she was in a wonderful position to collect, if you stop to think it over."

Keeler was talking too much, and Latham was now certain that there was something coiling and twisting in one of the obscure little caves in the fat man's mind. Keeler was as secretive as a mink, and it was not his nature to volunteer information without a definite motive. Latham decided to play along. It was a shock to him to realize that he actually knew very little of the last year and a half of Ruby's life, and he was hungry for information, which Keeler seemed very willing to supply, no matter for what reason. The reason would come out later.

"Maybe you're right," he said, trying to look discouraged. "I hadn't thought of it that way. People change."

"Now you're cooking, baby," Keeler said eagerly. "People change, and the chicks even more so, from one day to the next, and maybe this chick up and decided to get hers while the getting was good and went around with her hand out. And look at some of the guys she went around with—Ross McElroy that runs the crap game at the Beach Casino, pulling down five hundred a week easy; Harry Conley, the real estate guy, loaded; Frank Meyn, that owns the Palm Dairies, loaded; Doug Hemming, the Hemming Lumber yard, loaded; Stanley Wilfred Mays, treasurer of the bank, loaded …"

Latham blurted, "Mays!" and felt his stomach contract. Mays, that self-pitying, so-called blue blood, handsome enough on the outside, but just plain sludge on the inside. Latham felt a boiling fury at the thought of Mays with Ruby. Then suddenly he remembered that night Mays had been drunk and had wanted him to get a certain blonde for him. Ruby. He should have guessed, he should have known.

"Yeah, Mays," said Keeler. "I was surprised myself, but they kept it pretty much under cover, him being married and treasurer of the bank and all, and not a guy you'd expect to play around. But you see what I mean, baby? She was playing around with some guys that really had it, and if she said, 'Daddy, I want a diamond geegaw to hang around my neck,' any one of them boys could of bought it for her without thinking twice. See what I mean?"

"Yes, I see what you mean," said Latham heavily, thinking of Mays. Mays was one of the first with whom he was going to have a talk, a real talk, the bastard.

Keeler looked at the wineglass of bourbon that still stood on the counter beside the sink where he had placed it, and he picked it up and drained it in a single gulp. His hands were shaking a little. He looked down at them and quickly put them in his pockets.

"Now here's the way I figure, baby," he said. "You and me, we're both interested in the same thing—finding the guy that knocked her off. Right?"

Latham nodded, watching Keeler's face for he was sure the payoff on all this conversation was coming soon. Keeler had been leading up to it for a long while, and now it was getting close.

Keeler moistened his lips. "Here's the question—why was she knocked off? Jealousy? Hell no. She was the next thing to a call girl and everybody knew it. No offense, baby," he said quickly, "I'm just repeating the talk that's going round, and if we're going to get any place, we got to face the facts."

"She was sick." Latham felt sick himself, remembering her stricken face the last time he saw her. "She couldn't help herself. She should have gone to a psychiatrist."

"That's right, she was sick," Keeler agreed eagerly. "A nymph, there's something the matter with them. I read it in a book myself. She should of gone to one of them head doctors and gotten herself straightened out, but that's beside the point now. She didn't. But like I was saying, no guy in his right mind would of been jealous enough to knock her off, any more than you'd be jealous of a five buck mudkicker in a Tampa crib. It wouldn't make sense. So this is the way I figure, baby—she found out how easy it was to collect from these guys, most of them married, and she got greedy. She wanted more. She wanted big hunks of it, so she put the screws on, and that's where she went tangent. The minute you start that stuff, you got your hand in the fire. So I say she put the screws on just a little too tight, and the sucker backfired on her. She wanted more than he could cough up, he told her so, and then she says to him, 'Okay, baby, unless you kick in, I'm going to your missus and have a nice heart to heart talk all about you and won't that be nice?' By this time the guy don't have no more of them friendly feelings towards her, so he slips her the ice pick. Remember Wooten said she was having a scrap with some guy here that night? Well, there it is, plain and simple. She gave that screw just one turn too many and collected something she hadn't bargained for. But they never do, baby, they never do. Even a sucker has a breaking point."

Latham said, "Yeah," but grimly he was repeating to himself—Mays, Conley, McElroy, Meyn, Hemming—memorizing the names.

Keeler poured himself another drink from the bourbon bottle. He was very excited now. His eyes gleamed and he was speaking very rapidly in a high voice.

"Now let's say one of them guys even wrote her letters," he said. "That would be it, see? That would be the proof she could take to the guy's missus, and something the missus could take into the divorce courts and collect on and get custody of the kids and everything else. And that's what I want to get my hands on, baby, them letters. Now a smart chick like Ruby, she wouldn't keep anything like that around the house. She'd put them in a safe deposit box in some bank somewheres. She had hardly nothing in this bank in town, so we know she didn't use that one, so—" Keeler's eyes became very intent and bright, "—so I thought maybe you might know what bank she might of used, you being so close to her for a while back there. It would take from now on if we tried to go through every bank in the state blind. We have to have some kind of a lead if we want to get anywheres, and you're the guy that might be able to give it to us. Did she ever mention any bank to you—Tampa, St. Pete, Miami, anywheres?"

Latham said shortly, "She never had anything to put in the bank when I knew her."

"Wait a minute, baby, wait a minute. Take time out to think for a minute. She might just happened to of mentioned it at some time or other, like, 'Oh I got to go up to the bank in Tampa tomorrow,' or something like that. Just something she might of let drop, know what I mean?"

"If I knew, I'd tell you," Latham said angrily, "but I don't know."

"You don't want to let that guy get away with knocking her off, do you, baby?"

"I told you—"

"Sure sure sure. All I'm asking is for you to keep it in mind. Right now you're all upset and maybe you can't think straight, but it might come to you, know what I mean? All of a sudden you'll remember once she mentioned a bank in St. Pete, and that'll be it and we can put the finger on the guy. Right now there's too many guys and that makes it tough. If we can narrow it down, we'll have something to work with. So if the name of the bank comes to you, give me a buzz and we'll see what turns up. Of course," Keeler shrugged, "I might be barking up the wrong tree. Maybe there ain't no letters or nothing or even a bank, but it's an idea and right now we need ideas. The way it stands now, almost anybody in the whole damn town could of knocked her off as far as we know. She, well, knew an awful lot of guys, baby. If the name of the bank comes to you, call me. That's all I ask."

Latham was suddenly abysmally tired of Keeler and all this prodding, and he said wearily, not arguing any longer, "If it comes to me, I'll call you."

"Call me the minute it comes to you, even if it's the middle of the night. You can always get me at the house if I'm not at headquarters. I want to break this case, baby. I want to get that guy just as much as you do. Call me the minute it comes to you."

"I said I would, didn't I?"

"Sure, baby, sure," Keeler said in a conciliatory voice. "And I know you want to get this killer as much as I do. That chick thought an awful lot of you, Joe, and that's the honest truth. No matter what else she did, you were number one in her book. Do you know she was writing a note to you the night she was knocked off? It's a fact. Here, take a look—"

He brought out his wallet from his left hip pocket and took a sheet of white scented notepaper from it. It was wrinkled as if it had been crumpled and then smoothed and folded. In the top left corner was a small embossed R. The paper smelled faintly, just faintly, of lily of the valley. It was the notepaper Ruby had used as long as Latham could remember and somehow or other, despite the sick, frantic life she led, the paper was indicative of what she was really like inside—chaste and clean. Latham felt the sharp ache of remembrance as he took the sheet of paper and smelled the scent.

There was only one line on the paper, written in a very shaky hand. "My Very Dearest Joe—" Nothing else, but nothing else was needed. That one line told everything. "My Very Dearest Joe—" All of her love was in those four words, and nothing else had to be said. The letters quivered as if her hand had been shaking badly when she wrote it. She had either been under a terrific emotional strain or— Latham did not want to finish the thought, but it completed itself. Or drunk. He knew that Ruby had been drinking heavily during the past eight months.

He had not spied upon her or anything like that, but here and there a bartender would mention to him, "That old girl friend of yours was in here a little while ago and, brother, was she looping!" Or sometimes, "She had a crying jag on and kept asking if you came around anymore. I think maybe she was looking for you, Joe. It's none of my business, but I thought I'd pass it on to you, just in case."

And now this unfinished note, written on the day of her murder, "My Very Dearest Joe—"

But you can't keep crying over her and feeling guilty all your life, he told himself fiercely, *just get the bastard who did it, that's all!*

"It was in the wastebasket all rumpled up," Keeler said. "There was a couple others too, if you want to look at them, but she didn't finish none of them."

His face wooden, Latham took the two additional sheets that Keeler offered him. One just said, "Dearest Joe," but the other was more formal. "Dear Joe: I am going to leave this in the mailbox, hoping you'll get it. I know you will because I want so much for you to read it. I want to explain—" That was all. Whatever it was she wanted to explain was lost now.

Poignantly, Latham remembered the "mailbox" of which she had written. This was another facet of Ruby, romantic, sentimental, and deeply loving, and wanting him to know it all the time, wanting to show the depth of her devotion to him.

When they were engaged and he saw her practically every day, she still wrote him notes and left them in what she called the "mailbox," which had nothing to do with the United States Postal system. The "mailbox" was the huge banyan tree at the landward end of the dock to which the

Belan was tied. It was a tremendous tree, a hundred feet in diameter, its aerial roots forming a large labyrinth that could hardly be penetrated. It was among these roots, that came down from the overhead branches, in the very heart of them, that Ruby left her notes to him.

"Sometimes, darling," she had told him, "I wake up in the middle of the night and want to talk to you and tell you things, so I get up and write you a note and drive down and put it in the tree for you. It brings you closer when I write to you—"

She had never slept well, even a year and a half ago, but she had stubbornly refused to go to a doctor or take sleeping pills. He had tried to urge her to go to a doctor, but she had become irritable. "But I don't *need* any more than three or four hours sleep a night." And seemingly she didn't, for she had always looked fresh and alive, though he knew now what a torment those long, dark hours must have been to her, and he knew, too, that writing to him had in some way alleviated that torment. For a brief while, during their engagement, he had been the one steadfast thing in her life, a life that must have been as instable as water. *("I don't know what I'd do without you, Joe.")*

Gratitude. An abased emotion.

("You've been so patient with me, Joe, you're wonderful, I don't see how you can be so patient with me, I'm such an awful bitch, and I don't want to be, oh Joe!")

Patience. The most sterile of virtues. God! She had needed love and understanding and he had given her patience.

And now here on the eve of her murder she had written, "My Very Dearest Joe—" Latham started when Keeler took the three sheets of notepaper from his hand and replaced them in his wallet.

"I wish I could let you have them, Joe," the detective said with an air of regret as he put the wallet back into his hip pocket, "but Hanna would have my neck. For some reason or other, he's got half an idea you knocked the chick off yourself, and he's got his eye on you. In fact, if he knew you busted in here tonight, you'd be in the caboose before you knew what happened to you. He had a padlock put on the door, and nobody's supposed to come in here except me and him. I'm doing you a favor not running you in, believe me."

"Maybe I'd better beat it now before you change your mind," said Latham with heavy irony.

"You don't have to rush on my account, Joe. You play ball with me and I'll play ball with you. Being you didn't have nothing to do with messing up this joint, I won't mention to Hanna that you was in here tonight. He'd just get himself in an uproar and it wouldn't do nobody no good."

"Is the door open or do I have to climb out the window again?"

"You can go out the door, Joe. But get in touch with me if you happen to think of anything, okay?"

Latham said, "Sure," walked out of the kitchen, through the debris of the living room and out of the apartment, hearing Keeler call after him, "Your car's on the side street, baby." Latham did not remember leaving it there or even having driven to the apartment, and he grimly made a note that this was his last binge for a long, long time. He was about half way back to the dock where the *Belan* was moored when he glanced in the rear vision mirror and saw a black car following him about a block behind. The car passed beneath a street light and he caught a quick glimpse of the black and white police insignia on the door and the single driver behind the wheel. It was Keeler.

CHAPTER SIX

There was no doubt in Latham's mind that all of Keeler's seeming friendliness had a purpose that would become apparent later and that to take it at face value would be setting himself up as the patsy in whatever scheme the fat detective was hatching. Keeler had the reputation of being as devious as a cat stalking a covey of quail. Still, he was just about the best detective on the force, and if he took any graft from anyone it was so hidden that there had not even been a whisper a of that kind of thing against him.

Latham glanced at his wrist watch. It was ten minutes to one. He wanted to see Ross McElroy out at the Beach Casino, but there was plenty of time for that. He could have lost the police car by driving out to Pelican Key and disappearing in the maze of narrow, palmetto-lined roads that twisted through the northern end of the island like meaningless scrawls on a kindergarten blackboard, but it was much easier to lose Keeler another way. He drove straight to the dock and parked his car in its usual place under the banyan tree and then lumbered heavily up the dock to the *Belan* as if aching for nothing but a long night's sleep. As he stepped down into the stern cockpit of the cruiser, he saw Keeler's lightless car drift into the shadows of the huge tree and stop. Latham went into the cabin and turned on the light; knowing that Keeler would spot it immediately from the parking lot. Then he sat down on the edge of the bunk and lit a cigarette. When he had smoked it through, he turned out the light. He sat in the high chair at the wheel and watched the parking lot through the port. Keeler stayed a half hour before he turned on his headlights, turned around and drove slowly back into the quiet city. Latham smoked a second cigarette and waited another twenty minutes. He still had plenty of time. The gambling room in the Casino seldom closed before five in the morning.

The breeze had freshened and the boat rocked and tossed a little as the rising chop slapped against the lean hull. Before leaving, Latham checked the two lines that moored the *Belan* and hung two more fenders over the side to protect the boat from the timbers of the dock. The wind was coming in from the Gulf and the breakers were beginning to roar as they pounded the beaches. Latham glanced up at the sky, which was so studded with stars that it was like a handful of ground glass flung on black velvet. There were a few clouds in the northeast and it would shower before dawn, but the day would probably be clear and calm with maybe just a little chop, not enough to be uncomfortable. Better for fishing, actually, than a glassy calm day. He had a charter for six A.M., a Mr. Bispham from Ohio. Mr. Bispham wanted to catch a tarpon. Mr. Bispham was an executive type who owned some kind of factory in Cleveland. He wanted a tarpon that he could have stuffed and mounted and hung over the fireplace in his living room back in Cleveland. He was not going to be satisfied with just any old tarpon. He wanted a big one, and he was going to take it as a personal affront if his tarpon did not break the record. Mr. Bispham was the kind who, when he chartered a boat, had the idea that he automatically chartered all the fish in the Gulf, too. Of course, he had never done any deep-sea angling in his life, but he was a great trout fisherman, he had told Latham patronizingly. Trout fishing took skill, but this deep-sea stuff, why all you had to do was haul it in with that windlass and flagpole that pretended to be a rod and reel. There was no more sport to deep-sea fishing than turning a crank. Well, Mr. Bispham certainly had a surprise in store for him when the first tarpon took his hook and came up out of the Gulf, shaking itself like an enraged bulldog, every silver scale shining in the sunlight.

Latham looked at his wrist watch. It was now two o'clock, and Keeler was well out of the way, though probably not home in bed. Keeler liked to roam the city even when not on duty, and whenever there was an accident or a fight or trouble of any kind, no matter at what time of day or night, you could almost place a bet that Keeler would be one of the first at the scene. He and Hanna made a good pair.

It was two-thirty when Latham drove into the parking lot of the Beach Casino on Little Sister Key, the island immediately south of Pelican Key. The Casino was dark, but there were about thirty cars in the lot, and

Latham knew that the gambling room on the second floor was humming like a machine shop under full production. It was outside the city limits and Dean Odum, who, it was rumored, ran the place for a Miami syndicate, had full protection from the county. Latham slid his car into a slot between a Lincoln and a Cadillac, but when he got out to walk to the side door of the Casino, a burly man in a wrinkled seersucker suit barred his way, hemming him in the space between his car and the Lincoln. He was an ex-wrestler whom everybody called Mush. He waved Latham back to his car.

"Sorry, bud," he said, "all closed up for the night. Come back tomorrow." He had taken so many blows on the neck when he had been in the ring that his voice was hardly more than a hoarse whisper.

"Don't give me that, Mush. I didn't come out here to dine and dance, and don't tell me you don't recognize me."

"I ain't telling you nothing 'cept we're all closed up for the night, so beat it."

"I'm Joe Latham. I've been out here a dozen times in the last two months. What's the matter with you?"

Mush set himself solidly on his broad, flat feet and said truculently, "I tole you onct and I tole you twict we're closed up for the night, and I don't give a damn who you are, so get your tail out of here before I get sore."

"You know me, Mush. I'm Latham, Joe Latham."

"Latham-Schmatham, I never seen you before, so do like I tell you and beat it before I let you have it."

Latham pressed his lips together. This was one of Mush's bad nights. Most of the time he was good-natured and friendly, but every once in a while he turned sour and pugnacious and no one could do anything with him, except Odum himself. There was no use arguing with him, because once he had made up his dim mind that he didn't know you, nothing could move him.

Latham held up his left hand. "Just look at this for a minute, Mush," he said, and as Mush turned his head, he clubbed him heavily on the side of the neck with his right fist. Mush grunted and his knees buckled, but he did not go down. He made a groping motion with his big hands and Latham hit him again just under the left ear. Mush fell forward and Latham caught him and eased him down, propping him in a sitting position against the Lincoln. Latham said, "You poor lunk," stepped over his outstretched legs and walked to the side door of the Casino. It opened to a set of stairs to the second floor. There was another door at the head of the stairs and Latham pushed a buzzer button concealed on the side of the frame. Odum was not so much afraid of a raid by the law, but a year ago three gunmen from Detroit had tried a holdup. They had ended up dead before they reached the gambling room itself, but the gunplay had upset the customers and for two or three months afterward trade fell off badly and the profits were light. Odum had then installed two steel soundproof doors, the buzzer and a peephole.

Latham had to wait a few moments while he was being scrutinized, and then the door was opened by a tall, slender man in a white dinner jacket that was draped to conceal the gun under his left armpit.

He said, "Hi, Joe. Feeling lucky?"

"Something like that. I just had a little trouble with your boy down in the parking lot. Mush. He wanted me to go home and I had to clip him. I thought I'd tell you just in case it comes up later."

The man raised his eyebrows, looking no more than politely surprised.

"You really must be feeling lucky to take on that ape, and you were lucky to get away with it. He's been sour all day. He gets that way when the moon is full. You can go right in."

There was a small foyer with a checkroom and beyond that the door that led to the gambling room. The door was steel and soundproof and was opened only after the proper signal had been given by the doorman at the head of the stairs. Odum was a showman as well as a shrewd operator, and part of this display of security had been set up to give the customers the feeling that the management had spared no pains to protect them from annoyances, such as holdups.

There were about seventy-five people in the room. There were tables for card games, a roulette spread, a bird cage, which was a novelty dice game, a bank of twenty slot machines, and a craps table. A muted loudspeaker piped Strauss waltzes into the room and several waiters walked among the customers serving cocktails and hors d'oeuvres. There was a slight hum of conversation, but most of the customers played silently and intently.

A waiter stopped in front of Latham and offered a tray of martinis and Manhattans. "A drink, sir?"

Latham took a martini and stood at the door, staring at the craps layout. The man at the table was slight and of medium height with the ivory complexion and black polished hair of a Latin, very different from the big, florid, sandy-haired Ross McElroy.

"Is Ross off-duty tonight?" he asked the waiter.

The waiter glanced at the craps table. "I wouldn't know, sir. You'd have to ask Mr. Odum."

Latham said, "Thanks," and sauntered deeper into room, carrying his glass but not drinking from it. He stopped at the fringe of the crowd around the roulette table, where the play was the heaviest. There were only two players at the craps layout, and Ross McElroy was probably taking a cigarette break. He had wasted his time asking the waiter. He knew that the waiters had instructions from Odum not to answer any questions about anything except the direction to the johns. All questions were referred to Odum himself.

Latham stood watching the craps layout and waiting for McElroy to return. Someone touched his arm very lightly at the elbow and a quiet, uninflected voice said:

"Hello, Joe. I hear you had a little trouble getting in."

Latham turned. It was Odum, a tall, heavily-built man with a tight little smile that looked as if it were meant to conceal a toothache. His fleshy face was white and looked slightly floury, like that of a baker, but his eyes were black and hard and as direct as a blow. No one knew very much about him except that he ran the Casino with an iron hand and that the hired help always spoke of him as Mr. Odum and kept their shoes polished and their hair combed.

"I'm sorry you were inconvenienced," he said. "I'll have to get rid of Mush, I'm afraid. He's becoming very unreliable. In fact, I just had one of the boys drive him up to the bus station. He didn't attack you, did he?"

"He tried to stop me from coming in, that's all."

"Apparently you're a hard man to stop. You wanted to see Ross McElroy about something?"

Latham's eyes widened just slightly. Odum really had a tight rein on this place. That waiter must have reported immediately.

"Just something private," he said. "Nothing to do with the dice."

"You mean, no complaints?"

Latham was surprised to see that Odum was joking, which was highly unusual, for he had the reputation of being as humorless as a brick wall. The joke was that Latham gambled very moderately, seldom winning or losing more than fifty dollars, and there was no question of a complaint.

"No, no complaints," he said. "Is he taking a cigarette break in the lounge?"

"No, he's sick. He's been sick for the past three days."

"Something he ate?"

"I wouldn't know."

"He's got a cottage up on Pelican Key, doesn't he?"

"I never asked."

"You mean you're not running an information booth, is that it?"

"If you want to put it that way, yes." His eyes left Latham and he glanced around the room as if checking to see that all the operations were running smoothly. Then unexpectedly he said, "I was sorry to hear about Ruby, Joe. She was a good girl. She didn't deserve to go out that way."

This was Latham's second surprise. He had known Odum a long while but the gambler had never been anything but formal, as he was with all the other customers who came into the Casino. He was an aloof, dour and rather sinister figure—the man who operated the gambling room for the Miami Syndicate, the front man, the watchdog with a squad of strongarm men always within whistling distance. Latham had never heard him speak a personal word to anybody beyond a comment on the weather.

Odum went on in that musing, uninflected way of his. "I knew her pretty well, Latham. She used to come in here a lot."

"To see McElroy?"

"No, she was always with somebody or other."

"Who?"

"I don't know. I forget. Different people. We used to talk once in a while. I got to know quite a lot about her, one way and another." He took out a tooled leather case from the inside pocket of his jacket and offered Latham a slim, dappled green cigar. Latham shook his head and Odum selected one of the cigars with the care of a jeweler lifting a precious gem from a velvet tray. He cut the end with a small gold penknife and lit it with a matching lighter.

"I'd like to talk to you, if you've got a minute," he said with an abstracted air. "I know how you feel about Ruby and there are a few things ..." He let the phrase dangle and made a vague gesture with his hand. "Do you have a minute or two to spare?"

Latham nodded shortly. This was so much of a departure from Odum's usual manner that he was certain the man had something he wanted to tell him.

"Let's go in my office," Odum said, pointing toward the door with his cigar. "This crowd bothers me. I don't like people who gamble. I think there's something wrong with them. As far as I'm concerned, I'd rather take my money and throw it in the street and let the kids scramble for it."

"You're in the right business then, aren't you."

"If they want to throw their money away on the wheel or the dice, I'll take it. I don't mind. But I wouldn't bet a nickel on the turn of a card, even if I was sure it was an ace. I don't think gambling's smart, and I don't want anything to do with that end of it. Shall we go in my office?"

"Why not?"

"Good. I can't talk out here. By the way, you don't actually want that sludge, do you? You're a bonded bourbon drinker, as I recall."

Latham looked at the martini he was still holding. "I was just minding it," he said. "The waiter looked as if he had too many on the tray."

"I'll get some bourbon and we can have a drink while we're talking. I wouldn't use all the martinis in the world for a mouth wash. Excuse me a moment."

He walked over to the bar in the corner and returned with a bottle of bourbon and two glasses, his wintry smile still fixed, unchanged, on his face. He nodded at Latham and led the way to his office, which was immediately behind the cashier's cage. It was a purely functional room, his office. There was a green steel desk with a swivel chair, a large impregnable-looking safe, also green, and a bank of green steel filing cabinets. The only other article of furniture was an office chair beside the desk. The office was small, only eight feet by ten feet in size, and the floor was laid in two tones of green rubber tile. It was a workroom and nothing more. Odum took the chair behind the desk and indicated the other chair with a slight lift of his chin. He carefully poured exactly one inch of bourbon into each glass, pushing one across the desk to Latham. He seemed like an ordinary, methodical business man in an ill-fitting dinner jacket except for his hard, black eyes, which made all the difference.

"As I was saying," he continued, as if the conversation had been interrupted only a moment before, "I got to know Ruby pretty well during the past year. I know, for instance, that she was carrying the torch for you. She didn't say so in so many words, but she was always talking about you. In fact, it was only three nights ago that she was in here, and from the way she talked I had the impression that you two might get together again."

Latham shook his head. "This is the first I knew of it."

"Well, maybe she was working up to something. She seemed very happy, which was unusual for her. I asked her if she had just broken the bank at the dice table, and she said she hadn't, so I asked her why she was so happy. I mean, she was never really gloomy, but she drank too much and was usually that kind of happy. You know what I mean, that she could just as easily burst into tears as into a laugh, but this night she was really and genuinely happy. So when I asked her, she kind of winked and asked if I'd be surprised if she went on a honeymoon one of these days. I said that I was surprised that she hadn't gone on one before this and then asked if you were the lucky man. She just smiled and said that it was going to be a big surprise, but a little later on she mentioned your name in such a way that I knew you were the one she had in mind." Odum droned on and on in his monotonous voice, without emphasis of either tone or gesture, his hands resting inert on the desk before him, brutal hands without finesse. "I was really hoping you two were getting together because it meant a lot to her, and I think you would have done her a lot of good. I got the idea that she was going to get in touch with you the very next day."

With a sharp pang, Latham remembered the three letters that Ruby had started but never finished, and this was the explanation. Perhaps she had really made up her mind to go to a psychiatrist, the one in Miami whom Latham knew, and take a course of treatments as he had suggested. His hands tightened unconsciously on the arms of his chair and he said harshly, "She didn't get in touch with me."

Odum regarded him stolidly, and though that fixed, spurious smile did not change, his eyes were very sharp and clinical.

"If I were going to bet on anything," he said finally, "I'd have bet that she was going to get in touch with you the next day, she seemed so sure of it herself. The next day or very shortly thereafter."

In the same harsh voice, Latham said, "She was interrupted."

Odum blinked. "That's true. I hadn't forgotten, but—well, I was sure she was going to get in touch with you. From the way she spoke, I'd have bet everything was all set between you. I had the impression that you were going to get married and would be off someplace by the end of the week." His smile disappeared for a moment, and his face looked as hard and expressionless as a tombstone without an inscription. "I'm seldom wrong about people but—" The frigid smile reappeared again.

"As you say, the circumstances are very unusual this time. Very unusual."

He was staring very hard at Latham, who demanded angrily, "What's the point of all this, anyway?"

Odum looked down at his hands and flexed the thick fingers. "There's really no point," he said vaguely. "I liked Ruby very much, that's all. I guess that's what I wanted to tell you, knowing how you feel about her. At a time like that, I think it helps to know that not everybody in this tank town judged her at face value. There was a lot more to Ruby than appeared on the surface, and I really wanted to see her get straightened out."

"Why? She was just another customer to you, wasn't she?"

Odum considered this thoughtfully, raising his glass to his mouth for his first sip of whiskey. "I wasn't one of her men, if that's what you mean," he said woodenly. "I had plenty of chances, but I wouldn't steal pennies from a blind man's cup, either. Maybe that's the reason she liked to talk to me. She knew I wasn't trying to get anything from her. She was a very lonesome girl, Latham, whether you know it or not. That's one of the reasons she kept going the way she did, drinking and all the rest of it. You could have straightened her out."

"I tried, damn it!" said Latham violently.

"I know. She told me. That doctor down in Miami. But do you know why she didn't go? She was scared stiff. She was afraid he'd tell her she was crazy. Did you know her father went crazy and had to be locked up when she was about six years old? That's what she was afraid of."

Latham looked numbly at the stolid, hard-faced man across the desk from him. Ruby had never told him about her father, nor anything about her past except that she had lived on Jefferson Avenue in Jersey City, and had moved from there to Belleville before coming to Florida. She had always given him the impression that she had come from a quiet middle class family. He shook his head, feeling a little sick at what Odum had told him. Sick and shamed and guilty, for he had thought that part of Ruby's trouble had been her revolt against the restrictive, dull and unimaginative life her family had led.

"I guess maybe I was the only one to whom she ever talked about her family," Odum said, tapping the ash from his slim cigar in an onyx tray. "Her father killed her mother and tried to kill her, but the neighbors heard the screams and saved her. She didn't tell me many of the details, but I gathered that it was very messy. He killed her mother with an electric iron. They didn't even try him for murder. They put him in an asylum where he died about ten years ago. Ruby went to live with an aunt and uncle in Belleville, New Jersey, and they never let her forget where her father was. It must have been a hell of a life for a young kid. And the funny part of it is, she loved her father. She said her mother drove him crazy. He was in the insurance business. He never did very well and the mother nagged him all the time to make more money and, well, you know how it goes. She never went to see her father in the asylum, though. She said she wouldn't have been able to stand seeing him locked up there like an animal, and furthermore she said he wasn't really her father anymore, his mind gone and all that. She talked a lot about him, how he used to take her to Coney Island and the Bronx Zoo and the Statue of Liberty and Bear Mountain, but the mother never went along with them. Yeah," Odum pursed his thin mouth, "I don't think a kid ever thought more of her father than Ruby did. She said she cried for a whole year after they locked him up in the asylum, and I believed her, too. She carried a picture of him in her wallet and she showed it to me. He had gray hair and was kind of stout, but not fat, and you could see from the picture that he was the dreamy type that would never amount to anything. She thought the world of him, though."

"Damn it!" Latham cried. "What are you telling me all this for?"

Odum turned over his hand in a peculiar gesture of intimacy as if he and Latham had become more than just casual acquaintances.

He took a breath and said, "Well, maybe because we both loved her. That must sound funny coming from me, but it's the truth. We loved her in different ways. She always seemed so damned young to me, young and scared and sick, and I wanted to help her get straightened out. I'm a bastard in a lot of ways, Latham, but if I had a family, I'd see that they got everything they wanted. Even a wild animal loves its young. Ruby wasn't my family, but sometimes I had the funny feeling that she talked to me as if I were her father. You know what I mean."

Latham said thickly, "You—you were the one who paid for her funeral then."

Odum's eyes widened just a trifle. "Who told you that?"

"Nobody. I wanted to take care of it, but Younk said it had already been paid and wouldn't give me the name."

"So you think I was the one?"

"Yes, damn it, I think so."

"Nobody'd believe it if you told them, Latham. They'd laugh in your face. Everybody knows I don't give anything away for nothing."

"I'm paying for it, you understand? How much was it—eight hundred? Nine hundred? A thousand? How much?"

Odum regarded Latham's flushed face reflectively. "Fifty-fifty," he said at length.

"I'm paying for the whole damn thing! How much?"

"Is there any sense in our fighting over this, Latham?" Odum asked very quietly. "I told you how I felt about Ruby, so give me the satisfaction of paying at least half. Give me that much. You and I were the only real friends Ruby had in the world, so let me do this last thing for her. I'm not trying to take anything from you, even the memory of her, but let me pay half."

Latham hesitated. "How much was it?"

The telephone rang before Odum could answer. When he hung up, he looked at Latham for a long silent moment and then he said, "Ross McElroy's dead. Somebody hung him on his closet door with an extension cord."

CHAPTER SEVEN

Latham stared. He said incredulously, "What!"

Odum's fingers drummed on the desk. "He's dead. Somebody hung him. It wasn't suicide. There wasn't any chair or anything around that he could have stood on."

"But when?"

"No more than two hours ago. What difference does it make? He's dead." Odum stood up. Now he was obviously impatient to be rid of Latham. "We'll talk about it some other time. I have to get back outside."

"Wait a minute," Latham stood up slowly. "Who was it that found him?"

"What difference—"

"Who just called you? The guy you sent out to warn McElroy that I was looking for him?"

Odum glanced toward the door and then shrugged. "Actually," he said, "I was doing you a favor. You were all set to beat McElroy up, and what good would that have done?"

"All I wanted to do was talk to him, damn it!"

"About what? Ruby? That would have done a lot of good, too. She didn't give a damn about him, and he didn't give a damn about her. As far as he was concerned, she was just another pushover, and that was the way he liked them. With him it was a different woman every night whenever he could manage it. Ruby was just one of the crowd. He couldn't have told you a thing about her or why she was killed or anything else. There was only one thing he cared about, and when he got it, he moved on to another woman. There was nothing there for you, Latham. Talking to McElroy would just have been a waste of time."

"You know," said Latham, dangerously calm, "there's nothing makes me so sore as people trying to tell me what to do and what not to do. I wanted to talk to McElroy, and you stalled me here till you could get him under wraps. I don't like that, Odum. I don't like that even a little bit. All that pitch you gave me about Ruby was just a stall."

"Put it that way if you want to," Odum said indifferently, "but you're still barking up the wrong tree. You think maybe he had something to do with killing Ruby. Pal, you couldn't be more wrong. In the first place, he didn't care enough about any woman to knock her off. And in the second place, he wasn't sick. He was on one of his periodic binges, and when he goes on a binge, Latham, all he does is lock himself in a room with a case of liquor and stay there till it's gone. I know all about it. He goes on one of those toots about twice a year, and if he weren't one of the best dice table men in the business, he'd have been out of here long ago. And, brother, when he gets that way, he can't move. It's one drink after another till he's paralyzed. He started drinking the night before Ruby was knocked off, and inside of four hours he couldn't have swatted a fly if it crawled under his hand, so just exactly what did you expect to get out of him? Hell, man, if you'd seen him tonight, he wouldn't have understood a word you said much less give you any answers. Whoever hung him on that door didn't have a bit of trouble. All they had to do was wind that extension cord around his neck and hoist him up. He couldn't have lifted a finger to defend himself. I've seen him in the middle of one of those toots, and I know."

"You know a lot about everybody."

The ghost of amusement appeared behind Odum's frozen smile. "In this business you can't afford to make mistakes about people. You, for instance. McElroy was one of the guys who had gotten to your girl friend, so tonight you got yourself an overdose of conscience because you kicked her out, and you were all set to beat the living daylights out of Ross McElroy. Well, I wasn't going to let you do that. His getting drunk is one thing; he usually sobered up in about a week and was back at work as good as ever. But having his ribs kicked in and winding up in the hospital is something else again. Let me emphasize, Latham, that I don't give a single solitary damn about Ross McElroy personally. If he didn't work here, you could beat his brains out, for all I care. But when he's on the job at the dice table, he's money in the bank for the house, and I wasn't going to let you ruin a good property for me. Now why don't you go home and get a good night's sleep and forget about Ross McElroy. There's nothing you can do about that now anyway, so forget it."

"And Ruby," said Latham in a savagely controlled voice, "you knew all about Ruby, too. Was she a property, a shill for the house, or were you one of the boys who had gotten to her, too? And don't try to tell me that you loved her like a father. I wouldn't believe it twice. What was it between you and Ruby? You know, as sick as she was, there were some men she wouldn't let lay a finger on her. Were you one of those men, Odum? Were you one of those who couldn't get to first base with her?"

Odum stiffened and seemed to grow larger and fill out the wrinkles in his badly fitting dinner jacket. His fixture, the frigid smile, was gone from his face, and his eyes were tiny, glittering points of jet in his pasty face.

"Go home, Latham," he said heavily. "Go home. All you want to do tonight is fight with somebody. Go home."

Latham placed both hands on the desk top and leaned forward over them, his own eyes glittering. "Or maybe it was something more, Odum. McElroy was getting to Ruby, and you couldn't stand that. In your book, McElroy was a jerk, but he had an inside track with Ruby and you didn't. Ruby was a girl who could drive you mad, sick as she was. She could keep you awake night after night and you'd just lie there in bed, clenching your fists and wanting to smash something. Was that the way it was with you, Odum? Did it just build up and build up till something exploded inside you? *Did you kill her, Odum? Did you have McElroy killed, too?"*

Odum swore harshly and swung his thick fist at Latham's face. Latham laughed as easily he warded off the wild blow, stepped to the corner of the desk and hit Odum savagely on the point of the chin. Odum's eyes glazed and he fell back against the wall. Latham hit him again and he slid slowly down the wall to the floor in a sitting posture, his helpless legs sprawled before him. But he was not unconscious. His eyes cleared and, though he could not move, he glared up at Latham with blazing hatred. His mouth twitched and he mumbled thickly.

Latham bent over him, his mouth a thin line of grim satisfaction. "What are you trying to say, Odum? Make it a little clearer. I can't hear you, and I'm interested. You're a great conversationalist, Odum, and I'm interested in everything you have to say. Is there something on your mind?"

Odum struggled and painfully he managed to whisper, "Sucker ..."

"Come on, Odum, you can do better than that. You were talking a blue streak only a few minutes ago. Don't you have any more to say about Ruby or McElroy? Come on, speak up. You have my undivided attention."

Odum closed his eyes and turned his head slightly away from Latham.

"Is that all, Odum?" Latham asked mockingly. "Are you all finished for the evening? Have you finally run down, all talked out? That's a pity because I was just getting started. Keep that in mind, Odum, I'm just getting started, and if I find out that you killed Ruby or had her killed, I'm going to nail you to the cross, so help me God. That's a definite promise. I'll get you if I have to go through that whole squad of watchdogs you keep around here."

Odum's eyes remained closed and he made no answer. There was not a sound in the little room except the breathing of the two men— Odum's shallow and rapid, Latham's slow and heavy. The office was windowless and the door was steel, and no sound came in from the outside. Latham stood up when it became apparent that Odum was not going to say anything further. Someone knocked on the door and Latham turned swiftly. The knock was repeated and Latham stooped and quickly patted Odum's armpit to see if he were carrying a gun. There was no gun. Latham pulled open the right-hand drawer of the desk, and there was a snub-nosed .38. He picked it up and went to the door. He opened it and stepped back and to one side. It was the cashier, a mild, bookkeeperish man with glasses. He was carrying a steel strongbox, obviously part of the night's receipts, and with him was one of the guards from the gambling room. The guard's hand darted inside his coat, but Latham lifted his gun and grinned.

"Come in, boys," he said softly. "Come in and close the door. This isn't a holdup, so let's leave guns out of it."

The cashier sidled into the room, clutching the strongbox, and the guard followed him slowly, his eyes never leaving the gun in Latham's hand. He kept his hands away from his sides and closed the door with his foot. Latham gestured with his gun.

"Over there against the wall, boys, and you can take your money box with you. I don't want any part of it."

The two men moved warily across the small room and stood with their backs against the tall green filing cabinets. The cashier's mild eyes widened when he saw Odum on the floor behind the desk. The guard's eyes flickered once in that direction, but returned immediately to the gun in Latham's hand. There was a heavy, clumsy noise of movement behind the desk and Latham took a step toward the door so that he could command the entire office.

A hand appeared over the edge of the desk, a forearm, and Odum painfully hoisted himself to his feet and stood there swaying, holding the edge of the desk with both hands. He put out one groping hand, felt the chair and sat down heavily. He looked at Latham and then at the two men backed against the steel filing cabinets.

"It could have been as easy as that," he said in a clotted voice. "He could have taken it away from you just as easy as that."

The cashier looked frightened, but the guard shook his head, "Not if you hadn't brought him in here yourself. I had my eyes open. You brought him in yourself and nobody came in after you. You've talked to people in here before."

"Why didn't you wait to bring in the cash?"

The cashier bleated, "But you made it a rule that every night at exactly—"

"Shut up. You didn't use your heads. You're finished here, both of you. You didn't use your heads, and I don't allow any mistakes, not even one."

Latham watched warily, hardly believing that Odum could be so coldly controlled. His only thought seemed to be for the efficiency of the organization he had built up in the Casino. Latham's presence was important only because it had showed a flaw in the routine. The two heavy blows in the face seemed to have been forgotten entirely, but Latham knew better when Odum turned his head and looked at him with smoldering eyes.

"Thanks for showing me the hole, Latham," he said. "But as for the rest of it, we'll take that up some other time."

"There's no question about that, Odum."

"No, there's no question about that, and you'd be doing yourself a favor if you went home now. I wouldn't come back here again if I were you."

"I'll be back. Don't worry about that."

"Suit yourself."

Latham's last glimpse of Odum as he backed through the doorway were those two black, pitiless eyes. No one stopped him on his way to his car in the parking lot.

CHAPTER EIGHT

McElroy had lived on the north end of Pelican Key, but Latham did not know exactly where the house was. However, Pelican Key was sparsely settled at that end because there were neither telephone nor power lines, though it was included on the rural free delivery route. There would be a mailbox on the road and Latham did not think that he would have much trouble finding the right cottage. He did not doubt that McElroy was dead and that he had been killed in exactly the way that Odum had described. Odum would not have lied about that. But Latham did not think the police had been notified, and he wanted to go through the cottage before the police cleaned it out. He was snatching at straws, he knew, but he had a feeling that the two killings were connected, and there just might be something in McElroy's cottage that could give him a lead. So far there was nothing to indicate why Ruby had been killed, and Wooten's story about a quarrel over a crap game did not make sense. There was a false ring about it. Ruby had not been a compulsive gambler and she had never cared enough about the game to quarrel over it. She liked the movement and excitement in the Casino, but she would never have played crap at home. It had to be something else, something else....

As he was approaching the causeway to Pelican Key, he heard a police siren keening behind him and he pulled over to the side of the road and turned off his lights. A minute later, a Sanibar police car flashed past him and thundered over the planked bridge. The key was out of the city limits but the sheriff's department might have called in the Sanibar police because the two deaths were linked. Latham swore softly. There was no point in going out to McElroy's cottage now. The place would be swarming with police, and when they got finished, there would be nothing left for him. They were not stupid and they would certainly pick up anything even remotely resembling a lead. McElroy had been one of the ill-fated Ruby's random lovers, and that would be enough to tie the two killings together.

Swearing monotonously and with futility, he turned his car and drove back to the dock in Sanibar and parked under the monstrous banyan tree. He was tired, and the back of his neck felt as if it had been locked in a garrote. He plodded up the dock, listlessly unbuttoning his shirt as he went. The thing to do now was go to bed and get some rest. He swore again when he remembered that the *Belan* had been chartered for a day of tarpon fishing and that he would have to be up by five-thirty. It was now after three. Inside the cabin of the boat, he threw his pants and shirt over the back of the tall chair at the wheel, dropped his shoes and socks on the deck and rolled into the bunk.

About a half hour later, still sleepless, he heard footsteps thumping hollowly on the dock and he sat up, listening. The footsteps stopped outside the boat. It was low tide and, peering through the port beside the bunk, he could see two pair of legs standing close together and could hear the voices. One was Hanna's and the other Keeler's. He could not distinguish the words, for the port was closed, but Keeler's voice sounded pitched in protest against something that Hanna was saying. Latham reached up and turned on the light. He opened the port.

"All right, come on in," he said. "Let's get it over."

By the time they walked to the stern of the boat and stepped down into the cockpit he had pulled on his swimming shorts and had lighted a cigarette.

Keeler looked as sloppy and sleepy as ever, still wearing the same wrinkled clothes, but Hanna's dark narrow face had a predatory sharpness as he looked quickly around the small cabin and ducked his head to enter through the low door.

"When did you get in?" he asked abruptly.

Latham, knowing what was coming, shrugged and said carelessly, "About a half hour ago. Why?"

"Where were you?"

Keeler stood unhappily in the doorway, slouched there, chewing on a toothpick. His hands were sunk in his pants pockets and he stared down at his dusty shoes. He looked once at Latham and shrugged as if to say that their coming had been none of his doing and that Hanna was the cause of it all.

"I was out at the Casino," Latham told Hanna. "You can check with Odum if you want. I was with him. We were having a little talk."

"Where were you before that?" Hanna stood at the opposite side of the narrow cabin, watching Latham intently.

From the tail of his eye, Latham saw Keeler shake his head and he said, "Here and there. I can't say exactly. I had a load on. I just sobered up a little while ago." He tilted his chin to indicate the coffee pot on the gasoline stove in the tiny galley. "The last gin mill I remember being in was the Cypress Room on West Orange Avenue. After that I was here on the boat and had some coffee, and then I went over to the Casino."

"Why'd you go to the Casino?"

"I wanted to talk to Ross McElroy, but Odum said he was out, sick, then later he told me he was off on one of his periodic binges, so I talked to Odum instead."

"About what?"

"Ruby, Hanna. We talked about Ruby, and we didn't call her a whore or a Jezebel or any of those things you called her, you bastard. We talked about how sick she was and how scared she was of going to a doctor because she was afraid he might tell her she was going crazy."

Hanna's face seemed a shade paler, but he said crisply, "What I thought of her is entirely immaterial. Why did you want to talk to Ross McElroy?"

"I wanted to talk to him about Ruby, too," Latham said, knowing that he was punishing Hanna with every mention of Ruby's name. "He was one of Ruby's pickups, one of the men she picked up when she couldn't help herself, or maybe he picked her up. He was that kind of guy. He'd pick up anything in skirts, just to add it to his score."

"You were sore at him. You wanted to do more than just talk to him, didn't you? You had an idea he might have been the one who was playing craps with her that night, and you thought maybe you could beat an admission out of him. Wasn't that the way it was, Latham? Wasn't that what you set out to prove?"

"But that's your job, isn't it, Hanna?" Latham drawled. "I'm not on the police force. I don't have to prove who killed Ruby. You're the one who has to dig into that muck, and I hope you enjoy every minute of it, talking about Ruby to all the bastards who took everything they could get from her. That's your job, friend."

Keeler sighed audibly and Hanna gave him a sharp, hard glance.

Then, suddenly wanting to end this, Latham said, "I know McElroy's dead. I was in Odum's office when he got the news. That was between two-thirty and three o'clock. Before that, your fat friend over there was tailing me around town, and it was about one-thirty when he followed me here to the dock. Right, Keeler?"

"Just about," Keeler sighed.

Hanna looked angrily at Keeler, who was again staring unhappily at his dusty shoes.

"Take his fingerprints," Hanna ordered.

Latham laughed without humor and submitted while Keeler squirted ink from his fountain pen on a sheet of paper from a small notebook and then took Latham's prints on other sheets of paper from the same notebook, identifying the prints of each finger in a surprisingly neat handwriting. The ink was black and the paper took perfect prints.

"Naturally," Latham said, "the killer left a perfect set of prints on the kitchen door, or was it on the toilet seat? You won't find my prints there, Hanna. I've never set foot in McElroy's cottage."

Keeler said mildly, "Talking to the Captain like that ain't going to do nobody no good, Joe, so why don't you cut it out? Do you think we're kicking around in the middle of the night and no sleep just because we like it? And you ain't got no alibi as far as I know. McElroy was knocked off around midnight."

"Let him talk," said Hanna. "Let him talk any way he wants." He was regarding Latham with a brooding expression which gave his dark, narrow face an edged fierceness. He shifted his glance to the fat, perspiring Keeler. "Wait for me at the car, Keeler. I'll be down in a few minutes."

Keeler's hands were shaking a little and he mumbled to Latham, "That ain't waterproof ink, Joe. You can wash it off with soap and water. I—didn't mess you up."

Latham knew then that Keeler was afraid he would force his alibi, for it had been just about midnight that Keeler had found him unconscious on the floor of Ruby's apartment and Keeler had not reported it to Hanna. Keeler was scared to death of what Hanna would do if he found out. He could scarcely deny it for the whole thing had undoubtedly been witnessed by Wooten, the besotted peeping Tom. Keeler was squirming. Latham looked down at his ink-stained fingers.

"No mess, eh? I can depend on that?"

"Sure, Joe."

"Good. Then it'll all come out in the wash."

Keeler said, "That's right," and sidled out of the small cabin putting his notebook with Latham's fingerprints back into the inside pocket of his wrinkled jacket. He stopped outside the doorway and looked back into the cabin, a little flustered, saying unnecessarily, "I'll be at the car, Captain." He still hesitated. "I'm clobbered," he mumbled. "I can hardly see straight." He closed the door and climbed clumsily up to the dock and Hanna and Latham listened to his receding footsteps.

Latham said, "You work your hired help too hard, Hanna. He didn't seem to know if he were coming or going. You'll have a nervous wreck on your hands if you're not careful."

Hanna said, "Don't worry about Keeler," but he gave the door a narrow, thoughtful glance.

Latham sat down on the edge of the bunk and lit a cigarette. "He's your worry, not mine, Hanna." He felt unutterably tired and he wanted to sleep.

Hanna stood for so long in silence that at length Latham looked up and said irritably, "Well, what is it? What do you want? Let's get it over so I can get back to bed."

"I was just wondering about you, that's all, Latham."

"Then go home and wonder. I want to go to sleep."

Hanna said softly, "You and McElroy were the most notorious of Ruby's seducers. You both flaunted her in public when everybody knew her for what she was. Now McElroy is dead. Has it occurred to you that you might be next, Latham?"

"Me?" Latham took a listless puff from his cigarette. "No. Why should it?"

"Your punishment will surely come. You've already begun to suffer. The mark is on your face."

Latham raised his head and looked at Hanna's taut face. "You're doing a little suffering over Ruby yourself, friend," he said dryly.

"You can't make me angry again, Latham. I pity you, that's all. However," his voice picked up a crispness, "there have been some further developments in Mays' death and—"

Latham jerked to attention. "Mays' *what?* You mean Stanley Wilfred Mays?" He tried to arrange the jumble in his sleepy mind. "The Mays who's treasurer of the bank? Dead?"

Hanna's face sharpened with suspicion. "You didn't know? It's been in the papers since yesterday afternoon."

"I haven't seen the papers. But how dead—"

Hanna shook his head. "He wasn't murdered. He did it himself. He went down to his beach house, locked himself in, put the muzzle of a shotgun in his mouth and pulled the trigger with his toe. In fact, you were in my office when I got the news."

Latham remembered now how Hanna had cut that interview short and had rushed out after barking a half dozen orders over the telephone. With a chill, he remembered, too, that Keeler had told him that Mays had been one of Ruby's lovers. He stared bleakly at Hanna with the question open in his face.

Hanna was inexorable and to Latham, sleep-drugged, the police captain seemed suddenly a tall, dark priest of a savage sect, towering there with the words of doom in his mouth.

Hanna said with slow emphasis, "It was Ruby again, Latham. He was another of her seducers, but snared in his own trap; calling it love, deluded, a vain and weak man, rotten inside. Ruby put the mark on all of you!" Then abruptly he was Hanna the policeman again. "But he didn't kill himself for love or grief. There wasn't enough to him for that.

The minute it was learned that he had blown his brains out, they started digging into the bank records. He embezzled something like two hundred thousand dollars out of trust funds and negotiable bonds left for collateral. The bank examiners were coming next week. He couldn't hide the theft any longer and he couldn't replace the money, so he committed suicide."

"The poor bastard," said Latham heavily. "The poor gutless bastard."

"Pity, Latham?" asked Hanna with thin irony. "Pity for a man who shared the bed of a harlot, a bed that you wanted all to yourself? Pity? You surprise me."

"You've got a lot of surprises in store for you, you cold-blooded crut," said Latham but without much interest. "You've got the surprise of your life in store for you someday. You're going to find out that you're not super-human but just plain human, or maybe sub-human, and all the pseudo-righteousness in the world won't help you then."

"The trouble with people like you, Latham, is that you think being human is an excuse for anything, and the worse it is the more you think it proves your case. However, Mays didn't die loving Ruby. He died hating her. He left a note cursing her and—" he made a contemptuous gesture with his long, narrow hand, "—practically naming her as his accomplice in the theft."

Latham started to his feet, his hands clenching his knees, but he sank back on the bunk. "He was a liar!"

"But why should he lie, Latham?" Hanna leaned forward, watching the other man narrowly. "He was about to commit suicide when he wrote that note, so what could he gain by lying?"

"He was excusing himself," said Latham angrily. "He took the money and spent it and couldn't stand the gaff. He was just excusing himself. He was lying."

Hanna shook his head. "Not this time, Latham. His whole life was a lie, yes, but he died with the truth. Every word, every curse in that note was the truth. He hated her for what she had done to him and for the theft itself. There was one line in the note, 'I gave you everything, damn you!' That wasn't a lie. He meant that."

"He was talking about something else," said Latham, tight-lipped.

"Oh no he wasn't. He meant the money. He stole it and gave it to her."

"She wouldn't have taken it, not Ruby."

"But she did take it. They were planning to live in South America. That was in the note. Ruby had the money when she was killed."

Latham said contemptuously, "It's easy to blame a dead woman. She can't defend herself. Ruby wouldn't have touched a penny—"

"How well did you know her during the past two months, Latham? She was drinking very heavily, every day. She drank so much that Mays couldn't keep her in the bank as his secretary any longer. She came in drunk every morning. She was following the familiar pattern of every tramp in the world, so why should it surprise you that she was an accomplice in a theft? She had rotted away inside and there wasn't even conscience left. You saw her last week in the Flamingo Bar, Latham—"

"And she was sober, damn it!"

Hanna shrugged. "According to the bartender, that was the second time she was there that day. She was in for lunch at about twelve-thirty and had four martinis before eating a sandwich. Which she didn't finish, by the way. How sober could she have been with four martinis and only a half sandwich in her stomach? Why did you meet her there that day, Latham?"

Latham said stolidly, "We went all through that once. I met her by accident and it was the first time in a year and a half. I was already there when she walked in. Ask the bartender. He heard the whole damn conversation. We were the only ones in the bar and his ears were standing out like a broken gate. Not that you haven't already questioned him up and down, crosswise and in and out. You know every word we said, so why go into it again?"

Hanna said, "Why indeed?"

"Or maybe you think she slipped me a suitcase containing the two hundred thousand. Naturally, the barkeep wouldn't have noticed a small thing like that, even though we opened it and counted all the money right on the bar. Of course we tipped the son of a bitch with a ten thousand dollar bill, and that's why he kept his mouth shut about it."

"Very amusing, Latham."

"I thought you'd die laughing."

Hanna regarded him for a long, somber moment, that brooding expression on his dark, narrow face again. Then he shrugged and stood away from the side of the cabin against which he had been leaning.

"The picture keeps changing all the time," he said in a musing tone, as if half to himself. "Right now you're just a little out of focus, Latham, but we'll bring you in again sharp and clear. You're part of it."

"Good night, Hanna."

Hanna nodded. "Good night, Latham." He walked to the door and went out and a few moments later Latham heard his footsteps moving briskly down the dock.

Latham sat motionless on the edge of the bunk, his hands dangling between his spread knees. He turned his arm and looked at his wrist watch. It was twenty minutes to five and in fifty minutes he would have to start readying the boat for Bispham.

He muttered, "The hell with that," and lurched heavily to his feet. He trudged down the dock to the public phone booth and called Bispham at the hotel. Bispham answered sleepily but became sharply indignant when Latham said that he could not take him out tarpon fishing that day.

Latham interrupted the sputtering to say curtly, "I'm sorry, Mr. Bispham, but there's been a death in the family."

He hung up and walked back to the boat. He took the first aid kit out of the locker in the galley. There were some pills for seasickness. He swallowed four of them with a glass of water. They would put him to sleep. He pulled the blind over the port and stretched out on the bunk, staring up at the ceiling and waiting for the first drowsy waves of sleep to come.

CHAPTER NINE

Latham awoke around noon and the first thing of which he was conscious was the rich fragrance of newly made coffee that filled the cabin. Puzzled, he sat up and sniffed and a gangling boy of sixteen with sun-bleached hair and a lean, solemn face, peered out of the galley at him. It was Chet Akin, the kid who went out on charters with him to bait hooks, cut bait, fetch beer from the ice chest, take the wheel if necessary, and otherwise to make himself generally useful.

"You been rakin' around for the last half hour, Cap'n," he said gravely, "so I thought I might as well boil up some coffee for when you came awake. Want a cup now? It's done."

Latham drowsily knuckled his eyes which felt as if someone had been dribbling sand into them all night. He felt sodden, too, heavy and listless. He nodded.

"Yeah, a cup of coffee would go good, kid," he said. "Black."

"And how about some bacon and eggs, Cap'n?"

"Nah, don't bother with it."

"No bother, Cap'n, no bother at all. They're right here and all I got to do's dump them in the frying pan. It'll only take a minute, Cap'n."

Latham saw that the boy was eager to perform this small service so he said, "Sure, that sounds good, kid," though he did not feel much like eating at the moment. "But the coffee first."

He sat up on the edge of the bunk, wondering why he felt so listless and sodden. Then he remembered the heavy dose of pills he had taken. They always left you feeling this way if you took too many of them, and he had taken four. The coffee would fix that up. The kid brought the coffee in a plastic cup. It was as black as tar, strong and hot, grainy from the flecks of coffee that floated in it. The kid had literally boiled it, disdaining the drip pot that stood on the small gasoline stove. Latham sipped gingerly at the scalding liquid and the boy lounged against the high chair at the wheel, regarding him with that solemn, sixteen-year-old gaze of his. He had on a pair of once-white tennis shoes, faded blue jeans and a white T-shirt. His hipless, boyish body was as lean and tough as piano wire. He had a deep affection for Latham which he disguised behind an elaborately casual manner.

"The bacon's doing," he informed Latham. "You look like you been up rasslin' alligators all night, Cap'n."

The coffee was flooding out the sodden drowsiness and Latham said, "That I was, Chet, that I was. Big ones and little ones. I think I won, but I'm not sure."

"Aaaah, you wouldn't have no trouble with 'gators, Cap'n. I rassled one onct and all the thing wanted to do was go to sleep."

"Sure. And then you woke up."

"No, honess to God, Cap'n," the boy said earnestly, "I rassled one onct. A six-footer, down one of them Seminole villages on the trail. A friend of mine, Joe Meola, he's an Indian, he took me down. There ain't nothing to rasslin' a 'gator. All you got to do is not let them sock you with his tail. Joe said he got a broken leg that way onct."

Latham looked incredulously at the slim, still unformed boy. *My God*, he thought, *this must be a tougher generation than the one I grew up in.*

"You're a better man than I am, kid," he said. "I wouldn't grapple one off those lizards if you paid me."

"You wouldn't have no trouble, Cap'n, not with your build. They're only mediocre. I could show you how in just a couple minutes."

Latham knew that the kid was bursting with pride, so he shook his head and said, "No thanks, Chet. I'll do all my 'gator wrestling in my sleep. That way nobody gets hurt. Say, this is good coffee, kid. How's the rest of it coming?"

The boy gave the galley a startled glance and fled to the stove, swearing luridly. Latham chuckled. The kid had the words, but the tune was all wrong. It was a phase that would pass. A few minutes later the boy returned to the cabin with a plate on which the creamy scrambled eggs were garnished with strips of crisply brown bacon and buttered toast. He lounged against the chair at the wheel again.

"It's only mediocre," he said. "What you ought to have with that is grits." Then quickly, before Latham could praise the food, he asked, "What happened to Mr. Bispham. He PO on us?"

"I cancelled the charter," said Latham, eating hungrily. The kid was really a good cook. And a good kid, too.

"Yeah, I kind of figured."

"You did? Why?"

"Oh," and the boy looked embarrassed, "on account of what was in the papers this morning."

Latham paused with a forkful of scrambled eggs half way to his mouth. "What was in the papers this morning?"

"Well—maybe I ought to let you see it."

"Yeah, let's see it."

Chet went into the galley and came back with the morning edition of the *Sanibar News*, which he handed Latham with the same air of embarrassment.

Latham finished his bacon and eggs and then opened the paper. As he expected, the killing of McElroy was the lead story on the first page, and there was nothing in that that he did not already know. The secondary story, run as a sidebar to the McElroy murder, concerned the suicide and embezzlements of Stanley Wilfred Mays from the South County Bank, the figure being given as approximately two hundred thousand dollars. The story quoted Captain Hanna, who linked Ruby with both the embezzlement and the murder of McElroy, though the statement was so vaguely worded that there was no real information in it. At the end of that was a rehash of the killing of Ruby, and then Latham saw the paragraphs that had embarrassed young Chet Akin.

Captain Hanna disclosed also that on the eve of her death, Ruby Lake had written three unfinished notes to her former fiancé, Joseph Latham, captain of the charter boat *Belan*. The notes, found in the wastebasket of the girl's apartment, according to Hanna, indicated that the girl was attempting a reconciliation with Latham, although they had never been mailed. Hanna said further that the handwriting of the notes showed plainly that Ruby Lake had been under great emotional strain whet she wrote them.

Hanna commented only briefly on the fact that the girl was attempting a reconciliation with Latham while she was still Mays' paramour and had been an accessory to the embezzlement. 'Latham denies that any reconciliation took place or was even attempted to his knowledge,' he said.

The story concluded with another statement from Hanna. "Of course we questioned Latham, just as we have been questioning everybody who was or had been associated with the girl, but he is no more a suspect than anyone else. Our primary concern in the Mays suicide is to find out what happened to the two hundred thousand dollars, and to date we have found no trace of it."

Latham folded the paper thoughtfully and laid it on the bunk beside him. He lit a cigarette. "Any more coffee, kid?"

"Sure, a whole potful, Cap'n," the kid said eagerly. He snatched up the empty cup and darted into the galley.

When he came back, Latham took a sip of the steaming coffee before asking, "Now what was there in the paper that made you think I'd cancel Bispham's charter, kid?"

"Oh—nothing," the boy said evasively, his face flushing a little. "Just the way they put it, I guess."

"I didn't see anything wrong with the way they put it. And what are you getting yourself in an uproar about?"

The boy's face was crimson and he blurted, "They put it like you had something to do with it, stealing that money from the bank, I mean."

"Your imagination's running away with you, kid. They didn't put it that way at all." Latham was watching the boy narrowly. "Whatever gave you that idea?"

"Well, they hinted, didn't they?"

"They didn't even hint, as far as I could see, so what's it all about?"

"But that's the way they put it!"

The boy was very agitated and, for the first time, Latham noticed a slightly swollen bruise on his tanned left cheekbone.

"Come clean, kid," he said. "You didn't read that in the paper. It's something somebody said to you. Right?"

"Well—you know how some guys talk."

"What guys?"

"Just some guys downtown. Dopes. Who cares what they say?"

"But you got in a fight about it."

"Well, I kind of took a poke at this one jerk. I never liked him anyway. He thinks he's real cool but he ain't even mediocre."

"What did he say, Chet?"

The boy was in an agony of embarrassment and his face and neck were fiery. "Well—" He looked everywhere in the cabin but at Latham, twisting his long, lean hands together, pulling at his knuckles. "It's just a lot of flap, Cap'n, that's all. They, well, they said you and that Miss Lake kind of got together and took old man Mays for all that money. See what I mean? It's just a lot of flap. I know you wouldn't do nothin' like that, and these dumb guys, they don't know you, and they're just repeating a lot of stuff they heard around, that's all." He raised his eyes and for a moment looked appealingly at Latham, begging him not to continue the questioning any longer, and begging also for a word of reassurance, something that he could fling back into the teeth of the adolescent gossip-mongers.

"It's just as you say, kid," said Latham, speaking very carefully, "it's just a lot of flap. In a case like this, everybody concerned is bound to get himself talked about. It's to be expected. People like to talk about the things they read in the newspapers. Sometimes it's foolish talk, and sometimes it's all right. Neither the police or the newspaper said I had anything to do with that stolen money. People just made that up. Somebody probably said to somebody else, 'That Latham guy, he knows more than he's telling.' Well, the police know everything I know, which isn't much, and if they thought for a minute that I knew anything about that money I'd be down at headquarters with a half dozen cops firing questions at me from all angles. So when you hear anymore flap, kid, don't pay any attention to it. It isn't worth getting in an uproar about. Okay?"

"Sure, Cap'n. But it's just that—well, I won't, that's all."

"And don't get in any more fights either."

"Aaaah, that wasn't a fight, Cap'n," the boy grinned suddenly. "I smacked him, he smacked me, I smacked him and he smacked the dirt. You couldn't call that a fight."

"Well, no more of it, anyway, unless you want to make me sore."

"Is that an order, Cap'n?" Chet was grinning widely now, happy that Latham had confided in him.

Latham stood up and stretched. "I'm going to take a swim, kid, and then I have to go into town for a while." Then, seeing the disappointment in the boy's face, he added, "But I'd like you to stay aboard in case anybody comes up for a charter. We're open tomorrow and the next day, but booked solidly for a week after that."

"Sure, Cap'n," the boy said eagerly. "And the decks could stand a washing and I could polish up some of the chrome and a couple other things around."

Latham tousled the kid's sun-bleached hair and said, "I'm glad I got somebody I can trust aboard," knowing that the boy would have spent every waking hour on the *BeIan* if permitted. He put on his trunks, went out to the deck and dove over the side into the clear, warm water of the bay, swimming in lazy circles. When he climbed back aboard, Chet was washing the forward deck with fresh water out of the hose from the dock. Latham grinned affectionately at him and went into the cabin to dress.

Before he left for town, he said to the kid, "Take care of anything that comes up, Chet, okay?" knowing that the request, which really meant nothing, would keep the boy as happy as a dog in a boneyard for the rest of the day.

As he walked down the dock he kept thinking of Chet. The kid had attached himself to the boat about six months before just by hanging around and running an errand or two, gradually working himself aboard until he was now the "mate." And the affection wasn't all one-sided, either. It was almost like having a kid of your own, with everything that went with it, the responsibility included, and it was a good feeling, too. What was it about strays, human or animal, that brought out the paternalism or maternalism in people?

As he approached his car parked under the leafy spread of the huge, exotic banyan tree, he saw a police car drawn up beside it and then made out Keeler sitting behind the wheel, nervously smoking a cigarette, which he flipped away the moment he saw Latham approaching. The detective beckoned furtively and Latham walked over to the side of the police car. Keeler looked terrible in the light of day. His face was pouched and had faint discolorations of yellow and red. His eyes were bloodshot and the pouches under them were a mottled brown.

"What'd Hanna have to say after I left last night?" he asked quickly. "He didn't say a damn word to me all the way back to Headquarters, and then he just told me to go home and go to bed."

Latham could see that the man was frightened, but he had no pity for Keeler. He shrugged. "We didn't talk about anything you can't read in the paper this morning. It's there."

"Is that all? I mean, he didn't say anything about me after I left?"

"No."

Keeler let out a heavy breath of relief. "You know, I didn't sleep a wink. I thought sure you'd spilled to him about me finding you in Ruby's place, and that would of meant my neck. So thanks, pal, I won't forget it."

"Don't worry. You won't forget it—pal. Just pray that I won't need you for that alibi for midnight last night, because it'll be your neck and not mine."

"Sure, Joe, sure, but you can forget that angle. I'll steer Hanna clear of that."

Latham rested his hands on the sill of the car window and looked steadily into Keeler's puffy, anxious face.

"You know something?" he said at length. "You're one cute son of a bitch."

Keeler grinned wanly. "Hell, I've been handling Hanna all my life. I can lead him around by the nose."

"I'm not talking about Hanna. I'm talking about a little matter of about two hundred thousand dollars."

Keeler blinked. "Two hundred thousand—oh, you mean that chunk Mays carved out of the bank. What's that got to do with it?"

"You wouldn't know?"

Keeler shook his head, his face loose. "I don't get your pitch, Joe." His expression was that of puzzlement heavily larded with fatigue, his eyes hiding behind drooping lids.

to This time Latham was not at all fooled. He had not been fooled by Keeler before but the issue had been obscured behind a cloud of devious words that had masked the real motives.

"I kind of remember a pitch you gave me last night," he drawled. "It was really inspiring: we're working for the same thing, we both want to get Ruby's killer, so let's work together, hand in hand, or something. It was quite a pitch. You did everything but raise your right hand and recite the Boy Scout Oath. Remember, Tubby?"

"Why sure, Joe, and it still goes, every word of it. I wasn't giving you a pitch."

"Not at all, Tubby—except maybe for one little item, that part about Ruby's safe deposit box. Let me see now, it was something about Ruby blackmailing somebody who had written her some Indian love lyrics which she had salted away in a bank someplace. That was it, wasn't it? This alleged guy had written her some alleged love letters and she had him on the hook because he was married and she was putting the squeeze on him. I've got it straight now, haven't I, Tubby?"

Keeler's eyes were bright, malicious slits behind his heavy lids, but when he spoke, his voice was earnest and still a little puzzled.

"It was an idea I had, sure, Joe. It might not have worked out, but you have to cover all the angles."

"That's right, and you even tossed me the names of three married men in the important money bracket who might have written her those tender little notes. You covered that angle like a blanket."

"So?"

"Of course you had no thought of that two hundred thousand dollars. Or don't you believe that Mays gave her that money, the way your boss does?"

Keeler spread his hands on the wheel. "Nobody hands a dame two hundred grand, Joe," he said blandly.

"Hanna thinks so. Or maybe it's just that he has a low, suspicious mind."

"Even a damn fool wouldn't give a dame two hundred grand. Mays wasn't a damn fool. It's only a side issue anyway, unless—" he added significantly, "—somebody thought she had it and that's why she got knocked off. There's another angle, Joe."

"You've got more angles than a billiard game, haven't you? But tell me something, suppose I did come up with the name of Ruby's bank, exactly how did you expect to get the money out of that safe deposit box? There'd be a line of witnesses from here to Miami. How'd you expect to get away with it? Or do you have an angle on that, too?"

"You've got it all wrong, Joe. All I'm interested in is the guy that knocked—"

"Don't give me any more of that!" Latham said violently, "You've had your eye on that money from the minute you heard about it, and you tried to suck me in. Well the hell with you, Keeler. I'm warning you off. Don't come around me again with any more angles or, by God, I'll stuff them down your throat!"

Keeler sighed as if he were too tired to defend himself. "I don't think that dough's ever going to turn up, Joe. I think Mays futzed it away one way or another, stocks and bonds, the ponies, the wheel out at the Casino, or a half dozen other ways, but I know damn well he didn't just turn it over to any dame, lock, stock and barrel. No guy could be that dumb."

Latham said, "Oh hell," and turned his back and walked to his own car, smoldering, paying no attention when Keeler called after him, "Think it over, Joe, and you'll see I'm right."

Latham backed his car and drove out of the lot without giving Keeler another glance. The anger in him was a slow-burning bed of coals. Ruby was dead but they were still fingering the corpse, prying and poking at it, turning in their obscene ghoul hands to see what more they could get from it, as if she hadn't given far too much when she was alive. Keeler was after the money, all right. Then another thought struck Latham and he said, "By God!" There was Odum, too, and that odd and unexpected friendliness of his last night. Odum would have known of the money. Two hundred thousand dollars floating around loose was a rotten plum that would attract a lot of flies. *If* it was floating around loose. Ruby would never have touched that money. Never. Mays had gambled it away or spent it, but Keeler was right about one thing, he would never have handed it over to Ruby as if it were a box of candy or a bouquet.

He glanced in his rearview mirror to see if Keeler were following him again, but he could not spot the police car in the line of light traffic behind him. He drove to the garden apartments where Ruby had lived and parked around the corner from it in the shade of a live oak. A squirrel dashed frantically across the sidewalk, leaped for the tree and peered brightly at Latham around the trunk, making small chittering noises. Latham lit a cigarette and looked at it, shaking his head.

"Not yet, squirrel," he said. "I'm not ready for your warehouse yet."

He got out of the car and walked around the corner to the entrance of the apartments. Wooten's apartment was directly across the small patio from Ruby's, Keeler had said. There was a small vestibule and Wooten's door was on the right. Latham pushed the buzzer and waited. There was no answer and he pushed the buzzer again, listening with his ear close to the panel of the door. He heard a radio faintly playing hillbilly music, but there was no other sound. He tried the knob and the door opened. Suspecting that Wooten was napping in the midst of his perennial drunk, Latham walked into the apartment, closing the door behind him. This was an efficiency unit, smaller than Ruby's apartment. There was one large room, fourteen by eighteen, with a kitchenette and a bath off the side of it. There was a rumpled bed against the wall beside the door, beyond that a dinette table with four chairs, and under the wide window, facing Ruby's apartment, was a studio couch on which Wooten lay sleeping, breathing shallowly as if panting. He was a skinny, gray-faced man, unshaven, clad only in a pair of dirty light blue walking shorts. The ribs plainly slatted his almost emaciated chest and he looked sick. He twitched continually as he slept and occasionally an unintelligible mumble bubbled from his slack mouth. On the floor before the studio couch were two empty bottles of bargain rum and an almost full can of tuna fish with a spoon lying across it, Wooten's untasted lunch or breakfast or it might even have been his dinner from the night before. A souse like Wooten would not eat if he could avoid it.

Latham did not attempt to wake him up immediately but went into the kitchenette, which was off the living room at the foot of the studio couch. It was a tiny room into which was crammed an electric stove, a sink, a dish closet and a refrigerator. There was a pot on the stove, half full of soup, and beside it was a loaf of bread, long stale. On the shelf of the dish closet was an opened can of beef stew, but it was full and had not been touched and the top of it was green with mold. Apparently Wooten stirred himself once in a while to make a gesture toward eating, but probably had gone right back to the bottle for another drink or two or three and drowned out his appetite. There were over twenty empty rum bottles on the floor of the kitchen. Latham looked into the refrigerator. It contained nothing but a gallon jug of port wine, but on the shelf over the refrigerator he spied a large jar of instant powdered coffee. That was the thing for which he had been looking. When he awakened Wooten, he wanted to feed him strong, hot coffee to snap him out of that hangover. If possible. People like Wooten did not have hangovers. They were just perpetually drunk. He put some water on the electric range to boil and then went back into the living room. Wooten had turned and was now sleeping on his back, snoring hoarsely through his open mouth. His legs were the white of peeled potatoes, so skinny that his bony knees looked like deformities. There were more empty bottles on the living room floor—beside the bed, beside the rocking chair, beside the lounge chair. There was an empty bottle wherever Wooten could sit and reach it.

The room had the sickly-sour smell of undigested rum fumes, soiled bedding, and a body that had long been without a bath or a shower. Latham grimaced and opened the casement windows. A bit of paper fluttered from the dinette table and Latham bent automatically to pick it up. He saw with a slight shock that it was a picture of Ruby, clipped from a newspaper. It was just her neck and head clumsily cut from the paper with a pair of scissors. He glanced at the table. It was covered with pictures of girls torn from magazines—girls in bathing suits, girls from lingerie ads, girls with their skirts lifted to show and advertise stockings. And there were several other neck-and-head pictures of Ruby, clipped from newspapers. Wooten had carefully placed these pictures over the faces of the girls in the advertisements, and Ruby's face looked up at him from incongruous bodies in various stages of undress. The texture and color of the heads cut from the newspapers did not match the glossy white paper of the magazines from which the other pictures had been torn, and the display was too unreal and childish to be obscene. It was morbid, but mostly fumbling and sad. Some of the bodies were too small for the heads, though apparently this had made no difference to Wooten's sodden mind. In the very center of the table, as if in a place of honor, was a picture in color in a rich green evening gown standing against a glowing red velvet drape. Ruby's newspaper face looked gray and macabre against the living colors, though it had probably been beautiful to Wooten's bleary eyes.

Latham raised his arm as if to sweep the pictures from the table, then slowly lowered it and looked at the wasted figure crumpled on the studio couch. "You poor son of a bitch," he thought. Of all the people who had used Ruby one way or another this clumsy array of the drunkard's was probably the most harmless. There was not a nude among them, though magazines of "art" poses could be bought for a half dollar apiece at almost any magazine stand in the city. Wooten had not done that to Ruby, and the picture of the girl in the rich green evening gown showed that in some way Wooten had not wanted to shame her, even if only in secret and only to himself.

Latham went back into the kitchen. The water was boiling. He took a cup from the dish closet and put two heaping teaspoons of powdered coffee into it. He poured the water over it and carried it into the living room. He put the cup on the floor and sat on the edge of the studio couch. Wooten did not at first respond when Latham shook him, but by degrees he opened his melancholy bloodshot eyes and looked numbly at Latham. He tried to close his eyes again, but Latham sat him propped against the back cushions and picked up the cup of strong coffee from the floor.

"Come on," he said, holding the cup to Wooten's bloodless lips, "drink it down but take it easy. It's hot."

Wooten tried feebly to push the cup away, but Latham made him drink it, sip by sip. Wooten did not utter a word all this while, and Latham had an idea that he was accustomed to having someone feed him coffee from time to time in the vain effort to sober him up. He just kept staring at Latham with lacklustre, incurious eyes.

"Now how do you feel?" asked Latham when the coffee was gone.

Wooten drew a shuddery breath. "Sick," he mumbled.

"Want to go to the bathroom?"

Wooten nodded dully and when Latham took his arm to help him up, he said, "I can make it."

"I'll make you another cup of coffee if you're going to vomit that one up."

Wooten shrugged and stumbled across the room to the bathroom. There was enough hot water left for another cup of coffee, and Latham made it just as strong as the first. Wooten seemed a little better when he came out of the bathroom, but he was very shaky and sat down on the couch as if collapsing. Latham again had to hold the cup for him as he drank. Wooten's hands fluttered like dying butterflies.

"Just a little at a time," he mumbled. "I don't want to get sick again. What do you want, anyway? People always want something when they try to sober me up."

"I'm a friend of Ruby Lake's."

An odd gleam appeared momentarily in Wooten's blurred eyes. "She had no friends," he said thickly.

"I was a friend of hers all the same. I tried to help her, but I didn't go about it the right way."

Wooten peered hazily at him for several seconds and finally shook his head. "I don't remember you."

"It was a year and a half ago, before you moved in here."

"Oh."

"Captain Hanna said you saw a man with Ruby the night she was killed."

"He did?" A spasm convulsed Wooten's face and he choked. "Excuse me." He pushed himself up from the couch and lurched across the room and into the bathroom again. He was in there about five minutes and looked much better when he came out.

"Sorry," he said to Latham, "but I haven't eaten anything today and the coffee must have hit me the wrong way. I think I'll be all right now," he laughed shakily. "Lord knows there's nothing left to come up out of me." With the thickness gone from his voice, he spoke softly and quietly and with an intonation of a cultural and educated man.

He sat in the rocking chair that obliquely faced the couch on which Latham was sitting. "Yes," he said, "I did see a man with Ruby that night. I told Captain Hanna about it. They were kneeling on the floor and playing crap. May I have the coffee, please. I'll see if I can keep it down this time."

Latham handed him the cup. "I was told that you thought there was something familiar about the man you saw with her that night."

"I think I remember saying something like that, but," and his mouth bunched with sardonic self-scorn, "as you have probably deduced from the number of empty bottles lying around this hutch, I am a confirmed and dedicated alcoholic. I'm not apologizing, Mr.—?"

"Latham. Joe Latham."

"Mr. Latham?" A small frown clouded Wooten's eyes. "The name sounds familiar. Ruby must have spoken of you, or perhaps it was someone else. Things have a tendency to become vague, but it doesn't really matter. What was I saying? I think I was propounding something of importance. Oh yes, the bottles." He waved a limp hand to indicate the empty bottles lying on the floor. "I was making the somewhat redundant observation that I am a dedicated and unapologetic alcoholic," he laughed shortly. "I drink because I like to drink, Mr. Latham, and not because of any great tragedy in my life, no blighted love, no ruined career. Everyone has his own notion of utopia, and I have found that it can be most easily achieved through the consumption of alcoholic beverages. Of course, it does odd things to the body and possibly the mind, but it takes the spirit at least to the gates of paradise and sometimes the gates open for a while."

"I think you should eat something," Latham said. "Do you want me to go out and get you some eggs and milk and vegetable juice and some things like that?"

"Later, later. I was trying to make a point, but it seems to have evaded me for the moment."

"You told Captain Hanna that there was something familiar about the man who was with Ruby that night. I want to find out what it was."

"Are you with the police, Mr. Latham?"

"No, I—"

"Yes, yes, I remember. You are a friend of Ruby's. You see, I can remember some things if I make an effort, though it usually isn't worth it."

"Do you remember anything about this man? Was he tall or short, fat or thin, dark or blond? Maybe it was voice you heard, or maybe it was the way he moved his arms."

Wooten shook his head. "Frankly, Mr. Latham," he said ruefully, "I don't even recall telling Captain Hanna that there was, as you put it, something familiar about the man. That is one of the penalties of approaching paradise. Mundane things have a tendency to lose any semblance of importance, and one forgets all too easily. I may have told the Captain that I thought the man familiar, and someday I might even remember what it was, but I doubt it. My memory has ceased to be a pack rat, storing useless odds and ends in a cluttered nest. My memory has wings ..."

"Then you're not even sure there was a man with Ruby that night," Latham said impatiently, "or it may have been another night that you saw them. It might even have been a month ago, or you might have dreamed up the whole thing!"

Wooten smiled, gently and sadly. "No, I didn't dream it up, Mr. Latham. And I remember the date very clearly because earlier in the evening Ruby brought me a bowl of chicken soup and a small casserole made, as I recall, of elbow macaroni, ground beef, mushroom sauce, onion and grated cheese. You see, my memory does function. At times, at times. Every once in a while Ruby would do that, bring dinner to me and sit with me until I ate it, and I have never forgotten any of the times she did that, Mr. Latham. In a way, our spirits were very much alike, Ruby's and mine, both seekers after a random paradise."

"You're positive of that—the date?"

"Beyond any shadow of doubt, Mr. Latham. You see, I was sober for a while and I resented it. After Ruby left, that is. If she had stayed ..." He made a vague, dismissing gesture with his skinny hand. "But it wouldn't have made any difference really, even if she had stayed. However, when she left I opened a fresh bottle of rum and lay down on the couch on which you are now sitting. I have found that it is much easier to slip from one world and into another while lying down. I was approaching the most delightful stage when the spirit begins to become less body-bound when I noticed a light in Ruby's apartment. This was unusual, for she was seldom at home at night. So I glanced across the patio and saw her and, well, her gentleman friend kneeling on the floor and apparently playing crap and quarreling."

"How were they quarreling?" Latham asked quickly, knowing how easily Wooten went off on by-paths and lost the point of what he was saying.

"We-ll ..." Wooten pursed his lips. "The gentleman's voice sounded loud and angry and Ruby sounded not exactly frightened, but she seemed to be pleading with him to stop the quarrel. I remember thinking how odd it was that anyone should want to play crap with Ruby and actually quarrel over the game. She was a beautiful woman, Mr. Latham, and it struck me that to play games was such a waste of time, don't you think? I mean, it seemed so childish, or perhaps I mean irrelevant."

"Go on," said Latham woodenly. "How did the quarrel end?"

"Then Ruby became angry and I heard her say very clearly, 'I don't want to hear any more. I'm going to have a drink!' and she walked into what I believe is the kitchen of her apartment. The gentleman followed her. He seemed to be pleading with her. I could not hear what he was saying, but I judged that he was pleading from the motions he made with his hands. I watched for a while but they did not come back into the living room. I heard Ruby's voice just once more. She said irritably, 'Stop it please, I'm sick of it.' Apparently he stopped for I did not hear their voices again. They stayed in the kitchen and I decided that the quarrel was over and that they were having a drink on it. So I lay back and ..." He smiled dreamily and indicated the bottles on the floor. "Let's say I had a drink with them."

He looked into his coffee cup, which was still almost full, and raised it to his mouth. He took two swallows but gagged on the second and hurriedly put the cup down on the floor beside him.

"Excuse me, please," he said and made a beeline for the bathroom, closing the door behind him.

Latham sat staring down at his hands. There was no doubt that Wooten had seen Ruby and a man in her apartment on the night of the killing. Ruby had been killed in the kitchen of her apartment and Wooten's story of the quarrel gave the background, though Latham did not understand that dice game at all. It wasn't just odd; it was crazy. But Wooten had been admittedly drunk. That business about the spirit becoming less body-bound was nothing but double-talk. Wooten had been pretty well soused, though his account of the quarrel seemed clear enough. Latham turned his head and looked across the patio at the windows of Ruby's apartment. They were no more than thirty feet away. With the light on in Ruby's living room, the features of both Ruby and the man would have been very plain—yet Wooten could not describe the man who had been with her for the simple reason that he probably hadn't been able to see straight. Wooten's testimony, even if he finally did manage to remember what had been familiar about the man, would be worthless in court. Even a fair defense attorney would make hash out of him in thirty seconds.

Good God, thought Latham disgustedly, *even I wouldn't believe him now if he put the finger on the guy and swore on a case of Scotch!*

Still, he waited for Wooten to return from the bathroom. Wooten was in there about ten minutes and then the toilet flushed and the man came back into the living room. There was some color in his face and he seemed much revived.

"I'll have to eat something in a little while, Mr. Latham," he said, reseating himself in the rocking chair. "But I'll walk down to the store and get it myself. Once in a while I do like a breath of fresh air. Not too often, mind you, but once in a while it's rather pleasant in a depressing sort of way. Whenever I take a walk, I'm always very glad to get back to my apartment."

"Did you see them leave the apartment by any chance?" Latham asked.

"No, I thought they were pleasantly drinking in the kitchen so I lay back on my couch and pleasantly drank here, to join them *in absentia*, so to speak. She was a lovely, beautiful, tragic girl, Mr. Latham, beautiful and sweet and lovely," Wooten said dreamily. "She used to bring me dinner once in a while. Did I tell you? She did. Once she brought me a bowl of Bahamian fish chowder and a broiled red snapper filet and a carton of coffee. She had bought it especially for me in the Fishhouse Grill, a fine place to eat. I ate there many times when I was interested in eating, though it seems such a waste of time these days. She was a lovely, beautiful, sweet girl and she used to talk to me by the hour. She would sit beside me and hold my hand and talk to me in that lovely, clear, high, sweet voice of hers. She called me Eugene. I never liked the name until she used it. Nobody ever called me Eugene except Ruby. Everybody else called me Gene. But she called me Eugene. She used to bring dinner to me once in a while. I recall a bowl of Spanish bean soup and a lovely steaming platter of shrimp enchilada. I never told her that I loathed shrimp. They always reminded me of insects. But we talked and talked and talked. She had a beautiful voice, low and rich like a 'cello. She told all about her friends and how happy she was—"

"Did she say who she was meeting that night?" Latham interrupted quickly.

"That night?" Wooten looked a little confused as if the sound of Latham's voice had broken a trance. "Oh, that night. She did mention a name. An old friend, she said, an old delinquent friend. The name is right on the tip of my tongue. Latham, that was it. Latham, a delinquent friend. He wanted to help her but he went about it the wrong way."

"You damn fool," said Latham angrily, "*I'm* Latham, and that's just what *I* told you."

"Well, perhaps it was another name then. But it was of no importance. I did not love her friends. I loved her. She used to come to me in the night, wraith-like through the walls and shimmer above me on a bed of moonlight and say, 'I love you, Eugene.' Did I tell you that she used to bring dinners to me? Clam chowder and filet mignon. I told her of how I had found the way to paradise and she wanted to lie beside me and hold to me while my spirit took wing, but something happened, I don't know—" Wooten looked confused and troubled. "Something, something. Something very bad. Did you say your name was Latham? It sounds very familiar. I think she spoke of you, but I hope you'll pardon me if I say that I wasn't much interested. She was as beautiful as a dream woven of snowflakes. Do you know something? I dream of snow quite a lot, lovely white soft snow. Snow in drifts or falling from the sky like frozen kisses, and snow a bed for Ruby and me, a lovely world of pure white snow. Ruby and I talked often of the snow. She felt about snow the way I did, to lie in it and dream."

He pushed himself up from his chair and stood there for a moment with a vague, half formed smile on his lips. "Excuse me, please," he said and walked to the bathroom, staggering just a little. Latham stared after him and then jumped up and strode to the bathroom door. Wooten was standing in the middle of the small tiled room with a bottle of rum tilted to his mouth, drinking greedily. He swayed and put out one hand to the wash basin to steady himself. He was quite drunk, and Latham knew that this was the reason for those frequent trips to the bathroom. Wooten was suddenly aware of Latham and his eyes became stricken.

"Just—just a little pickup," he stammered.

Latham said, "You poor son of a bitch," and walked of the apartment.

CHAPTER TEN

As Latham drove away from under the shade of the live oak he thought he had a glimpse of a police car behind but when he turned the street was empty except for a lumbering orange-colored delivery truck of the Palm Dairy. He was almost certain he had seen a black sedan with the police insignia on the door, but after that slightly nightmarish session with Wooten he could easily have imagined it. After a session with Wooten you could imagine almost anything. Wooten, who longed to die and was killing himself with alcohol.

Latham drove slowly, pondering over the crap-shooting scene. It still made no sense to him. It was possible, of course, that the man had been McElroy. McElroy had been a gambler by profession and compulsion. He would gamble on anything and it was well known around town that many times he had gone straight from the Casino to a stud game or a crap game in one of the hotel rooms and had played right through until it was time for him to go to work at the dice table in the Casino again. No matter what bar he went into, he would inevitably offer to match coins with the bartender for the drinks, double or nothing, and once when cashing a check at the bank had made the teller the same offer— double or nothing. And he always had a pair of dice in his pocket, and there was the classic bit of gossip that once he had gotten a parking ticket and had gone straight to the chief of police and had rolled the dice across the desk blotter with the words, "Be a sport, chief. The best two out of three rolls, double or nothing." It was said that the chief had accepted and lost, throwing a six and a four against two sevens by McElroy, but Latham knew that this story was pure fabrication. Chief Hulse was a hard-bitten, humorless cop and he would have had McElroy thrown out of Headquarters on his ear had such an offer ever been made. Still, McElroy's reputation was such that many people actually believed every word of it and repeated it at every opportunity as a good joke on the chief.

But it was possible that McElroy had offered to roll the dice with Ruby for something or other that night. Perhaps Ruby wanted to go out and McElroy wanted to stay in the apartment. That would have been like McElroy, too. He could not be with a woman for five minutes without making a pass at her. And it would have been like Ruby to have become annoyed if he persisted. Despite the thing that ripped and tore at her emotions, she would never have consented to roll the dice or flip a coin on such an offer. Or, Latham continued to torture himself, there may have been another motive for the crap game and the consequent quarrel. Latham now admitted that he knew very little of what had happened to Ruby during the past year and a half. It was possible that she had changed, and it was possible that there was some truth in the story that she had been a partner in Mays' embezzlement. Frightened of insanity and drinking heavily, God only knew what had happened to her during the past eighteen months. Add to that the shame and black remorse she had always felt after her sickness had flamed up in a torment of desire, as it had periodically. Perhaps at the end she had just given up, unable to fight it any longer. Everyone had his limit, and perhaps she and McElroy had taken Mays for that two hundred thousand, and perhaps McElroy had offered to roll the dice for all or nothing. That could have been when Ruby said irritably, "I don't want to hear any more. I'm going to have a drink." That could have been the cause of the quarrel between her and McElroy, Ruby resisting out of remorse, guilt and shame. Later, according to Wooten, Ruby had said, "Stop it please. I'm sick of it."

Sick of what? Sick of McElroy's offer to roll the dice for the money, or sick of the whole sordid thing? If there had been a flash of the old Ruby then, Latham knew, she would have told McElroy bluntly that she was going to return her share of the stolen money to Mays and would have ordered McElroy to do the same. A man could kill under those circumstances, a man like McElroy....

A sudden fierceness swelled up in Latham and violently he struck the seat beside him with his clenched fist, saying savagely, "No!" Ruby would never have entered any such partnership with McElroy and she would never have been an accessory to the embezzlement. The whole theory was ridiculous.

Still, there was Mays' suicide note implicating Ruby.

Desperately, Latham wanted to learn more about Ruby, how she had lived for the past year and a half, what she had thought and felt, and he remembered the three men named by Keeler—Harry Conley, the real estate man; Frank Meyn, who owned the Palm Dairy; and Doug Hemming, who operated the lumberyard. Those three had known Ruby, but had they been her lovers? They were all older men and Frank Meyn had white hair.

Latham had been driving aimlessly, but now he turned his car toward the downtown business district of Sanibar. The business office of the Palm Dairy was on Sorrento Street. It was a large building with a garage for fifty of the distinctive orange-colored delivery trucks. The office itself was small and the only one in it was a dark-haired girl wearing a sun-back dress, strapless and snug. She was typing peevishly when Latham walked into the office and did not stop to look up until she had typed several more lines.

"Yes?" she said as if irritated at being interrupted.

"I'd like to see Mr. Meyn."

"He's not in."

"When will he be back?"

"He didn't say."

She was scarcely polite and, annoyed, Latham said, "Look, I'm a friend of his and I want to see him, so relax and give me some answers. Where can I get in touch with him?"

Sullenly the girl said, "He called up this morning and said he was sick. He hasn't been in all day."

"Is he home?"

"That's where he said he could be reached if anything came up during the day, but he said not to disturb him unless it was something important."

He said, "Thanks," and walked out of the office and back to his car. Meyn had an old-fashioned verandah style house on the bay at the southern end of town. That was the exclusive residential area and the half acre of ground on which the house stood was worth about twenty-five thousand dollars, though the old house itself was not worth very much.

Latham was acquainted with Meyn who had chartered the *Belan* several times during the tarpon run. He knew him well enough to call him Fritz, Meyn's nickname among his friends, just as he knew Meyn's wife well enough to call her Tante Minna. Though Meyn was known as a solid family man, Latham was not too surprised that he had made a play for Ruby. At the yacht club dances, Fritz liked to put his arms around the women, the young girls especially, and give them noisy and ostensibly paternal kisses.

The house was screened from the road by a high hedge of cajeput trees, sometimes called punk trees, which grew very thickly and had cream-colored flowers that looked like bottle brushes. Inside the hedge, the grassy grounds were as neat as a billiard table. Latham's ring at the front door was answered by Meyn's wife, a short, plump woman with white hair, red cheeks and happy blue eyes that reminded one of Mrs. Santa Claus.

"Ach, Joe Latham," she cried, recognizing him immediately. "Every time I see you, you get bigger and bigger, and soon you are a giant. You eat your Wheaties every morning, I bet." Though she had come to America from Germany forty years before, she still had a strong accent.

"I heard Fritz was sick, Tante Minna," Latham said.

"Sick? Maybe. I think today he is lazy and does not want to work. All day he is in bed with the shades pulled down. But he is a little sick, ja, but no temperature. It is his stomach. Last night he eats too much bockwurst and sauerkraut, today he suffers. The next time he knows better."

"I'm sorry to hear that, Tante Minna. I always thought he had a digestion like a barracuda."

"Well, he is not so young, not so young. You wanted to see him about something, Joe?"

"It's personal."

"I go up and tell him you are here. All day he makes like he is sleeping when I go into the room, but I know better. When he sleeps, he snores.

Come in and sit down and I will tell him that you are here."

She led him into a spotless but gloomy living room crammed relentlessly with massive Victorian furniture. She made him sit on a horsehair sofa that was as hard as cement and pointed to a bowl of dried fruit on the ornate coffee table.

"Eat some," she said, "they are good for you, dried fruit. I will tell Fritz."

"Tell him it's personal, Tante Minna."

"Ja, ja, I will tell him. Dried fruit is better than fresh fruit. It does not spoil so easy."

She left the room and Latham stood up because the sofa was exceptionally uncomfortable. He was pretty sure he knew why Fritz was sick, and it had nothing to do with bockwurst and sauerkraut. He was just plain scared that the police investigation would bring publicity on his relationship with Ruby. Latham reseated himself on the sofa when he heard Tante Minna coming slowly down the stairs.

"Well," she said as she walked into the room, "he did not want to see you but I told him it would do him good to talk to somebody. It's time he gets up soon anyway, laying in bed all day." And then in a different, softer tone, "I am sorry to hear about your young lady, Joe."

He said, "Thanks, Tante Minna," not wanting her condolences, well-meant though they were.

She nodded, "I know, I know. You can go up the stairs. It is the first bedroom on the right."

Fritz Meyn was sitting up with two pillows behind him when Latham walked into the bedroom. He was a stocky man and his white hair was cropped short, which made him look a little like the pictures of Bismarck, without the intensely military moustaches, though the iron expression was much the same.

"How are you feeling, Fritz?" Latham asked.

Meyn glowered and barked, "Close the door, close the door. I'm getting a draft."

There was no draft, but Latham closed the door. Meyn continued to glower.

"Well, what is it you wanted to see me about?" he growled. "What is this something personal?"

Latham took the straight chair beside the bed and lit a cigarette, despite Meyn's scowls. "Ruby, Fritz," he said.

Meyn's square, knuckly hands jerked on the sheet that covered him to the waist. He moistened his lips. "Ruby?"

"That's right. Ruby Lake. You knew her, didn't you, Fritz?"

"A little, a little," Meyn said hurriedly. "She came to visit Tante Minna once in a while."

Latham said incredulously, "She what?"

"Ja, ja, she came to visit Tante Minna." Like everyone else, Meyn always called his wife Tante Minna. "Every once in a while she came to have a talk."

"Well," said Latham, watching him narrowly, "that must have been a shock, the first time she came. I'll bet you damn near fell through the floor, didn't you, Fritz?"

Meyn's florid face turned quite white and he blustered, "Fell through the floor? Why should I fall through the floor if Ruby comes to visit Tante Minna? Lots of people come to Tante Minna when they are in trouble and need advice," Now his hands were shaking a little, rippling the sheet.

"Who're you trying to kid, Fritz?"

"Kidding? Kidding? Do I look like I'm kidding? What do you mean, kidding?"

"You were playing around with her, taking her places and doing things."

"That's a lie!" Meyn said loudly, but his eyes flickered uneasily toward the closed door.

"You never took her out, Fritz?"

"Never! I'm a married man with two grown children, married too. Who says I was playing around?"

"And you never saw her except when she came here to visit Tante Minna?"

"Never!"

"Do you know Captain Hanna from Headquarters, Fritz?"

"I have met him, yes."

"And Floyd Keeler, the police detective?"

"The fat one. Yes."

"And they asked you some questions about Ruby, didn't they, Fritz?"

Latham kept looking at him with an expression of mild interest. By this time the old man should have told him to go to hell, but Latham could see that Meyn was desperate to find out how much he knew about his affair, if it could be called that, with Ruby.

Meyn's hands were now tightly clasped together on the sheet and he said, "They asked me some questions about her, yes, and I told them how she used to come and visit with Tante Minna, and then they came and talked to Tante Minna."

"Why did they ask you questions about her in the first place, Fritz, if you hardly knew the girl?"

Meyn's jaw dropped. He had let Latham talk him into a dead end. "They—they are asking questions of everybody," he said weakly. "In a case like this they—they have to find out as much as they can. Maybe somebody told them she used to come here to the house. They have to ask these questions. It is their duty. That is what we pay taxes for."

"But didn't they ask you if you had an alibi for the night of the murder, Fritz? Wasn't that one of the questions they asked you? Didn't they ask you to prove it?"

"I was right here in this very house with Tante Minna and the Keyserlings from Bradenton, and I don't have to prove it. The Keyserlings were here till after midnight and we were looking at the television!"

"Why did they ask you that if you hardly knew Ruby, Fritz?"

Meyn glowered at him and his face set stubbornly. He had obviously decided that Latham was only fishing for information.

"The police have to ask questions," he said curtly. "That is their job. But I don't happen to remember that *you* are on the police, Latham, so what right do *you* have to ask me all these questions? I am not going to answer any more, and I will thank you to go away now, please."

Latham crossed his legs and looked thoughtfully up at the ceiling. "Let's see now," he said. "You'd hardly take her out here in Sanibar. There are too many people who know you. So when you took her out, I'd say you went up to Tampa. Ruby was crazy about Spanish food, so if you took her to a restaurant it would probably be either Las Novidades or the Columbia. Ruby was very fond of both places. I know because I used to take her there myself. She liked El Presidente cocktails and her favorite dish was paella and after dinner she always took a pony of chartreuse, but it had to be green chartreuse. She liked the color. She spoke Spanish very well and would always joke with the waiter. She was one of the favorite customers and the waiters always remembered her."

Meyn listened open-mouthed as Latham added detail after detail. Latham smiled thinly.

"Do you know what I think I'll do, Fritz? I think I'll hire a private detective and find out how many times during the past few months you took Ruby to Tampa. A good private detective could find out a thing like that in a few hours. But do you want me to hire a private detective, Fritz? It could cause some talk and the newspapers might even find out about it. It's hard to keep things from a good newspaper reporter, especially when there's a murder case in the background."

Meyn had slumped back against his pillows and was staring at the foot of the bed in dull defeat. It was a long time before he spoke and when he did, each word was labored.

"I am an old man. I am over sixty, but I have always told myself that sixty is young and that you are only as old as you feel. I feel very old and my brains are not very smart. I built up the dairy by myself and I thought, you are a smart man, Fritz Meyn, to make such a success. But I was smart in just one thing, to make money." He took a heavy breath. "In other things I am not smart at all. A man is not smart in the head to go around with a young girl at my age. What can he give a young girl except tell her how much money he has made? Yes, I went out with Ruby to Tampa. For five months I went out with her once a week. I told Tante Minna I had to go to Tampa on business. I knew it was foolishness and I said to myself to stop it, but I kept on doing it all the same, telling myself that foolish thing, that you are only as old as you feel."

"I'm not interested in that part of it," Latham said brusquely. "All I want to find out is what Ruby was like during the five months you knew her."

"What she was like?" Meyn looked blankly at him. "She was a young girl. She was happy and it made you happy to be with her."

"She was always happy, every time you saw her? I don't want any rosy pictures, Fritz. I want to know exactly what she was like."

"Well, sometimes she was sad, yes."

"And she drank too much."

"Well," Meyn said reluctantly, "yes, sometimes she drank a little too much."

"Most of the time, wasn't it?"

"Yes, most of the time," Meyn said sadly.

"What did she talk about when she was drunk? I mean, during the past month or so."

"I don't remember. She—I worried because she was drinking too much and I told her it was not good for a young girl to drink so much."

"Did she laugh at you, or what?"

"No, no, she did not laugh at me. She said, 'I'm just having a last fling, Papa.' She always called me Papa. And she said soon she was going to give up drinking and that soon maybe she was going to live in South America."

Latham started. In his suicide note, Mays had said that he and Ruby had planned to live in South America on the embezzled two hundred thousand dollars. He felt a little sick, hearing the confirmation of this from Meyn.

"She actually said she was going to live in South America?" he demanded.

"She said maybe. She was in love with somebody, she said, but he did not have very much money. He worked for a living and that was all he had. I wanted to give her some money, I have plenty, but she said, 'No,

Papa, I don't want you to give me money.' She would never let me give her anything, except sometimes a box of candy or a bouquet of flowers. But she was very happy the last time I saw her, two days before—before they did that to her. 'You are very happy tonight,' I said. And she said, 'Yes I am very happy, Papa.' And I asked her if everything was all right now with her and her young man, and she laughed and said everything was going to be wonderful. I asked her if she was going to South America with him like she said, but she just laughed again and said it was all still a big secret. She was not very drunk that night, though people looked at her because she was laughing so much, but she was just happy."

"Then she didn't tell you any more about this trip to South America with this man?" Latham asked heavily.

"No, it was a secret, she said. 'Oho,' I said, 'then you are going to surprise everybody, eh?' And she laughed again and said yes, everybody would be very much surprised, but that was all she would say."

Latham was silent. He had never expected such complete confirmation that Ruby had planned to go to South America with Mays and that she had been a party to the theft of the two hundred thousand dollars. He felt as if he had been hollowed out and scraped.

Finally, as if just to say something to break the intolerable silence that was filling him, he asked, "Did she say where she was going to get the money to go to South America?"

"No, she said that was a secret, too. Then I told her when she was married she must give up all this drinking and go to church every Sunday. She said yes, she was going to give up the drinking but she would never go near a church. I told her she shouldn't talk like that. I scolded her and said she did not know what she was saying and that all decent people went to church. Then she gave a funny laugh and said that was why she would not go to church, because she was not decent and she was a wicked sinner and never prayed when she went to bed at night and God would never like her very much. And she said that she had it on very good authority that God had it in for her and was just waiting for the first chance to knock her on the head and make her suffer. I told her she was talking foolishness, but she said she knew all about God, the one that lived in the churches and He was a man with a big stick, and that was why she would not go to church, because the minute she set foot inside He would grab her and hit her with the stick and she was not going to take any chances of that happening. I told her she was crazy."

"She was kidding you," said Latham. Ruby had never talked like that before and, in fact, when they became engaged, she had been looking forward to a big church wedding.

("With all the trimmings, Joe, the organ playing, a fat soprano singing O Promise Me, bridesmaids and flowers and you standing up there at the altar in striped pants and a Prince Albert coat, so tall and handsome, and oh Joe, won't it be wonderful!")

Meyn said cautiously, "No, I don't think she was joking too much, but yes, she laughed, so maybe she was joking. I am not very good at jokes myself and I cannot always tell when people are making jokes to me. Is there anything else you want to know? I am very tired. My stomach is very upset."

"No," said Latham, getting heavily to his feet, "you've told me just about all I want to know."

"And you—you don't have to hire one of those, a private detective now?"

"No, I just wanted to find out how Ruby was, that's all."

"She was a fine girl if only she didn't drink so much."

Latham said, "Yeah," and turned abruptly and walked out of the bedroom.

He had his hand on the knob of the front door when Tante Minna called to him from the doorway of the living room.

"I would like to talk to you for a minute, Joe, all right?"

He said, "Sure, Tante Minna," and went into the living room with her. She closed the door very carefully. She was very serious and her blue eyes were not smiling as they usually were. She stood at the door with her hands folded at her comfortable waist.

"I don't want you to think too badly of Papa, Joe," she said.

He made a small gesture of negation and shrugged.

"I know, I know, Joe. You do not like him very much now because he took Ruby to dinner once in a while. He does not think I know but I knew before people were so kind as to tell me. There are always kind people like that who wish to tell you things. Papa is of the age now when he thinks it is wonderful to take a young girl out to dinner, but he is over that now, I think. I'm glad it was Ruby, she was a good girl. He might have picked somebody who was not so good, who would make him spend money and leave home and do other foolish things. So when I knew he was going out with Ruby I said to myself, let him have his little fling, it is his last one. Do you think I am foolish?"

"No," said Latham without much interest.

"Also, I know Papa is very safe with Ruby and she will never make him leave home. She was in love with you, Joe. She told me."

Latham said, "Yeah," thinking of the plans Ruby and Mays had made for living in South America on the stolen two hundred thousand dollars.

"Please, Joe, she was," said Tante Minna earnestly. "When she first came to see me, all she did was cry. I had the feeling she wanted to tell me something, and it was later that I found out that Papa was taking her out to dinner, but she told me herself the next time she came. She was crying and she begged me to know that—there was nothing wrong between her and Papa but begged me to forgive her."

"But she kept going out with him all the same," Latham said harshly.

"Yes. I asked her to. It was something that Papa had to get over and done with, taking young girls out, and it was best that he went out with Ruby because she would see that Papa did not do anything wrong. I did not have to ask her. I knew she would not let Papa do anything foolish. After that she came sometimes and visited with me in the afternoons. She loved you but did not think that you loved her. No, no, that is not quite right. She did think you loved her but she did not want to be a burden on you with doctor bills and expensive things like that. She did not tell me what she was sick from, but from little things I knew it was going to be an expensive operation and maybe a long time in the hospital."

"Did she say when she was going to have this operation?"

"No, and she seemed very much afraid of it. But Joe, listen to me, that girl, she loved you even after you broke the engagement. Maybe she did not tell you this, but she told me and her eyes, they were very honest. You can lie with your mouth, but the eyes, they tell the truth."

Latham said, "Yeah," and glanced at his wrist watch. "I have to go now. I have to meet some people down at the boat."

"What's the matter, Joe? Are you still mad with Papa?"

"Not at all."

"Or are you mad with Ruby for going out to dinner with Papa?"

"No, I'm not mad about that either. I'm not mad about anything."

"Ah, yes you are, Joe. You are very mad. Your eyes are like thunder and lightning and they are dark with clouds."

"I didn't get much sleep last night, Tante Minna, that's all. And if you see any thunderstorms in my eyes it's only because they're watering."

"Ah, such a joke," she said dryly. "With such a joke the executioner chops off a head. Maybe you should go home and get some sleep. When you wake up you will feel better and not be so mad with everything."

She went to the front door with him and before he left she put her hand on his arm and smiled gently. "I talk too much that is not my business, but Ruby loved you, Joe."

She wanted him to believe it but the best he could manage was, "It's possible," and walked down the verandah steps to his car. The shining sun seemed a little unreal and he had the vague feeling that it should have been night. It seemed hours that he had been in the house.

CHAPTER ELEVEN

On his agenda there were still Harry Conley, the real estate man, and Doug Hemming, the lumber yard operator, to see, but Latham felt too depressed to talk to either of them about Ruby. He had wanted information about her and Fritz Meyn had served it up seasoned with bitter herbs, a dish that turned his stomach. And what further could either Conley or Hemming add?

They were both older men, and the pattern of their friendship with Ruby had probably followed that of Fritz Meyn. Both were married, both were supposed to be solid citizens, and neither had ever been known to have been a chaser. With Ruby they had probably found a fleeting illusion of springtime amour, but like Meyn both were in their sixties and not especially vigorous. Conley had suffered a heart attack two years before and since then had been able to work only an hour or two in his office in the morning, and the business was actually being run by his son-in-law. Hemming was an excessively shy man and spoke with a stammer. Both had grandchildren. Neither of them would have picked up Ruby in a bar or any of the usual places, including Dean Odum's Beach Casino, but it was hardly likely that they would have met Ruby in any other way. Unless—

Latham gripped the wheel of his car as the thought formed unpleasantly. Unless Ruby had picked them up. That would have been the only way. She had picked them up. But why, for what reason? Because they all had money? They were damned well off, all three of them. But Meyn had said that Ruby had refused any gifts from him except the mere token gifts of flowers or candy. It didn't make sense. Or Meyn could have been lying out of shame that he had let Ruby take him for a good healthy slice of his bank account. That could be it. A man like Meyn would lie about something like that, refusing to admit that he had been played for a sucker.

Latham's face hardened. Yes, Ruby had changed in the past year and a half, since the breaking of their engagement. She had been in on the embezzlement with Mays, so why couldn't she also have played those three aging, wealthy men for suckers?

He glanced at his wrist watch. It was three o'clock, too late to see Conley, who had to lie down and nap for a few hours every afternoon because of his heart. But there was Hemming, who would be in the office of the lumber yard until five. Hemming was better anyway. Latham had known him for a long time and could talk to him. He drove over to the lumber yard on the railroad siding beyond the station. Hemming was alone in his office. He was a heavy man, gray-haired. He was a shrewd businessman but his shyness with strangers made him seem unsure of himself. He was different with people he knew and greeted Latham cordially.

"I haven't seen you for a long time, Joe, not since that fishing trip down to Boca Grande. What's on your mind?"

Latham took the chair beside the desk and said bluntly, "I want to ask you a few things about Ruby."

Hemming was silent but looked steadily at Latham. "How did you find out about that, Joe?" he asked at length.

Latham shrugged. "Somebody mentioned that you knew her."

"I suppose it's all over town."

"Not that I know of. I didn't hear it that way."

"No? Then how did you hear it?"

Latham shrugged again. "I forget."

"Did you hear it from Ruby?"

"Is that important? I just want to ask a few questions about her—"

Hemming interrupted quietly. "It's important to me, Joe. I was possibly very foolish to, well, have met Ruby as I did, though our relationship was on a father-and-daughter basis and nothing else."

"Did she call you Papa, too, the way she did Fritz Meyn?" asked Latham brutally. "And Harry Conley probably."

Hemming's eyes widened a little when Latham threw the two names at him, but his voice remained quiet. "Once in a while. But I'm interested in how you learned this. If there's talk, I want to know. I don't want my wife to be upset by this."

"You should have thought of that sooner."

"I don't understand why you're trying to quarrel with me, Joe. Were you in love with her?"

"That was all over a year and a half ago," Latham said harshly. "Over and done with. I'm just trying to get a line on her, that's all. I've been sucked into this and I want to find out where I stand. It was Keeler who told me about you and Ruby."

"Keeler? Oh yes, the fat detective with Captain Hanna." Hemming's face flushed. "Well, well. I think I'll have a little talk with Captain Hanna about that. I don't think policemen are allowed to gossip, especially in a case like this, and I think Captain Hanna should know about this. Keeler had no right to talk to anybody about our conversation."

"He didn't say anything about your conversation. He just mentioned that you, Conley and Meyn were three of Ruby's boy friends. I was interested at that time in finding out who killed her and he wanted me to give him a hand. And furthermore, I don't want you to go to Hanna right now. You can do it later if you want, but I need him for an alibi until the case is broken. Put it down as a favor to me."

"Are you asking me or telling me, Joe?"

"Asking."

"Can you give me any assurance that this Keeler is not going to gossip all over town?"

"I don't think you have to worry about that. Keeler was giving me a pitch. For personal reasons. He was trying to suck me into something. I don't think he's going to do any more blabbing to anybody else."

Hemming drummed on the desk top with his hard, mottled fingers. "Well, all right," he said finally. "But if I hear any more gossip about Ruby and me, I'm going straight to Captain Hanna with a very strong protest. Now what did you want to know about Ruby?" Hemming's gray eyes were frosty and his manner was no longer friendly.

Latham did not care and asked bluntly, "It was Ruby who picked you up instead of the other way around, wasn't it? I want to know."

"Not in that sense of the word," Hemming said coldly. "We met on the beach quite casually. It was not a pickup by any manner or means."

"You met on the beach several times and then you started taking her out."

Hemming stood up. "I'm not going to answer any more of your questions, Joe. You're in a quarrelsome mood, and I don't have to take this from you or anybody. Come back some other time and perhaps we can talk about it."

"Damn it!" cried Latham violently. "She was involved in that bank embezzlement with Mays—"

"I read it in the papers but I don't believe it."

"Oh it's true all right," said Latham, suddenly very weary as the belligerence drained out of him. "Captain Hanna told me first and then Fritz Meyn practically confirmed it."

Hemming sat down slowly, his expression incredulous. "Fritz confirmed it?"

"He didn't know he was confirming it. She told him that she was going to South America very shortly, and he couldn't have known that she was planning to go with Mays because that part of the suicide note was not printed in the newspapers."

Hemming's incredulity faded and he looked genuinely shocked. "Mays said in his suicide note that he and Ruby were planning to go to South America with the stolen money?"

"According to Captain Hanna. Did she ever mention anything about going to South America to you?"

Hemming nodded heavily. "Yes, several times during the past few weeks. She—made quite a mystery about it. I—I can hardly believe it of her."

"I could hardly believe it too, but at that time the returns had not come in from the outlying precincts. What did she say to you about it?"

There was shock and sadness in the slight movement of Hemming's old hands. "Not very much, Joe. I—had the impression that she was going to South America to be married, but I never dreamed that it was to have been with Stanley Mays. It's still hard to believe, Joe. I mean, he was her employer and we spoke of him a few times in the ordinary course of conversation and she appeared to think him a little ridiculous."

"Maybe the two hundred thousand dollars changed her mind."

"Yes, that's possible, Joe."

"Did she ever try to 'borrow' any money from you?"

"I—had the impression at one time that she might be leading up to something like that, though she never really asked. She talked vaguely about some heavy expenses to come, medical bills it seemed to me, though she never fully explained. We only talked about it once or twice and then she never mentioned it again, so I thought I must have been mistaken."

"Medical bills," said Latham cynically. "That's the old gimmick. Medical bills, rent, a sick mother—every moocher in the world has used those gags at one time or another. So you thought she was really setting you up for a 'loan,' eh?"

"At the time I thought so, but as I said, she dropped the subject entirely, so I thought I must have been mistaken."

"Was that recently?"

"Within the last six weeks or so."

"That must have been just about the time Mays started getting sticky fingers at the bank."

"It would seem so," Hemming agreed unhappily.

"Did she ever talk to you about Ross McElroy, that gambler from the Beach Casino?"

"The one who was killed last night? Yes, we spoke of him several times, but that was about four months ago. She said he had asked her to marry him. I was quite surprised. I'd met McElroy several times and he did not seem the marrying sort. However, I made some inquiries and learned that he had asked several women to marry him, and it turned out to be his particular approach to seduction, a not unusual one. I told Ruby and she laughed and said she knew that but thought he was serious this time. She said she didn't love him but that he was fun to be with. I told her that he was an unscrupulous scoundrel but she replied that all she wanted was a short life and a merry one. That's why I was surprised when you said she was planning to go to South America with Stanley Mays. I thought it was Ross McElroy."

"It could have been. She and McElroy could have teamed up to take Mays for that two hundred thousand and skip to South America with it."

"That I will never believe," said Hemming flatly. "Ruby was not capable of a foul thing like that."

"You didn't know her very well."

"I knew her quite well. She was wild and drank too much, but she had had a very unhappy childhood, a tragic childhood with her father going crazy and killing her mother—and that was the essence of our friendship, Joe. It sounds trite, but I tried to be a father to her. If she could have given up drinking, she would have been a much different girl. I always had the feeling that if I had been her real father, I could have influenced her more. As it was, I was just a substitute and a not very good one or I might have persuaded her to give up drinking so heavily. Liquor, that was her tragedy."

Latham looked sharply into Hemming's face and saw that the older man did not know about the other tragedy in Ruby's life, the sickness that drove her to liquor. There would be no point in telling the old man of all the men in Ruby's life. She had never shown him any of that, and he believed her to be as lovely as Latham once had, lovely inside and out. It was with a stabbing poignancy that Latham remembered how lovely she had been. And Hemming could be right at that; it could have been the liquor that finally unbalanced her.

But there was nothing more to be said. From what Hemming had told him, it now seemed very possible that Ruby had teamed up with McElroy to take Mays for that two hundred thousand. That would seem to make McElroy her killer, but who had killed McElroy? Was there a third person involved in their scheme? Perhaps McElroy and someone else had teamed to make a sucker out of Ruby, which would make it a double double-cross.

Latham rose to go and Hemming walked to the outer door of the office with him. Like Fritz Meyn, Hemming too seemed to have aged that afternoon. Lovely, lovely Ruby, Latham thought savagely, destroying herself and everyone who knew her! Hemming stood looking at the sun-drenched street lined with the dusty palms that made dry, withered noises as the faint breeze stirred their fronds.

"I loved her as a daughter," he said in a bemused voice, "and that's what she actually seemed to me. A daughter. I'm afraid, Joe, that if you offered me all the proof in the world, I would still not believe this of

Ruby."

Latham thought of the record—Mays a suicide, McElroy murdered, Ruby murdered and the cold finger of the tragedy touching both Meyn and Hemming, and God only knew what other men Ruby had trapped within it. None of them believing that she could have enmeshed them.

"It'll take time," said Latham grimly.

CHAPTER TWELVE

Across the street from the lumber yard was a tavern called Joe's Joint. It was a hangout for truckdrivers and the crackers who had farms or cattle ranches in the palmetto and rattlesnake country east of the Tamiami Trail. At night it was a tough, brawling place and during the day it catered to a steady stream of beer drinkers who were either nursing hangovers or just warming up for the more serious drinking that would begin about seven-thirty, right after dinner. The bar was made of plywood and topped with dark green Formica and tacked to the wall behind it were various signs, all on the same general theme:

> You ask for credit
> I no give,
>   You get mad.
> I give credit
> You no pay,
>   I get mad.
> DAMSITE BETTER YOU GET MAD!

Latham leaned against the bar, paying no attention to a knot of beer drinkers clustered at the end in a noisy argument about the World Series larded with insults at Joe, a tall man with the narrow, pointed face and bored eyes of a disillusioned fox.

"Hey, Joe, when you puttin' in TV?"

"Hell with TV."

"Aaah, you cheap bastard, you wouldn't even put out two bits for a flower on your mother's grave."

"Hell with flowers."

"What a crud."

"Hell with you."

"Come on, I'll match you for beers, Joe."

"Hell with that, too."

His nose wrinkled as if something smelled bad, he moved away from the group and toward Latham.

Latham said, "Hit me," the usual order for a shot of 'shine. Joe had a license for beer and wine, but he made his own 'shine in a still well hidden in the palmetto on a branch of Ax Head Creek. He poured the drink from a jug under the bar and set the wineglass of yellowish oily liquid in front of Latham without saying anything but the short customary, "Hi." Latham pointed to a new sign over the cash register. It said, "We have an agreement with the bank, They don't sell liquor, And we don't cash checks."

"Still taking no chances, eh, Joe?"

Joe shrugged, picked up Latham's quarter and started to walk back to the group of beer drinkers. Latham scowled. "Hey, wait a minute," he said.

Joe looked back. "Yeah?"

"What's the matter with you?"

"Me? Nothing. Why?"

"That's what I want to know. Why the brush-off?"

"I didn't give you no brush-off."

"What do you call it then?"

"I don't call it nothing. I'm just going down to talk to the boys, that's all. What do you want me to do, stand here and give you my life history? You wouldn't be interested."

"Tell me about the weather, Joe. I'm very interested in the weather. Come back and tell me it's a nice day."

Joe came back and rested his hands on the edge of the bar. "I don't want no trouble with you, Latham, that's why I was leaving you alone. You walk in here with a face on you like the first word out of somebody he gets a poke in the snoot. Okay. If that's the way you feel, that's your business, only you ain't starting no fights with me. It's too early in the day. Come back tonight and there'll be a half dozen guys only too glad to oblige. That answer your question?"

Latham looked at the reflection of his face in the mirror behind the bar. His brows came down in menacing knots over his eyes and his mouth was a thin, curled belligerence, and he realized that he would have welcomed a fight at that moment. Not just a fight but a savage toe-to-toe slugging match, just to have something in front of him with which he could slug out his smoldering fury. But now that Joe had called the turn, he could not build a fight in cold blood, deliberately. He drank down the shot of 'shine and pushed the empty glass toward Joe with his forefinger.

"That's all over now," he growled. "Hit me again. We'll start all over again. It's a nice day, isn't it?"

Joe relaxed and poured another drink under the bar. "Yeah," he said, "but we could use a little rain." He set the drink warily before Latham, watchful with his cynical fox eyes. "I'd settle for a hurricane if it'd blow half this damn town off the map and this joint with it."

"You've been saying that for the past four years."

"Well, one of these days—but you got troubles of your own, so let's forget it." Joe hesitated and then mumbled as if it were something that he felt he had to do, "Sorry to hear about Ruby."

Latham said, "Thanks," with deliberate indifference to discourage further conversation on that subject.

"It's quite a while since you went around with her though, ain't it?"

"That was way back when."

"You were lucky and didn't know it. She was nothing but grief. She used to come in here once in a while stewed to the eyeballs, and I had to drive her back to her apartment or some of these jerks around here would of dragged her in the bushes. A dame like that, she must of been nuts running around alone and plotzed. She used to hang on the end of the bar hardly able to stand up and these jerky mutts here, they'd crowd in on her and try to get real close to her and all that stuff, but I busted that up but fast. That's all I'd need, for her to start yelling rape, and you know some of these jerks around here, they would of raped her, given half a chance."

Latham listened to this with mounting astonishment. "She came in all by herself?" That didn't sound like Ruby, not in a joint like this.

"Yeah, usually around one or half past, just before closing when she could be the most trouble and I had to take her home. Once she came in with just a nightgown and a coat and I hustled her out but fast. She was stewed as usual and tried to tell me that she was supposed to meet you here, but I knew that was the malarky. That was about four nights ago, now that I remember."

"Four nights ago," said Latham, "I was down at Boca Grande with a charter fishing for tarpon."

"Yeah, that's what I figured. But that was her usual line when she came in. She just come to meet you, and the first few times I believed her, soused as she was, on account of she kept watching the door like she really expected you to walk in any minute. But you never showed and finally it dawned on me that this was just something she dreamed up whenever she got really soused. But she was so damn convincing. She said, 'Lath likes it here because it's the only place he can get a good drink of 'shine,' she said to me. And me, I know how you like a good drink of 'shine once in a while, so I believed her at first. But like I said, I got wise to her. Or maybe she expected to run into you by accident or something, but who can figure out a female rummy. I gave up a long time ago. You were just plain lucky you didn't really get tangled up with that dame."

"That was a dead end," said Latham mechanically. "That was a dead end a year and a half ago."

"She was carrying the torch for you, or maybe that was only when she got liquored up."

"Probably."

"So you never did have any of them dates with her, eh?"

"No."

"That's what I figured. And I told the cops I never seen you meet her here."

"The cops?" Latham looked up to find Joe watching him with an unaccustomed intentness, which was immediately veiled behind his usual bored indifference.

Joe nodded. "Yeah. It was that fat cop, what's his name—"

"Keeler."

"Keeler, that's the one. He was trying to tie you up with her in some way, but I told him you never met her here. What's he trying to do, suck you in?"

"Something like that."

"Well, he didn't get anything from me on account of there was nothing to get. I told him that Ruby was in here a few times on her own, but I didn't mention that she was looking for you. But he's a jerk, that Keeler. I wouldn't tell him what way was up if he was in the bottom of a well. He's a tricky son of a bitch anyways."

"Let's forget it. As far as Ruby's concerned, I've been out of it for a long time and there's nothing to talk about with you or Keeler or anybody else, so let's drop it."

"I know just how you feel. Dames are a pain no matter how you look at them. She sure took that dumb jerk Mays for plenty, didn't she? Two hundred grand. He must of had it bad."

"So they say," Latham said wearily.

"They're still checking on it. According to the paper this afternoon, they don't know what the hell did happen to the dough. They've checked Mays backwards and forwards, the stock market, gambling and all that, but they can't find out a thing and they figure he turned the dough over to Ruby, only they can't find out nothing on her neither. I wonder what the hell they did do with all that dough? You can't spend two hundred grand without somebody noticing it, if you know what I mean. If they blew it in on the ponies or even on the wheel out at the Beach Casino, word would of gotten round. The only thing I can figure is that they stashed it away. How do you figure it?"

"I don't and I don't give a damn what they did with it. Maybe they bought the Empire State Building."

"You know what I think? I think that jerk Mays got cold feet at the last minute and went to the dame and wanted the dough back. He wanted out, but she laughed at him, as what dame wouldn't when she had it socked away. And when she told him to go take a running jump for himself, he blew his stack and stuck an ice pick in her and then went out and did the Dutch. He wouldn't be the first guy. When you figure it out that way, it really adds up, right?"

Latham shrugged. "Could be."

"But that still leaves the question, what'd she do with the dough? If you ask me, she had a safe deposit box someplace under a different name. A dame smart enough to take a guy for two hundred grand would be too smart to bury the dough in a hole in the ground."

Latham had drunk only a sip or two of his second 'shine but he put down his glass on the bar and pushed it away from him. Slowly he took out a cigarette, lit it and puffed at it but with no evidence of satisfaction, keeping his ironical gaze on Joe until the bartender shifted uneasily.

"Well," said Latham at length, "you were a long time getting around to it."

"Around to what, Lath?"

"Let's see now. What could Ruby have done with that money? Did she buy U.S. Savings Bonds? No, wasn't the saving type at all. She'd rather blow her money on a movie and an ice cream soda than put it in the bank. No Savings Bonds for her. Maybe she bought a yacht. Do you think she bought a yacht, Joe?"

"Very funny. I'm laughing."

"No, I guess she didn't buy a yacht. She wasn't fond of the water. Why even a bath in the bathtub made her seasick. But there were other things she could have done with a bankroll that size. She was crazy about Mexican food so maybe she bought herself the biggest damn mess of chili and frijoles in the world and sat down and ate it all by herself. That's just the kind of thing a dame would do, eat it all herself and not give anybody else a bite." Then, mimicking the bartender, "When you figure it out that way, it really adds up, right?"

"Anything I hate, it's a comedian," said Joe, turning his head to spit on the floor in disgust.

"Wait, I just thought of something else," said Latham, snapping his fingers as if a sudden bright thought had burst upon him, "something else she could have done with the money. She could have given it to me for my birthday. She was always very sentimental about birthdays, Ruby was. Every birthday I could count on a card from her, special delivery air mail, even before I knew her. She was crazy about birthdays. Yessir, that's exactly what she did with that money she got from Mays; she gave it to me for my birthday. When you figure it out that way, it really adds up, right?"

"Aaah ..."

"Of course my birthday won't be for a couple of months yet, but I'm not worried. When the mail comes around, there it'll be, two hundred thousand dollars all done up in tissue paper, pink ribbons and bows and a lovely birthday card with paper lace all over it." Deliberately Latham ground out his cigarette on the Formica top of the bar. "That's what you were nosing around about, wasn't it? Was I in on that deal with Ruby or wasn't I? You'd give your right arm to know, wouldn't you?"

Joe did not look bored. There were small angry glints in his foxy eyes. "Man," he said softly, "you're riding for a fall and don't know it. Yeah, I been wondering if you and Ruby were in together on that deal, but so's the rest of the town, comedian. A lot of people are wondering, and some of them are saying that if you were in on that deal, you've made yourself the biggest sucker of the lot and that one of these days you're going to open your eyes and you'll be staring right smack in the middle of the eight ball."

"That's very interesting," said Latham, "only I seem to have heard most of it before."

"And you'll hear it again before you're finished, sucker. And you'll more than hear it, too. You'll never have a chance to lay a finger on that dough, because the minute you do, your next stop's the electric chair. The minute they can tie you in with the dough they can tie you in with Ruby's killing, and that'll be the end, man, that'll be the end. And maybe McElroy's killing, too. How do you like the view from behind the eight ball, comedian?"

Latham looked up at the cypress-paneled ceiling. "Oh, I don't know," he said thoughtfully, "maybe I've got an out."

"Don't make me laugh. That dough's hottern the hydrogen bomb."

"Yeah, yeah, but I still think I could have an out. It could be worked."

Joe said, "Don't make me laugh," but now he was watching Latham intently. "You can't work this one."

"No? Well, suppose I said to you: the money's in such and such a place. You pick it up and I'll meet you in Buenos Aires in six months. Of course if you were caught with the money, you'd be behind that eight ball, but for a fifty-fifty split, it'd be worth the chance. To protect myself and to make sure that you'd be there in six months, I'd have you sign a little paper saying that you'd stuck the ice pick in Ruby. I'd give you the paper back when you handed me my hundred thousand. Simple, isn't it? And it could be worked."

Joe's pale tongue darted across his lips. "It could at that," he whispered. "Sure it could."

"Is—this a proposition, Lath?"

"A proposition?" Latham's brows lifted in obviously simulated surprise. "Hell no. I just said *if* I knew where the money was, that's the way it could be worked, but I don't know where it is. Ruby and I were washed up a long time before this ever happened."

Joe's hand jerked and his knuckles whitened as his fingertips dug hard against the edge of the bar. "Washed up, eh?" he said thickly.

"A year and a half ago."

"And you didn't see her or give a damn about her or nothing, eh?"

"Right."

"And you didn't meet her none of those times she was in here looking for you. As far as you were concerned, she could drop dead." Joe was breathing a little heavily and his eyes were laden with the hate born of disappointment and the knowledge that Latham had played *him* for a sucker. "You didn't give a damn about her."

"That slate was wiped clean a long time ago."

"That's what I thought, or I wouldn't of touched her with a ten foot pole. You know me, don't borrow money from a friend and leave his women alone. But things being the way they were, what the hell, I figured if it wasn't me it'd be the next guy."

Latham felt the blood beat in his face as if his cheeks were clenching and he said, "You're a liar!"

"I am? What do you think I drove her home for those nights, the ride?"

Latham swung at him. The bartender saw the punch coming and he rolled with it but still it caught him high on the cheekbone. He staggered back, instinctively throwing out his arms to break a fall. He fell against the back bar, knocking several bottles of wine to the floor. He glanced a little dizzily at the sawed-off baseball bat under the bar but steadied himself and remained where he was, out of reach of Latham's fists. He laughed thinly.

"All washed up with her, were you?" he jeered and then pointed at the knot of beer drinkers who were staring silently up the bar at them. "This'll be all over town in an hour, chump."

Latham turned and walked out of the bar, hearing the bartender's "Sucker!" just before he slammed the door.

CHAPTER THIRTEEN

It was four-thirty when Latham walked down the long municipal dock to the *Belan*. The geodetic survey ship, the *Sosbee*, had come in and there was a small crowd of tourists curiously looking it over and talking to the crew. There was another crowd around the crossbeam from which hung four large tarpon. The fisherman, a paunchy, beaming middle-aged man, was having his picture taken with his catch. The kid, Chet Akin, was up on the flying bridge of the *Belan*, busily polishing the chrome work.

Latham looked up at him and said, "Don't you ever let up, kid?"

The boy grinned. "This is fun, Cap'n. This ain't work."

"How many charters you get for me while I was gone?"

"None, but—wait a minute. I'll be right down."

Latham jumped down into the stern cockpit, fitted with the two swiveled fighting chairs, and went into the cabin. Chet came in a few minutes later as Latham was taking off his sweat-streaked sport shirt.

"A guy was here to see you," the boy said a little breathlessly. "A cop."

Latham hung the shirt over the back of the tall chair at the wheel. "A fat, sloppy guy?"

"No, a tall dark one. He told me his name but—"

"Hanna? Captain Hanna?"

"Yeah, that's right. He was here about a half hour ago. He's tough, ain't he?"

Latham frowned. "He didn't give you a bad time, did he, kid?"

"No no, nothing like that. It was just the way he talked."

"What'd he say?"

"Well, first he asked if you were here and I said no so he said he'd wait and he went down into the cabin. I didn't want to let him, Cap'n, I don't let nobody on the boat when you ain't here, but he was a cop—"

"That's okay, kid. What else did he have to say?"

"Well, he hung around for about fifteen minutes or so and I kind of peeked in at him once or twice to see what he was doing, but he saw me and told me to beat it and I didn't argue with him. I mean, I didn't want no trouble with him. Then he came out, I was up on the bridge, and he looked up at me and gave a kind of nasty laugh and said to tell you that God had His eye on you. What'd he mean by that, Cap'n?"

"He was being funny," said Latham, knowing that Hanna had been anything but funny. "What was he doing in the cabin when you peeked in on him?"

"Nothing. Just sitting there reading out of a little book. Hey, he left it—"

He picked up a small, black book from the bunk and handed it to Latham. It was a pocket edition of the New Testament. Chet leaned forward to peer at it.

"It's a Bible," he said.

"Yeah," said Latham dryly, "Captain Hanna is a very religious man. You didn't see him search the cabin or anything like that, did you, kid?"

"No, both times I peeked in he was sitting there reading—and kind of talking to himself, it looked like. He looked mad. I thought he was sore at you."

"That's his normal expression. But that's all he said, that God had His eye on me?"

"That's all. And then he walked away and, you know how a guy walks when he's mad, coming down hard with his heels, that's the way he walked. I watched him and once somebody got in front of him and he just pushed him out of the way and kept going. You could see something was eating him, Cap'n."

"Something's always eating him," Latham growled. "He was born that way. You can knock off now, kid. It's almost five."

"Not before I finish the chrome up on the bridge, Cap'n. It's only half done."

"You can finish it tomorrow. You've worked enough for one day."

"Oh, I ain't got nothing else to do, Cap'n. My mother had to go to Tampa and she won't be back for two days ..."

"Okay, sure," said Latham quickly, seeing the loneliness and pleading in the boy's eyes. "Finish up the chrome and then we can have dinner together down here. Okay?"

"Sure!"

Latham smiled a little wryly as the boy darted eagerly out of the cabin. It was rough when you were that young and it took so little to make you happy because most of the time you weren't. Some home life the kid must have had. He had just changed into a pair of khaki shorts when he was startled by a heavy thumping on the side of the boat, followed by Chet's shrilly angry, "Hey, cut that out. You're making marks in the varnish."

A heavy voice rumbled, "I want to talk to the guy that runs the boat, kid."

Latham zipped up his shorts and went quickly out to the stern cockpit. Two heavy-set men in plaid sport jackets and a vivid but sullen-looking girl with black hair were standing on the dock beside the *Belan*.

"What's going on?" Latham demanded.

"He was kicking the side of the boat, Cap'n," Chet said defensively.

"Sorry, friend," the taller of the two men said; he was the one with the heavy rumbling voice. "I was just kind of knocking at the door. I didn't mean to hurt nothing. This boat's for rent, ain't it?"

"That's right."

"I thought so," the man lifted his chin and indicated the For Charter sign. "Me and my friends'd like to take a little boat ride."

Chet laughed and the man scowled up at him. "What's so funny?"

"You've got the wrong boat," Latham told him. "You want the *Jungle Miss*, the sight-seeing boat. It leaves from the end of the dock every morning at nine. This is a fishing boat."

"So what? It's for rent, ain't it? We want to go fishing."

"Then you've got the right boat," Latham kept a straight face. "A charter is fifty dollars a day."

"Fifty bucks a—" the man turned and looked at his two companions. "Is he kidding, Coot?"

"I think the man means it, Russ."

Russ turned back to Latham. "You mean it's fifty bucks a day just to go fishing?"

Latham smiled a little. He got many inquiries like this and it always amused him to see the look of incredulity that came over the faces of the would-be fishermen when he quoted the price.

"The boat you really want is the *Doris*," he said. "That's a party boat. They only charge six dollars a day and take you out to the grouper banks and guarantee that you'll catch a fish. This is a sportfishing boat."

"That's what I want—sport," said Russ. "But what kind of fish do you catch for fifty bucks a day? Whales?"

Latham laughed. "Tarpon, and when you hook one you'll think you've got a whale. There isn't a better fighting fish in the Gulf of Mexico."

"For fifty bucks a day they should fight Rocky Marciano. How's about it, Coot? You want to go out and fight some of them tarpons?"

"I'd just like to *see* one. They must be gold-plated."

"How's about you, Lila?"

"Crazy about it," said the girl in a voice of infinite boredom.

"Okay, friend," Russ told Latham, "you got a deal. When do we start?"

"Tomorrow morning."

"Why can't we go out now? I feel like fishing."

"It's too late. Anyway, the fish bite better in the morning." This was not true, but it was obvious that these men had never fished before and he did not want to take them out at night.

"Oh." Russ hesitated and looked at Coot, who shrugged. "Well, how's about a little ride out in the ocean for say a half hour or so? The little lady ain't never been out on a snappy boat like this."

"In that case, the little lady will get all of that she wants tomorrow, and if I were the little lady, I would bring along a bottle of pills for seasickness. If there's a chop or a heavy ground swell, she might need them."

The girl looked at Latham with interest. It was a lazy, sultry glance that lingered on his wide shoulders, the depth of his chest and the muscular legs.

"I don't think the little lady has anything to worry about," she said, "or is the captain going to rock the boat?"

"But how's about it, Cap?" Russ asked impatiently, "How's about taking us out for a little spin?"

"Sorry, not tonight. We're all cleaned up."

"I'll pay for it, if that's what you're worrying about."

The girl, Lila, tapped Russ on the shoulder. "Relax, junior. You can have your lollipop tomorrow." She smiled at Latham, a lingering and languorous smile. "What time should we be here, Captain?"

"At six."

"Six!" Russ looked disgusted. "At six you'd have to wake up the damn fish before you could catch them. Make it nine, Cap."

"Anytime you say, but it's still fifty dollars a day. In advance. If I were you, I'd leave at six. The fish bite better in the early morning."

Chet gaped down at him from the flying bridge in open-mouthed astonishment.

Russ grimaced at Coot. "The Captain says six o'clock, Coot."

"So he does, Russell, so he does. Maybe the Captain knows what he's talking about."

"But do you think the Captain will be here at six A.M., Mr. Coothelbert?"

"Personally, Mr. Bones, I think the Captain will be laughing into his pillowcase at six A.M."

"That would be very distressing, Mr. Coothelbert. That would distress me very much. That would irk me no end. That would raise my ire."

"Where there's smoke, there's ire, Mr. Bones. If the Captain is pounding his ear at six A.M. I personally would be in favor of giving him the old hot foot."

The girl sighed and sat down on the dock with a lazy show of long tanned legs. "Aren't they wonderful?" she said to Latham. "Aren't they refreshing? Now you know what killed radio. You might as well relax. They go on like this for hours. Don't ask me why."

"Now don't be like that, Lila," said Coot. "We're looking for a sponsor. But come clean, Cap. Will you be here at six A.M.?"

"I sleep on the boat," said Latham.

"Hm," said Lila, leaning forward to peer into the cabin, "how cozy."

Russ grinned and patted her on the head, winking at Coot. "Well well well," he said, "there's the answer, Coot. We'll leave Lila on this little dream boat just to make sure that the Captain will be here in the morning."

"It might not be a bad idea at that," the girl drawled, giving Latham a lazily appraising glance, which he met stolidly.

"Are you going to be here at six?" he asked Russ.

"You talked me into it, Cap," Russ took out a well-filled wallet and handed Latham a fifty-dollar bill, adding another ten a moment later. "The ten's for a bottle of Scotch and some club soda, Cap."

"Sorry, but I have a rule that liquor and fishing don't mix. I'll put some beer on ice if you want, but no liquor."

"We got to keep in training for them fighting tarpons, Russell," Coot said. "Let's get out of here before the Captain says we got to go to bed at nine with a glass of hot milk."

The girl rose to her feet with another lazy show of legs and a slow smile at Latham. "Pleasant dreams, Captain," she said.

Latham watched them walk down the dock, the two burly, heavy-footed men and the dark, slim girl. He looked thoughtfully at the sixty dollars in his hand. Chet stared round-eyed from the flying bridge.

"Well ain't that something!" he said.

"What?"

"I never thought you'd take that charter, Cap'n."

"Why not?"

"Well, I've seen you turn down guys that wasn't as bad as them. They don't care nothing about fishing. All they want to do's go out and get drunk just like a lot of them. I betcha they bring a bottle aboard anyways."

"Probably."

"Then why'd you take them, Cap'n?"

Latham held up the two bills he still had in his hand. "Fifty dollars is fifty dollars, kid. And anyway I feel like going out tomorrow."

"Yeah?" the kid jeered, grinning. "I betcha I know why, too. That dame."

"Not this time, sonny."

"You can't kid me, Cap'n. I saw the way she was giving you the eye. And she was really stacked too, wasn't she, Cap'n?"

"You notice a hell of a lot for a kid your age."

"Oh I been around, Cap'n," the boy boasted. "And you're going to have fun with them two guys tomorrow too—I don't think."

"I wouldn't be surprised," said Latham vaguely. "I'm going down for a case of beer and you get washed up and ready for dinner. You can sleep on the boat tonight if you want, being we're going out at six."

"Honest, Cap'n?" asked the boy eagerly. "You really mean I can sleep in one of the bunks?"

"No, I'm going to sling you over the side in a minnow net. Now get cleaned up for dinner."

When Latham returned about twenty minutes later with a case of Tropical beer, the boy was in the galley frying two redfish fillets which he had first dipped in batter.

"This is a surprise," he told Latham proudly. "A school of reds went through this afternoon and I snagged two of them in a minute and a half. The other one's in the refrige. I'm having string beans and hot buttered noodles with it. How's that?"

"You're some cook, kid."

"It's on account of my mother had to work since the old man died. I cook the dinner."

Latham patted him on the shoulder. "You're a good kid," he said and, kneeling, began to load the case of beer into the small refrigerator. He remembered now that Chet had told him that his mother was a demonstrator for a line of electrical appliances and had to travel from town to town showing them to women's clubs. Some kids would have run wild under those circumstances, but this was a good kid.

The dinner was surprisingly good and afterward Latham turned on the ship-to-shore radio and they listened to the fishing boats talking to each other out in the Gulf. The tarpon were running strongly at Boca Grande and though here had been no record catches, everybody was getting fish.

Chet said gleefully, "Won't those guys, Coot and Russ, be surprised if they really catch a fish tomorrow! I can't wait to see their faces when they hook into something big. I betcha they fall right out of the boat."

Latham said vaguely, "Maybe."

"I betcha those guys never caught a fish in their life. You ever catch any marlin, Cap'n?"

"A few, off Bimini and down in the Bahamas."

"Would you take me the next time you go, Cap'n?"

"Well, we'd have to ask your mother about that."

"Oh, she'd let me go. And I could be a big help to you, Cap'n. I been studying navigation and I can handle the boat and cut bait and I know all the kinds of rigs you have to have for different kinds of fish, like bonefish for marlin and crabs and mutton minnows or lures for tarpon. I wouldn't be in the way, Cap'n, honest. I know I can't run the boat as good as you, but I can run it as good or better than most guys."

"I know you can, kid, and if I go down to Marathon or Bimini, we'll talk it over with your mother. Hey, it's nine-thirty. We better turn in. We got a big day ahead of us tomorrow.

After the lights were out, Latham could hear the boy turning and fidgeting excitedly in his bunk, but in the darkness the sadness about Ruby came again more strongly and it was worse because the memory of how she had been before she went to pieces was alive and poignant in his mind.

It was about an hour later that the police came, two of them tramping on the dock. Latham got up when the flashlights glared in the ports and one of them said, "This is the boat all right. He must be asleep."

Chet was sleeping soundly in the other bunk and Latham went out to the stern cockpit. There were two uniformed policemen on the dock and one of them was preparing to jump down into the cockpit when Latham appeared.

"What's on your mind?" Latham asked.

"Your name Latham?"

"That's right."

"Keeler wants to see you."

"What for?"

"I wouldn't know," said the policeman. "He just said to pick you up."

"Pick me up?"

"This isn't a pinch. He just wants to see you."

"Why didn't he come himself?"

"You can ask him when you see him."

"The hell with him."

"Now don't be like that, Latham. If he wasn't tied up he would have come himself."

Latham hesitated and then shrugged. "I'll be with you as soon as I put some clothes on." Something had happened, he knew, or Keeler wouldn't be tied up. And Hanna had been looking for him that afternoon too. Now what? he wondered sourly.

He went back into the cabin and changed into slacks and a T-shirt in the dark, careful not to awaken the sleeping boy. Chet's lean young face looked even younger in sleep, softened by a slight smile instead of that pseudo-knowing grin he affected sometimes. He slept curled up, holding his pillow to his chest with both arms. His cockiness erased by the truth and innocence of sleep, he was just a defenseless young kid.

Cryptically, only half knowing what he meant himself, Latham thought, *"Don't worry about it, kid, don't ever worry about it."* Buckling his belt, he went out to the dock where the two policemen were waiting.

The police cruiser was at the foot of the dock in the parking zone. Latham sat in the back, and the police beside the driver half turned in his seat so that he could keep an eye on him.

Latham growled, "I'm not going to jump out the window, for God's sake. What's Keeler tied up with?"

"He'll tell you all about it when you see him."

Latham knew that it was useless to ask any further questions. These two were just stooges for Keeler and they wouldn't know anything anyway. He lit a cigarette and leaned back, yawning. He hoped it wasn't going to be another long session. He had that charter coming up at six and he wished now that he had let them come at nine as they had wanted. But you didn't do things like that if you had any pride in your business. You didn't let yourself get sloppy.

He was suddenly aware that they had turned away from the road to the downtown section of Sanibar and police headquarters. They were on the road to the south end of town. Latham sat up more alertly and watched the street signs. They made another turn and he knew that they were on their way to Ruby's apartment. Five minutes later they stopped in front of the scattered units of the garden apartments, but it was in Wooten's apartment that the light was on, not in Ruby's.

The two policemen got out of the car and one of them held the back of the front seat down so that Latham could get out. Police cruisers were all two door cars for obvious reasons.

The policeman said, "Let's go, Latham," and they walked into the apartment with him, one on either side. If this wasn't a pinch, it was the next thing to it.

Latham knew what he was going to find when he walked into that big, untidy room, and the first thing he saw when they went through the doorway was the body of Wooten on the studio couch, a lamp cord imbedded in the swollen flesh of his skinny neck. He had been strangled and his cyanotic face and protruding tongue made his death a mask of horror. Keeler looked out from the kitchenette at the sound of their entrance. He looked terrible. His eyes were completely bloodshot and his face had the appearance of kneaded, unbaked dough.

"Sit down, I'll be with you in a minute," he mumbled and turned back to the kitchenette, from which came the mutter of two men in low-voiced conversation.

He came out in about five minutes with two other men in plain clothes, one of whom carried a camera and a tripod. Keeler said, "Thanks boys, and get those shots developed as fast as you can." The two men left the apartment, giving Latham a flat, incurious glance as they went. Keeler also dismissed the two uniformed policemen and closed the hall door, leaving himself alone with Latham. He tilted his chin at the body on the studio couch.

"There goes your alibi, Joe," he said.

"You're my alibi, remember?" said Latham woodenly.

"Uh-uh. I was your alibi only as long as Wooten was alive. As it stands now, only you and me know that you were in Ruby's apartment while McElroy was being knocked off. Just you and me, and sometimes I have a very bad memory."

Before Latham could answer, there was a knock on the door and Keeler opened it to admit two men carrying a long, coffin-like basket.

"Take it away," he said, waving his hand limply at the corpse on the studio couch. "We're done with it."

Latham watched them carelessly lift the body of Wooten into the basket and carry it out. Keeler closed the door again, this time snapping the spring lock. All his movements were heavy as if he were bone-tired and marrow-tired, though his blood-red eyes, darting at Latham, were very much alive.

"That's the way it is, Joe," he said. "No more alibi unless I feel like giving you one."

"It'll take more than that to pin the McElroy killing me," said Latham in the same wooden voice.

"Maybe. But you don't know Hanna. He's just aching to pin that on you."

"I thought I'd find him here. Or is this something else you didn't tell him about yet."

"He's working on something of his own."

Keeler's manner was evasive, and Latham wondered why. He knew that Keeler wouldn't dare conduct this investigation without notifying Hanna. Keeler was evasive, but there was something smug and satisfied in his manner, too.

"Sit down, Joe," he said. "Let's forget Hanna for the minute. This is just between me and you. What's the matter?"

Latham was staring at the table on which, not eight hours before, he had seen those pictures and the heads of Ruby that Wooten had cut from magazines and the newspapers. On the table now was a gray and black heap of curled ash, as if someone had crumpled the pictures before burning them.

Latham said, "Nothing."

Keeler followed Latham's gaze and looked at the heap of ash on the table. "You look as if you knew something about that."

"I don't know a thing."

"The hell you don't. I happen to know that you were in here to see

Wooten. We got your fingerprints on a coffee cup, the doorknob and a couple other things. Did you burn that stuff when you were here?"

"I don't know the first thing about it."

"Why make it tough for yourself, Joe? That stuff might have been important. What was it?"

"Okay, I'll tell you," said Latham, sourly anticipating Keeler's reaction. "They were just some pictures of girls that Wooten had cut out of a magazine. They were spread out on the table when I saw him this afternoon."

Keeler stared, unbelieving. "You expect me to believe that?"

"I don't expect anything. You asked, and I'm telling you. If you don't believe me, have the ashes analyzed or something."

Keeler said peevishly, "You know damn well we don't have the equipment for that. Pictures out of a magazine! What kind of sense is that supposed to make? And why burn them in the second place?"

"That's your problem, not mine. I'm just telling you what I saw this afternoon, pictures cut from a magazine." He did not add that the newspaper pictures of Ruby's head had been superimposed. He knew what kind of obscenity Keeler would make out of that, though there had been nothing obscene about Wooten's pitiful display.

Keeler looked sharply into Latham's face. "If that's all it was, why burn it?" he demanded.

"Your guess is as good as mine. Maybe Wooten set fire to them accidentally. He was pretty drunk when I left him. He might have tried to light a cigarette and dropped match on the table."

"Nuts. You can see by the ash that they were all crumpled up before they were set fire to. Somebody did that on purpose. Sit down, Joe. I want to talk to you."

"And suppose I don't feel like talking, what then?"

Keeler looked significantly at the closed door. "I could call in the boys and have you taken down to Headquarters, and I got enough on you to take you in for questioning. Can't you get it through your head that I'm actually giving you a break. Look, you were in to see Wooten this afternoon, and now we find him knocked off and your fingerprints all over the place, and Wooten was the only one who saw the guy with Ruby that night. Together with a few other odds and ends I picked up, we could make a nice little case against you, if you believe it or not. For instance, I happen to know that Ruby was in Joe's Joint saying she had a date with you three or four times during the past few weeks. How do you think that would sound in front of a jury? Be reasonable. I could run you in right now, but I'm giving you a break. Don't you realize that I'm just about the only guy in the whole town that can really help you out of this mess? You're in it up to your neck, pal. All I want to do is talk to you and the first thing you do is get on your high horse. Use your head, will you?"

"Okay," said Latham, "let's talk."

"You could of said that in the first place," Keeler grumbled. "You can see for yourself I'm giving you every kind of a break. Sit down and relax."

Latham shrugged and took the armchair while Keeler sat on the studio couch which had so recently held a grimmer burden. Keeler's hands were shaking a little as he struck a match and held it to the cigarette in his mouth. He blew out the match and dropped it on the floor.

"Look at it this way, Joe," he said. "Maybe I'm the only friend you've got left in this town, the only friend that can do you any real good. I think that should be worth something to you."

"You wouldn't have your hand out, would you, Keeler?"

"Not for nickels and dimes, Latham," said Keeler softly, "not for nickels and dimes."

Latham stretched out his legs before him and lounged down in the chair. "I've been waiting for this pitch. Go on, let's have the rest of it."

"I'll make it short and sweet. I'm talking about two hundred thousand bucks."

"That comes as a big surprise," said Latham dryly.

"I'll bet. I want in on that, Latham. I want in for a fifty percent cut."

"But wouldn't that come under the head of bribing an officer of the law?" Latham mocked him.

"Let's not backfire into a wisecrack," said Keeler angrily. "I'm not kidding about this. I want in for fifty percent."

"I'll think it over."

"There's nothing to think over. I want yes or no."

"Being friends with you isn't exactly a bargain at those rates, is it?"

"It's a real bargain when you consider that I could rig the damnedest case against you that you ever saw. And I wouldn't have to do much rigging at that. You're backed into a corner that's getting tighter all the time."

"I could buy a dozen lawyers for a hundred thousand dollars. Your price is a little high, isn't it?"

"Don't you believe it, Latham," said Keeler grimly. "You'd need a dozen lawyers, the case I could make against you. And on top of that, you don't have a prayer of getting near that two hundred thousand bucks. There'd be somebody watching you for the rest of your life even if we couldn't stick you with a murder rap. Think that one over for a minute or two."

Latham shifted in his chair, pretending to be uneasy and troubled. "I don't see how you can take the heat off unless you can wrap the case up and how can you do that?"

"That's tailor made and here's how it can be done. Some of that two hundred thousand is in municipal bonds. We'll take about five thousand of that and 'find' it someplace in McElroy's shore cottage. That'll automatically put him in on the deal with Ruby and from there on in it'll be easy to show that him and Ruby had a scrap about the money and he knocked her off."

"Yeah, but who knocked him off?"

"A guy in McElroy's business, he'd know some pretty tough characters now, wouldn't he? Some of the guys he knew'd knock off their own mother for a sawbuck, and I'm not kidding about that. That part of it'd be easy."

"But there's still Wooten. Why should he get knocked off? That has to be taken care of, too."

"It's all the same thing. Let's say it wasn't McElroy that knocked off Ruby but this pal of his. It can be done."

"Not by just saying so. You'd have to have somebody in mind."

Keeler winked. "I said it could be done, didn't I? If we planted another few thousand of those bonds, there'd be no question."

"You mean—you'd frame somebody for *murder?*"

"Brother," said Keeler bluntly, "for a hundred thousand bucks I'd frame this whole damn town for murder. I've been an honest cop all my life and I don't give a damn if you believe it or not, but it's the truth. Some of the other guys in the department have had their hands out all over the place, but for my money that's nickel and dime stuff and they're suckers to stick their neck out. But this is different. This is big money, and with my cut of it, I can tell Hanna and all the rest of them what to do with themselves. Well, how's it sound to you?"

Latham pretended to worry the plan in the teeth of his mind. "Well," he said finally, "there's only one trouble with it."

"There's no trouble with it," Keeler said impatiently. "I can handle this one with my eyes shut."

"But there is one trouble and unless you can figure an angle on it, we're stuck."

"What is it?"

Latham grinned savagely. "I don't know where the money is, you bastard!"

Keeler sat very still, his cigarette half raised to his mouth His face was mottled and seemed to swell. Without a word he got up heavily from the couch, walked across the room, opened the door and went out into the small hall. He stood with his back to Latham, staring out at the darkened patio. It was so quiet that the faint dry rustling of the palms sounded like a man crumpling stiff paper in the next room. Latham waited for Keeler to summon the two policemen parked in the prowl car at the curb but the detective just stood there snapping his fingers in a sharp, angry rhythm. His shoulders were hunched and his round head sunk between them. Finally he turned and came back into the room, closing the door behind him. His face was hard and his mouth was a mean, thin slit.

"I'm going to give you twenty-four hours, Latham," he said in a voice devoid of expression. "At the end of that time if I don't hear from you, I'm going to have you picked up and booked for murder."

"You might as well do it now, hot shot."

"And I'll tell you one more thing, just to let you know what you're up against. You went to see Fritz Meyn this afternoon."

"That's right. And Doug Hemming, too."

"Well, Fritz called Headquarters a little after six and said you asked him a lot of suspicious sounding questions. He said you acted as though you were trying to find out how much Ruby had told him about her and you. That's going to sound swell in front of a jury, together with all the other stuff I got on you. He's going to make a good witness for the prosecution, Latham."

"If you can get him to testify. He's scared to death of his wife and that she'll find out he was running around with Ruby. You'll never get him up on the witness stand."

"There's one little detail I forgot to tell you. It was his wife that called first and said Fritz had something to tell us. She was the one that made him call. It seems she was listening at the bedroom door when you were talking to Fritz, and she has the idea that you're trying to get him mixed up in the killing. Between her and Fritz and the guy that runs the gin mill down near the lumber yard, the jury is going to get the idea that you've been running around trying to lay a neat cover for yourself. I wouldn't want to be in your shoes for the whole two hundred thousand, once you're up there for trial. And don't forget those half-finished letters from Ruby to you. We have it in her own handwriting that she was nuts about you right up to the very end. And here's Wooten dead and your fingerprints all over the place. The prosecutor's a bright boy and he'd just love to go to court with a case like that against you. But if you think you can beat the rap, go right ahead. Let's see how you feel when the jury comes back and hands you a couple thousand volts as a going-away present."

Latham looked at him curiously as he might have looked at someone caught performing a particularly disgusting act.

"Tell me something off the record, Keeler," he said. "Do you think I killed Wooten or Ruby or McElroy or all three?"

Keeler sniggered contemptuously. "Frankly, chump," he said, "I don't think you had the guts. I think it happened just the way I told you, with a few slight changes. I think McElroy and some other guy found out that Ruby and Mays were tapping the bank. Ruby had a habit of talking a little too much when she got stewed. I think McElroy tried to cut in but he had a lousy temper and lost his head when he stuck that ice pick into her. And I think his pal didn't quite believe him when he said he didn't get anything from Ruby, and that was the end of McElroy. And I think you and Ruby were the ones who took Mays over the bumps and you know damn well where the money is. So that's the way we'll let it stand for the next twenty-four hours, and in the meantime I'll probably pick up a few more things the prosecutor'll be glad to have when he brings you to trial. And don't think I'm kidding you because I'm not. Think it over. I'll be waiting." He tipped his hand from his forehead in a mocking salute and walked out of the apartment and a few minutes later Latham heard two cars drive away, Keeler's and the prowl car.

Latham calmly lit a cigarette and sat staring at the heap of ashes on the table. Twenty-four hours, he thought, twenty-four hours. He did not doubt that Keeler meant every word of his threat, but he did not think of it that way. He had twenty-four hours in which to explode that threat in Keeler's face. He did not know how it could be done, but he had twenty-four hours.

He found himself regarding the heap of ashes with growing bafflement. Keeler had been right about one thing—it didn't make sense. They had been only pictures cut from magazines and newspapers, nothing that anyone would want to destroy. There was no clue there, nothing that meant anything to anybody except the pathetic Wooten. But it had to have a significance or the killer would not have bothered burning them. Wooten himself would not have done it any more than he would have destroyed Ruby herself. It didn't make sense.

It was not until he left the apartment that he remembered that he did not have his own car. The prowl car had brought him there. It was a long walk back to the dock but Latham did not feel like calling a cab. He wanted to walk and not think about anything except the physical thing of walking fast into the soft, cool night. In a cab it would be just sitting and thinking. It took him a half hour of brisk walking to reach the long black finger of the dock that pointed across the bay to the muttering Gulf to the west of the Key. As he crossed the shadowed street a voice thickly called his name from a car parked under the spread of a royal poinciana tree. Latham approached warily until he saw that it was Hanna sitting behind the wheel.

A very drunk Hanna!

Latham put his hands on the edge of the window and looked at the swaying, disheveled man inside. The smell of undigested whiskey was sour in the air.

"Well well well, Captain," he said, "did the devil take you to a mountaintop and tempt you?"

Barely able to sit upright, Hanna looked owlishly at him. Finally in an alcohol-slurred voice he said, "You're Latham. Joseph Latham."

"That's right, Captain. But who are you, one of the fallen angels?"

"You are mocking me, Latham, but you don't know, you don't know." Hanna took a heavy breath. "I've been wrestling with myself, Latham, I've been wrestling with the devil that is in myself. Every man, Latham, every man in the whole world has a devil in himself. Did you know that? You've got a devil in you and I've got a devil in me. People don't know they've got a devil inside themselves, but they have. You hear of somebody doing something bad, Latham, and people say, well he's only human, but that is not so. The devil makes a man proud, Latham. God wants a man to be humble, but the devil makes him proud and he thinks he is something better than he is. Do you know what I'm talking about, Latham? I've been wrestling with myself, Latham, wrestling with myself and the devil that is in myself."

"You've been wrestling with something all right, but if you ask me, it came in a bottle."

"You have a right to mock me, Latham," Hanna's voice droned thickly. "You have a right to mock me because I was proud and I realized I was proud and then I was ashamed."

"Look, pal," said Latham, becoming a little disgusted with this now, "why don't you go home and sleep it off? I'm tired and I'm going to bed."

"You don't know what I'm talking about, do you, Latham?"

"You're drunk and you don't know either. Go home and sleep it off. And tomorrow morning," he added cynically, "you'll be ready to crucify me because I saw you this way."

"You're wrong, Latham, you're wrong." Hanna lifted a wavering hand. "I have waited here to talk to you. I know I'm drunk, I know, I know, but that's of no importance. I did it to humble myself. I hated you, Latham. That was the devil inside of me. I hated you. I thought you were rotten with lust, filled with the maggots of desire, lies and filth. But I was blinded with pride."

Latham lit a cigarette and leaned against the car. "Boy," he said, "you're really something. Do you get like this very often? I didn't think you were very fond of me."

"I was wrong, Latham, wrong, wrong!"

"You mean you don't think I've got maggots anymore?"

"In my pride, Latham, I closed my eyes to the thing you told me, the thing that showed me that you did not lust after her like the rest of them. I have wronged you, Latham, and I humble myself before you."

"If you think you're humble now, wait till that hangover gets hold of you in the morning. That'll really bow you low."

"I wanted to save her soul and you wanted to save her body, but we both loved her, Latham. We loved her. I know, Latham, how you tried to take her to a doctor to be cured. I was told how you pleaded with her and how she scorned you. We loved her, but she was bad and we cast her out in our pride. We are the ones who should be punished, Latham. We are the ones on whom the wrath of God should fall, but there might be some grace for us for we did not lust after her. There is forgiveness in the Lord. Our punishment is that we failed, but there is forgiveness in the Lord if we but bow our heads and humbly ask His mercy. The way of the transgressor is hard and the wrath of God shall be visited upon him. Come to the Lord, Latham—"

Latham turned suddenly from the car and strode toward the dock.

Hanna cried thickly after him, "Latham, Latham, blessed are the pure in heart—"

"Go home!"

"I'll pray for you, Latham. I wronged you and I will beg forgiveness."

Latham strode on and did not look back again though Hanna's drunken voice continued to cry after him. When he reached the boat, he stepped softly into the stern cockpit. He opened the cabin door very quietly and then froze, staring incredulously at the wild disorder within.

Every locker and cabinet had been opened and emptied on the deck and the bunks, and even the door of the small refrigerator in the galley hung open. The mattresses of the bunks had been ripped open and the feathers from the gutted pillows were everywhere. There was a faint knocking from the head, which lay forward of the galley and, swearing, Latham leaped for the door. The boy, Chet, lay curled inside, tied with fishing line, a wide strip of white adhesive tape across his mouth.

CHAPTER FOURTEEN

Snatching up a carving knife from the galley, Latham went down on his knees beside the boy and swiftly cut the lines that bit deeply into the kid's thin wrists and ankles. The boy's eyes were tremendous and there was a thin trickle of blood from a lump on his forehead.

"Are you all right, kid?" Latham asked anxiously. "Do you feel okay?"

Chet nodded, but there was pain in his eyes when he tried to move his hands and legs. Latham patted his shoulder soothingly.

"That's just the circulation getting back into your hands and feet, kid," he said, trying to sound reassuring. "Just lie quietly for a minute or two and you'll be all right. I'll let you take that tape off your mouth yourself. I don't want to hurt you."

He breathed a silent prayer and felt a flood of relief when at last the boy sat up and picked gingerly at a corner of the adhesive tape.

A towering fury was mounting in Latham, but he kept his voice quiet and soothing, for the shock was still naked in Chet's distended eyes. "I'll get some rubbing alcohol, kid, and we'll peel that thing off by degrees. You don't want to pull all the skin off your mouth."

It took about five minutes of slow, patient work and the boy took off the last half inch of the tape with a sudden jerk. He gave Latham a shaky grin.

"It was a tough fight, Mom," he said, "but I lost."

"What happened, kid?"

"I don't know, Cap'n. I was asleep and then I heard a noise and the next thing I knew I was all tied up in here."

"How's your head feel?"

"My head?" Chet raised a wondering hand and winced when his fingers touched the bump on his forehead. "They smacked me!"

"Let me help you up."

The boy swayed when Latham helped him to his feet. Latham helped him out into the cabin and cleared one of the debris-laden bunks with a savage sweep of his arm. "You lie down, kid. I'm going to get a doctor."

Chet protested weakly, "I'm okay, Cap'n."

"I know you are," Latham growled. "It'd take a Mack truck to hurt one of you thick-headed crackers, but I want a doctor to look at that bump anyway. Now you lie down till I get back, and I don't want any arguments."

He strode out of the cabin, swearing under his breath. He glanced down the dock and saw Hanna's car still parked under the royal poinciana tree. "*I'll be with you in a minute, bud,*" he thought grimly. He stopped at the public phone booth on the dock and called the doctor, then strode down to Hanna's car. The man was asleep with his head on the wheel. Latham jerked him upright and slapped his face sharply until Hanna opened his eyes and feebly tried to push Latham away. A car door slammed and Keeler came lumbering from the parking lot.

He saw Hanna inside the car and whistled under his breath. He snatched a blackjack from his hip pocket and swung backhanded at Latham's head. Latham ducked and, taking a short step forward, hit Keeler heavily in the stomach. Keeler fell against the fender of the car and hung there, gagging. Latham kicked the blackjack into the darkness across the street and turned to Hanna again. He jerked open the door and pulled Hanna out of the car, slapping him across the face, back and forth. Hanna's head lolled, his hands pawed helplessly and he tried to protest but his voice was only an inarticulate mumble.

Latham snarled, "Damn you!" and as he drew back his fist he heard Keeler say sharply, "Hold it, Latham!" The fat detective was propped against the car, his left hand holding his middle, a gun in his other hand.

"Let him go or I'll blow your legs out from under you," he ordered.

Latham glared at him but gradually the hot red mist of fury cleared out of his brain. He released his grip on Hanna's shirt front and the detective captain's knees sagged and he fell to the pavement. He rolled on his side, gave a sigh and fell asleep with his head cradled in the crook of right arm.

"Now what was that all about?" Keeler demanded.

"The son of a bitch ransacked my boat and beat up the kid who was sleeping there."

Keeler said flatly, "You're nuts."

"The hell I am. And when he sobers up, cop or no cop, I'm going to beat the hell out of him."

"I still say you're nuts. You don't know Hanna. If he wanted to go through your boat he'd have had a search warrant and he'd of made damn sure you were there when he did it."

"Maybe he had the same idea you had, Keeler. Maybe the thought of that two hundred thousand was a little too much for him, too."

"You don't know him if that's what you think, Latham. Money don't mean a thing to him."

"Don't make me laugh."

"If I didn't have a personal interest in you for the next twenty-four hours I'd let you tangle with Hanna, but I don't want nothing to happen to you, so I'm telling you money don't mean nothing to him and I can prove it."

"This should be good, a cop with no interest in money."

"You're looking at one, Latham, you're looking at one. He's been making good money for the past ten years or more, but he ain't hardly got a cent in the bank, and you know why? He gives it away to the church and the missionaries. He practically supports the missionaries. It ain't no secret and you don't have to believe me. Just ask the minister of his church. Ask him who's the first to kick in with a good substantial hunk of dough every time there's a special collection. And he wouldn't touch a cent of that two hundred thousand."

"Maybe he wanted to give it to the missionaries."

"Be yourself, chump," said Keeler, taking him literally. "How could he get away with a thing like that? Anyway, take a look at him. Is he in any shape to beat up anybody, even a kid? He's slopped to the eyeballs and out cold. He couldn't even make trouble for a midget. And hell, it's only a little over an hour since I had the boys pick you up. They picked you up at ten-thirty and it's only quarter to twelve now."

"What's that supposed to mean?"

"He just wouldn't have the time to go through your boat, beat up somebody and get soused too, would he?"

"You're sure trying hard, aren't you?"

"Only for the next twenty-four hours, chump, that's all."

"Well, take good care of your boss because I'm going to find out if he was on that boat tonight, and if he was, I'm going to beat the living hell out of him!"

He turned and walked up the dock, ignoring Keeler's jeering laugh. When he stepped aboard the *Belan* he found that the cabin had been completely cleaned and put in order and Chet was just sweeping up the last of the feathers from the gutted pillows. The boy started and grinned defensively when Latham walked in.

"I just thought I'd clean up the mess a little, Cap'n," he apologized.

"I thought I told you to lie down in the bunk and stay there."

"But I feel all right, Cap'n—"

"Sure, till you keel over. Now lie down until we hear what the doctor has to say. And the next time you do as I tell you or I don't want you on the boat at all," Latham said gruffly, disguising his relief that the boy had felt well enough to clean the cabin.

Chet obeyed meekly and stretched out on the bunk. "You're not sore with me, are you, Cap'n?"

"You'll have to learn to do as you're told. I don't want to have to worry every time I give you an order."

The doctor came aboard a few minutes later, sleepy-eyed and yawning. "Is that the patient?" he grumbled, looking at Chet who grinned at him from the bunk. "He doesn't look like an emergency case to me."

"He got a bad bump on the head," Latham said.

"Well, a head bump isn't anything to fool around with. Let's take a look at this terrible wound, son. You might be dead and don't know it."

Chet continued to grin while the doctor felt all around the bump with sensitive fingers.

"It's a bump, all right. How'd it happen, son?"

"I got up in the dark to go to the head and ran into the door to the galley," the boy said quickly.

"Well, you'll live. There's no fracture. I don't think we'll have to put your head in a cast after all. But do me a favor, will you, son? The next time you feel like running into a door, do it in the middle of the day so a man can get some sleep."

Latham walked out of the cabin with the doctor and up on the dock he said, "Is he really okay, Doc? I mean, should he stay in bed for a day or so or anything like that?"

"You'd probably have to tie him hand and foot if you tried it. I doubt that he'll even have a headache in the morning."

"Well thank God for that!"

The doctor looked at him curiously. "Well well well," he said, "I never thought I'd see the day—the tough Joe Latham acting like an anxious papa. That wouldn't be one of your wild oats by any chance, would it, Joe?"

"Cut it out, Doc. I was just worried about the kid, that's all."

Both men turned and stared down the dock as a speeding car braked with screaming tires and came to a stop on the Bay Shore road. Keeler's sharp voice came clearly over the water, "Just do as you're told, damn it, and keep your fat mouth shut!" A few moments later the headlights of three cars swept the dark waters of the bay as they turned and headed back toward the city.

"Well," said the doctor wonderingly, "what was that all about?"

"I imagine," said Latham, "that it was Floyd Keeler and the prowl car taking Captain Hanna home. Captain Hanna had a snootful."

"Hanna? Hm, that's unusual. The last time he took a drink was seven years ago when his wife died."

"What was he doing, celebrating?"

"No, he wasn't celebrating," said the doctor in a quietly rebuking voice. "He was suffering. He thought he was taking his wife down the path of righteousness, but instead it was the road to hell. He has the common delusion that God is a kind of super-policeman and the poor woman couldn't take it. The death certificate said she died of pneumonia, but she just didn't have the will to live anymore. I think Hanna realized that and that's why he went off on a bender. He's not as tough as you are, Joe."

"Whatever gave you the idea that I was tough, Doc?"

"It took a pretty tough man to slap Ruby Lake down the way you did when you broke your engagement to her."

"I wanted to help her but she didn't want to be helped," said Latham shortly.

"I tell you something, Joe. Half the people I treat don't want me to help them, not really. They just want me to hold their hands, but I have to help them in spite of themselves, and some of them would die if I said, 'Well if you don't want to be helped, the hell with you.' The way you did with Ruby Lake. She was close to a nervous breakdown when you broke the engagement. I know you wanted to help her, but the only thing you did was scare the poor girl out of her wits. If you'd had a little more patience or hadn't been so tough about it, she'd have come around. I know because I had her on my hands for a month after you broke it up. She'd have done anything for you."

"Oh sure, except go to a psychiatrist and get the kind of help she needed."

"She shied away because she had the idea that you thought she was going crazy, and she couldn't face that. But she would have done even that for you, Joe, given a little time and understanding—instead of being told flatly that she had to do it your way or else."

"You just plain don't know what you're talking about, Doc, so let's drop it."

"Yes, you're right. I can be wrong too. Maybe Ruby couldn't be helped. Go back to your boy inside. He's somebody you can help, and I was glad to see that you were worried about him."

"He's a good kid."

"I know, and he thinks the world of you. Don't get tough with him."

The doctor plodded down the dock and Latham went back into the cabin of the boat. The boy was sitting up the bunk, looking at Latham with wide, troubled eyes.

"Is everything all right, Cap'n?" he asked. "You were out there such a long time."

"You're okay, kid. The doctor said you won't even have a headache in the morning."

"Then I can go out on that charter with you?"

"Sure, why not?"

"You're not sore at me anymore?"

"I never was sore at you, Chet. I was just worried about that bump on your head. You should have stayed in the bunk till the doctor got here. You might have had a fracture and moving around the way you did could have made it worse. Do you feel like talking?"

The boy grinned happily, "Sure, Cap'n!"

"Did you get even a glimpse of the guy who slugged you, kid."

"I didn't even get a peek at him, but—"

"But what?"

"There's something I been trying to remember, but I can't think of it.

I mean," his hands moved in a bewildered gesture, "there was something I knew I should remember, but all I can think of is a party and that ain't the thing."

"Well, don't worry about it, kid. Maybe it'll come to you tomorrow."

"I'll try, Cap'n."

"No, don't try and don't worry about it. Just let it come and if it doesn't, that's okay too."

Latham noticed that the boy was watching him with an air of suppressed excitement and had several times started to say something but had held it back as if waiting for Latham to give him a lead.

Finally Latham asked, "Is there something on your mind, kid?"

"Well, I was kind of wondering, that's all. Why that guy searched the boat, I mean. You know, all that talk about you and Miss Lake, maybe he thought you had the money or something. Do you think that's what he was looking for, Cap'n?"

"I wouldn't be surprised, but forget it."

"I—I been thinking, Cap'n—"

Latham was about to tell him abruptly to forget it for once and all, but that would have been a slap in the face to the kid, so he said, "Thinking about what, Chet?"

"Well—I know you didn't have nothing to do with it and all that, but some of the guys say this Miss Lake was really crazy about you and all that and it got me to thinking. They say she didn't care nothing about that Mr. Mays down at the bank, but she was really nuts about you." Then timidly, "You don't mind me saying this, do you, Cap'n? I mean, I'm just telling what the guys say."

"I don't mind, but you shouldn't pay any attention to that kind of talk, kid."

"Oh, I don't, Cap'n, but it just got me to thinking, that's all. Not about you but about Miss Lake.

"Well there was this dame in school. She was a real hot dog. I mean she had feathers in her brains and she was nuts about Vic Toomey on account of he's quarterback on the football team and makes all the touchdowns, only he wouldn't give her a tumble. Then he started finding all kinds of things in his desk, a fountain pen, a fishing reel, a wrist watch strap, and like that, and he didn't know what the hell and he started asking questions and somebody told the principal and the next day they caught this dizzy dame sneaking in ahead of class and putting a cigarette lighter in his desk. So they took her up the principal's office and when they got finished she was bawling her eyes out and said she'd been shoplifting the things all over town on account of she didn't have no money and she wanted to give Toomey presents so he'd fall for her. She was real dizzy, but they didn't do nothing to her 'cause Toomey didn't use none of the stuff and they gave it all back."

Latham stared into the serious face of the boy and then burst into a guffaw of laughter. "And you think that's what Miss Lake did, kid, hide the money in my desk without my knowing it?"

"Well," said Chet sheepishly, "I know it sounds kind of screwy, but if one dizzy dame did it, another one could do it too, couldn't she? I mean, if she wanted you to fall for her."

Latham reached out and patted the boy's knee. "I didn't mean to laugh, kid, but I don't think Miss Lake left any two hundred thousand dollar presents around for me. A cigarette lighter or a fountain pen, well, they're different, but—"

He stopped as if the words had frozen on his lips in a sudden blast of petrifying cold. Ruby had not been normal these past few months, and then there were those half-finished or just-started letters that Keeler had found in her wastebasket, the ones that she had intended to put in the "mailbox." Only it wasn't the ordinary dark green mailbox of the street corner; it was the huge banyan tree that spread over the parking lot at the foot of the dock. That was the "mailbox" in which she had left her midnight notes to him when they had been engaged. Latham felt the cold heavy on the back of his neck and he thought, "Oh God!"

He heard the boy's voice saying something and vaguely he asked, "What was that, kid?"

"I just said I hope you weren't mad with me. I mean, it was a screwy idea."

"Yeah, yeah, but we all have screwy ideas at some time or other, so don't worry about it. If you're going to be up by six, you'd better hit the sack. I'm going to take a little walk on the dock. I'll be right back."

He left quickly, not wanting to answer any more questions except the one big one that was coiling and straining in his mind. He walked down the dock, looking back every few steps as if afraid the boy might be following him. The huge banyan tree was a cave of black in the darkness of the parking lot. There was no moon in the sky and the blackness there seemed beyond that of night, a waiting and engulfing thing.

Latham was aware of the slow hammer of his pulses as he felt his way among the thick aerial roots that made an almost impenetrable maze of the tree. The "mailbox" was at the very heart of the maze, a niche in the main trunk. He groped his way slowly until his hands encountered the massive bole and then he felt along very carefully until he found the niche. He did not immediately reach into it. The palms of his hands were sweating and he wiped them down the sides of his thighs. He reached into the niche and there was an oblong box there, wrapped in something smooth like plastic. It seemed as if he stood there for an eternity with his unmoving hand just resting on the box. His heart continued its slow, steady thumping. His fingers examined the box. It was tied tightly with rough twine, wound twice around the length and width of the box. He turned the box and underneath he felt the outline of an envelope held in place by the twine. His mind was working at possibly its lowest level—this is a box, it is wrapped in plastic, it is tied with twine, this is an envelope, there is a note in the envelope. He hesitated, breathing shallowly through his slightly parted lips, and then pulled the envelope from under the bristly twine. He folded it very carefully in half and put it into his hip pocket. He did not touch the box again and when he turned to grope his way back through the labyrinth of roots, the box remained in the niche. He had no conscious reason for doing this. He simply left it where it was. It was as if his mind were locked, permitting the exit of no thoughts except the merest essentials.

Outside he leaned against the fender of his car and was vaguely surprised to see that his hand was trembling when he held a match to his cigarette. He had a note in his pocket. It was from Ruby. He wanted to read the note. He could go into the car and turn on the dashboard light and read it there, but as he opened the car door he heard a footstep crunch in the shell that covered the parking area and Keeler's voice asked;

"Going someplace, Latham?"

Latham said casually, "Left the keys in the car. Bad habit," and reached into the car as if removing his keys from the ignition lock. "Get the Captain home all right, Keeler?"

"Fine, Latham, fine. Were you worried?"

"It made me very sad to see a fine upstanding man like the Captain in such a condition."

"I'll bet. If you want to take a little drive, go right ahead, Latham. You won't get far in twenty-four hours."

"But I like Florida, Keeler. I have no intention of leaving it. I've been thinking about that money, too."

"Change your mind?"

Latham could see Keeler now, a slouched figure leaning against a tubby cabbage palm, fifteen feet to his left.

Keeler wanted the money.

Good.

Now he had found a real use for Keeler.

"I don't know where the money is," he said, "but I might be able to find out." He could almost see Keeler smile in the darkness.

"Fine," said Keeler. "Maybe by this time tomorrow night you'll have it all figured out."

"Maybe. But I'll need some help."

"You won't need any help, baby. You'll be able to figure it out all by yourself. Just keep thinking of that little old electric chair and you'll be surprised how much you can figure out for yourself."

"No, I'll need help. From the guy who killed Ruby."

"Are you drunk?"

"Cold sober, Keeler, and I don't know where the money is. Keep that in mind and listen. I knew Ruby better than practically anybody in town. I knew how her mind worked, and there's a chance, with death staring her in the face, that she tried to tell the killer where it was hidden, only he was too excited to realize it. Everybody wants to live, Keeler, even if it's only for two minutes longer, and when she saw the killer coming at her with the ice pick, I'm betting that Ruby tried to tell him. Maybe the words didn't mean anything to him, but I knew her. Maybe she managed to get out only one word before he let her have it. It wouldn't mean anything to him, but it might mean something to me. It might lead us right to the money. The killer was after that money, too; now suppose the word got around that with a clue or two, I might be able to put my hands on it and would be willing to split. I'll give you odds that the killer will get in touch with me the minute he hears it. What do you think?"

Keeler leaned forward as if trying to pierce the darkness to see what lay in Latham's face.

"I'm giving it to you straight," Latham said. "I don't know where the money is, but I think it can be found and you can help by passing the word around."

"If this is just a stall, Latham—"

"It isn't."

"Okay. I'll see that the word gets round, but you won't be making yourself a thing if this is just a stall."

"You do your part and I'll do mine." And as he walked the length of the dock for the second time that night, Latham felt the letter in his pocket and thought fiercely, "I'll get the bastard for you, Ruby, I promise you I'll get him!"

CHAPTER FIFTEEN

Latham knew that Chet would not yet be asleep, so instead of going to the boat he walked to the far end of the dock and sat down under the lamp on the right that threw a steady green beam over the dark restless water of the bay. Across the dock burned a red lamp. Beneath him, the slight chop that had risen with the wind slapped fretfully at the pilings and occasionally there was a sharp splash out in the darkness when a mullet jumped.

He lit a cigarette, postponing the opening of the letter. It was not going to be an easy or a good letter to read. The money—he felt sick at the thought of it. There had always been a part of him that did not believe that Ruby had had anything to do with that or with Mays, despite all the evidence to the contrary. There had always been a smoldering hope that even at the end Ruby had not rushed headlong into her own disintegration and destruction. But now there was the money, an almost exact parallel to the story young Chet had told him about the high school girl who had brought stolen gifts to the football player, and it was a horrible thing to find a comparison between Ruby and that feeble-minded adolescent, who at best had had an atrophied conception of right and wrong. Ruby could not possibly have been in her right mind to have believed for an instant that he would accept that money, or to have thought that he would not question the source. But she had been sick, sick, worse than he had thought.

Heavy-hearted, he took the letter from his pocket and turned toward the glow of the green light over his head. Something had been written on the envelope but the ink had run so badly that the words were indecipherable. It had rained several times during the past week. The envelope came apart in his hands for the glue had been entirely dissolved, and the letter inside, except for a few disjointed phrases, was unreadable. She had wrapped the money so carefully in plastic but had forgotten to protect the letter the more important of the two. Oh Ruby Ruby! Latham thought wretchedly.

He spread the sodden sheet of paper on the dock and tried to make some sense out of the blurred words.

".... together now .... will be expensive but .... to help .... please take me away from .... honestly will try .... hounding me, driving .... going crazy if .... go anywhere you .... my very dearest I .... please ...."

There was a blur at the end that must have been her signature.

The letter was Ruby's last despairing plea.

Latham sat staring over the water. He was calm but it was the ominous kind of calm that lay in the eye of a hurricane, the stillness that awaited the unleashing of the terrible winds again.

Knowing what he did, most of the letter was quite plain to him. With this money Ruby believed that they could be "together now." By "will be expensive but" she probably meant the course of psychiatric treatments, hence the money "to help." She wanted him to "please take me away from" this life she was leading and she was willing to "go anywhere you" wanted to take her. That much was obvious, but what was "hounding" and "driving" her? Probably her own fears—but that didn't sound right. She wouldn't be "hounding" herself. Something or somebody was "hounding" her. Mays? McElroy? Meyn or Hemming? Or possibly Odum out at the Beach Casino. Whatever or whoever it was, she was frightened and thought she was "going crazy if" it didn't stop. Or if Latham did not take her away. Latham crouched over the letter, muttering to himself as futilely he tried to decipher one more phrase or even just another word. But it was no use. The words were as meaningless as spilled ink on a blotter.

But was somebody "hounding" her or was that part of an alcohol-fevered nightmare in which she was living? Judging from the few words that could be read and the uneven up-and-downhill scrawl of the lines, it was fairly plain that Ruby must have been quite drunk when she wrote the letter. The words were overly large and the letters shaky and badly formed, as if written by a six-year-old.

"Hounding" her.

A delusion?

No.

Because there was the terrible realization of her fears in the fact that somebody *had* thrust an ice pick into her heart. Somebody *had* been hounding her. Her fear had been real and not part of a mounting nightmare.

God, if only the rain had not gotten at the letter! Ruby must surely have named the one who had been "hounding" her. Desperately Latham went over the smears again, hoping to find even just a letter that might give him a clue, but everything but those few words were irrevocably washed away. The thing to do now—but what was the thing to do now? That plan for trapping the killer that he had told Keeler was as flimsy as if it had been built of egg crates. The money was there and the killer wanted it, but he certainly was not going to walk up in broad daylight and say, "I got your message, Latham. Let's sit down and talk it over." That was not the way it would happen, if it happened at all. It would happen like a defective gun exploding in your face when you pulled the trigger. It would happen like a ladder breaking after you had climbed it half way to a tall roof. It would happen like meeting a truck head-on on a blind curve when you were speeding at eighty miles an hour on a dark highway. Three had been murdered—Ruby, McElroy and Wooten—and the fourth killing would be the easiest of the lot.

Latham folded the letter very carefully and put it into the watch pocket of his slacks. Well, there was one thing he could do now. Wait.

CHAPTER SIXTEEN

At five-thirty in the morning, in the gray streak of pre-dawn, the daily pattern of movement and sounds began on the dock. A boat motor coughed a few times, muttered drowsily and then roared in bursts as the owner revved it to warm it up. Like the answering barks of dogs in the night, the motors of other boats followed suit, one after the other, rumbling, sputtering, spewing blue smoke and driblets of water from their exhaust pipes. The captain of the *Tacona*, tied up beside Latham's *Belan*, shambled out into the stern cockpit in a pair of seersucker pajamas, rumpling his hair as he lifted his head and looked sleepily up into the sky to judge the on-coming weather. Captain Widlund of the *Skidoo*, across the dock, appeared in a pair of baggy khaki shorts and went through a routine of arm-swinging calisthenics, unabashed by either hoots or stares. At the end, he slapped his curly gray chest with a satisfied, "Hah!" and ducked agilely back into his cabin. Others appeared, some still sour from sleep, some cheerful and chatty between sips of steaming coffee from unbreakable plastic cups, calling from boat to boat.

"Just talked to the *Gulf Girl*. They're biting like fury down Boca Grande. Pulled one in last night that'll go a hundred and fifty easy."

"The *Flyaway* says the schools're moving north. Got three off Englewood."

"... and where the hell's the ice ..."

"... lots of black grouper and ..."

"... a hundred and fifty bucks worth of tackle all shot to ..."

"... so there he sat flat on his tail while that lousy tarpon took off for ..."

"I'm telling you, the next time I live I'm going into a business where I don't have to get up in the middle of the night."

"Dammit, how many times do I have to tell you, where's the ice?"

"... Hell, a nickel apiece for mutton minnows at ..."

The dawn became more glowing as night seeped off into the western horizon.

Latham sat at the controls in the cabin, warming up the twin Packard motors of the *Belan* until they purred powerfully under the deck like contented tigers. Chet was in the cockpit, chipping up the hundred-pound block of ice that Latham had brought aboard from the self-service ice house at the landward foot of the dock. He was whistling *The Stars And Stripes Forever*. The doctor had been right. The kid did not even have a headache.

Latham cut the motors and went out to the cockpit. The fishermen were going aboard the other boats now and, looking toward the parking lot, Latham saw Russ, Coot and Lila. The men were in slacks and T-shirts but the girl was more scantily clad in very short shorts and a halter, carrying a large straw bag. The bag sagged heavily from its straps and Latham guessed that there was at least one fifth of bourbon in it.

"What the hell," said Russ, as he came up to the *Belan* and jumped down into the cockpit, "does everybody in this whistle stop get up in the middle of the night just to catch a lousy fish?"

"They're not lousy," said Coot, following him into the cockpit. "They're gold-plated. They cost fifty bucks a day." Latham held up a steadying hand to the girl they had left standing on the dock with her heavy bag, and she stepped from the dock to the rail and then dropped lightly to the deck.

"You shouldn't do that," she said to Latham. "It confuses me. I'm not used to gentlemen."

"In her book," Russ winked, "a gentleman is a guy that apologizes after he smacks you in the puss. Well, we're all set for our boat ride, Cap. What do we do now, weigh the anchor or what?"

Chet was standing near the cabin door, wearing a troubled frown, and Latham glanced sharply at him.

"Feeling okay, kid?"

"I'm all right, Cap'n."

"Cast off and let's get out of here, then."

Latham ducked down into the cabin as the boy sprang up to the dock and released the stern line then ran forward and held the bow line until Latham got the boat in position to back off. The boy leaped to the nose of the boat and busily began coiling the bright new yellow manila line on the deck. The boats in a line as if in formation moved slowly across the placid bay toward the pass to the Gulf. Russ and Coot sat in the two fighting chairs and Lila leaned against the transom, smoking a cigarette, her bag under her left arm now. She had long slender legs that flared softly at the thighs and her halter decorated rather than concealed her full breasts. The two men with their muscular arms and heavy chests looked as thick and solid as bulldozers. They were both smoking cigars and looking serenely around them, watching the other boats with interest.

Latham guided the boat through the winding, tricky channel that was so narrow in places that you could look down the side of the boat and see the weedy bottom of the bay a bare foot below the surface. It was a little rough in the pass, for the tide had just turned, and the *Belan* pitched and rolled, the high ship-to-shore radio antenna whipped wide circles against the sky.

"Hey, watch them bumps, Cap," Russ called from the cockpit, and Lila said, "I thought it was against the law to rock a boat."

But it was calm again when they gained the wide water of the Gulf and Latham opened the windscreen and called to Chet.

"Take the wheel up on the bridge, kid. Follow the *Skidoo*. That's the gray and white boat dead ahead."

Latham watched the boy scramble up the deck, a little surprised at the obvious lack of eagerness. *I hope that head's not bothering him*, he thought. The boy definitely did not look happy, and Latham called up to him.

"How's the head, kid?"

"*It's* all right, Cap'n," the kid answered.

"Feel all right?"

"*I'm* fine."

Latham frowned. There was something wrong with the kid. Maybe an upset stomach from excitement. Probably hadn't slept a wink all night. He'd go up to the bridge and have a talk with him a little later and see if he'd calmed down. He lit a cigarette and watched the bright plain of the Gulf for signs of tarpon feeding and splashing on the surface. There was a brief glitter far off to starboard and he watched intently but it did not come again. Most likely it had been a large ray, jumping to escape an attacking shark. The shark always swarmed when the tarpon came and many a record fish had been mangled in voracious jaws set with teeth like jagged glass. Sometimes the waters were so thick with shark that they attacked almost every tarpon you hooked and ruined strike after strike. They were swift, sinewy killers and gluttonously hungry all the time. Latham hated them, as did all charter boat captains, and he kept a rifle and an Army .45 on board and blasted them out of the water every chance he got. There were no more splashes and the *Belan* moved steadily southward toward Boca Grande. The kid could handle the boat fine and knew the waters as well as Latham did, the bays and creeks and inlets and channels, and he had a rare instinct for finding fish. In a few years of growing up he'd be as good a guide as the best of them. He was still a little too young and excitable, but a few years would calm him down.

Then he found himself thinking about old Fritz Meyn. He had never expected Fritz to get panicky and run to the police, but he should have known about Tante Minna. For all her white hair and motherly appearance, she was still a tough German *hausfrau* at heart and the most important thing in her life was her home and husband, in that order. If Fritz were threatened, the home was threatened, and she would never stand for that. She was frugal, hard-working, sentimental, kindly, warm, but would be utterly ruthless and perhaps unscrupulous as well if she thought her security menaced. She was the real danger, not Keeler. Keeler could be handled, but Tante Minna and Hanna could crucify him. Latham did not have to be told what an impression she could make on a jury. She would remind every man on it of his mother, and her testimony, no matter how twisted and garbled, would be the most damning of all. If it came to that. Latham thought of the money hidden in the maze of the banyan tree and knew how close he was walking to a narrow edge. And his fingerprints all over that plastic wrapping. If Hanna knew about that, it would really be the end. The smart thing would be to get rid of it, to mail it anonymously to the bank, to play it safe. But the money was the one thing that would bring the killer to him sooner or later. The money was the heart of the matter.

Oh Ruby—

Latham shook himself. Don't think about that now. Let it rest. Give yourself time to incubate. You've been running at top speed and getting nowhere. Relax so you can start thinking again. You've been too close to this damn thing. Stand back for a while and maybe you'll be able to see something of the things you've overlooked, the little things that you can add up. You're still running the same tight little circle, wearing a groove in it. Now cut it out.

He walked aft to the cockpit where Russ and Coot were lounging in the fighting chairs and Lila sat on the transom, watching the three boats that followed, cutting through the water with a lace of froth at their bows.

Russ took the cigar from his mouth and pointed at the shore. "I hope we ain't going to stay in this close all the time, Cap," he complained. "Hell, this near I might just as well be on the Staten Island ferry and it wouldn't cost me no fifty bucks neither."

"We have to go where the fish are if you expect to catch any," Latham said.

"Fish!" said Russ. "Look, I'm going to tell you something, Cap. When I was a kid I used to go down to the Battery up in New York and watch the big boats going out, and I used to think to myself what's out there in the ocean the other side of the Statue of Liberty, and I still'd like to know. What the hell *is* out there?"

Latham looked to starboard. "There's nothing out there but about a thousand miles of water before you reach Mexico."

"Yeah yeah yeah, I know all about that, but what's it *feel* like to be out there with nothing but water all around you? The longest boat ride I ever took was up to Bear Mountain on the Hudson River Day Liner, and I was I further away from shore then than we are now. What's it *feel* like to be out there? That's what I want to know."

Latham shrugged. "Some people think it's lonesome."

Lila looked at him and laughed. "Not for me it wouldn't be," she said. "Not with three strong men and a boy aboard. Hey, Coot, wake up. Did somebody hypnotize you?"

Coot was staring off to starboard with an odd expression on his broad-jawed muscular face. "There's something out there," he said. "My God, it looks like a submarine."

At almost the same moment, Chet's shrill boyish voice cried out, "Shark to starboard, Cap'n. A big 'un!"

Latham sprang to the rail. The sharp, distinctive dorsal fin was cutting the water about thirty feet off and the huge grayish-white body was clearly visible just beneath the surface. It was about fifteen feet long and keeping pace with the boat. Latham swore and jumped for the cabin. He reached for the rifle in the scabbard over the port bunk, but the scabbard was empty. He swore again and felt behind the control panel for the holstered Army .45 rolled up in a web belt on a shelf there. He ran out to the cockpit. Russ, Coot and Lila were all standing at the rail, staring wide-eyed at the huge fish. Latham steadied himself and fired three shots at the eye of the shark. Lila screamed as the water boiled. The fish thrashed and sounded, diving straight down.

Russ stared at the big gun in Latham's hand. "You get him, Cap?"

"I don't know, but I hope I spoiled his appetite."

Lila said shakily, "And that was a shark? I didn't know they came that big."

"They come bigger, too," said Latham, buckling on the web belt and settling the holster against his thigh just below his right hip.

"Well well well," said Russ, still staring at the gun. "Now it's Roy Rogers we got. I thought we were going fishing, not playing cowboys and Indians."

Lila looked pale and her tongue slid nervously across her lips. "Do you *have* to wear that thing, Captain? Guns give me the jitters. They're always going off and killing somebody when they're not loaded. After all, we're not going to be attacked by sharks, are we? If so, I want to go home right now. I thought we were going for fish and not vice versa."

"Yeah," said Russ, "put that machine gun away, Cap. It makes me nervous, too."

"I don't even like the shooting galleries at Coney Island," said Coot.

"Do we *have* to go fishing?" Lila asked. "After seeing that thing out there, I don't want any part of it. Suppose you get one of those on your hook, then what? No thanks."

Russ stared at the water, unruffled again, now that the shark had sounded. "Yeah, me too. From now on I'm doing all my fishing in Central Park with a bent pin and a worm. Let's just go for a boat ride, Cap."

"I'll take you back to the dock," said Latham. "This isn't a sightseeing boat."

"Well ..." Russ looked at Coot. "I'll tell you what, Cap. Take us for a little drive around the ocean and then we'll go fishing. Give us a little time to forget that shark or whatever it was. Okay?"

"Just for a little while?" Lila asked. "I'd really love to see what it's like out there."

"The next time," grumbled Coot, slouching down in the fighting chair, "I'm taking all my boat rides on the Forty-Second Street ferry."

Latham hesitated, then shrugged. What difference did it make? And, too, he understood this yearning for the open sea, even among these city dwellers.

"Take her due west for a while, kid," he called to Chet up on the flying bridge.

The boat did not turn and Latham called, "Did you hear me, kid? Take her due west."

"Could—you come up here for a minute, Cap'n?" The boy's voice was a thin squeak. He sounded a little sick and scared.

Latham said quickly, "Coming right up, kid," and climbed the ladder to the top deck over the cabin.

The boy was standing at the wheel looking pinched-faced over his shoulder.

"What's the matter, kid?" Latham asked. "The head bothering you again?"

The boy put his finger to his lips, beckoned urgently. Latham went over to him, surprised to see that the boy's thin hands were shaking.

"What is it, kid?" he asked quietly.

The boy whispered, "Remember what I said about last night, something I was trying to remember that reminded me of a party and couldn't think of it?"

"Yes. Well?"

I just thought of it. It's that dame down there, the cologne she's got on. The smell of it, I mean. That's what reminded me of a party."

"Come again?"

"It reminded me of a party. You know, the girls always wear cologne to a party. And that's what I smelled last night, the cologne that dame's got on."

Latham looked sharply toward the stern, his eyes narrowing. "You're sure of that, kid?"

"I'm positive, Cap'n. And there's something else, too. Just before you come out of the cabin I saw her take a cigarette out of that big bag she's carrying. She's got two guns in that bag, Cap'n. I saw them. I could look right down in the bag and she's got two guns in there, chrome-plated. I saw them shine."

Latham compressed his lips. He did not doubt the boy's word because now it explained a lot of things—Russ' willingness to pay fifty dollars for the charter though he and Coot were obviously not fishermen, their urging him to go out into the open Gulf where they would be absolutely alone. Then suddenly he remembered a third thing—that black bobby pin on the floor of Ruby's kitchen the night he had been slugged when he crawled in through the window. Ruby's apartment had been ransacked and the boat had been ransacked, and it all added up to the same thing. A package containing two hundred thousand dollars.

"What—what're you going to do, Cap'n?" Chet whispered. "You don't want to go out in the Gulf with them, do you?"

"I think I do, kid," said Latham slowly. "I think that's exactly where I want to go."

"But Cap'n, they—"

"Take her out into the Gulf, kid. I'll handle the rest of it." He looked down into the cockpit before descending the ladder. The two men were in the fighting chairs again and Lila sat on the transom, nervously puffing at a fresh cigarette. The big straw bag was clasped under her arm and Latham could see how the bottom of it sagged from the weight of the two guns. Good. She hadn't slipped them to Russ and Coot yet. He dropped down into the cockpit and sat on the transom beside her.

"You letting that kid take the boat out in the ocean all by himself, Cap?" Russ asked. "That's taking a chance, ain't it?"

"He can handle it."

"He didn't sound like he thought he could handle it when you told him to turn."

"That was something else," Latham drawled. "He got a bad bump on the head last night when a couple of sharpshooters and a woman came on board." He turned suddenly and hit the end of Lila's bag with the heel of his hand. It shot out from under her arm and disappeared into the frothing wake churned up by the twin propellers. "What were you looking for last night, Russ—two hundred thousand dollars maybe?"

He was not prepared for the speed with which the two bulky men could move. They dove at him from their chairs and if the cockpit had not been so small they'd have pulled him down in the first rush, but Coot tripped over Lila's feet and sprawled against Russ, throwing him off balance.

Lila flung herself on Latham, pinning his arms and crying, "Take him, take him!"

Latham swung his body and threw her at the two men on the deck just as they were scrambling to their hands and knees and they went down in a tangle again, but as he jumped down from the transom, Russ' foot shot out and knocked his legs from under him and he went down on top of them in a melee of flailing arms and thrashing legs. Latham was hit twice on the jaw but, though a little dazed, he rolled clear of them and sprang to his feet. Cursing, Coot dove at him with arms outstretched to grasp him around the waist. Latham straightened him up with a blow to the chin and then hit him heavily on the side of the head. Coot staggered against the transom and with a hoarse cry fell over the stern into the water. Russ was still on his hands and knees and Latham clubbed him across the back of the neck with his fist. The man surged into him and tried to grapple, but Latham seized him by the wrist and, whirling, threw him across his back, out over the rail and into the Gulf. He turned on the girl who backed away from him, her red mouth terror-stricken, holding out her arms to ward him off.

"You're next, sister," he said heavily. "Can you swim?"

She shrieked as he grabbed her arm and dragged her toward the transom. The heads of the two men bobbed astern and they were crying out frantically and their arms thrashed the water as they tried to swim after the boat.

The girl screamed hysterically, "The sharks the sharks the sharks—"

"A whole Gulf full of them, sister," Latham snarled. "On your way!"

"*Nononononononononono!*" She clung to the port rail with her free hand.

Latham released her and she fell to the deck, moaning. "Who put you three up to this?" he demanded.

"Nobody, nobody—"

"Don't give me that, sister. You three clowns never dreamed this one up all by yourselves."

"We—we read it in the paper—"

"Sure. In the comic section."

The girl huddled across the cockpit from him, her eyes as huge and dark as those of a cornered animal. Latham glanced over the stern.

"Your two friends are still swimming back there. Would you like to join them?"

"Pleasepleasepleaseplease—"

She was shaking uncontrollably and Latham knew that if he took a step toward her she would pass out completely from sheer terror. She was very close to that now. He leaned against the rail.

"Who're you working for?" he asked. "And I'm remembering how one of you slugged a kid last night when you went through the boat. If it was all your own idea, sister, you're going over the side and the hell with you."

"It was Russ that did it—Russ!"

"But who told Russ to do it?"

"I don't know. Honest I don't know I don't know I don't know."

"But there is somebody."

"Russ knows. He's the one. He knows. He knows all about it. Even Coot doesn't know, but Russ does."

It was not a pretty thing to have to do, to browbeat this girl made ugly by terror, but this wasn't a girls' school and Latham remembered the two guns she had concealed in her bag and had been ready to slip to Russ and Coot.

"Well, we'll find out in a few minutes, sister," he said.

"I'm telling you the truth, honest I am." She was huddled against the side of the cockpit, looking piteously at him. "We were supposed to make you take the boat to a certain place and meet somebody. That's what Russ said. We were supposed to make you meet somebody."

"Who?"

"I don't know. Russ knows. He's the one."

"We'll find out, sister." Latham turned to the bridge and called, "Take it back to where those two fellows are swimming, kid."

The boat turned in a tight half circle. Russ and Coot could still be heard yelling faintly, and as the boat drew nearer they swam frantically toward it. Latham went up to the flying bridge and took the wheel. The boy stood aside and regarded him with wide, admiring eyes.

"Golly, Cap'n," he said, "you sure clobbered those two guys but I thought for a minute they were going to get you."

"So did I kid, the way they jumped me."

"But I was going to help you, Cap'n. I was all set."

Then Latham saw the underwater gun, with its lethal harpoon cocked, leaning against the rail and he said, "My God!"

Then sternly, "Look, Chet, no matter what happens, I don't want you shooting at people with that thing, understand?"

"But, Cap'n, if they—"

"No ifs. You're too young to get mixed up in this kind of thing, and nobody ever gets old enough to start killing people. Remember that."

When Latham was close to the swimming men, he cut the motors to idle and drifted up to them. They swam to the side but it was too high for them to climb back into the boat without aid. They beat against it with their fists, they swore at him, they ranted, they threatened, they begged. Latham waited until they were pleading and then leaned on the rail and looked down at them. They were clinging to the rub-rail that ran the length of the boat a few inches above the water line, their heads turning every few seconds to look fearfully at the Gulf behind them.

"Who're you working for, Russ?" Latham asked.

Russ looked up, his mouth gaping. "I—I don't know, Captain. Honest to God, but let us in the boat, don't leave us out here."

"Sure. When you tell me who you're working for."

"But I don't know, Captain. That's the honest truth. A guy contacted us in New York and said to come down here and then another guy got in touch with us in the hotel by phone and we never even seen him. That's the truth, Captain, honest to God, that's the truth."

"He said, go out and pick up that two hundred thousand and trusted you because you have honest faces."

"A double-crosser don't live long in this business, Captain. Specially with that kind of dough, but for God's sake, let us in the boat, *will you!*"

"Where were you supposed to meet this guy?" Latham asked stolidly.

"A place called Indian Pass. I don't know where it is but he said you would. It's down the shore someplace."

Latham knew Indian Pass. It was one of the inlets to the Hosakka River, a dreary, desolate place of stumps and dead trees bearded with gray moss. An isolated place seldom used because of the treacherous stumps that lay beneath the surface of the water waiting to rip the bottom out of a boat. A perfect rendezvous for this kind of thing.

"Throw them a line, kid," Latham told Chet. "Tie it to the rail before you drop it to them, then come back up here, and I mean right away."

Grinning, the boy swarmed agilely down the ladder and ducked into the cabin. He returned a few moments later with a coil of half inch manila line. He tied one end to the cockpit rail and dropped the other end to the men in the water. He sprang nimbly up the ladder to the bridge. Latham watched the two men laboriously climb the rope and drop exhausted and dripping into the cockpit.

"You know where Indian Pass is, kid?" Latham asked.

"Sure do, Cap'n. It's about two miles below that fishing village."

"Take her down there, but stop outside the Pass and I'll take over."

Latham sat at the end of the deck overlooking the cockpit. Russ cursed him weakly, but Coot just sat against the transom with his eyes closed, his chest heaving.

Lila crouched in her corner of the cockpit, shivering. "You can throw us a cigarette, can't you?" Russ said sullenly to Latham.

Latham took three cigarettes from the package in his shirt pocket and threw them down into the cockpit, together with a package of matches. Russ picked them up and lit one, not offering any to either Coot or Lila, neither of whom looked as if they felt like smoking at the moment. Russ sprawled in one of the two fighting chairs and smoked silently.

It was a 45-minute trip southward to Indian Pass. The Pass itself was between two small Keys, barren except for palmetto and a few scattered cabbage palms. Beyond was one of the outlets of the Hosakka River, a dismal, swampy place. There was an eagle's nest, larger than a bushel basket, tucked in the crotch of one of the high, skeletal trees. Long ago a top-fire had swept through the area, blighting and blackening the tall trees, but below the shores were thick with tangled mangrove that marched into the water on their arched, spider-leg roots on which oysters grew. The mangrove masked everything except the thready, stump-studded channel to the main body of the river. Latham touched the boy's arm.

"I'll take over now, Chet," he said. "You keep an eye on the cockpit and if any of those monkeys move, let me know immediately."

"Yes sir, Cap'n," the boy said eagerly.

Latham smiled ruefully. This was just a game to the kid. Pirates, Long John Silver, and he was intrepid young Jim Hawkins—and concealed back in the trunk of that big banyan tree was Treasure Island.

Latham turned the boat and, looking watchfully over his shoulder, backed it through the pass and into the dangerous thready channel. He saw the glimmer of something white among the mangrove to starboard and immediately cut the motors. Now he could sketchily make out the outlines of a cabin cruiser about thirty feet in length.

"Hey, you in there!" he bellowed. "This is the *Belan*."

A voice came clearly over the water. "Is that you, Russ?"

"That's right, and Latham's here too."

"Be right out."

The boat's motor coughed and muttered. Latham cocked his head. It had just one motor, his experienced ear told him, and not a very powerful one at that. The boat moved cautiously from the screen of mangrove. It was a thirty-foot Chris-Craft, blue and white with mahogany decking, a dependable boat but not very fast, compared to the *Belan* with its souped-up twin Packard motors. The tide was coming in and, keeping the motors at low speed and the bow facing the current, Latham kept the boat stationary.

In a startled voice, somebody cried, "That's Latham up there at the wheel! What the hell—"

Latham laughed. "That's right, Odum. And the next time don't send Boy Scouts to do a Marine's job. I've got your Boy Scouts tied in knots, and their Campfire Girl, too."

Odum appeared on the deck of the other boat, the name of which, Latham noted, was *Floradora*. Odum's heavy, bearish body was encased in a dark blue business suit, which was as shapeless as usual and looked as if it had been cut by a tailor's apprentice with a lawnmower. His square face was impassive.

"You're turning out to be a bad risk, Latham," he said. "This is the second mistake I've made about you."

The two boats were drifting closer, but Latham had the .45 in his hand and he lifted it and showed it to Odum. "Just in case," he said. He looked down into the cockpit. "Over the side, you three. Your boss'll pick you up. If he isn't mad at you. And you, Russ, take the girl with you. I don't think she can jump by herself."

Russ glowered but, without a word, Coot mounted the transom and dove awkwardly into the water, splashing his way to the *Floradora*.

"Help him up," said Odum to someone in the cabin.

The fat Keeler came reluctantly out of the cabin and, leaning over the rail, held out a hand to Coot and grunted when he hoisted him out of the water. For all his fat, Keeler was amazingly strong.

"Well well well," said Latham, grinning at Keeler, "old home week. You sure have yourself a wonderful office staff."

Keeler stood lumpishly in the cockpit of the other boat and looked at Latham with pure hatred. Latham laughed and waved, then looked down into the cockpit.

"I said jump," he said sharply to Russ. "We're not serving lunch today."

"She can't swim," said Russ, tilting his chin sullenly at Lila.

"Then tow her, but get out of here. You can swim."

Russ gave Latham a look that promised violence, then stood and picked up the limp, all-but-unconscious girl. He threw her over the rail as if she were a bundle of discarded rags, then jumped in after her. One-armed, he swam clumsily to the *Floradora*, pulling Lila along beside him. Keeler helped them into the boat and he and Russ stood together, talking in low tones, watching Latham.

Odum said, "I'll make a deal with you, Latham."

"Fifty-fifty?" Latham mocked him.

"Fifty-fifty, and if you think it over, it's a bargain. I can have you covered from now on, Latham, day and night, and you'd never get a smell of that money. Fifty-fifty."

"But I told your friend, the pudgy policeman over there, that I didn't know where the money was. That still stands."

Odum made a gesture of disbelief, waving the statement aside.

"I know what you want, Latham, and I'll throw it in as part of the deal. I'll give you Ruby's killer."

Latham was more than startled but concealed it. "Oh sure, Odum. But who'll you throw me? Russ? Coot? Keeler? Who'll be the patsy?"

"That's part of the deal," said Odum with a small, iron smile. "And this isn't a transaction in which anybody's giving away any samples."

"I won't settle for a patsy, Odum."

"You won't get a patsy. You'll get the man himself." Latham had the feeling that behind Odum's impassive face, the man was laughing at him.

"Now I get it, Odum," he said. "You'll give me the name, but I won't be able to do anything about it. Is that it?"

"That part of it's up to you. I'm not going into court as a witness."

"That's no deal."

"I'll give you the name and all the rest of it—when, where and how and why. That's better than fumbling around in the dark, isn't it?"

"You could pick a name out of a hat."

"No hats and nothing up the sleeve. There won't be any doubt in your mind when I give you the name, Latham."

Latham jerked up his gun and snarled, "You'll give me the name right now!"

As if expecting this move, Odum dropped out of sight behind the sheltering side of the cockpit before Latham could fire.

At the wheel behind Latham, Chet screeched, "Look out, Cap'n!"

At the very last instant Latham saw Keeler leveling a gun at him but he could not swing his own gun around in time. There was a dull thud of plunging darkness—

CHAPTER SEVENTEEN

It was still dark when he opened his eyes, but it was a star-pierced darkness and the sky was above him and he could feel the gentle motion of the *Belan* as it rocked at the end of its mooring. He was lying in the cockpit on a mattress taken from one of the bunks and there was a pillow under his head. Chet's thin face was a pale oval hovering over him.

"How—how do you feel, Cap'n?" the boy asked anxiously.

"What time is it?" Latham asked thickly.

"Eight o'clock, Cap'n. Eight P.M. You been out a long time. I was almost scared to death."

Latham's head throbbed painfully and when he put his hand to it he found the swath of bandages that the boy had wound clumsily around it.

"You were only creased, Cap'n," Chet gulped, "but I thought you were a goner, all that blood. I put ice on it and it stopped. The bullet just kind of glanced off. You feel all right?"

"Dandy, kid, bully. Where are we?"

"Inside Indian Pass. They won't find us. We're hid way back in the mangrove. They'd tear the bottom out of their boat if they try to come in here. It's tricky, but I know the side channel. It leads to Bullfrog Creek. I come down here lots of times for frog legs."

Latham sat up and swayed, but the dizziness passed.

"I'd of put you in on the bunk," the kid said apologetically, "but I couldn't lift you. You're too big."

"How—how'd we get away from them, Chet?"

"The minute that guy shot, that fat cop, I gave her the gun and got out of there. They came after us but I kept going straight out in the Gulf, swinging a little north like I was going back to the dock in Sanibar. They didn't have a chance. The *Belan* can really step, can't she? I'll bet she's the fastest boat around. I lost them and hung around the Gulf, moving around, till it got dark and then I came back in here. I thought this was the last place they'd look."

Latham started, "You're a smart kid—" and then he saw the underwater gun lying on the deck of the cockpit. The harpoon had been discharged. He looked up at Chet.

The boy looked frightened. "I didn't mean to shoot him, Cap'n, honest I didn't. When he shot you, my finger just kind of tightened on the trigger and—"

"Who was it, kid?"

"That fat cop—the one you called Keeler."

"Did you hit him?"

"In—in the throat," the boy mumbled. "Just—just the side of the neck. It wouldn't of hurt him bad but he let out a yell and jerked the harpoon out and you know that big barb at the end—"

Latham compressed his lips. He knew that big barb at the end of the harpoon. It was there so that the lanced fish could not shake loose. If Keeler had jerked it out of his neck, it would have ripped his throat wide open. He said no more to the boy about it. The sight of that was something that was going to stick in his memory for a long time.

"Well," he said, "let's get out of here, kid."

The boy stammered, "We—we can't, Cap'n. I run out of gas. I had to pull the boat back in here by the branches of the mangrove."

Latham grunted. There was the ship-to-shore and he could radio for help, but that was the one thing that Odum would be sure to have covered, that wavelength. It would be better to wait until morning when it was light and they could see.

He rose painfully to his feet. His head throbbed and the outlines of the cabin and the bridge swam before him in liquid distortion as if they were dissolving before his eyes. He clutched the rail to steady himself and felt the boy's anxious hand on his arm.

"Are you all right, Cap'n?"

"I'm fine—no, I'm not. I'm dizzy, but I'll be all right after a while. It's just what I told you last night so take a look at me and remember it—when you get a bump or a cut on the head, take it easy and don't try to be a hero by pretending it's nothing at all. Remember what the doctor told you, don't take any chances with a head wound. I'm going inside and take a look at it. I'm not going to die, so don't worry about that. Put this mattress and pillow back on the bunk."

He went unsteadily into the cabin and into the head.

Latham crouched and looked into the small mirror over the hand basin as he unwound the clumsy bandage on his head. He winced as he pulled it loose from the dried blood of the wound. The gash was about three inches over his left ear and he tilted his head away from the overhead light to look at it. It was about four inches long and shallow, less than a half inch wide. The bullet must barely have touched the bone as it whispered past him. Carefully, he felt all around it, but the bone was solid. He washed it with hot water, swabbed it with mercurochrome and made a sterile pad of gauze, which he bound expertly in place with bandage. He had a double shot of bourbon before he went back to the cockpit, thinking to himself—sure, don't take chances with a head wound. One of the things you weren't supposed to do was drink alcohol. This thought would never have crossed his mind except for the kid, who was now perched on the rail regarding him with solemn and owlish concern. Latham grinned reassuringly.

"You can't kill a thick-headed monkey like me, kid," he said. "But how's about rustling up some dinner. I seem to remember your saying something about some redfish fillets in the refrigerator. Would you like to broil them and serve them up with a can of brussels sprouts and a handful of potato chips? We'll eat out tonight, kid, out here in the cockpit."

Chet jumped down from the rail. "You got some catsup and stuff, I could make a barbecue sauce," he said eagerly. "I can cook almost anything. In my scout troop—I'm an Eagle Scout—I'm always the cook when we camp out."

"Okay, Boy Scout," Latham chuckled, "but don't tie yourself in knots."

The boy darted into the cabin and very shortly Latham heard him singing in a high treble that broke into a baritone croak at disconcerting intervals. *I can't keep this up forever with him*, Latham thought unhappily, *he's got a home and mother of his own; I can't just up and keep him like a puppy or a stray cat.*

He slouched in one of the fighting chairs and moodily sucked on a cigarette. All around him the tall dead trees were stark silhouettes, leafless and gaunt against a faintly luminous star-clustered sky. From deeper in the swamp that lay between the creek and the mouth of the river arose all the night sounds, natural things that had become alien— the shrill shrieking of the tree frogs, the rumble of the bullfrogs, the muted and empty complaining of the owls, the cry of a wildcat, the occasional bellow of an alligator, the high bark of a fox.

The swamp was a living thing, peopled with deer, geese, 'coons, 'possums, rabbits, skunk, squirrels, quail, ducks, and a quivering womanish scream told him that there was a lone panther in there, strayed north from the Everglades, probably.

The boy made a picnic out of dinner, bubbling happily, and Latham turned on the ship-to-shore and Chet listened delightedly to the chit-chat between other boats anchored for the night out in the Gulf, talk of fish caught or fish lost, the movement of the great tarpon schools, personal conversations, light banter.

"Could I talk to one of them too?" Chet asked timidly. "I mean, you don't mind, do you? Cap'n Slater of the *Gulf Girl's* a kind of uncle of mine."

"Sure, kid." Then warningly, "But don't say where we are."

"Oh, I know that, Cap'n. If he's in Boca Grande, I'll say we're anchored off Englewood."

They went into the cabin and, unused to the mike, Chet talked in a stilted voice but happily to his uncle aboard the *Gulf Girl*, riding at anchor in Charlotte Harbor, and afterward they went back to the cockpit again, before turning in for the night. Latham smoked a cigarette and was silent.

"Are you thinking about that Miss Lake, Cap'n?" the boy asked, hesitant.

"Just thinking about things in general," Latham lied vaguely.

"She was beautiful. Even the kids said she was beautiful. But she had it tough, too."

"Everybody's got it tough one way or another, kid, but you don't let it get you down."

"Sure, but—yeah, I guess you're right."

But Latham was alert now. The boy had been about to say something but had changed his mind, probably with the diffidence of an adolescent in the presence of an adult.

"What do you mean she had it tough, kid?" Latham asked.

"Oh, you know, she didn't have it easy."

"In what way?"

"Oh—you can't have fun all the time, even kids."

"I know, but what makes you think Miss Lake had a bad time of it? I used to go around with her, and you know how it is when you go around with a girl, you're interested in her, even afterward. You're the same way, I'll bet."

"That's right. I went around with this dame a couple months ago and then we broke off but sometimes I find myself thinking about her. I thought it was, well, just kid stuff. You know."

"You'll have the same thing when you grow up, kid, believe me. Take me, for example. I broke up with Miss Lake a year and a half ago, but I still think about her. What makes you think she had a tough time?"

"Well, it's not me, Cap'n. I actually don't know nothing about it. It's this other kid—Brud Moran. He lives near Miss Lake and he used to go to the store for her once in a while."

The boy was still hesitant but more at his ease, and Latham said carefully, "What'd he say about Miss Lake?"

"Well, Brud likes to go fishing. He's a regular fishing bug, not like the rest of us kids. He likes to go fishing all the time. That's all he wants to do is fish. So this first night he was fishing on Pelican Key. There's a bar there and when the tide comes in you can catch all kinds of stuff. So he was fishing and he hears this yelling, and he knows Miss Lake and he recognized her voice. It was dark. Fishing ain't much good when the moon's out and he could just about see her and this guy up the beach. He was scared to go closer 'cause they were having a fight or something and she was crying and begging the guy and he kept yelling at her. Brud says he was sure the guy was going to kill her and he was so scared he couldn't move. The guy made her kneel down and told her to pray and kept yelling about blood and dying and I'm telling you Brud was scared stiff, honest. Finally he made a break for his boat to go for the cops, but he was just about half way acrost the bay when along comes this other boat with Miss Lake and the guy in it and she was still crying, so he knew she was all right, or not killed anyway and the next morning he went to see if she wanted anything from the store and she was all right and not hurt or nothing like that, but that guy sure had given her a bad time, according to Brud, and he don't make up things the way most kids do."

A rising excitement filled Latham's chest but he concealed it, knowing that it might only frighten the boy.

"You said 'the first time,' kid. Do you mean that Brud saw them out there at other times too?"

"He saw them out there a couple times more and it was always the same. This guy called her all kinds of names. He was really mad with her, Brud said. Brud always went away when he heard them, scared of what the guy might do if he caught him listening in."

"Did he say who the guy was?" Latham asked tensely.

"He didn't know and it was dark and he couldn't really see them except he knew Miss Lake's voice. This guy wanted her to do something and she wouldn't do it and they had some awful fights. Then they never came back again and Brud said Miss Lake seemed a lot more cheerful after that but sometimes she was—" Chet stopped and looked away pretending interest in a splash in the darkness of the water. "Sounded like a mullet jumping," he said hurriedly to cover the break. "Sound like a mullet to you, Cap'n? There's 'gators in here too sometimes."

Latham knew what the boy had been going to say, that Ruby was sometimes drunk when Brud went to see if she wanted anything from the store. The kid would shy away from saying something like that. Latham felt as if every nerve in him had been honed to a glittering razor edge. He did not have to ask the boy any more questions or wring any further information from him. It was all there now, the dark and final answer, the hidden thing. It had still not been proven, but it was all there.

The thing now was to erase it from the kid's mind, so he flipped his cigarette over the stern, rose and stretched and yawned.

"About time we turned in, kid," he said, as if drowsy. "We have a long day ahead of us tomorrow. And don't tell me you're not sleepy."

"I'm not, Cap'n, honest."

"Well, I am and it's time we were both in bed so let's go."

Later, Latham lay sleepless in his bunk. No wonder Odum had seemed to be laughing when he offered to tell him the name of the killer. Odum knew who it was, and knew too that he couldn't do anything about it.

It was almost dawn before Latham dozed off into a fitful nap.

CHAPTER EIGHTEEN

It was ten after seven by his wrist watch when Latham awakened, and he could hear the boy bustling in the galley, making coffee.

"Hey, kid," he called, "suppose you take the casting rod and see if you can catch us a couple of trout or bass for breakfast. They're thicker than ants on a lump of sugar in here. Or maybe you can even get us a snook. I heard them striking into a school of minnows last night before I fell asleep."

Chet came grinning from the galley. "Where's the lures, Cap'n?"

"In the tackle box over in the corner."

Latham waited until the boy went whistling out to the cockpit, and then he reached up and switched on the ship-to-shore, waited until the tubes warmed up and then spoke quietly into the mike.

"Charter boat *Belan* calling Sanibar police headquarters, charter boat *Belan* calling Sanibar police headquarters. Come in, Sanibar."

He waited a few minutes for the call to be relayed and then the answer came.

"Sanibar police to *Belan*, Sanibar police to *Belan*. Come in, *Belan*. What's on your mind?"

"This is Joe Latham, charter boat *Belan*. I want to talk to Captain Hanna. Did he come in yet?"

"Hi, Joe. This is Sergeant Moke. The Captain ain't in yet. Having trouble or you just want to talk to him?"

"Get hold of him and have him call me back, Sarge. It's important that I talk to him."

"He won't like being waked up—"

"Tell him it's about the Ruby Lake killing and it's important."

"Oh brother! Will do, Joe. Keep your receiver open."

Latham glanced out at the cockpit. The boy was casting over the transom into the glassy still water but so far had not had any luck. Latham nodded. The tide was ebbing and the fish would not be striking too eagerly, which was exactly the way he wanted it. He wanted to keep the boy out there in the cockpit until after he talked to Hanna.

"Any nibbles, kid?" he called.

"Well, the tide's kind of going out, Cap'n."

"Just keep trying. I got a mouth for fish for breakfast."

Glancing around the cabin, Latham suddenly remembered the ten gallon can of white gas he kept on hand for the stove, the refrigerator and the Coleman lanterns. It wasn't much, but it would take him where he wanted to go if he ran on just one of the twin Packard motors. But God help him if this thing blew up in his face. With only ten gallons of gas in the big tank, he'd be as helpless as a wounded duck out there on the Gulf.

About twenty minutes later the voice of Sergeant Moke crackled out of the ship-to-shore.

"Sanibar police calling the *Belan*, Sanibar police calling the *Belan*.

Come in, *Belan*."

The sergeant's voice was stolid and formal and Latham knew that Hanna was standing beside him. He flipped the switch and spoke into the mike.

"Joe Latham, charter boat *Belan*. Is Captain Hanna there?"

"This is Hanna, Latham. What do you want?"

"I want to talk to you about the Ruby Lake killing, Captain."

"Come in to headquarters. I'll talk to you here."

"I can't. I'm almost out of gas and stranded."

"Where are you? I'll send you some gas."

"It's better if I talk to you out here, Captain. I might have an 'accident' coming in."

"What? What do you mean, an accident?"

"I mean accidentally on purpose. Somebody would see to that."

"What are you talking about, man? Are you drunk?"

"It's like this, Hanna," Latham drawled, "I happen to know where the money is, all two hundred thousand of it, and I want to live long enough to give it back to the bank. Do I make myself clear?"

Hanna did not hesitate. "Where'll I contact you?" he asked crisply.

Latham calculated the distance between the Sanibar dock, where the police boat was tied up, and Indian Pass and added ten minutes for the time it would take Hanna to get to the dock from Headquarters.

"Sail south," he said, "and I'll get in touch with you by radio in exactly three-quarters of an hour. And look. Half the boats in the Gulf and somebody else are listening in to this call, so you might be followed. Keep your eyes open."

"I can take care of that, Latham," said Hanna curtly.

"All right. Leave now and I'll call you in exactly three-quarters of an hour."

Latham reached to switch off the radio then changed his mind and left it switched over to "send." He walked out to the cockpit where the boy was still doggedly casting and retrieving. There were no freshly caught fish flopping on the deck.

Chet shook his head apologetically at Latham. "The tide's going out, Cap'n, and they're just not biting."

"Well, okay. There's some bacon and eggs in the refrigerator. Let's have that if you can whip it up in twenty minutes."

"It'll be on your plate in fifteen, Cap'n!"

They were finished with breakfast in a half hour. Latham knew that he had to get the boy off the boat, but he did not want to tell him why. It would either frighten him or make him resentful, but time was passing and he *had* to get him off. Odum and Keeler had monitored that call to Headquarters, he knew, and he could not take any chances of the kid being hurt. He was still wondering how to go about it when he glanced aft through the cabin door and saw the unkempt heads of a cluster of cabbage palms beyond the shore fringe of mangrove.

"You know what I got a mouth for, Chet," he said casually, "heart of palm, good old swamp cabbage to go with the fish we're going to catch for lunch. How's about taking the hand ax over there and chopping out a half dozen or so?"

Swamp cabbage was the bud in the center of the fronds in a cabbage palm, common enough in Florida, but a real delicacy for very few took the trouble to hack them out. "You know how to chop them out, Chet?"

"I been doing it all my life, Cap'n," said Chet, his eyes shining. This was just like camping out, only better.

"Okay, but don't try climbing any of the big trees and break your neck. Get them from the little trees. They'll be more tender anyway. Better get a dozen. They'll be pretty small."

"I'll get you a bushel of them in no time at all, Cap'n!"

"Good." And then so that the boy would not worry, Latham said off-handedly, "I found a ten-gallon can of gas I keep around for the stove, so I'm going to take a little run to the Pass and see if our friends are still hanging around out there in the Gulf. I'll be back in about an hour or so. You don't mind, do you?"

"What'll you do if you see them, Cap'n?" the kid asked eagerly.

Latham grinned. "Duck back here as fast as I can. I don't want anything to do with them today. They play too rough."

"Not for you, Cap'n. You can handle the whole bunch of them."

"Oh sure, with one hand tied behind my back."

"Well, almost. The kids always said that when you get mad—"

"Kids talk too much. Now climb on that ax and get me the bushel of swamp cabbage you were talking about."

Latham helped the boy over the stern and watched him walk carefully on the arched roots of the mangrove to the firm ground beyond. Then he went back into the cabin and warmed up the engines. He inched down the stump-studded channel. He cut the motors before he reached the Pass and let the boat drift behind a thicket of sea grape on the bay-side of the smaller Key. He tied up and, taking the binoculars with him, swung ashore on the heavy branches. Crouched in a clump of palmetto fans, he scanned the Gulf to the north, watching for the gray police boat.

It was ten minutes before he saw the narrow hull knifing through the waters toward him and in another five the powerful glasses placed the boat almost at his fingertips. There was only one man aboard—Hanna. Latham went back to the *Belan* and started up the motors and, leaving them idling, he went to the ship-to-shore and switched over to "send."

"The *Belan* calling Captain Hanna, *Belan* calling Captain Hanna. Come in, Hanna."

There was a very brief pause and then sharply, "Where are you, Latham?"

"I'll contact you in five minutes."

He left the radio on "send" and strode over to the cabin controls. It was much easier to get to the Pass from here for the water was deep and there was no danger from submerged stumps as in the shallower channel to the east. He ran on one motor and chugged out into the Gulf. Hanna saw him the moment he emerged and the police boat angled sharply. Within a few minutes it was alongside and Hanna leaped aboard the *Belan* as Latham made the other boat fast so that it would not rub the white side of the cabin cruiser.

"Well," said Hanna curtly, "what's it all about, Latham?" His thin face looked drawn and his mouth was hardly more than a crease.

Latham nodded at the cabin. "Let's talk in there." He was wearing a loose sport shirt to hide the .45 stuck in the waistband of his jeans. He took the port bunk and waved Hanna into the other one beside the ship-to-shore. There was no hum to betray the fact that it was operating. Hanna sat down.

"Let's go," he said. "How'd you get the money?"

Latham hesitated. He had carefully rehearsed everything in his mind, but it was still going to be rough. He was going to have to say things that would be hard to get out of later, but it had to be done.

"I want to make a confession, Hanna," he said, mumbling in the hope that it would not be picked up by the mike. By this time, everybody in that area of the coast would be listening, and particularly Odum and Keeler. "I thought I could go through with this, but I can't." His mumble dropped into a still lower key. "Ruby and I took Mays for that two hundred thousand," he whispered.

The muscles bunched on either side of Hanna's narrow jaws. "Then you lied," he said harshly. "You *were* seeing her!"

Latham nodded, looking miserable. "I never stopped seeing her, Hanna, even after we broke the engagement. She was the one who broke the engagement a year and a half ago. I didn't want to break it, but then I thought, what the hell, why should I marry the dame if I can make her love me for free, know what I mean? As far as I was concerned, it was a perfect setup."

Hanna's hands twitched and the blood drained from his face, leaving it pale and pinched. "Keep going," he said harshly. "So you've been seeing her ever since, even when I was engaged to her myself."

"Oh I knew that wasn't going to last," Latham whispered hastily. "I knew you wouldn't marry her, once you caught wise. She was nothing but a tramp. And anyway, I thought you were making out okay too, so what the hell."

"So all that time—" Hanna said in a strangled voice.

There was a madness in his eyes, and covertly Latham slid his hand under his shirt, scratched his ribs and unobtrusively dropped his hand to the big grip of the heavy gun in his waistband.

"Well," he said, "you know the kind of dame she was, free and easy, especially both, if you know what I mean, and we had some pretty wild times." Latham winked lewdly into Hanna's congested face. "She really had something, Hanna, I'm telling you. She was one of the best. I'm telling you, one night I got six guys together—"

Hanna ground his teeth. His eyes were almost insane. Latham leaned forward.

"You don't seem very interested in the money, Hanna," he said softly. "You don't even care about it, do you? It's been Ruby all the way and that hyped-up way you felt about her. This is driving you out of your mind, isn't it, Hanna?"

Suddenly there was a gun in Hanna's hand and he gave Latham the bare skeleton of an insane grin. "Take your hand away from the gun under your shirt, Latham," he said in a glittering voice, "or I'll shoot you down this minute."

Latham stared, unbelieving, at the gun in Hanna's hand, then slowly withdrew his hand from under his shirt. He felt cold, glacially cold.

"What are you waiting for, Hanna?" he managed to ask. "You didn't give McElroy a chance. Or Wooten. You got them when they were drunk. Did you give Ruby a chance before you killed her, Hanna?"

"I gave her a chance to repent," said Hanna in a strange, exalted voice, "and she mocked me." And then he chanted in a skirling voice, "'When I say unto the wicked, thou shalt surely die; and thou givest him not warning, nor speakest to warn the wicked from his wicked way, to save his life; the same wicked man shall die in his iniquity; But his blood will I require at thine hand!'"

"You killed her, then, didn't you?"

"Yes!" cried Hanna, exulting, "I killed her. 'In flaming fire taking vengeance on them that know not God, and that obey not the gospel.' I killed her to save her soul before her iniquities carried her beyond redemption." His gun was unwavering.

"And McElroy?" asked Latham; he seemed to have trouble breathing. "Were you saving his soul, too?"

"He was an adulterer, a fornicator and a boaster," said Hanna sternly, "and I hanged him like a dog. He reveled in his wickedness, he wallowed in his filth and would have destroyed her in the pit of adultery, boasting and laughing."

"But Wooten. He was just a sot, Hanna—"

"He looked upon her and there was lewdness in his eyes and he lusted after her flesh." Then with a kind of mad calm, "I had never thought of him until I saw those pictures of undressed women he had cut from magazines and placed the picture of her head upon them. His was a filth that rotted within him. He would have destroyed her in the lewdness of his filth. I placed my hands at his neck until he died." He looked somberly at Latham. "You sought to save her, but you wanted her for yourself and when you could not have her, you made a beast of her. Repent of your sin, Latham."

There was a slight jar as if the boat had run aground and Latham said, calm now, "That'll be Odum and maybe Keeler. They'd like to get their hands on that money Ruby got from Mays."

Hanna twisted on the bunk and stared out the port behind him. Latham swiftly pulled his own gun from his waistband. Hanna leaped to his feet and ran out to the cockpit. There was a snarling burst of gunfire and Latham sprang to the starboard port. A speedboat was made fast to the police boat. Keeler hung limply over the thwart and Odum stood swaying, his face convulsed with the terrific effort of trying to raise the rifle in his hands. He crumpled slowly and fell over the side. Hanna lurched back into the cabin. There was a flaming sheen of blood down the right side of his white shirt and he held his gun in his left hand. His face looked suddenly gray.

"And the wicked shall perish from the face of the earth," he said in a dulling voice.

"But how about you, Hanna? You didn't kill Ruby to save her. You killed her because she threw you over and you couldn't have her. And you wanted her, didn't you? It was torture when you couldn't have her."

Hanna leaned weakly against the door frame. "You lie," he whispered.

"No I don't. You're a cop; you've met a lot of girls like Ruby but you didn't kill them to save them, so why did you kill Ruby? I'll tell you why. You were half out of your mind because she didn't want anything more to do with you. You tormented her and hounded her and drove her nearly crazy, and when she told you she was finished, you killed her. You wanted her!"

Hanna swayed. His eyes were glassy. "Yes—yes," he whispered. "'The same wicked man shall die in his iniquity.'"

Latham cried out and leaped toward him, but he was too late. Hanna put the gun in his mouth and pulled the trigger.

"The train's late," said Chet, staring up the empty track. "She should of been in five minutes ago."

"It's coming," said Latham; they were the only ones on the platform of the station. "Can't you hear it?"

"Yeah, now I can hear it. Gosh, wait'll I tell her about you and—"

Latham put his hand on the boy's eager shoulder. "No, Chet," he said. "If she didn't read it in the paper, we won't say anything about it. It's something we both should forget."

"All right, if you say so, but—okay, sure, Cap'n. But say, can we take Mom out on the boat sometime? We don't have to take her fishing or anything like that, just around the bay or maybe a little bit out in the Gulf. She's never been on a boat. I mean a real boat like the *Belan*."

"Any time you say."

The train pulled into the station and the boy remained at Latham's side with a pretense at adult dignity until a slim, blonde woman stepped down from the last car, and then he darted forward, crying out to her.

The woman walked toward them and she was very beautiful, the way she looked at the boy with shining eyes.

THE END

**Lorenz Heller Bibliography
(1910-1965)**

As Frederick Lorenz

Novels:
A Rage at Sea (Lion, 1953)
Night Never Ends (Lion, 1954)
The Savage Chase (Lion, 1954)
A Party Every Night (Lion, 1956)
Ruby (Lion, 1956)
Hot (Lion, 1956)
Dungaree Sin (Chariot, 1960)

Stories:
Backbite (*Justice*, Jan 1956)
Big Catch (*Justice*, July 1955)
Living Bait (*Justice*, May 1955)

As Dan Gregory

Three Must Die! (Graphic, 1956)

As Laura Hale

Novels:
Wild is the Woman (Rainbow, 1951)
Lovers Don't Sleep (Falcon, 1951)
Kiss of Fire (Rainbow, 1952; reprinted in Australia as *Kiss Of Death*,
  Phantom, 1953)
Woman Hunter (Falcon, 1952; reprinted in Australia, Phantom, 1953)
Desperate Blonde (Beacon Australia, 1960)
Lessons in Lust (Beacon, 1961; re-write of *Woman Hunter*)
Sensual Woman (Beacon, 1961; re-write of *Lovers Don't Sleep*)
The Zipper Girls (Beacon, 1962; re-write of *Wild is the Woman*)
The Marriage Bed (Beacon, 1962; re-write of *Desperate Blonde*)

As Larry Heller

Novels:
I Get What I Want (Popular, 1956)
Body of the Crime (Pyramid, 1962)

Story:
Blood Is Thicker (*Guilty Detective Story Magazine*, Mar 1957)

As Larry Holden

Novels:
Hide-Out (Eton, 1953)
Dead Wrong (Pyramid, 1957)
Crime Cop (Pyramid, 1959)

Stories (alphabetical listing):
...And Death Makes Ten (*Detective Tales*, June 1947)
Another Man's Poison (*Shadow Mystery*, Apr/May 1948)
Any Corpse in a Storm (*Dime Mystery Magazine*, Aug 1949)
Anybody Lose a Corpse? (*Mammoth Detective*, Aug 1946)
The Big Haunt (*10-Story Detective Magazine*, Oct 1948)
Blackmail Means Homicide (*15 Story Detective*, Feb 1950)
Bloody Night! (*Dime Mystery Magazine*, Oct 1949)
Bodyguard (*Thrilling Detective*, June 1951)
Bullets for Beethoven [Dinny Keogh] (*Mammoth Mystery*, June 1946)
Coffin Key (*Detective Tales*, Oct 1951)
A Corpse at Large (*Ten Detective Aces*, July 1949)
Corpse in Waiting (*New Detective Magazine*, Nov 1950)
A Corpse to His Credit (*Dime Detective Magazine*, May 1947)
Criminal at Large (*Suspense Magazine*, Summer 1951)
The Crimson Path (*Detective Tales*, Sept 1947)
Cry Murder (*New Detective Magazine*, Oct 1952)
The Crying Corpse (*Ten Detective Aces*, Sept 1948)
Death Brings Down the House (*10-Story Detective Magazine*, Apr 1948)
Death Carries the Mail (*F.B.I. Detective Stories*, Aug 1950)
Death for Two! (*Detective Tales*, Dec 1952)
Death in Dirty Linen (*Shadow Mystery*, June/July 1947)
Death in Six Reels (*Doc Savage*, July/Aug 1948)
Death in Thin Ice (*Shadow Mystery*, Feb/Mar 1948)
Death Is Where You Find It (*Suspect Detective Stories*, Nov 1955)
Die, Baby, Die! (*Detective Tales*, June 1948)
Don't Crowd My Shroud (*10-Story Detective Magazine*, Dec 1948)
Don't Ever Forget (*Detective Story Magazine*, Mar 1953)
Don't Wait Up for Me (*Triple Detective*, Fall 1955)
The Eighteen Screaming Corpses (*Detective Tales*, Jan 1948)
The Expendable Ex (*Dime Detective Magazine*, June 1952)
Face in the Window (*Detective Tales*, June 1951)
Fall Guy (*Detective Tales*, Aug 1953)
Forger's Fate (*Dime Detective Magazine*, Apr 1951)
The High Cost of Chivalry (*Dime Detective Magazine*, Dec 1951)
Home for Christmas (*Thrilling Detective*, Dec 1947)
House of Hate (*10-Story Detective Magazine*, Apr 1949)
Humpty-Dumpty Homicide (*Detective Tales*, June 1949)
If the Body Fits— (*Dime Mystery Magazine*, Dec 1947)
If the Frame Fits— (*Detective Tales*, Dec 1951)
I'll Be Home for Murder! (*Detective Tales*, Apr 1948)
I'll See You Dead! (*Detective Tales*, May 1947)
In Her Mother's Best Bier! (*Detective Tales*, Dec 1948)
Keeping Honest (*Doc Savage*, Winter 1949)

Kickback for a Corpse (*All-Story Detective*, Apr 1949)
Killer's Kiss (*Detective Tales*, Aug 1949)
Lady in Red (*Detective Tales*, Oct 1948)
Lady-Killer (*Dime Detective Magazine*, Dec 1952)
Lethal Boy Blue (*Detective Tales*, May 1949)
Love Me, Love My Corpse! (*Detective Tales*, Aug 1948)
Make Mine Mayhem (*New Detective Magazine*, Jan 1949)
Man with a Rep (*Detective Tales*, Dec 1949)
Mayhem at Eight (*New Detective Magazine*, May 1950)
Mayhem's Mechanic (*Detective Tales*, Sept 1946)
Morgue Bait (*New Detective Magazine*, Dec 1951)
Murder and the Mermaid (*Dime Detective Magazine*, Oct 1952)
Murder Never Gets Too Old (*Private Detective*, Jan 1950)
Never Dead Enough (*New Detective Magazine*, Sept 1947)
Never Turn Your Back (*Mike Shayne Mystery Magazine*, July 1959)
Nightmare (*Detective Tales*, Oct 1952)
No Dead End (*Triple Detective*, Spring 1955)
On a Dead Man's Chest (*Thrilling Detective*, Apr 1953)
One Dark Night [Dinny Keogh] (*Mammoth Mystery*, Dec 1946)
One for the Hangman (*Suspect Detective Stories*, Feb 1956)
Operation—Murder (*F.B.I. Detective Stories*, Aug 1949)
Orphans Are Made (*Mobsters*, Feb 1953)
Out of the Frying Pan... (*15 Mystery Stories*, Oct 1950)
Port of the Dead (*New Detective Magazine*, July 1947)
Prelude to a Wake (*Dime Detective Magazine*, Feb 1952)
Red Nightmare (*Dime Mystery Magazine*, July 1947)
Sailor, Beware! (*Detective Story Magazine*, May 1953)
Save Me a Kill (*New Detective Magazine*, June 1953)
Self-Made Corpse (*Detective Tales*, Apr 1949)
She Cries Murder! (*New Detective Magazine*, June 1952)
Sing a Song of Murder (*Dime Detective Magazine*, Aug 1952)
Snow in August [Dinny Keogh] (*Mammoth Mystery*, Aug 1946)
The Spice of Death (*Private Detective*, Dec 1950)
Start with a Corpse [Dinny Keogh] (*Mammoth Mystery*, Jan 1946)
There's Death in the Heir [Dinny Keogh] (*Mammoth Mystery*, Aug 1947)
They Played Too Rough [Dinny Keogh] (*Mammoth Mystery*, Mar 1946)
This Shroud Reserved (*New Detective Magazine*, Oct 1951)
Those Slaughter-House Blues (*Mammoth Detective*, Feb 1947)
A Time for Dying (*Dime Detective Magazine*, Aug 1951)
Too Many Crosses [Dinny Keogh] (*Mammoth Mystery*, Feb 1947)
Tragedy in Waiting (*Invincible Detective Magazine*, Mar 1951)
The Trouble with Redheads (*Mike Shayne Mystery Magazine*, Apr 1959)
Two-Headed Killer (*15 Mystery Stories*, Feb 1950)
Undressed to Kill (*New Detective Magazine*, Sept 1949)
Vicious Circle (*Detective Tales*, Nov 1949)
The Voice That Kills (*15 Mystery Stories*, Aug 1950)
Wake of the Ermine Chick (*15 Story Detective*, Dec 1950)
When Cops Fall Out (*Detective Tales*, June 1953)
With Hostile Intent (*Fifteen Detective Stories*, Dec 1954)

With Love and Bullets! (*Detective Tales*, Feb 1953)
Written in Blood (*Ten Detective Aces*, May 1948)
You Can't Live Forever (*New Detective Magazine*, Aug 1952)
You Die Alone (*Fifteen Detective Stories*, Oct 1953)
You'll Die Laughing (*Detective Tales*, Oct 1950)
You're Killing Me (*Detective Story Magazine*, Sept 1953)

Dinny Keogh series:
Start with a Corpse (1946)
They Played Too Rough (1946)
Bullets for Beethoven (1946)
Snow in August (1946)
One Dark Night (1946)
Too Many Crosses (1947)
There's Death in the Heir (1947)

As Lorenz Heller

Novel:
Murder in Make-Up (Messner, 1937)

Stories:
Blood Money (*Suspect Detective Stories*, Nov 1955)
A Tasty Dish (*Suspect Detective Stories*, Feb 1956)
Twilight (*Short Stories*, Nov 1956)
The Hero (*Mystery Tales*, Dec 1958)
The Last Hunt (*Adventure*, June 1959)

As Burt Sims

Television Scripts:
1953: "Death Does a Rumba" (Season 2, Episode 12, *Boston Blakie*)
1953: "Island of Stone" (Season 2, Episode 1, *Chevron Theater*)
1954: "Tailor-Made Trouble" (Season 1, Episode 11, *Waterfront*)
1956 - 1959: Seven episodes of *Sky King*
1958: "Beautiful, Blue and Deadly" (Season 1, Episode 14, *Mike Hammer*)
1958: "Texas Fliers" (Season 1, Episode 18, *Flight*)

Rediscover the hard-hitting, character-driven fiction of

Lorenz Heller

The Savage Chase (as Frederick Lorenz) · $19.95
Three 50s noir thrillers in one volume. "...a sexually frank, violence
packed thriller with vividly crisp dialogue."—*GoodReads.*

A Rage at Sea / A Party Every Night · $19.95
"Lorenz's characters are what keep the pages turning."
—Alan Cranis, *Bookgasm.*

Dead Wrong · $9.99 · Black Gat Books #26.
"These interesting, well-developed characters propel this rather standard
crime-noir plot into something special and unusual."—*Paperback Warrior.*

Hide-Out / I Get What I Want · $15.95
"In Lorenz's fiction, it feels like he moulds the plot from organic character
confrontations, his writing is electric and alive with unpredictability."
—Paul Burke, *CrimeTime.*

Crime Cop / Body of the Crime · $15.95
"One of the better entries, outside of 87th Precinct, in the paperback
police school." —Anthony Boucher, *New York Times*

Woman Hunter / Kiss of Fire · $15.95
"What makes this one ding is not necessarily the plot, but the great
characterizations which serve to humanize all the players. A terrific
read."—Dave Wilde

"[One of] "the real pros of suspense."—Anthony Boucher, *New York Times*

"[Heller] writes in a hard, fast, crisp style and he has a feel for colorful
language and characters that makes the story sing."
—*Mammoth Mystery.*

Stark House Press, 1315 H Street, Eureka, CA 95501
griffinskye3@sbcglobal.net / www.StarkHousePress.com
Available from your local bookstore, or order direct via our website.

www.ingramcontent.com/pod-product-compliance
Lightning Source LLC
Chambersburg PA
CBHW061234210726
48293CB00003B/764